Sal Thomas likes to string words  amusing order. BBC Comedy or woman who keeps on sending us as a stand-up, starred in an Edinbu hand at film writing and sitcoms (all to zero financial acclaim) and finally settled on romcom novels as her genre of choice after realising the world can never have enough of the mirth-filled mushy stuff. She lives in Manchester, England, with her husband and son – the two loves of her life. Her side hustle is managing her rampant anxiety. She also works in marketing.

 twitter.com/_iamsalt

THE ACCIDENTAL HOUSEMATE

SAL THOMAS

One More Chapter
a division of HarperCollins*Publishers*
1 London Bridge Street
London SE1 9GF
www.harpercollins.co.uk
HarperCollins*Publishers*
Macken House, 39/40 Mayor Street Upper,
Dublin 1, D01 C9W8, Ireland

This paperback edition 2023
First published in Great Britain in ebook format
by HarperCollins*Publishers* 2023
1

A catalogue record of this book is available from the British Library

ISBN: 978-0-00-860939-9

This novel is entirely a work of fiction. The names, characters and incidents portrayed in it are the work of the author's imagination. Any resemblance to actual persons, living or dead, events or localities is entirely coincidental.

Printed and bound in the UK using 100% Renewable Electricity
by CPI Group (UK) Ltd

To Jimbob, who made this possible.
And Edgar, my other true love.

PART I
AUTUMN

Chapter One

We have few good mornings in this house. Those idyllic breakfasts where a smiling family sits around a table listening to cereal going *snap, crackle and pop* surely only exist in Marketing Land. Our kitchen table looks less like the focal point for quality time and more like a municipal dump.

This morning started particularly badly. Toddler Jack got up in the night, came to my bed and subtly willed me to wake up by shouting in my ear. My pelvic floor already hangs as raggedy as a Union Jack flag outside a derelict pub, but on this occasion it failed me entirely, so I spent the early hours trying to wrestle a king-size memory foam topper onto the washing line. Consequently, I am beyond tired, and it's only the first day of a new school year.

Still, Jack seems fine now, merrily smearing Weetabix on his groin, his dark eyes twinkling from beneath a wispy brown fringe that I keep on forgetting to cut. Okay, I have nine minutes before we have to get out. Provided no one needs an ill-timed dump, there's a chance we might make it.

'What do you want in your sandwiches?'

Eric, who discovered a copy of *Of Mice & Men* over the holidays and now pretends to be Lennie just to wind me up, has appeared.

'I'm gonna live off the fatta the land.'

I suggest paté.

'Is it smooth? I sure do love smooth things.'

And I sure would love to be George from the book and put him out of *my* misery.

'Hey, lady,' he says.

'Save the performance, Eric. We're in a rush.' I check the best-before on some salami. No, that's out of date.

'No, really, lady,' he says.

'Please, dude, just a minute, okay? I haven't slept and I have a headache.'

'But...'

'Today is going to be difficult enough without you giving it the amateur dramatics.' The cheese is looking a bit suspect too.

'But MOM!' In his frustration, the American accent is temporarily replaced by his standard mild Brummie one.

I slam the fridge door.

'What? What is it? What is so bloody important that it cannot possibly wait one moment?'

He doesn't so much as flinch, just gestures to the patio doors. 'Why is your bed outside in the rain?'

My mattress topper is starting to speckle and darken. It hadn't been raining seconds ago. 'Oh bollocks,' I say.

'Bollocks!' parrots Jack.

'No, don't you say bollocks,' I say.

'But you said bollocks,' Eric helpfully points out.

'And don't you say bollocks either, Eric. You're not a teenager yet. You're too young to swear.'

'You said bollocks again,' says Eric.

'I know I said bollocks, but that was in the heat of the moment. That doesn't mean you should say it.'

'And what if I said it in the heat of the moment?'

'Did you?'

'Yes.'

'Bollocks!' Jack shouts again, hitting the tray of his highchair.

'You're right, Jack; that is bollocks.'

Leanne walks in, her mop of kinky bleached curls still wet from the shower, her kohl-lined almond eyes narrowed. 'The no-swearing effort's going well then?'

I toss twenty pence into the already-too-full swear jar. Six minutes before we need to leave.

'Don't suppose you can rescue that, can you?' I ask Leanne, pointing at the mattress.

'Nothing would give me greater pleasure than to wring out a six-foot sodden sponge ... said nobody ever. But since it's your birthday...'

She produces an envelope from the patch pocket of her dress. Oh yes, it's my thirty-ninth birthday. Thirty-bloody-nine. The sum of the consecutive prime numbers $3 + 5 + 7 + 11 + 13$, which is pretty much the only thing to recommend it. I open the card. It's a handmade number, fashioned from a series of paper cuts and folds, signed by both my eldest. All residual annoyance melts away.

'Thanks, guys. It's lovely.'

Eric nods non-committally. Leanne gives me a hug.

'I haven't got you a present,' says Leanne, 'because you said not to, and I *always* do as I'm told.'

'Don't you just,' I say.

'But for your special treat, can I drop you off and take the car afterwards? I've got some bits to pick up in town before the big move.'

'I thought you were up early. Anyway, I'm not letting you go. I'm too bloody young to have a kid at university.'

She arches a pencilled brow and points to the swear jar. I find another coin to drop in.

'Too old to win in a fight though,' she says. 'And I am practically superhuman.'

She really is, but I've not got time to go into that now.

'Okay, but can you get Jack ready for me?'

'I'm the girl with all the gifts today, aren't I?'

She takes him upstairs whilst I finish off the lunch. Eric has disappeared into the front room, probably reading about some other character with which he'll torture me soon. As I drop his lunchbox into his school bag, I look at Gaz.

'I don't know what you think you're doing, sat on your arse over there. You have been absolutely no help to me this morning.'

He doesn't answer back. Being dead will do that to you. In fairness, even if all the known natural laws of the universe were to break down and the urn in the corner could talk, it's probably not even Gaz in there. Not entirely. Merely the dusty remnants of countless vaporised bodies churned through the 21st century death system, swept up and combined with the six pounds or so of his own pulverised bone that withstood the 1600-degree temperatures in the furnace. I begin to tell him as much. Leanne catches me, her sunny face clouding over.

'What have we said about this?'

'I know, I know. Come on, we're late.'

I find Eric and give him a kiss he doesn't want. I tell him not to forget to go to school. Or lock the door behind him. Or take his bag. And not to stay in character all day, because whilst school claims to encourage creativity, what they really want are compliant automatons that never question the status quo.

He rolls his pale blue eyes. 'I remember about the rabbits,' he says.

Thankfully our battered but faithful Volvo is having a good day and starts first time. Leanne wrestles Jack into his seat and we're barely out of the drive when she starts.

'We need to talk about you and Dad.'

'Let's not do this now.' I turn on the radio. She turns it off again.

'It's been over three years. When are you going to do something with his ashes?'

'I am doing something with them. I'm talking to them.'

'I mean something to help you move on. I know you miss him—I do too—but you're in a state of limbo. Dad's in a state of limbo. It's not healthy.'

The long silence that follows is suddenly pierced by the quacking of one of Jack's farts. Perfect comic timing, only Leanne doesn't laugh.

'Granddad said when Nan died, scattering her ashes made him feel his grief had become manageable, that it was okay to carry on. And look at him now, he leads a full and active life.'

'You make him sound like a well-fed dog!'

'You know what I mean. He's putting himself out there. Exploring his options.'

We stop at traffic lights and I pretend there's a smudge on the windscreen that needs wiping off. Leanne continues regardless.

'I'm only saying that come Saturday I won't be around, and apart from Sindy, it's not as if you've got loads of mates. You've got to think of your future.'

We've arrived at nursery, so at least I can temporarily ignore the leaden weight that resides in my chest when I think of her impending departure. I don't know what I'd have done without her these last few years.

Unfortunately the *Chic Clique* (aka the seemingly perfect moms of some of Jack's classmates), are clustered around the entrance. Every one of them is utterly unblemished, with their just-thrown-on clothes that no one's ever just thrown up on and hair in actual recognizable styles.

'Shall I come in?' asks Leanne.

'Blimey, no. Keep the engine running so we can make a quick getaway.' At last, she smiles.

The other moms watch as I get out the car. The pack leader, Belinda, lives on the same street as me, albeit in a much nicer house, but she has never once spoken to me. I used to think it was because I was widowed, that perhaps by reaching out I could pass my misfortune along like a virus, but I suspect that even before Gaz's death I wouldn't have fitted their mould. I open the rear door, determined to demonstrate that I can do poise and grace. But as I pick Jack up, he pulls my top down to reveal a greying bra, one strap of which is attached by a paperclip threaded through the lace trim. In my haste to pull it up, I punch myself hard on the nose. Thankfully the ensuing tears help to blur their doubtless disapproving gazes as I hurry past.

Up in the classroom I find Jack's keyworker, Gill, whom I love as only a woman desperately in need of a break from her youngest son can.

'Hey, buddy, I've missed you,' she says with genuine enthusiasm.

I swear they must all be given acting training before the First Aid classes.

'Did you enjoy the holidays?' she asks. Sadly my free childcare doesn't cover us for non-term time.

'We endured them.'

She smiles. 'Did you bring in the collage of what you've been up to?'

My look of total incomprehension is enough to tell her I have not.

'We said it'd be useful to help him settle back in after the long break.'

'Shit, I'm sorry, Gill. I forgot.'

'Oops, language Mrs Beckinsale.'

'Oh sh— sugar. We didn't really do anything. A couple of trips to a soft-play centre and the occasional picnic. Ask him about that. I've got to go.'

I kiss Jack, who's already occupied putting a Sticklebrick up his nose. I tell myself he'll be fine without a collage, at the same time feeling I have failed him again. I dash back out through the moms, who are still chatting like people who have lives to talk about, and climb back into the passenger seat.

'Quick,' I tell Leanne. 'I'm cutting it fine.'

In her haste she puts the car into fourth gear and not reverse, and the car lurches a mere fraction closer to the group as it stalls, but they recoil as if she'd deliberately tried to mow them down. She rolls the window down and flips them the bird, from which they recoil further as Leanne only has half a middle finger. She gets the car going again and pulls away. I drop down in my seat and beg the footwell to swallow me up.

'Oh, come on, they're total dicks,' she says.

'You might be right, but I bet they wouldn't have forgotten to do a collage.'

'For…?'

'A bridge between the holidays and the new term apparently. I'm a terrible mother.'

A taxi cuts in front of us and Leanne leans out of the window and shouts 'WANKER!'.

'Don't be so dramatic,' she says, settling back into her seat. 'Not sticking some paper onto some other paper doesn't make you a terrible mother. All the other stuff does that.'

'Oh cheers.'

But she's softened up again, all talk of Gaz forgotten for now.

'Jack's a handful, Mom, you're doing your best given the circumstances.'

'It's not only that. It's as if motherhood has moved on since I had you and Eric. I constantly feel I'm falling short of some ideal that I can't even quantify. That I should be doing, I don't know, *more*. More engaged play. More fresh air. More healthy food. More reading. It's as if those moms see the lack in me.'

'They don't know you. I bet you're way better than them. Smarter, funnier, less judgmental.'

'Saggier, poorer, more widowed.'

'Stronger, more resilient, open-minded. You need to stop caring what other people think of you and worry more what you think of yourself.'

We have reached the school and Leanne pulls up onto the

zig-zag lines. The school's lollipop lady looks on disapprovingly, but Leanne waves her disabled badge out of the window. I love that she is so defiant; it's what kept her alive all those years ago.

'You're amazing. We love you. Yada, yada. Now get out and think on what I said.'

———

I pause for a second at the gates. Brookdene Academy looms before me, a series of interconnected buildings resembling the result of an unholy alliance between the Sydney Opera House and a Portakabin. The building is only ten years old, but it's already starting to look tattered. Litter swirls in the air as abundant as Autumn leaves as I walk past a vandalised memorial bench. Apparently Brookdene wasn't always like this. Granted, it's on the wrong side of the tracks, whatever arbitrary line that happens to be, and it was never going to set any new records in educational attainment, but it functioned. But when the second in a row of Ofsted results wasn't what the original academy sponsor expected, they withdrew their funding and things started to spiral from there. Still, they gave me a flexible job when I really needed one after Gaz died, so it's not all bad.

I arrive at my classroom (well, not mine, it's Mr Powell's) and head inside. I take in the flimsy modern set-up, the spindly laminated tables, plastic stools, and chipboard cupboards more resonant of a corporate break-out area than a seat of learning. How different to the steam-punk labs of my youth, with their age-worn iroko benches and delicate brass gas taps, or the huge floor-to-ceiling antique fume cupboards lined in creamy grey asbestos. Yup, it's all change. Not least because now these kids do 'science', the three most fascinating subjects imaginable lumped together in a single box to be reluctantly ticked. I'm unpacking some glass beakers when the door opens. Mr Powell walks to his desk, clutching his battered briefcase to his chest as if protecting himself from an unseen foe.

'Morning Mr Powell. Good holiday?'

He drops into his chair. The knee of his right leg jiggles up and down so the heel of his unpolished shoe taps against the scuffed linoleum. It's as if it's gearing up to escape, if only it could summon the courage. Most of his hair has succeeded in its quest for freedom, thinned out until only a follicular dust bunny remains.

'Let's keep the verbals to a minimum, shall we? Not in the mood.'

This is the start of a professional waltz we do often. Mr Powell thinks I am less of a colleague and more paid help, there to speak only when spoken to.

'Any experiments you need me to set up?' I ask.

'Not necessary.'

'I've had an idea for demonstrating tensile strength using hair and a hairdryer.'

His waxy complexion reddens. 'I am perfectly capable of dealing with any requirements I may have. You keep the usual suspects in check.'

As a technician, my official capacity is to set up equipment and help manage the practical side of things. Unofficially, I take a subset of kids who he's labelled *special educational needs* (although I think they're just bored senseless) into a side room and do fun experiments and lessons with them. I got five out of six of last year's *no hopers*—his words, not mine—to pass their GCSE double science. Mr Powell takes credit for the marks, and I get to play teacher. It's funny, the idea of teaching isn't something that interested me when I was younger—I always imagined I'd be a researcher of some description—but if I had my time again, I'd definitely train to be one. It is beyond rewarding and I genuinely love finding new ways to bring the concepts to life for the kids.

I head next door. I've barely laid out the equipment when the door flies open. A toweringly tall boy with a buzz cut and a face full of angry acne careens in.

'Walking, please, Bradley!'

'But Miss, Harpal is lobbing Skittles at me.'

Sure enough a sweet flies in after him and somehow lodges in his gelled spikes. He fishes it out and pops it into his mouth.

'And what were *you* doing before he started throwing them?' This is a question I have learned to ask from having children of my own. It comes from understanding a fundamental law of the kid universe: *every reaction has a catalyst. You just need to find out what it was.*

Harpal appears. 'Miss, Brad's put my bag on top of the lockers and I can't reach it.'

See what I mean? Harpal is much more compact. He wears a Patka for religious reasons, but the others tease him it's to appear taller.

'Bradley, please retrieve the bag so he can go to his lesson with some sweets left.'

Bradley slumps by five inches and turns to do as he's told. Instant compliance? Perhaps it's going to be a good day. Harpal follows him.

'And choose your breakfast more wisely tomorrow Harpal,'

I call after him. 'Those will rot your teeth, poison your brain, make you fat, then give you diabetes.'

'You should be in marketing, Miss,' he shouts back.

Bradley returns, trailed by the rest of my little group. There's Jada, Hannah, Malik and Reggie, every one of them flouting the already-relaxed uniform regulations we have. Reggie has been particularly creative, by not wearing one.

'Where's your uniform?'

His eyes roll in such an exaggerated way that for a brief second only whiteness remains, contrasting completely with chestnut skin that has darkened and freckled over summer. He resembles something out of the *X-Men*, although this boy's mutant power would be backchat.

'Miss, uniforms are an outmoded tradition that seeks to oppress rather than liberate the people on whom they're imposed. We are not all robots that need to be programmed with the same code, you know.'

Really clever backchat.

'And what's so individual about a pair of jeans and a sweatshirt?'

'Choice,' he says.

He is my absolute favourite, even though he's a total pain and I'm not meant to have favourites. He's smart, but he has a few behavioural issues that means putting him with Powell is like trying to mix potassium with water.

'He's talking shit, Miss,' says Hannah. 'He's been staying at some aunt's and his mom forgot to pack it for him.'

'*I* forgot to pack it,' he says. 'It's not her responsibility.'

God love him. I think he may also be a feminist without knowing it.

'Well, if you can possibly embrace your conformist side

today, perhaps after this you can get a spare one from the office, so you don't get excluded on your first day back?'

He clicks his tongue in that way these kids have of saying *yes*, but not actually conceding defeat. It's enough.

'Right, are your mobiles switched off?'

A collective groan passes amongst them.

'Come on, I need proof. I'm not having you SnapTwatting your way through the lesson when you should be listening.'

Various devices, all far better than mine, are pulled out of pockets and fiddled with. More compliance? Blimey. Perhaps it's even going to be a good term.

Chapter Two

F ive days later, I'm sat in Leanne's new bedroom, unable
to stop crying. Thankfully the other two kids are with
their granddad, so they don't have to witness this mess of snot
and tears.

'For goodness' sake, get a grip! I've moved a hundred miles
away, not to Australia.' She drapes some fairy lights across a
bookshelf.

'I know,' I snort through the sobs, desperately sucking in air
to try and compose myself. 'But I can't get my head round that
I have to leave you here. All on your own.'

She stands before me, charged with energy, already restless
to get stuck into what student life has to offer. I know she will
attack it as she has attacked life so far, fearlessly, overcoming
its many challenges with a confidence I can't even come close
to achieving.

'I'm in halls. I'm surrounded by people!'

As if to prove this point, there's a knock at the door. She
opens it to a guy in tortoiseshell glasses and very skinny jeans.

'Hiya. I wanted to say hello, seeing as how ⲛ
to be...'

The sentence trails off. Seeing my daughter for
time often does that to people. It's not becaus
beautiful, although she is. It's not because she has ar.
willowy curves. It's not even because she doesn't so ⲛ
wear her clothes as *occupy* them. It's because she
prosthetic legs.

'Come on in!' she practically drags him into the room.

Poor kid. He can't take his eyes off the complex mix o
polypropylene, titanium and carbon fibre that makes up the
lower third of her body. A hundred questions tumble through
his brain and onto his face.

'Meningitis,' she answers him. 'When I was four. Had these
away too.' She raises her hands, displaying a set of fingers a
young child might draw, all lumpy and featureless, the joints
in all the wrong places.

Meningitis. Four tiny syllables that meant five days of Gaz
and me thinking we were going to lose her, six months in and
out of hospital and a lifetime of after-effects and rehabilitation.

'I'm Leanne. My hearing isn't the best either, which is why
I've got one of these.' She lifts her hair to reveal the small
plastic-covered transmitter of her cochlear implant.

He nods, slowly, absorbing this information. *Meningitis.*
One single word that means she will forever be subject to the
scrutiny of strangers in this way.

'I'm Jasper,' he says eventually. 'Best I have is a chicken pox
scar on the side of my nose. Look.'

And with that they are away, a flurry of questions passing
between them. *Where are you from? What are you studying? Are
you going to the Fresher's Fair? Have you seen the hall's bar yet? Do*

you want to go and get a drink with some of the other people on the
corridor after you've finished up here?

Leanne glances at me and then back at Jasper.

'Maybe in half an hour,' she says, starting the countdown
clock until I must go.

'Right-oh.' He stuffs his hands into his pockets and turns to
leave. 'I'll knock on shortly.'

'He seems nice,' I say enthusiastically, trying to keep more
tears at bay.

'Yeah, he does,' she says, chuffed to have made a friend so
quickly. 'Shall we get some fresh air?'

'Sure.'

We step out onto the manicured lawns that surround her
halls. Beyond us there is a gentle slope down to a duck pond
and we wander towards it, gazing at the late summer sun
glinting off the ruffled water. We watch in silence as the female
mallards enjoy some brief respite from the ferocious
insemination war to which they are subjected every spring and
winter, whilst the males peck and preen at their speckled flank
feathers.

'How does it feel to be the only person in the history of
your family to go to university?' I ask her.

'It feels great. It really does. I'm so grateful to you, Mom.'

'I didn't do anything.'

'I know how much you wanted to go to uni. And who
knows what might have been had I not come along and
thrown a spanner in the works.'

'You are a massive spanner.' I taste the saltiness of more
tears as I take her by the shoulders. 'But I'm so proud of you.
Of the child you were. The girl you are. The woman you're
going to become. And I know your dad would have been

stupidly proud of you too, if he was here to see this.' I wish so much he was here to see this.

We hug, clinging to one another in the hope that if we stay here long enough, we might will him back to existence. Leanne pulls away first.

'Are you gonna be okay?' she asks.

'I'll be fine,' although my leaking eyes suggest otherwise.

'Because if you're not, I can always come home. Do this another time.'

'No! I forbid you to even think like that.'

She searches my face. I know she's worried that without her there, I'll continue to tread water, just about keeping my head above the waves but never reaching the comfort of the shore.

'I'm going to get there.'

Her lack of conviction is plain to see.

'But it won't happen overnight.'

'At least promise me you'll do something, anything, to get out of the rut you're in. Don't let life pass you by.'

I mentally fast-forward through the next decade and a half, picturing myself waving goodbye to Eric, then to Jack. How quickly the last fifteen years have passed. I recall those times in hospital when Leanne was fighting to stay alive as vividly as if they were this morning. This life will be gone before I know it, unravelling like the stitches on a pulled jumper, until barely anything of its original shape remains.

Leanne hugs me again. 'If you're sure.'

I remember the constant twinge of concern I felt for my mother after Dad left us. I'd watch as she smoked and drank herself into oblivion every night. Bitterness ate away at her until the cancer took over, devouring with it whatever hope she'd had of a better life. I don't want Leanne to feel that way. I look her squarely in the eye.

'I promise you, as I stand here, that I'll have it all worked out before I'm forty.'

She eyeballs me back. 'You'd better. Or I'm quitting and coming back to supervise.'

'You can't do that.'

'Wanna try me?'

She is head-on to the sun, my silhouette reflected in her marble irises. My reflection shakes its head. I really do not want to try her.

'Good. Now go because there's some serious bonding-stroke-drinking to be done.'

I smile, relieved to be released from that penetrating gaze. 'No getting legless.'

She grins. 'Too late for that.'

'And no spending that scholarship all at once.'

'You know full well I'm getting it in instalments. Now go!'

I drag myself away from her magnetic pull and head back to the car, mulling over the promise I've just made her. Well, Cath. What exactly do you expect to happen in a year?

Chapter Three

'Vroooooooom vroooooooom.' Jack shoots past me.

'Come here. I need to check your nappy.'

'Chase me!'

I'm carrying one scooter, two helmets, one changing bag, one handbag and a comforter toy that absolutely must be cradled in my arms rather than put safely away. Yeah right.

We've come to one of Birmingham's city centre museums. This was a mistake. I'd forgotten that on weekends museums are like gimp masks: something people squeeze themselves into out of curiosity, but then it all gets a bit claustrophobic and you immediately want out again. Don't get me wrong, I love a bit of history, but nowadays most museums are effectively less well-informed versions of the internet, and there's only so much interest you can take in an Anglo-Saxon arrowhead before you need to counteract it with a video of a monkey sniffing its own bum.

'When Pop-Pops getting here?' Jack shouts, whizzing past a woman trying to look interested in the Iron Age.

'Not soon enough.' My patience is a little threadbare today, but thankfully we're meeting Geoff, Gaz's dad, who's treating us to lunch.

'Did you know it's best to stick a bayonet in the belly,' says Eric, who has just returned from the war section, 'because it doesn't get caught like it would in the ribs?'

'I was not aware of that.'

'Do you know how to light a fire with wet wood?'

'Nope.'

'You have to cut it and expose the dry bit in the middle. Then you use that as kindling for a small fire to dry out the bigger bits.'

'Oh.'

He looks down at an exhibit of a piece of iron ore and slowly runs his fingers along the braille descriptor. Without looking up he asks, 'do you think Dad would've known that?'

The question catches me off guard, like every question about his dad does. Another one in a tray marked pending that I'll be dealing with for the rest of my life.

'Absolutely,' I tell him.

The truth is Gaz could barely start a barbecue on a hot day using matches and lighter fuel, but a little white lie won't hurt.

'Come on, let's go and look at Space.'

The Space & Time Gallery is the only bit I really like. Whilst everyone else is crowding round the Vivarium, or marvelling at the reproduction dinosaur skeleton, this is the one area you get a bit of, well, *space*. There's nothing particularly interesting about it, but it's comforting to be reminded of my insignificance in the greater scheme of things.

'You might want to stop your son from doing himself a mischief.'

It's Geoff, pointing at Jack who has climbed a bookcase and is batting at a suspended model of Neptune like a cat might a ball of wool.

'Oh gawd. Time to eat.'

We head to the museum café, which for reasons unknown has an old-fashioned nautical theme, even though the closest body of water is a canal, and you're more likely to find a supermarket trolley than a boat in there. Geoff sits opposite me on a chair fashioned out of an oak barrel, sipping a milkshake from a copper tankard. His thick hair emerges untamed from his scalp like a silver firework, grey rings encircling bright blue corneas that are now moist with laughter from Eric reciting stanza after stanza of Spike Milligan silly verse.

'That's enough young man,' he says in his soft Yorkshire accent as Eric launches into the *Ning Nang Nong*. 'Why don't you take Jack to play on those game machines whilst I have a quick chat with your mam?' He hands Eric two pound coins and the pair run off delighted.

'You still faring okay without Leanne?' he asks.

'I can't believe it's been almost a month. I call her every week. Sometimes she even picks up!'

He smiles. He misses her too.

'Is everything alright with you?' He doesn't normally angle for one-on-one time.

'Everything's great,' he says, but his cheeks colour a little, and he doesn't meet my eye. 'Actually,' he says eventually, 'there was something I wanted to show you.' He reaches into his pocket and pulls out his mobile. 'I've signed myself up to this application thing. It's called Stitch.' He passes his phone over to me. 'It finds you people in your local area.'

'What, like tradesmen?'

23

'No. Like women.'

Geoff mistakes my surprise for horror because he immediately flusters and pulls a handkerchief from his pocket to dab his forehead.

'Not only women,' he says quickly. 'People. You know, for friendship or courting or days out.'

'And have you found anyone to go on days out with?' I sip my fizzy orange and try to relax my face into one of total composure.

'Not yet. But I have found one who wants to meet up for sex.'

Whoops! My drink flies out of my mouth and nose and onto the striped table in front of me. I grab a serviette and try and coax my eyebrows down from my hairline.

'Someone said that?'

'Rather more than that. I'll show you a picture if you want?'

'She sent you pictures! What did you say this app was again? *Snatch*Chat?'

It's Geoff's turn to look shocked. 'Only of her face!'

'How old is she?'

'Sixty-six. She's very attractive.'

'Are you going to meet her?'

'Nay, lass. I can barely get myself up in the morning, let alone the old fella!'

Geoff is not your typical belt and braces, you can tell a Yorkshireman, but you can't tell him much kind of man. Not any more at least. After the death of his only son, followed by his wife barely nine months later, he is a stone battered by the seas of life, the edges worn away, still solid but infinitely more strokable. Still, this is all a bit too open, even for me.

'But I wanted to ask you if you're okay with me dating again. You wouldn't mind?'

As surprised as I am by the methodology, I don't mind. 'Course not, you daft sod!'

'You don't think it's too soon after Janet?'

'Not one minute.'

'Only I do long for some companionship.'

'That's completely understandable.'

'And some kissing and cuddling wouldn't hurt.'

I cover my ears. 'No, you have to stop now!'

He smiles. 'Well, that's settled then. Thank you.' He briefly glances over at the boys who are now ploughing money into a sweet dispenser.

'Eric,' I call over. 'Don't eat any until after your lunch!'

Geoff studies me. 'Do you ever consider looking for someone else? You're only young and you're an attractive woman. You've got half your life left to live. No need to rush into anything, but…' the words continue to stumble out.

He means well, but this isn't a conversation I want to have. I just want a nice lunch in which I don't have to make any decisions other than *do I want crisps or chips with my sandwich?*

'I'm not ready.'

Gaz and I were practically kids when we met. I'd never dated anyone before him, and I've never slept with anyone else. The idea fills me with genuine horror. I wouldn't know what to do or say. It'd be like being a teenager again, and I didn't enjoy those years the first time around. And who in their right mind wants to take on a widow and her three kids? I have unfinished business. Unfinished love. It would be like having an affair.

'You won't know how ready you are until you try.'

I don't relish the thought of always being single. Having spent all my adulthood as part of a unit, to suddenly find myself on my own was shattering beyond belief, but the missing piece of my life is Gaz-shaped. Even imagining there might be a replacement feels disloyal.

Geoff puts his hand on my arm. 'If guilt's holding you back, it shouldn't. I know you weren't married, but you fulfilled every vow as if you were. Right up until '*til death do you part*. There's no rule that says you can't move on.'

For the umpteenth time recently, I get the tickly burning sensation in my nostrils that heralds tears. I fight the feeling, but my vision blurs regardless.

'It's what Gaz would want for you too, love. I'm sure it is.'

I pull my arm away. 'We'll never know that for sure, will we? Because we never got the chance to discuss it, did we?'

I hate it when people tell me what he would or wouldn't have wanted. What he would have wanted is to see his kids grow up, not be suspended in time so that one day they'll be older than he ever got to be. What he would have wanted was to be here, with us, answering Eric's questions, eating lunch and making plans for future lunches. What he would have wanted was to walk off the five-a-side pitch with his mates that day, instead of being surrounded by them as someone compressed his chest so hard his ribs broke.

Geoff's crestfallen look makes me feel instantly bad; he's only trying to help. I don't know what I'd have done without him these last few years, emotionally, practically or financially. But he got to say goodbye to Janet. What I got was morgue visits, coroner's reports, pathologist's notes and the chance to mentally reconstruct the horror of Gaz's final moments so that

I could replay them over and over in my head. Luckily a loud shout pierces the white noise of a grief unexpectedly revisited.

'Muuuuuuuuuuuuuum.'

It's Jack, frustrated at being held at arm's length by Eric who's teasing him with some sweets.

'Sorry,' I say to Geoff, digging the heels of my hands into my eyes to dab away the moistness. 'I'd better sort them out.'

Lunch arrives shortly after and so all talk of dating is left. Geoff can do whatever works for him, but there's as much chance of me going out and finding a man as there is of the right one dropping out of the sky and into my lap.

Chapter Four

I look wearily at the teeming mass of unsupervised kids that stand between me and the classroom where I absent-mindedly left my packed lunch this morning. It's my year eleven's fault. We'd been discussing why getting decent grades in science was important for the future. Not everyone had been convinced. Malik is slated to work in his family's tile shop, Bradley plans to be a chef in the RAF and Jada is hoping for an apprenticeship in a nursery.

'I'm going to do hairdressing,' Hannah announced.

'Understanding the chemical compounds in hair colourants could be useful,' I hazarded. She laughed, flicked her brittle bleached hair and told me there weren't any chemicals in hair colourants.

'What about you, Reggie? What do you want to be when you finally grow up?'

He cast his eyes around the table, mouth set into a grim line. 'I wanna be a nurse, Miss.'

The others burst out laughing.

'Ooh, I can see you in the little white dress Reggie,' Bradley said, lips pursed suggestively.

'It's fucking scrubs,' Reggie growled.

'Okay, everyone, settle down. Language please, Reggie.'

'I knew you lot would give me shit,' he said, shaking his head. 'I love that biology stuff. Like when you bought in cow eyes for us to cut up.'

'I think it's a great idea,' I said, as the bell rang for lunch and they all scampered off. Reggie as a nurse? I was so caught up musing on it that I left the classroom when I should have been collecting my sandwiches from the main lab's fridge.

I make my way through the noisy corridors, the cafeteria's unique smell of fried food and overcooked veg lodging like a lining on the back of my throat, but somehow not dampening my appetite. But when I open the door to the lab my lunch plans are once again derailed, only this time by the sight of Mr Powell, squatting on his haunches, hastily picking up pieces of a broken bottle as amber liquid seeps across the floor. The stench of whiskey fills the room.

'Damned thing fell out of my hands,' he says, as if this is ample explanation.

He continues to pick at the jagged pieces, tossing them into a bin as I process the scene in front of me. I say process; that's suggesting that I hadn't noticed the tremble in his hands, or the galaxy of crimson veins clustered on his cheeks and nose. But I'd assumed it was testimony to a poor lifestyle and self-neglect, not a drinking problem. Clearly, I've been naïve.

'You dickhead.'

He jolts at my words, initiating a forward movement that, due to a combination of middle-aged spread and momentum, he's unable to stop. His outstretched hand follows an arced pathway straight onto the largest of the upturned shards of glass. Surprised, Powell raises his fist as someone finding a precious jewel might, opening it and gazing with wonder at the artifact nestling in the middle of his palm, and seemingly poking through it. Blood oozes out, a meltwater of crimson disperses across the deep lifelines of his palm and drips so rhythmically into the wreckage of the booze below that for a second we're both mesmerised by its monotony. Then I come to my senses.

'I'll get a first-aider.'

'They can't see this.'

'It's a bad cut.'

'They'll know I've been drinking. Do you know what will happen?'

Yes, I know. Suspension. Enquiry. Dismissal. He's a hair's breadth away from being unemployable within education, and I'm in two minds as to what to do. I may not be keen on the man, but I do understand the desire to deaden the pain of existence, especially one as seemingly unfulfilling as his.

'Can you do something?' he asks.

He's never asked me for help before, and I'm taken aback by the sincerity of the question.

'Hold your hand up above your heart.' That's assuming he has one. 'It'll stem the flow of blood at least.'

He does so, revealing a darkened patch of pungent underarm sweat. The blood stops dripping on the floor and instead courses its way down his wrist.

'We need something to wrap around it.' I go and carefully feed handfuls of blue paper through the toothy wall dispenser. I loosely wrap it around the base of Powell's hand and tell him to apply pressure to his pulse line. I have absolutely no idea if this will have any effect, but it sounds a bit medical and, truth be told, now the initial shock has passed, I'm rather enjoying giving him orders.

'The kids will be back soon,' he says.

I check the clock. Five minutes until the lesson officially starts. Seven until anyone turns up.

'Go get someone to take you to A&E. I'll clean up here.' I open the windows as far as the bars will allow. We need some air circulating.

'But what if someone asks what happened?'

Is he kidding me? Someone is almost certainly going to ask what happened. In fact, by the time he makes it to the staffroom, around two hundred kids will have done.

'You broke a bottle. No one needs to know what type. I won't tell anyone.'

He slumps with relief. He cuts an odd figure standing there, his arms raised, hands clasped together. It's a strangely victorious stance for someone so defeated.

'Thank you, Catherine.'

It's also the only time he's ever thanked me, which means he must have had a fair bit of that bottle before he dropped it.

A week goes by before I can dissect the incident properly, because my best mate Sindy has been hunkered down with her hubby who was on R&R following his latest Army stint. We've come to the local bingo place, a once-elegant dancehall, stripped of all its original features and filled with Formica tables and the kind of soft furnishings that look like a three-year-old with a spirograph and some neon felt tips designed them. The game has stopped for a break.

'You need to dob him in. What if he accidentally leaves the gas on and then decides to have a cheeky fag? Kaboom. Pieces of kid, all over the school.'

Sindy is my oldest friend. We met at the local *outdoor* (what us Brummies call an off-license) trading our empty fizzy pop (carbonated drink) bottles in for the five pence deposit you got back on each one back then, which would promptly be spent on sweets or transparent bags of greasy crisps.

'Shall we treat ourselves to a bottle of wine?' I ask.

'I shouldn't drink too much; I'm meant to be doing Slimming World.'

'I've told you, diets aren't sustainable. Moderation is key.'

'Okay, I'll only have half the bottle!'

We head to the bar. 'Seriously, though. He's been an ungrateful douchebag since you started. Why protect him?'

'I feel sorry for him. No one grows up wanting to be a knob, do they?'

'He's a moron. End of.'

We order a bottle of Blossom Hill's finest and bring it back to the table.

'At least give him grief when you next see him. Tell him you're watching him or something.' She makes a V sign with her fingers and points towards her eyes in what's meant to be a menacing way, but miscalculates the length of her new acrylic nails and pokes herself in the eyeballs. I almost wet myself laughing and have to quickly nip to the loo. I probably do need to keep an eye on the situation, but Powell's not going to drink on the job again, surely? When I get back, Sindy's opening a bag of crisps.

'Quick, the next game's about to start.'

'What happened to the diet?'

'It wasn't sustainable.'

When we met, Sindy was pretty and tanned, and a bright green double-breasted jumpsuit clung to her plump frame. Her thick blonde hair was swept to the side in a diamante banana clip and her broad feet spilled out of a pair of woven plastic jelly shoes that showed tan lines when she kicked them off. To me, a bookworm dressed in hand-me-downs of much older cousins, she seemed insanely confident and therefore someone who'd naturally despise me. I was wrong. As we sat together, solemnly making our way through our bags of pick 'n' mix, we discovered that despite many differences, we had more than enough in common to declare ourselves the best of friends. I was nine, she was ten.

Thirty years later as she sits before me, waving a lipstick-smeared wine glass around, she's still larger than life. I'm not even convinced she wants to be slimmer, but weight loss is like a hobby for her now and it gives her something to focus on whilst Dave is off on manoeuvres.

'It's alright for you,' she says. 'Your brain consumes all your calories and tells your knockers to be great, so no one notices the rest of you.'

An older woman knitting on a nearby table glances over, grins broadly, and promptly returns to the baby jumper taking shape on her needles.

'*Told* my knockers to be big. Past tense. I fear Jack's sucked the life out of them. Once they were mighty and proud like twin Vesuviuses, now they lie flattened and destroyed like twin Pompeiis.'

Sindy shakes her head, puzzled.

'It's because I didn't decline the nouns correctly. It should have been Vesuvii and Pompeii, but it wouldn't have sounded right.'

'No, it's because you my friend are talking intellectual bollocks. Speaking of which, did you decide about your school reunion?'

I'm about to answer, but the first number gets called.

'I'll tell you in a bit.'

The school reunion. I got the call a week ago. I was in the hallway trying to wrestle Jack's shoes on when the phone rang. It was Gaynor, a former-school-friend-cum-nemesis-turned-hugely-successful-high-flying-travel-journalist with whom I've maintained sporadic contact over the last two decades, to tell me she was organising something.

'There's no way I'm going,' I whisper, when play stops for a call. 'Can you imagine what it'd be like?'

'No, I can't, but I didn't go to school with a load of posh twots like you did. Will there be a string quartet and canopies?'

'You mean canapés.'

'That's what I said.'

'No, it's a disco and drinks.'

'It'll be fun!'

A collective groan echoes around the vast hall. It's an incorrect call, but it may as well be the sound of my soul dying at the thought of the reunion. We play on until another call punctures the silence.

'These are people I've not seen in twenty years. People who are now brain surgeons, peace workers and Arctic explorers. People who were born great, or have gone on to achieve greatness, or else have had greatness thrust upon them. People who did more with their private school education than bastardise the odd Shakespeare quote.'

The hall's TV screens herald the start of a different game we don't have tickets for.

'No, it's a part of my life that's over,' I tell her.

'Every part of your life so far is a part of your life that's over.'

'That's very profound.'

'Stop being such a pussy.'

I am being a pussy, but I'm nearly forty and I've done nothing interesting with my life.

'It's not for six months. I'll consider it.'

'Well, whilst you're thinking, any chance you can refill this glass while I go and order some chips or something?'

She sashays over to the bar once more. Ah Sindy. You might not know Latin, but *te amo*.

Chapter Five

We're barely half a term in, but the staffroom has already reached a state of complete disorder. I gingerly make my way round dozens of battered archive boxes, haphazardly piled on top of one another, and head to the kitchen to find the lovely Mrs Abara (Daphne to us grown-ups), looking exquisite in a voluminous skirt made from bright Dashiki fabric.

'How was your half-term?' she asks.

'Distinctly average.' We can't afford much by way of holidays, so we'd spent the time chasing free family entertainment. 'At one point we drove twenty miles to follow an *urban art trail* that consisted of a brightly painted bench and a tree in a scarf.'

She laughs. 'I'm glad we only have dogs.'

'Very wise!' I yawn uncontrollably.

'Late night?'

'Jack's still not sleeping properly.' I should read up on how to stop his midnight ramblings, but by the time I've made tea, checked on homework, done household admin, got him into bed, planned my lessons and questioned my life choices, I'm absolutely knackered.

Daphne shakes her head, her long brass earrings tinkling as she does so. 'Again. I'm glad we only have dogs.' She passes me her coffee. 'Your need is greater than mine.'

'Thanks.'

'On the subject of money. Crazy question, but since Leanne's moved out, you don't want a lodger, do you? Graham's trying to find temporary digs for a kid who's coming from the States to study. Last minute decision. Might be a bit of dosh in it for you?'

'I'm always into the idea of extra money, but I'm not sure replacing one sassy teenager with another is quite the answer I'm looking for.'

'Fair enough. Have a think about it though. If you change your mind, I can always get you some more details. He's coming in the next couple of weeks. We haven't got the room or else I'd do it.'

I'm heading out of the kitchen with a coffee when the Principal, Mr Gerald, steps in front of me. He is a plump dumpling of a man, not fat as such, but more round than he is tall, and entirely hairless due to alopecia. Combined with a penchant for beige suits and gold-rimmed glasses, he has the appearance of a short-sighted dough ball.

'Ms Beckinsale. I wonder if you can come to my office for five minutes?'

'Is everything alright?'

'It's a private matter I need to discuss.'

I wonder if there's suspicion being thrown on Mr Powell's accident and I'm being called up for questioning. The whole matter was usurped by a Year Niner setting fire to the bike sheds, so there hasn't been the same level of interest I'd originally anticipated.

Mr Gerald ushers me into his spacious office. The walls are covered in clichéd motivational posters with words such as *EXCELLENCE* and *SUCCESS* and *AMBITION* sitting beneath images of sunsets and mountains and goldfish jumping out of bowls. There's also a picture of a man kissing a killer whale. I'm not sure what that signifies: *IDIOCY*, or maybe *BESTIALITY*.

'Please, take a seat, Ms. Beckinsale.' He motions to the chair opposite his desk.

'Please, call me Cath.'

'Okay. Well, Cath, I've called you in here today because there's been a very serious accusation concerning alcohol abuse on the premises.'

I knew it. 'Who told you?'

'It doesn't matter how I heard. The question is, is it true?'

Shit, shit, shit. What to do?

'I cannot stress the importance of honesty in this matter. We might not have much of a reputation at this school, but the children's safety remains our highest priority.'

I look at my hands. I don't have much choice. 'It's true,' I tell him.

He sighs, takes off his glasses and gives them a cursory wipe with his handkerchief. 'I'm very disappointed to hear that.' He puts his glasses back on and fixes me in his gaze. 'I know you've been under a great deal of emotional stress, and stress can make us all behave inappropriately, but this is entirely unacceptable. I'm afraid I have no option but to terminate your employment.'

My stomach drops and the metallic taste of anxiety floods my mouth. 'What?' I manage.

'I'm sure you appreciate that I simply cannot have technical staff, in charge of potentially dangerous chemicals and equipment, under the influence.'

I struggle to parse what he's saying, but then the penny drops. 'Hang on, there's been a mistake. I'm not the one who's been drinking.'

'You just admitted your guilt.'

'I thought you were talking about Mr Powell!'

He furrows his eyebrows and tilts his head to one side. 'No. You are the person against whom I've received the complaint.'

'From whom?'

'That's not your concern.'

I bark with laughter. 'You're sacking me based on an unfounded accusation and you're telling me it's not my concern!'

'My source has asked to remain anonymous, and I must respect that.'

I'm out of my seat. 'No, you bloody well don't.'

He shrinks back and instinctively reaches for the phone. What's he going to do, call for back-up?

'Try and remain calm.'

'It's Powell, isn't it?' The shifty, bloated, self-serving dickhole. I felt sorry for him!

'You seem very agitated. Have you been drinking today?'

I laugh again. This is ridiculous. 'Listen to me. I'm not the drunk. He is! Did you stop to think how he cut himself when I took over his lesson because he was getting stitched up in A&E? Only now I'm the one being stitched up!'

He runs a finger round the inside of his collar. 'I have

spoken to Mr Powell, and he informed me that he sustained the injury helping you to clear up your ... little accident. He was very reluctant to do so, but he felt it was in the best interests of the school to come forward.'

'And you're going to believe his word against mine?'

'He is a senior member of the team.'

'And I am...?'

He shrugs. 'Part-time support staff.'

My body sags and I sit down again. I sense this is an argument I cannot win. I take as deep a breath as my racing heart will allow. 'For the record, even if I *was* caught drinking during working hours, I'm pretty certain policy is to initiate a precautionary suspension pending an investigation.'

Mr Gerald's eyes widen. 'On full pay? For however long it takes? You know very well this school is already underfunded. That's not a course of action I'm in a position to take.'

'But it's in my contract.'

He inclines his head to one side, a grim smile playing on his pale lips. 'A contract that you have been in breach of, ever since you took it upon yourself to extend your duties beyond mere technical assistance.'

How long have they known for? But does it really matter? I've been doing a bloody good job, and it's only been necessary because of Powell's blank refusal to do *his* job properly. 'I'll take you to a tribunal. I haven't done anything wrong.'

'Come on, Cath.'

'It's Ms. Beckinsale.'

'Do you really want to make this official? Get the authorities involved? You have two young children. Do you want the details of your life picked over, or do you want to walk away now with two month's pay to see you through until you find alternative arrangements?'

'But what will happen with my year elevens?'

'If you care at all for these children, you should do the decent thing and let us find a replacement so that we can give them the continuity they need at this crucial time.'

Every ounce of my being rages at the injustice of what's unfolding, but I know that if I fight this thing, I'll be using up resources and money that the school doesn't have. And even then, I probably won't win. 'And you promise you'll get them the support they need?'

'You have my word.'

I stand up, barely, my body as uncontrollable as the wavy-hand inflatables you see on retail parks. 'Okay, I'll go.' My wobbly legs almost give, surely making me look like I *have* been drinking. I lurch towards the door, open it, but then stop, determined to give him a piece of my mind. I level him a gaze that I hope demonstrates that I'm back in control of the situation. 'But when that lying, conniving, urine-stain on the underpants of humanity shows himself for what he really is, I only hope you can forgive yourself for being such an absolute and total waste of life.'

I walk out and try and slam the door behind me, aiming for a loud and rapturous full stop to my postscript, but it's got one of those soft-closing mechanisms on it, so instead it slowly creeps shut as Mr Gerald's face disappears inch by inch. I turn, the sick feeling in my stomach growing by the second, the rush of blood in my ears almost drowning out the secretary who is asking me if I'm okay. I'm so wound up it takes me several seconds to realise that the last part of my outburst had been witnessed by Reggie, who is outside the office with a large cut on his lip. Has he been fighting?

'What's going on, Miss?'

Dear, brilliant Reggie. My best pupil who I now won't be able to teach. His eyebrows furrow, seeking an explanation that I can't find my voice to articulate.

'I'm sorry, Reggie.' I choke as I run past him. 'I'm so, so sorry.'

I break through the exit doors that lead onto the delivery bay at the back of the school, and take in gulps of air as a soft drizzle settles on my skin. I can't believe I've lost my job. What the hell do I do now?

Chapter Six

'I can't see you, are you video calling me from under the duvet again?' asks Leanne.

Every day for the last two weeks, after I've dropped Jack off at nursery, I've taken to crawling into bed and mainlining depressing boxsets on my laptop. At first, I thought watching fictional characters having a worse time than I was might be cathartic, but the only thing I'm achieving is getting a sweaty lap.

'Ugh. I know, I need to get over it, but it's so unfair.'

In the days immediately following my dismissal, I imagined that the school was going to call and tell me it had all been a terrible mistake, that I was welcome back with open arms, right until I remembered I'd drawn a penis on the bonnet of Mr Gerald's car using a marker I'd found in my handbag. Since then I've moved between anger, fear, resignation and currently frustration at the injustice of it all.

'Sorry, I'm feeling sorry for myself. I really shouldn't be burdening you with this.'

I had resisted telling Leanne about losing my job, knowing it would afford her another excuse to worry about me, but Geoff let it slip.

'Don't apologise. It's natural you're struggling. I've been reading up on unfairness and the brain.'

Leanne is really getting into her course and I love it when she gives me little snippets of what she's learned.

'Hang on, I'm going to make myself a cuppa whilst you tell me.' I get out of bed and head downstairs.

'Okay, so there's a researcher who gets two people to play a game. The first player is given a sum of money and told to offer some to a second player who knows how much they have. If the offer is rejected, they both end up with nothing.'

I fill the kettle and grab a mug from a vertiginous stack on the draining board. 'Okaaay.'

'Pure financial self-interest suggests the second player should accept any offer greater than zero, no matter how unfair he thinks it is, because it's better than nothing, right?'

'Right.' I open the tea jar on the side, noting with a sinking heart that it's empty. I find some camomile teabags that only went out of date two years ago.

'But in reality, most people reject offers that are less than around a quarter, because they don't think it's a fair split.'

'So, they cut off their nose to spite their face?'

'In effect, yes. They would rather go without than feel unfairly treated. But the interesting bit is what's going on in the brain when this is happening. There's heightened activity in an area associated with contempt or disgust.'

I pour water on the teabag and realise too late that I didn't switch the kettle on. *Gah* to the power of *arse*. 'What's your point?'

'You might think you should be able to get over it, but it's not the rational part of your brain that's dealing with it. It's more visceral than that.'

'So, I have your permission to continue to wallow in self-pity?' I sit at the table and prop my phone up against the cold tea. She tilts her head, her curls falling away to reveal a recently pierced patch of angry red cartilage.

'Nope. You really do need to get over it.'

'What an empathetic psychologist you're going to be.'

A fly settles on the edge of my mug. Its tiny proboscis taps at the rim in search of sustenance.

'Why thank you. Seriously though, what are you going to do?'

'I don't know. I don't have any qualifications. It's only because they were desperate that I got the job at Brookdene. Do you know how many jobs there are that are part-time, midweek and give you school holidays off?'

'You're going to be okay though, right? Financially I mean.'

'Of course.'

The only positive by-product of Gaz's death was, thanks to a life insurance policy he got through work, the mortgage got paid off when he died and we were left with a modest sum that covers about half of our monthly outgoings. *That doesn't mean I forgive you for abandoning us*, I mouth at the urn. Without any foreseeable income though, once my final wages run out, we'll be into savings, and I really don't want to touch those.

'You could always sell your body.'

'I beg your pardon!'

'I'm joking. I wanted to check you could still smile.'

'Hey. You don't need to worry about me, okay.' I knew she would. 'The only way I'd get cash for this bag of flesh would be for spare parts.' I force myself to sound as upbeat as possible. 'Actually, flogging a kidney on the black market wouldn't be such a bad idea.'

'Not your liver though. That's taken a bit of a battering.'

'You cheeky get! I don't drink that much. I barely go anywhere!'

She lets her face go all slack and stupid looking. 'Err. Again. Joking.'

I smile. Slightly less forced this time.

'Mom, I'm really sorry, I have to go. I've got a lecture.'

'Go! I love you.'

'I love you too.'

She disappears and the phone's home screen takes its place. I feel immediately glum again. What am I going to do? I look across at the urn, hoping it might offer some enlightenment. Gaz says nothing, as per bloody usual. Unless some fairy godmother offers me several hundred pounds per month in the coming days, I might have to take drastic measures.

―――――――――

A few nights later I'm still entirely out of options, but rather than do the sensible thing and look to see if there are any part-time jobs that might be suitable, I've fallen down a social media rabbit hole, scrolling through feed after feed of accomplished ex-school friends. I never have anything to post myself, but lurking on the sidelines is a form of masochism that I can't help but indulge in. Thankfully the doorbell rings to save me from myself. Sindy is here for our weekly movie night.

'What about this for an advertising slogan?' I say as I lead her into the kitchen. '*Twitter: makes your life shitter.*'

'It's catchy.' She hands me a cold bottle of Pinot Grigio and places another one on the countertop. Looks like she's staying for the night. She shrugs off her denim jacket and gets some glasses from the cupboard.

'Perhaps I *should* get into advertising,' I muse.

'I think you're meant to *sell* the products you advertise.'

'Yeah, but I bloody hate social media.' I open a bag of bear-shaped crisps, the only vestige of savoury snack I have in, and empty them into a bowl. I'm sophisticated like that.

'As a science lover, aren't you meant to like all techy developments?' she asks.

'Only the ones that advance our society.'

'What about emoticons and text speak? That's a brand-new language created in barely a few years.'

I take a big swig of wine. 'That's the *worst* thing about social media.'

'Why? They save you loads of time.'

'But where's it going to end? By the time Jack reaches adulthood, will human language be reduced to a series of symbols and strokes on our *Apple EmotiPads* linked to our cerebral cortexes and shown to one another via 3D projections from our sphincters?'

'If that is what happens, Steve Jobs will be sad he missed it. Speaking of jobs, if you don't find anything soon, I can lend you some cash.'

'You are a true pal, but I need a reason to get out of the house.'

'At least let me bring you the occasional wine parcel. And some better crisps.'

'Accepted. Come on, let's watch something to take my mind off it all.'

One romantic comedy and half a tub of ice cream later and I'm altogether more relaxed. It wasn't even a great movie—the standard fodder of girl meets boy, girl hates boy, some incident forces boy and girl together, girl warms to boy, some calamity forces boy and girl apart and then both boy and girl decide they can't live without one another. But no matter how unlikely the story, there's something about watching happiness unfold on-screen that infuses you with the sense there are still happy endings to be had in real-life.

'One of my old work colleagues called this week to persuade me to take on a lodger.'

'What? Really? How come?'

I'd just got back from dropping Jack off this morning when Daphne rang. I'd been resolutely ignoring her calls since I got sacked because I felt embarrassed by what had happened, but I accidentally answered and immediately felt bad about ignoring her because she was lovely, told me everyone who mattered knew I would never do the thing I was accused of, and then reiterated the offer of the lodger, because apparently some other arrangements they'd made had fallen through.

Sindy, who up until this point has been lying slumped inside a blanket with her head hanging off the end of the sofa, suddenly perks up. 'Why not do it? It's easy money!'

'Hmm. I'm not sure I like the idea of a stranger in the house.'

'They're practically a kid though, right? Probably some wet behind the ears geekoid who needs someone to cook and clean for him because he's never been away from home.'

'Or the teenager out of *We Need to Talk About Kevin*, all serious glaring and murderous intent.'

'Get his name and we'll see if we can find him online.'

'We can't go stalking people on social media.'

'Says the woman who was stalking people on social media earlier.'

'Fair point. I'll message her.' I grab my phone and type out a quick message asking for details and telling her I'm considering it.

'Go get the laptop. And that other bottle of wine.' She waves her empty glass at me.

No sooner is my message delivered than Daphne starts typing a reply.

Dan Stanford-Sturgess fr Kansas. Apparently lovely. Let me know what u think.

This is probably a terrible idea, but I drag myself from the comfort of the sofa and negotiate countless toddler-placed obstacles to do Sindy's bidding. Once returned I flip the lid and search the name. I should probably go easy on the wine as it takes a few attempts to get it right, but then the screen fills with a list of Dan Stanford-Sturgesses.

'Isn't a sturgess a type of fish?' Sindy asks as she plonks next to me on the sofa.

'That's a sturgeon.'

'Is that the one that operates on all the other fish?'

I dig her in the ribs then study the list of profiles. At first it had looked like hundreds, but in fact there are only a handful spelled in the same way.

'Ooh, check out that one.' Sindy points at a picture of some floppy-haired Poldark type with a smouldering selfie.

'Wrong state. Location is Little Rock. Didn't that have something to do with the de-segregation of schools in the 1950s? Anyway, we're looking for Kansas.'

'Yawn. Facts. Yawn. You know things. Let's have a proper looksie. He is fit as!'

'May I remind you that you're a married woman?'

'And Dave's away, so some light ogling of a stranger is not doing any harm.'

She grabs the laptop and scrolls through Little Rock Dan's feed. It's not been updated for a while, but there's plenty of nausea-inducing photos of a guy who got an extra helping of good looks and knows it. There's Little Rock Dan in skin-tight wetsuit with surfboard; Little Rock Dan clutching a guitar; Little Rock Dan staring into the middle distance by a campfire; Little Rock Dan with a succession of identikit hotties; Little Rock Dan in close-up, beaded necklace à la Patrick Swayze in *Point Blank* encircling his neck.

'He is beautiful.' She strokes the screen. 'Any of him in trunks?'

'Oh please. The guy is clearly a douchebag.'

'Why, because he's hot and carefree?'

'How old is he?' I check his date of birth and struggle to do the mental arithmetic in my head. I am very squiffy. 'He's what, thirty-six-ish? Old enough to be that last girl's dad!'

'They might be friends. Or relatives.'

'Yep, and I might be Jennifer Lopez.'

'Are you telling me that if you weren't totally against the idea of ever dating again, and he walked into your life, you wouldn't fancy him?'

'Definitely not!'

'Even though he looks like an older version of the guy in the movie we just watched, and you were all like *"ah, he's so cute"*.'

'That's different. He *was* cute. Look at this guy with his self-satisfied grin and his faux ruminative poses. I bet in real life he's as profound as a fart in a yoga class.'

I reclaim the laptop, close Little Rock Dan's profile with an emphatic mouse click and review the other profiles. It's the last name with that exact spelling that I click on that delivers the goods. Dan Stanford-Sturgess. Eighteen. Kansas City. His profile picture shows him in a dark blue cap and gown, high school diploma in hand with a broad grin and thick rimmed glasses on his pale benign face. 'Now he's cute. Not in that way, obviously.'

'And how much of his college fund is he prepared to spend for B&B?' Sindy asks.

'Six hundred pounds per month, apparently.'

'And how much were you getting for working three days a week?'

'Just shy of eight hundred, after tax.'

'Er, it's a no brainer.'

'I'm not sure.'

'Think about it. It's only, what, six months? He'll probably sit in his room playing games when he's not at lectures. Or chit-chat with Eric about drones, or clones, or thrones, whatever nerds are into now. It'll give you some breathing space at least. You won't be ploughing into your savings so quickly.'

'I'd need to get Leanne's permission. It's her room.'

She shakes her head sagely. 'No biggie.'

'And the probabilities of it being as straightforward as you make it sound are very slim.'

'Pah! That's just maths.'

I roll the idea around in my head for a few seconds. 'This could be the universe gifting me the chance to do something different, couldn't it?'

'It could. You could get a degree.'

'You know it takes longer than six months to get a degree?'

She waves a hand noncommittally in my general direction. 'There's no rush.'

'But I might be able to do something in that time.'

'You almost certainly could.'

'Einstein said if you always do what you've always done, you'll always get what you've always got.'

'That's so like him.'

'I'd have to check the tax implications of renting out the room.'

'You're losing me with the detail now.' She reaches for the wine bottle.

'Screw it. Why not? Why the hell not?' I type out a quick message to Daphne then drop my mobile as if I'm dropping a mic. What was I so worried about? This is a great idea!

Sindy stands up and raises her glass. 'Today is the first day of the rest of your life, Catherine Beckinsale. Onwards and upwards from here on in!'

I get to my feet and clink her glass emphatically with my own. 'I'll drink to that!'

Chapter Seven

O f course, it's only the following weekend as I'm on the way to the airport that the full force of what I've let myself in for comes rushing at me like a tidal wave of *WTAF?* I've left Jack and Eric at home with Sindy, who assured me that inviting someone I know barely anything about to come and live in my house without so much as having had a conversation with him, is a great idea. I guess it happens all the time on Airbnb, right? And Daphne wouldn't have put me in touch with some psycho. Still, my stomach is doing all manner of odd things as I pull into the car park ten minutes before the plane is due to land. I figure there's half an hour before Kansas City Dan emerges from customs, which is just as well, because I need to tidy the car up. I gingerly toss bits of biscuit, crisp packets and dried-up curls of satsuma peel into a plastic bag. Most surprising is the amount of dirt that has accumulated in the rear foot well. It's as if the boys have been conducting their own *Great Escape*, secreting soil in their turn ups and emptying it out into the car when no one is looking. I'll have to check for holes behind their *Star Wars* and *Paw Patrol* posters later. I make a quick name sign using the inside of an empty tissue box and head into arrivals.

Minutes after I get to the gate a stream of people starts to emerge from the exit, their weary faces lighting up as they spot waiting relatives. I check the photo of Dan I saved to my phone. No sign yet, but he's probably slowly lolloping his way from the plane, peering through his hair curtains and taking in a brand-new country. As I'm watching it all unfold, a man, I'd say in his mid-thirties, emerges from the exit carrying a large rucksack and a guitar. He's over six-feet tall and archetypically handsome, a mop of loose brown curls framing an elfin face rescued from femininity by a defined jaw and strong straight brows. His cheeks dimple as he smiles at the striking young air stewardess walking alongside him. I can't make out what he's saying, but she is lapping it up as she overtly throws her head back in amusement and lightly touches him on the arm.

As he gets closer, I have the strongest sense I recognise him, which is odd because I don't tend to knock around with tall, dark, handsome men. He could be a former school friend, one of the pupils from the boys' school next door with whom we'd shared a hockey pitch, older now and hard to place in this incongruous setting. But that can't be right because I've seen this face more recently. He could be someone well-known, off the television perhaps? But that doesn't check out because whilst he's drawing a few subtle head turns, they don't seem to be of the tap-the-person-next-to-you-because-that-guy's-famous variety.

He gets closer still and I take in the whiter than white teeth, the full mouth with the natural upturn at the edges. And then he unzips his puffer jacket and I spot a shell bead necklace poking out from the collar of his T-shirt. Oh. My. God. It's not possible, is it, that when Sindy and I were messing around online that night, we got the wrong guy? That Little Rock Dan is my new lodger? A wave of sickness engulfs me. I break into a hot sweat and my hands go clammy. It must be a coincidence. Or I'm mistaken. Shell necklaces may be all the rage in America. It only looks like him. Any second now, Kansas City Dan will appear, pushing the hair out of his face, and Sindy will howl when I tell her what initially went through my head. But this guy really does look like an older version of the cute guy in that film. And what of my message exchange with Daphne. Did I ever ask for definitive details? Did I tell her about our search? Not that I recollect. Shit! Why did I not think to check exactly who he was? Why did she not tell me he was a mature student? Why would someone like him come to somewhere like this? And why do I not have a cyanide pill tucked about my person for this precise eventuality? I would run away, but my legs have stopped working, and besides, Little Rock Dan has spotted the bloody sign I'm still holding up, bids farewell to the stewardess, and makes a beeline for me.

'Hey, you must be Cath.'

Before I realise what's happening, he leans in for an air kiss, but a combination of misjudging his angle of descent and having to stand up on my tiptoes to try and greet it means I land a smacker straight on his mouth.

'Shit! Sorry!' I'm only wearing a baggy sweatshirt and some leggings, but it is several layers too many for how hot I've gone.

He steps back. 'Wow. Fine. Okay.'

The distance gives me a chance to take him in properly.

He's ridiculous. He's just stepped off a flight and yet could equally have stepped out of a frigging photo shoot for some hipster magazine. *Today, ladies and gentlemen, Dan has styled his crisp white T-shirt with a red & black plaid shirt, close-fitting mid-blue jeans, a navy puffer and a pair of well-loved black & white converse trainers.* I, by contrast, look like I've just stepped out of a hedge.

'I wouldn't normally … I wasn't expecting a…' I'm doing so much gesticulating I'm creating a draught. 'Honestly. Even a handshake is practically foreplay for me nowadays!' *WTF?* I am only two sentences in, and not only have I accosted him, but I've also told him I have no sex life. What if he thinks the two things are related? 'Shit! That's not the reason why I … you know, I wasn't trying to…' I need to stop digging— figuratively, and with my hand movements.

He smiles broadly. His teeth are so straight. 'It's fine. Do you want to start over?'

'No, I want a plane to crash on my head.'

'Continue to wave your hands around like that, you might attract the attention of one.'

He has a mild southern accent. Not even close to cowboy, but the faintest of drawls that rounds out into such a softening of the 's' into 'shh' that he could probably whisper a horse into submission. But it's his face that's really hypnotic. I can't take my eyes off it. It's so symmetrical; impossibly so. You could trace a dotted line down the centre of it and each side would be a mirror image of the other. It's uncanny. Oh no, I'm staring, aren't I? He doesn't seem to mind. He's probably used to being stared at.

'Do you have a ride?' he asks, 'Or should I climb onto your back and you'll fly us home?'

I take his guitar and point him in the direction of the busy lifts that lead to the multi-storey carpark. We wait there in silence until we spot an opening. Dan gets in after a bunch of other people, and I follow on, squeezing myself into the corner and turning to face the door so I'm not distracted by Dan's eyes. His irises are almost as dark as his pupils. As the doors begin to close, despite the lift already being full, some bloke in a pinstripe suit jumps the queue and crams his way in. He extends his arm towards me exposing a fancy watch and diamond cufflinks, and his hand comes very close to my boobs.

'Can I press one?' he says, impatiently.

'Not unless you want me to kick you in the balls,' I say, as my brain clocks he means the panel of buttons next to me.

Dan sniggers behind me. I pray for a painless death.

Once we're out of the lift I try and regain my composure, but my brain is bouncing between embarrassment and puzzlement. How could I possibly have ended up with Little Rock Dan? Why in heaven's name would he want to stay with a middle-aged woman and her two children? And where the bloody hell is the car? As I'm losing hope of finding it, I spot its bonnet poking out from behind some top-of-the-range Jeep and almost groan with relief.

'This is us.'

'Nice wheels.'

He thinks I mean the 4x4. 'No, not that one. This one.'

He takes in the battered brown paintwork, the rusting body, the plastic roof box we lost the key for that's now so sun-damaged, it's just an ill-fitting bleached hat.

'This is cute too.'

'It's as aerodynamic as a fridge-freezer, but it goes. Mostly. And there's room for the kids.'

'The kids?'

Oh shit-a-doodle-do. He doesn't know I have kids.

'You didn't know I have kids?'

'I did not. Do they live with you?'

'Two thirds of them do. One's at uni. It's her room you're meant to be having.'

'Okaaaay.' His brows knit like squiggled parentheses.

'I was under the impression you were a teenager.'

I desperately want to call Daphne and ask her if she knew this was the fella or whether we've both been labouring under the same misapprehension. But that'll have to wait.

'Let me get you back to mine and we'll take it from there.'

Whilst he pops his stuff in the boot, I check myself in the mirror. Lots of strands have escaped from my already messy bun, and I really need to pluck my eyebrows. At least my teeth are food-free. As he climbs in, I snap the sun visor up and start the car. Trouble is, I'm somewhat disconcerted at having an attractive man in the passenger seat, and despite me telling them to behave themselves, my brain and body have gone into some evolutionary mode of fluster and suddenly my ovaries are driving. I bunny-hop three times on pulling out of the parking space and then stall the car altogether.

'It always does that,' I lie, cursing myself that I will now have to replicate that every time I happen to give him a lift anywhere. I regain control of my arms and legs enough to see us safely out of the car park and on our way home.

At first Dan is happy to look out of the window, which is perfect because it gives me time to agonise over how much of a numpty I've acted so far. But then we hit the motorway and any visual interest that he may have pretended was holding his attention falls away, to be replaced by four lanes of stop-start traffic on a so-called *smart motorway* currently being used by morons.

'It's the shockwave effect,' I utter, for wont of something to say.

'What is?'

'The speeding up and then slowing down. It's how you get tailbacks even when there are no visible causes.'

'Oh,' he says.

Terrible opening chat gambit, Cath. Shut it down.

'Yep. Scientists have shown that when motorways, or freeways as you call them, are at capacity, even the slightest bit of bad driving, like braking too hard, has a knock-on effect that can stop traffic for several miles behind you.'

'Right.'

Meaningless drivel alert. Back track.

'Yeah, it was discovered in Exeter, which is only about a hundred miles from here.'

Change the subject. To literally anything else. Quick.

'Yeah, it's fascinating really…'

It isn't Cath. It really isn't.

'Even more fascinating…'

Nope.

'…is that we've known how it happens for years, but we're no closer to preventing it.'

He shifts in his seat and sits up straighter. My mouth takes this as interest before my brain registers that his bottom is probably numb from the seat's shot-to-buggery springs, but I'm committed now.

'I'm really interested in how, despite understanding the

SAL THOMAS

ramifications of our actions, we still do the very thing we know will have a negative impact on us.'

'I see.'

We come to a standstill once again, the traffic a metaphor for this conversation.

'And tell me, Cath, do you have any other hobbies?'

I'm several minutes into a manic soliloquy about currently being obsessed with quantum computing and explaining the limitations of modern digital PCs by way of an old Indian legend involving chess and grains of rice, when I realise the question was meant as a joke. At least we're off the motorway and back onto a faster-moving A road.

'I can't imagine how this cock-up could have happened,' I say, moving to safer territory. 'What were you told about your new living arrangements?'

'A pal of mine said he knew someone who knew someone who was looking for a roommate. You?'

'Undergraduate, called Dan, coming from Kansas.'

'I'm from Arkansas.'

Hmm. I see what might have happened here. Stupid text messages.

'Did you not ask for any more information?' I ask.

'I've travelled a lot. You're never sure what you're going to get into, but that's part of the fun. How about you?' He tucks his hair behind his ear.

'I did some research. Only of the wrong person.'

The car falls quiet again. We pass a park, a huge cemetery, then Sarehole Mill where J. R. R. Tolkien hung out as a child.

'Obviously you won't want to stay now you know I have kids.'

'Why not?'

60

'Erm. Because even I don't want to stay half the time, and they're my flesh and blood.' Now I sound like a bad mom. But Dan laughs.

'I stayed with a host family in Guatemala a few years ago, and that was great.'

'For a year?'

'No. But I could have done. And do you not need the money?'

Blimey. I heard Americans could be frank, but asking about someone's financial situation when you've only just met is next-level forthrightness.

'That's not your problem.'

'But I still need somewhere to stay, so what's stopping me doing you the favour and going through with it?'

Has he got some kind of benevolent Jesus complex? That might explain the hair.

'Because that's not how the world works.'

'People can't do favours for one another?'

'People can. Strangers, nah.'

'You let a stranger in line back there. That's an act of kindness.'

'That's different.'

'What about giving money to charity?'

'Are you saying I'm a charity case?'

'No.'

It's starting to rain. I cringe as the wipers scrape noisily across the windscreen.

'It's just that lots of people are bell-ends, aren't they?' I say.

'What's a bell-end?'

Oh god. Me and my potty mouth. 'It's the … the erm… It's…' It's only a body part, Cath. Not like you've shied away from sexual references already. 'It's what we call the end section of a penis.'

'Bell-end,' he draws the words out. 'Really? I don't get the similarity.'

'What about those little jingle bells with the little ... you know...'—we hit a red light—'... slitty hole bits at the end.'

He's looking directly at me. Is he smirking or smiling? I never thought I'd miss the shockwave effect chat. It's suddenly hot in here. I crack a window to prevent the windscreen completely steaming up and try to ignore the rain dripping onto my arm.

'Just because some people are, as you so eloquently put it, bell-ends, doesn't mean everyone is. I think it's possible to be altruistic.'

'Hah!'

We're finally pulling into our road.

'I'm guessing you don't.'

'I think you can have the illusion of altruism, but really people always act in their own self-interest. Biologically we're here to survive and replicate.'

'Story time with you must be so much fun. *And the fairy godmother waved her magic wand but absolutely nothing happened. "Screw you, Cinderella," she shouted in the startled girl's face. "Don't you know it's every man for himself!"'*

'I just don't think you'll get much out of staying with us.'

'I already know *bell-end*. And *cock-up*. Such rich visual imagery. This truly is the land of Shakespeare.'

We've arrived home. I park up outside the house.

'I mean anything worthwhile.'

'Then it really would be an act of altruism, wouldn't it?'

Damn it. He's got me on a technicality. Still, I know what he's letting himself in for and he won't last the week.

'Fine,' I say. 'You can stay if you want.'

'Great,' he says. 'Let's see what happens.'

I spot my eldest son at an upstairs window and feel a cold flush of anxiety at how he'll react to this turn of events.

'Apart from your Guatemalan family, do you have much experience of children?' I ask as I open the front door.

'Not much.' He leans his guitar against the wall. 'Is that one?'

Jack, dressed in a clown mask, angel wings and nothing else, is at the bottom of the stairs poking a finger into the end of his penis. He doesn't even look up as we go inside. I take my coat off and try to place it over his lap.

'It's a stage he's going through. He's obsessed.'

'With clowns, or his johnson?'

'The latter.'

'You know that's not just a stage, right?'

I kneel, take Jack's mask off, kiss the top of his head and ask him where Auntie Sindy is. The toilet flushes upstairs.

'I'm coming,' she shouts, 'I was on the loo. I thought I only needed a wee, but then…' She looks up from buttoning her jeans and clocks Dan, shock and awe fighting for precedence on her face.

'Holy shitting hell! You're the other guy.' Her hands go to her cheeks. 'You're the Dan we stalked and were saying was well fit!'

Dan casts me a quizzical glance.

'I didn't say you were fit.' Which is true, but I'm not sure the disclaimer is either required or appropriate. I widen my eyes at Sindy in remonstration.

'Where's the eighteen-year-old?' She bounces down the stairs to get a better look, stopping at the bottom step.

'We got the wrong guy.'

'You were stalking me online?' asks Dan, eyebrow raised.

'We were looking up the Dan I thought I was getting, but we might have come across your profile.'

'I practically did come across your profile,' says Sindy. 'If you know what I mean. You must get that a lot.'

'No one's ever really … gee … thanks, I guess.'

'Bollocks. You get that all the time. You're like a cross between the lead singer of the *Stereophonics* and, I don't know, someone tall. Or the love child of Cillian Murphy and, well, someone tall. Or Patrick Dempsey, if he was about six inches taller.'

'Are you sure you don't just think I'm tall?'

'Holy shit. This is insane. Can I get a selfie with you?' She whips out her phone, and takes a selfie, lips puckered up to Dan's cheek. I must admit, for a man whose day hasn't gone according to plan, he's taking it in good humour. Then again, he probably flourishes under flirting conditions.

'Dan, this is my best friend, Sindy.'

'Best friends,' says Dan, like he'd heard a snake announce it was best friends with a mouse. 'Hmmmm.'

'I get that a lot,' says Sindy. 'Did she go maximum nerd on you in the car? She can't help herself. She bored you senseless, didn't she?'

'We may have touched on the lack of rationality in humanity, exponential numbers and the genetic nature of selfishness.'

Sindy shakes her head. 'She doesn't get out much.'

'Well, you're going to have to point me in the direction of

someone who does, because I was hoping to have some fun whilst I'm here.'

'*ANYWAY*,' I say, a little too brightly and a little too loudly. 'I'm sure Dan is super tired, so I'm going to make him a cuppa and show him to his room.'

'Do you want me to tuck you in?' says Sindy. 'It's absolutely no problem.'

'I'm good, but thank you for your fine English hospitality.'

I open the door for her. 'You are free to go, my lovely. Will I see you on Friday?'

Sindy backs out of the door, nodding vociferously, all the while looking at Dan. *I would so do that* she mouths at me.

I know you would I mouth back.

'I said, I would so do that,' she enunciates, out loud this time

'I know, I lipread you the first time.'

Dan laughs behind me.

'Call me. We need to discuss … that!'

'You know he can still hear you?'

She shakes her head, still not quite getting it round how this Dan is in my hallway. That makes two of us. I close the door to find Jack gone and Eric in his place.

'I'm Eric. I see you have a guitar. Is it classical or electric?'

'It's classical.'

'Great. My dad has one of those. Can you teach me how to play it?'

'I could try. Will your dad mind?' asks Dan.

'I doubt it,' says Eric.

'Come through to the kitchen,' I tell Dan. He should probably meet Gaz too.

Chapter Eight

B angs, fizzes and woody smoke aromas filter in on the crisp autumnal air through Jack's bedroom window. The neighbourhood is alight with Bonfire Night celebrations, and Sindy arrived twenty minutes ago in readiness for our own cheapskate display, an annual tradition in which we light a selection of disappointing supermarket-bought fireworks rather than head to a properly organised thing at which I would probably only lose Jack. I hear her raucous laughter echoing up the stairs despite the noise outside. Dan's drifts up in response.

Dan has been around for precisely seven days, and he's not showing any sign of leaving. For my part I've been doing my best to avoid him when I can. I'd like to say that this is for his sake, that given the circumstances I'm giving him space and letting him acclimatise, but the truth is it's me struggling with the new dynamic, feeling hamstrung by his ease and confidence as he moves around the house with the self-assurance of a seasoned traveller. Sindy clearly has no such issues; they sound like they're having a whale of a time.

It was always going to be odd having someone new in the house, but when that someone looks like he's stepped off the cover of *Men's Health* magazine, it is way harder. It doesn't matter how many times I tell myself he simply got lucky with his DNA, my own DNA does something stupid like mistakenly assuming he's out and breaking wind loudly whilst shouting 'a little bit more choke and you'll get it started!' Gaz used to say it to amuse the kids. That was an hour ago and I've been hiding out ever since.

'Want fireworks,' says Jack, who has grown bored of stuffing soft toys into my jumper.

'Okay, Son.' I suppose we should head down.

Dan and Sindy are sat at the still very messy kitchen table. Sindy is telling Dan about hubby Dave and how he fought in Iraq alongside the US Army. I busy myself moving some cups from the breakfast bar to the sink.

'Where have you been?' asks Sindy. 'I thought you'd got lost!'

'I was just…' I let the sentence trail. *Avoiding Dan* would sound too pathetic. I'm going to have to style the whole bottom burp thing out. Pretend nothing happened. This is my house after all. I sit down and, with a bit of a tussle because the lid is on very tight, open the fireworks I bought earlier to check there's a taper inside. There is. I pop the lid back on again, but air escaping through it makes a sound just like a fart. I instinctively look at Dan, who pretends not to notice, but I feel myself flush from my chest upwards anyway. Fortunately his attention is quickly diverted to something behind me. Phew.

'Hey buddy,' he says. 'Interesting hat.'

I turn, expecting to see Eric in some new literary-inspired ensemble, but Jack is there wearing a pair of my pants on his head. And not a pair of my good pants. He's managed to uncover a pair of massive greying pregnancy pants, crotch bit turned out across his nose, two amused eyes staring out from the baggy leg holes.

'I think those need to go on the fire.' Sindy chuckles.

'Give me strength,' I mutter.

I make to grab them, but Jack quickly skitters across the room and pulls them more firmly onto his head, stretching the crotch even tighter across his nose. I don't have time to chase him around, and besides, it's nearly seven and if we don't get the fireworks underway soon, I'll never get him to bed. I open the box again because I need something to do with my hands, only this time I pull a little too vigorously to avoid more wind noises and send the fireworks scattering to the floor. I crouch down to pick them up at the same time as Dan does, and our hands and gazes meet. I move my hands to one side, but Dan's go in the exact same direction, so our hands touch again. Then we do the same thing in the opposite direction. My face lights up like a Roman Candle.

'Ooh, would you look at the fireworks between you two,' jokes Sindy.

'Very funny,' I manage. Both Dan and I know the only chemistry between us is the audible gaseous emission from my bottom earlier.

'What exactly is Bonfire Night?' Dan asks once everything is back in the box.

'You know,' says Sindy. 'Remember, remember the fifth of November.'

Dan shakes his head. 'Nope.'

'Oh come on,' she says. 'The fifth of November, gunpowder treason and plot.'

'No idea.'

'Seriously?' Sindy says flabbergasted. 'Guy Fawkes. Wanted to blow up Parliament?'

'Why?'

'Because,' she says, eyes bulging. 'Becaaaause... Do you know what, I haven't the foggiest.'

Dan laughs. 'Cath? Do you know?'

Both heads swivel towards me.

'It was a religious thing. Several hundred years ago Catholics were being persecuted, so decided to blow up the Protestant King. Guy Fawkes, the ringleader, was discovered before the deed was done.'

Sindy mimes me having a big head.

'You asked! To celebrate not being burnt to death, the King decreed everyone should set off small unlicensed bombs in his honour. Which, if you ask me, is a bit like surviving a plane crash and then getting someone to fly a microlight at your head every year.'

Dan laughs, his face creasing into an abundance of eye crinkles and straight white teeth. I hadn't meant it as a joke. It's an inherently stupid thing to do.

'How do you know all this stuff?'

'I told you, she doesn't get out enough,' says Sindy.

'You can't repeatedly do something and not think about why it is you're doing it.'

'Oh, I don't know!' says Dan.

He and Sindy share a high five and a knowing look. I'm immediately fifteen years old again, when for a brief period

Sindy and another neighbourhood girl temporarily bonded over losing their virginity. I hadn't, and resented every minute they'd spent talking about something I didn't yet have the vocabulary for.

'What are you high-fiving over?' Eric has wandered in.

'Nothing,' they both say at the same time.

Eric grunts. 'I hate it when adults say that.'

Yeah, me too, son.

'Did you buy toffee apples Mom?'

'No.'

'Oh Mommm.'

'Just open your mouth so wide your jaw locks, and then shatter a glass of the apple juice that's in the fridge into it. It's practically the same.'

Dan laughs again. 'Your mom's pretty funny.'

I find this statement unaccountably irritating. It's not like I need his approbation.

Eric shakes his head, appalled. 'She really isn't.'

'I do have marshmallows and the firepit is all set up. Wanna go light it?'

'Okay.' He heads outside.

'Dan, why don't you join us?' says Sindy. 'It'll be your first authentic British experience.'

I give Sindy my hardest stare that she fails to notice, but I'm pretty certain Dan clocks it because he says he doesn't want to intrude.

'Cath doesn't mind, do you?'

I can't exactly say that I do mind, because that would be churlish and unreasonable and I'm not sure why I would mind, except I guess the way this evening is panning out, we won't need a Guy because I'm either going to combust with embarrassment or petty jealousy.

'Sure, why not?'

By 8pm we're all done. No one lost an eye or a finger, but I almost certainly hurt Dan's feelings when he offered to assist with the fireworks and I told him I wasn't some damsel in distress that needed a man to help me. Shortly afterwards I hammered the Catherine wheel into the fence too tightly, so rather than looking like a cat's anus exploding, it looked like an off-kilter fountain which set fire to the panel. Not quite the finale I was looking for. Naturally Dan was the first to it with a pan of water, thus undermining my point entirely. I mumbled my excuses and took Jack straight up to bed, where he dicked around for forty-five minutes whilst I replayed Dan's crestfallen look in my head.

I don't know what's up with me. I wonder if it's because he's so bloody comfortable in his own skin. Or he finds it so easy to ingratiate himself to people. Whereas I am awkwardness squared. I never used to be this way. Sure, I've always had a knack for saying the wrong thing or making an inappropriate joke here and there, but with Gaz around the spotlight of attention was never fully on me, and I never had reason to feel self-conscious. But when he died my personal identity went through the shredder. I've painstakingly pieced it back together so it's broadly recognisable, but the joins are still visible. After several attempts, Jack finally drifts off to sleep and I reluctantly head down. I should try to make amends but without actually apologising. I could offer him a biscuit, that always seems to work with the kids. At the bottom of the stairs I hear my name mentioned through the cracked kitchen door. Naturally I do whatever self-respecting adult with integrity would do: I position myself out of eyeshot so I can hear what they're saying about me.

'She doesn't not like you,' says Sindy.

'Really? Because I'm trying not to make a nuisance of myself, but...' he trails off.

'Just give it a bit of time. It's gonna be weird having a bloke around again.'

'How long ago did Gaz die?'

'It's been over three years.'

It's been three years and two months.

There's a pause.

'But doesn't that mean... How old is Jack'?

'She was pregnant when he died.'

'Oh jeez.'

'Yeah.'

'And there's been no one else since?'

'No one.'

'What was he like?'

'Gaz? He was an absolute belter.'

'A what?!'

'It means a great bloke. He was funny, really funny. He made her laugh a lot. Kind, but not in a soft-arsed, overbearing way. Handy around the house. Hardworking. Loyal. Doted on Cath and the kids, but again, not in a soft-arsed, overbearing way. He loved her quirks. Shared her interests.'

I smile. Clearly he was so much more than that, but she's nailed the basics.

'They were equals, you know? Intellectually. Emotionally. All of it. They just got on. And they got on with it. Cath's always just got on with it, even before Gaz died.'

She gives Dan a whistlestop tour of some of the other

defining moments of my life. My dad leaving when I was ten. Leanne's illness. Nursing my mom when she was dying of cancer. She then tells him about me being sacked. It's like I'm listening to a podcast I've heard a hundred times, the details utterly familiar, and yet, I feel oddly removed from them. I'm going to kill her when I get her to myself, but I can't drag myself away.

'No wonder she comes across as pretty fearless,' says Dan.

Sindy scoffs. 'Hah! You think?'

'You don't?'

'It's all a front. She's vulnerable as. Reckon she got so good at coping. She's worried that if she stopped, there'd be nothing left of her.'

'What do you mean?'

Yeah, what do you mean, Sin?

'Oh, I don't know. Cath's smart. Really smart. But beyond this posh school she went to, she's never had to prove it to anyone. I know there's been the kids and everything else, but she's always ended up in jobs that she was too good for. I sometimes wonder if she was scared she wouldn't live up to her early promise.'

Ouch.

'I suppose if you don't try, there's no chance you can fail,' says Dan.

'But she has the time to mix things up now.'

'That's what I'm doing.'

Yeah, but you don't have three kids and imposter syndrome, Dan.

'I don't think she'll take the leap though. The really annoying thing is, I really do believe she can do anything she puts her mind to.'

'What makes you so certain?'

'It's obvious, isn't it?'

There is a brief pause.

'Because she already has?' hazards Dan.

'Exactly.'

Something catches in my throat. I really need to clear it, but I can't give myself away. I swallow it down.

'What are you doing?' Eric is looking down on me from the top of the stairs. The conversation stops.

'What have I told you about using your indoor voice when Jack's in bed?' I hiss.

'That's not an answer.'

'I was coming down for a cuppa.'

He eyes me suspiciously. 'The kettle's *inside* the kitchen.'

'Which is where I'm heading now.'

The kitchen door opens fully.

'Cath?' Sindy eyes me suspiciously.

'I was coming down, but then I thought I heard Jack.'

'Is he awake?'

'No. False alarm.'

'Do you want me to go and check for you?'

And leave me alone in the kitchen with Dan when I was so clearly listening at the door. Not likely. 'No, it's fine.'

'I don't mind.' Her eyes widen. 'You can keep Dan company.'

'He is actually awake,' says Eric.

'No, he's not,' I say confidently.

'Er, he is.'

I turn to Eric. 'Really?'

'I thought you thought you heard him,' says Sindy. She is

messing with me. She knows full well I was listening at the door and will totally not let me get away with it.

'He just walked into my room wearing one of your bras,' says Eric. 'Which is disgusting.'

He means any sight of my underwear is abhorrent to him, but Sindy says, 'Well if it's anything like the pants.' Dan stifles a laugh.

'I'll sort him out,' I say, half relieved, half narked off the little terror is out of bed again. I take the steps two at a time.

About an hour later, I'm sat on Jack's floor watching his sleeping form in the cot next to me pondering on what Sindy had said when I hear her leave and her car door opens and closes. My phone screen lights up. I read the message.

I stand by everything you'll claim you didn't hear. As Geoff would say, 'It's time to shit or get off the pot'.

Sindy is right: I haven't lived up to my earlier promise, but loads of people don't. We all have big dreams that we think we can sculpt in our own image, but then before you know it circumstances have taken over the tools and they get gradually chiselled away until they look nothing like you imagined they would. I check the time. It's nearly ten, late enough to head straight to bed. I sneak out of Jack's room and have made it to my own without any further close encounters of the Dan kind, when my phone lights up again.

You know you're going to have to engage with him eventually, right?

Sindy only lives a five-minute drive from us, so I'm guessing she's already home.

Why bother? Sounds like you told him everything he needs to know.

Stop being such a baby. He thinks you're fearless!!!

Er, I think you disabused him of that notion.

I wait for a reply. I know I'm also sulking about how well they're getting on. Which is truly pathetic. A couple of long minutes pass without so much as her typing. I'm about to go and clean my teeth when another message pops up.

Sorry for delay. Was looking up disabused.

A mutinous laugh emerges from my mouth. I can't stay mad with Sindy for long.

He seems like a decent bloke.

I can't believe you've fallen for the handsome face/roguish charm thing so easily.

Hah! I can't believe you HAVEN'T!! It's only a matter of time.

A winky face appears.

Not a chance!

Well, you're gonna have to pretend to be nice, because you totally need the money.

Ugh. That's true. Okay, I'm going to have a proper word with myself in bed and then tomorrow I'm going to try to be more accommodating.

Chapter Nine

'What are you doing?' Leanne asks.

'I'm sorting out my underwear drawer.'

'What a time to be alive! So, dare I ask how it's going?'

'Oh, it's fine.'

'So why doesn't it sound like it's fine?

When not at uni, Dan has continued to make every effort to slot into the household. He has offered to make cups of tea, has taught Eric some scales, and last night I found him reading a book to Jack. But rather than appreciating the effort he's making, I find myself resenting it. I've even started running to get out of the house when he's around and the kids aren't.

'He's been here for barely a fortnight and he's already won Jack, Eric and Sindy over. Your granddad met him this week too. Said he was a lovely lad.'

'And isn't he?'

I pick out a greying bra that has several pairs of tights tangled up with it. I start to pull them apart.

'He's a bit too good to be true, you know?'

'You have such a negativity bias.'

'And what's that, Little Miss Freud?'

'Just that the brain is hard-wired to notice the bad instead of the good. Show it a picture of a bombed-out house and it lights up like Oxford Street at Christmas. Show it a picture of a family picnic and it's like, *yeah, whatever* … zzzzzzz.'

'Couldn't that be because of a difference in intensity of the event itself?'

'Nope. Even if they were evenly ranked emotionally, the rubbish ones will always form a stronger impression than the nice ones.'

That must explain why Gaz could never remember Leanne's birth, but he always remembered the poo that popped out moments beforehand.

'And then there's your confirmation bias.'

'Which is?' I move on to pairing my socks.

'Our brain's tendency to search for, favour and recall information that confirms or supports its prior beliefs, even in the face of conflicting information.'

I may have mentioned that I thought Dan was a self-centred douchebag when I saw his online profile.

'Or perhaps you're jealous because he's getting a degree and you're not.'

'Woah! Where did that come from?'

'Oh come on. He's doing the very thing you've wanted to do since you were a kid.'

'I never wanted to do media studies!' Talk about a Mickey Mouse subject.

'Don't play dumb. What about picking Open University back up?'

My OU course. Another failed attempt at self-improvement from way back when.

'You could do teacher training if you got a degree.'

I picture myself at the front of a proper classroom, children's rapt faces turned towards me, but the image pops like a bubble, leaving a sprinkling of dust dancing in its wake.

'Where would I find the time?'

'You're sat cleaning out your underwear draw! And I'm sure Granddad or Sindy would help out with Jack.'

'He's my responsibility, not theirs.'

'It's okay to ask for help.'

'I know it is.'

'Do you though?'

I find an old maternity bra and sling it into a mound mentally marked for the bin. 'And it's not cheap. I've been tightening my belt so much, my vagina's gone numb.'

'Have you not got any savings you could dip into?'

'I'm ringfencing them for an emergency.'

'How many more emergencies can happen to one family?!'

'I owe it to you guys to save for your futures.'

'We don't care about the money. The only thing you owe us is to be happy.'

Gulp. My daughter really knows how to pile it on. 'Any points I'd accrued have probably all expired by now.'

'I thought the whole point of OU was to take as long as you needed.'

'That depends on whether the course is still taught.'

'They're hardly going to stop teaching science!'

'The curriculum might have changed.'

She pulls a goofy face and leans into her screen so only her crossed eyes are in view. 'Duh. You could always find out.'

'Hmm. What I really need is a job.'

Leanne sighs. 'Will you at least think about it?'

I fold the remaining underwear as Marie Kondo might, neat little packets of cotton rolled up into repurposed plastic fruit boxes. 'I will.'

'Will you though?'

'I will. Promise. In the meantime, any hot tips for overcoming all my biases?'

'Yep. Stop being so bloody negative.'

'What a compassionate mental health practitioner you're becoming.'

'I'm starting to wonder whether some people aren't beyond help.'

'Same time next week, doc?'

'Hmm. I'll check my appointment diary.'

Perhaps Leanne is right. Perhaps part of my problem with Dan is that he's bitten the bullet on the uni thing. He's not let age, or an ocean, get in the way. But he doesn't have the baggage I do. Or the self-doubt. Sure, I used to be strong academically, but that was twenty-odd years ago. My brainpower is nose-diving faster than my fertility. We sign off and I put the drawer back, feeling happy that at least I've imposed order on something in my life. I really need to go and wash up the breakfast stuff, but Dan's not left for uni yet. I might go for a quick run. The upside of being a coward is at least I'm getting fitter. I'm even fitting my pelvic floor exercises in.

I'm in the hallway, wondering whether to take a fleece, when a cry of '*Jesus Christ!*' comes from the kitchen. Perhaps he's opened the salad drawer. I've been meaning to clean it for a while, but why put off until tomorrow something that you can do equally well the day after? I really don't want to have to interact over some liquefying lettuce leaves and mummified carrots, so I carefully ease the latch. I'm almost through the door when a gust of wind catches me unawares and it flies open, knocking over the umbrella stand with an almighty clatter.

'Cath! Are you there?' There's a note of dismay in his voice. Perhaps he's discovered the breadbin too?

I sigh, close the door and head for the kitchen. Dan holds his palm out, motioning me to stop.

'Walk over here, very slowly.' He's acting like there's an unexploded bomb in the room. 'Look at the table.'

Okay, that looks like a bomb has already gone off on it. 'Sorry, I know. It's a mess. I've been meaning to deal with it.' I really wish I could afford a cleaner.

'No. Look!'

He slowly moves behind me and angles me so I can see what he sees. His hands are touching my bare skin. His face is so close to my right shoulder I can feel his breath on my ear. It's an oddly intimate gesture, but I doubt he's thinking about that because his attention is consumed by something on the table. A rat. A massively fat rat, sat on its hind legs, front paws propped up on a box of cereal. Shit. That's something else I'd been meaning to sort out; we have rats.

Now before you imagine I live in abject squalor, be assured that the house enjoys a standard level of mess and grime. No chicken carcasses flung directly into the back garden onto a pile of disused furniture and despair. In fact, the garden looks like something out of a catalogue, and so it should, Gaz and I bought it out of a catalogue. About four years ago we were having a good summer, came over all Mediterranean and decided we should get some decking, a wicker sofa and a chiminea. But I recently read that decking is like the Ritz to rats, and a few days ago I thought I spotted one taking full advantage of the wooden five-star lodgings on offer. I snuck some humane traps under there, stopped feeding the birds and hoped it was an isolated incident, but now one's in the house helping itself to the buffet breakfast? I should have called pest control straightaway.

'Can you see it now?' he whispers.

Oh god. Is there some regulation I'm breaking by taking money from him for unsuitable lodgings or something? Could he sue me? They like that in America, don't they? I need to say something.

'Ah, yes.'

Ah no. That was way too casual. Like he'd pointed out a bird in a tree, not vermin on the table. I should have feigned panic. Or shock. Yep, shock is definitely the correct reaction to discovering you have rats. You can't get sued for something of which you've only just become aware, can you?

'What's it doing there?' he asks, so softly that I get a static-like sensation running from my scalp to my neck. Must take care with my next response.

'Reading the nutritional information?' FFS. But I can't be expected to concentrate having him so close behind me.

'How can you be so casual?

Not feeling all that casual tbh. In fact, feeling pretty bloody horrified, but not sure that's going to help the situation.

'Cath, did you *know* you had rats?'

His tone has shifted from surprise to suspicion. He's on to me. What to do? I should probably come clean. At least tell him I'd taken action and hoped it would then take care of itself. Not the rat. That's clearly capable of taking care of itself.

'Of course. The truth is…' Go on Cath, politely explain that now you have a confirmed sighting, it won't require another one to take evasive action. '… it's our pet rat.' Okay, I may have a pathological condition, but I don't want him being all judgy about it.

'You have a pet rat? Nobody mentioned anything.'

He is barely an inch away from me. If you could smell lies, he'd be getting a lungful of eau du deceit right now. I should move, but my skin is alive. It's the exact feeling I used to get when being read a story as a child.

'Yeah.'

'What's its name?'

'His name's…'—come on, synapses, ignore the bubbly feeling and help me out here—'… Jack.' Is it possible to officially disown your left hemisphere?

'Jack?'

'I know, right. What a coincidence!'

'But didn't you name the rat yourselves?'

'No. It was adopted.'

Even the rat smells a rat at this and turns towards us. The tickly sensation passes all the way down my spine. I shiver uncontrollably.

'Blimey. Is it me or is it cold in here? I should probably go and put a jumper on.' I need to get out of this room and think about how I'm going to extricate myself from this blunder. I'm two steps from freedom, the sensorial spell broken, when Dan stops me again.

'Shouldn't Jack be in his cage?'

'Yeah, probably.'

'So he doesn't have free rein of the house?' His face is unreadable.

'No. Definitely not. He lives in the shed. Free rein? That would be disgusting!'

'Aren't you going to put him back? He's moved onto the bread.'

Bugger, that was our last loaf. But more pressingly, he's expecting me to remove the goddamned rat from the table.

'Yeah, that's fine. I'll sort this. You go.'

'I'd love to, but I'm going to need my wallet.'

Dan's wallet is on the table, right next to the seeded batch the rat is munching on.

'Oh right. Great. Well, you stay there and watch me pick up the rat then.' I'm going to have to pick up the rat.

The rat turns around in the bread bag and pokes its head back out and eyes me suspiciously. Don't panic, Cath, this isn't a problem, chances are if you stride towards it purposefully it'll run off in fright. I walk towards the table with a confidence I don't feel, painfully conscious of Dan eyeing my every move. I mentally run through the list of diseases rats might carry. Is the plague still a thing? Have I had a rabies jab in the last ten years? What about monkey pox? I reach out my hand, hoping the movement will spook it into scarpering, but it stands its ground and stares right back at me. I hover, uncertain what to do, in that bitter line between truth and lies, caught between a rat and a hard place.

'He's a bit hand shy.' The words come out in a croak. 'I'm going to…' I grab the large plastic tub that had all of Jack's felt pens in before he scattered them on the floor this morning, and in one swift motion drop it over the rat. I tease it to the edge of the table onto a cutting board, lift the whole thing aloft and make for the patio door. Then Eric appears.

'Why aren't you at school?'

'Problem with the water.'

I give him a look that attempts to convey that the rat I'm carrying is not a feral one from our garden, but his pretend pet that he must feign knowledge of.

'Why've you got a rat in a box?' he asks.

'Because...' I turn to Dan and then wish I hadn't.

'Cath...?' He lets the question hang, head cocked slightly to one side.

Brilliant. I really am going to have to come clean. 'Okay, fine! I lied! This isn't our pet rat. I thought that if you thought we had actual rats that you might, I don't know, sue me.'

I can't read his reaction. Is he revolted? Indignant? He looks a bit smirky, but he can't possibly be finding this amusing. Then he full-on laughs.

'What's so funny?' asks Eric.

'Your mom was trying to persuade me that was your pet rat.'

'We don't have a pet rat.'

'I know.' He laughs again.

'You knew?'

'Yeah. I went into the shed yesterday. No rat!' He's properly enjoying himself.

'So why did you let me...'

'I was interested to see how far you'd go.' He wipes away a tear.

I nod to the rat, who is trying very hard to escape its confines now; in fact it might be suffocating. 'Seemingly this far.'

86

'Can I keep it?' asks Eric.

'No!'

He instantly loses interest and heads upstairs. Dan saunters to the table, picks up his wallet, pops it into his back pocket and tells me he'll be back later.

'Are you not disgusted?'

He shrugs. 'In some places in India rats are considered sacred and eat at the same table as guests. But yeah, it would be better not to have to share with it I guess.' He leaves the kitchen.

I lift the rat so the two of us are face to face. 'Ooooh. I once went to Indonesia and there were rats and I'm so bloody cool with everything, absolutely nothing phases me.'

'It was India,' the rat says without so much as moving its lips.

Oh. My. God.

'Also need my keys,' comes Dan's voice from behind me.

I only breathe out when the front door closes. 'Okay, rat. I'm looking up what you might be carrying, and if any of those diseases are fatal in ten minutes or less, you have free rein to gnaw away at me.'

Chapter Ten

The great thing about not having to work is that I don't have to drop Jack off at nursery as early as usual and can thus avoid bumping into the uber-moms. Dan is out, so since returning home I've dug out all my old text and notebooks from when I first attempted to get a degree and have settled down to do some sums and check out the curriculum. It makes for mixed reading. The credits I accrued from the last time are still valid, so that means I don't have to pay the full whack. Financially we could scrape by for the first year, but if I don't want to take out a loan, and I really don't, it means using savings. If Dan left—he's still pig-headedly hanging in there—that means I really would have to find the kind of flexible job that I'm not sure exists. Or become a permanent landlady.

Then there's the timeframe; I'm staring down the barrel of four years of study, plus at least a year of teacher training, so I'd be forty-four before I qualify. Jack would be at primary by then, so I'd have time to work alongside studying, but I'd need to pay for wraparound care for him. And what about the actual work? I love science, but it's been years since I last wrote an essay, and planning lessons is very different to being on the receiving end of one. Since having kids, momnesia has set in, and I can barely concentrate enough to complete a crossword let alone a degree. Flicking through these old maths textbooks, it's hard to believe that the person who had written out the formulae in meticulously neat handwriting is the same person sitting here now, struggling to make sense of the jumble of symbols.

Britney Spears' 'Oops!... I Did It Again' comes on the radio and I'm instantly transported back to an even earlier version of me: Cath, post A levels, on one of mine and Sindy's frequent trips to the disco at the Red Lion Pub. We would dance like lunatics, making the most of our time together before I left for pastures new. It was where I spotted Gaz for the first time, a tall skinny boy wearing an oversized T-shirt tucked into his belted stonewashed jeans. He had a mop of dirty blonde hair that fell in curtains across clear aquamarine eyes. He gave me an unassuming yet flirtatious grin that suggested he found something especially enjoyable about the way I was jumping around to Kriss Kross. He was back living with his parents having recently graduated from a degree in Engineering and he invited me to a play (a play!) that some of his mates were putting on in the Arts Centre in town. He was so thoughtful and philosophical but could also make me howl with laughter, so it was no surprise when, in the space of a few short weeks, I'd decided I wanted to be with him forever.

Gaz knew I wanted to make something of myself. I was going to break a longstanding tradition in my family and have a career. I was going to be different. Trouble is, in an ongoing and concerted effort to be different, I decided to be one of the six people in the UK who thought female condoms were a good idea. Gaz was happy to comply—even the most respectful of boyfriends still wants to get his end away—and who cared that it looked like you'd lined your cervix with a plastic bag? Or that the failure rate was significantly higher than most other forms of contraception?

After I fell pregnant with Leanne, I entered a state of quiet despair; I wasn't ready to have a child, but I wasn't ready to get rid of one either. And then Gaz announced he'd got a job; nothing amazing, he counselled, merely a graduate placement with a manufacturer on an out-of-town industrial estate, but it meant he had prospects and could afford to keep all three of us, if that's what I wanted. We could muddle through for a year or two, and then I could go back to university, perhaps not in London as planned, but we could always visit at weekends. He told me he loved me and that this was simply a fork in the road, but that the direction we were headed in was still the same. But the forks got wider, the adventure more perilous. Leanne was born, but then she got sick and by the time we'd come out of the other end it was time for another child, planned this time because we longed for an unremarkable parenting journey without turbulence or incident. When Eric started at school, I started OU, ready to get things back on track. But fate had other plans. Mom was diagnosed with lung cancer. Dad was long gone by then, so it was up to us to watch endless rounds of chemotherapy slowly erase her body and then her spirit. By increments we lost sight of the life we'd once envisaged and settled into the one we had, happy enough so long as we got to see it out together. Well, that didn't happen, did it? His heart, which would soothe my soul to listen to after a tough day, was another ticking time-bomb, detonated prematurely by a simple kick-about with his mates.

I flick through the course notes again. Can I really do this? I'm not the girl I was back then. My resilience reserves are running on empty.

The urn is damning in its silence.

'It's okay for you; you don't have to decide anything anymore.'

I sometimes wonder if having to make all the decisions is the most exhausting aspect of being on my own. There's no one to outsource all that thinking to, not even for a day. The brain is a cognitive miser, reluctant to expend too much energy on processing choices, preferring instead to rely on intuition and gut feel. So what's my gut telling me? I close my eyes and settle into my chair. An image of Dan pops into my head. If he can do it, why can't I? I might not be as quick as I used to be, but I could still run rings around Powell. I don't need to be an A grade student to be able to do the job; I just need to be diligent and patient. And what else will I do with the next five years if not this? Leanne is right: I can't carry on the way I have been. Jack will get easier as he gets older, and I'll be able to get a part-time job when he starts school. Plus, I'm a budding scientist, goddammit; out of anyone, I should know that everything is theoretically impossible until it is done. At least if I try, I'd be testing the hypothesis. And having an excuse to hide myself in my room for as long as Dan is here can't hurt.

'This would all be a damned sight easier if you were here,' I say to Gaz. 'Give me a sign if you think I should do it.'

The urn sits resolutely mute in its corner.

'That's fine. I've got a couple more weeks before I need to apply.'

I close the folders and pile them on top of one another. I think I'm going to do it. I'll let the idea build momentum in my head first, just to be certain, and I need to check a few more things before I make it official, but I'm already excited to tell Leanne that I might finally be following in her footsteps.

Chapter Eleven

'J ack!' I call up the stairs. 'Your lunch is ready.'

Jack's had a cold for the last three days so I've been forced to keep him off nursery, even though his only symptom has been a glistening slug of mucus perpetually crawling out of his nose. He's not even been tired, more's the pity. The weather has been awful the whole time, like someone has positioned a giant slushy machine over the whole of Moseley, and great clumps of sleet have fallen endlessly from an invisible sky, trapping us in the house together. I left him fifteen minutes ago having a tantrum because I wouldn't let him stick a crayon in his ear, but now it's gone suspiciously quiet.

'Jack! Come and get your sandwich!'

Still no answer. Hmm. I wonder if he's fallen asleep. I tiptoe up the stairs, because if he is asleep, I am totally eating his sandwich and finding an episode of Columbo to watch. I gently open his door. No sign.

'Jack!' I shout a bit louder. I hear a faint giggle. My room? I go and check. Nope. I return to the landing. 'Jack! Come and eat your sandwich and you can have a treat.' There's another giggle. It's coming from Dan's room.

'Jack, darling. We're not allowed in there sweetie. That room's private.'

'Find me!'

'I can't, sweetheart. That's Dan's room and remember what we said about not going into Dan's room.' I have no idea how he reached the handle. It's at least a foot higher than his stretch height.

'Find me!'

His voice is a little more insistent, like he could be about to have another strop. I really need to get some food into him.

'Jack. I'm going to count to three and I want you to come out okay. One … two…' There are no sounds of movement. 'Two and a half … two and three quarters…' Who am I kidding? 'Two and seven-eighths.' Another giggle. 'Three. Okay, I'm going to have to come and get you.'

I open the door, wondering what the room will look like. I've not been in here since he arrived, and he insists on cleaning it himself. It's actually looking pretty good. Far tidier than how Leanne kept it. There are barely any personal effects on show. Only the guitar, a laptop, some textbooks and a modest stack of paperbacks on the bedside table. I run my eyes down the spines: *Shantaram. Flowers for Algernon. Confessions of a Philosopher. The Selfish Gene. The Immortal Life of Henrietta Lacks.* And at the bottom, *In Search of Schrodinger's Cat* by John Gribbin. I pause. Surely not *the* Schrodinger's Cat. I lift the other books off the top and read the front. Blimey. It is. It's a book about quantum mechanics.

'Come and get me!'

I hastily pile the books back up and drop to my knees. Jack is under the bed, lying front first alongside Dan's rucksack.

'Come on sweetie,' I coax. I look back up at the book. He must have bought it to try and look intelligent. Like that massive art book I bought for the coffee table but never read, so Gaz ended up using it to prop up our broken bed frame.

Jack wriggles under the bed some more.

'Baby, please come out.' I reach under the bed. 'We shouldn't be in here.'

He wriggles further back. I don't want to grab and drag him and risk another meltdown, so I wonder if driving him out from behind might work.

'I'm coming to get you.' I go to the other side of the bed, get down flat on the floor and commando crawl towards him on my front. He turns, sees me, and starts to squirm away. Brilliant. I squeeze in a bit further. He laughs and writhes forward some more. I'm almost fully under the bed when he wriggles free and wanders out of the room. Perfect. I attempt to follow him the same way, and my head is almost out the other side of the bed when two things happen. The first is I get stuck on something. The second is that the front door opens and closes. Shit. Dan's back. I awkwardly swivel round to see what it is that's stopping my exit. One of the slats has slightly cracked and it's caught in the belt loop of my jeans. I wriggle backwards to try and free it, but the wood groans like I'm making the crack worse.

'Hey, Dan,' Jack shouts.

'Hey, buddy,' he replies.

I need to get out of here before he comes upstairs. If having rats isn't bad enough, flagrant trespassing in his room must surely break some code of landlady-ery. I tentatively shuffle backwards, but now the wood seems to have the loop in a vice like grip. I cannot be found in Dan's room; I'd never live it down. I'm going to have to take the jeans off and cut them free when no one's looking later. I lift my hips the minimal distance they will go in the confined space so I can unbutton the fly and take down the zip, not easy with one hand. I've managed to wriggle out of them without further damaging the bed when the sound of Dan's footsteps on the stairs stops me from moving any further. Unless he goes to the bathroom, there's no way I can sneak out of here undetected. I pray really hard to a god I don't believe in, promising I will be a model citizen for the rest of my days if they can delay Dan coming in here for two minutes. I hold my breath, cross my fingers and try to control the ridiculous things my heart is doing when, because fate never ever has my bloody back, a pair of adult feet pad into the room. I tell my racing pulse we just need to wait it out. He will leave again shortly, and I can make my getaway. Only he doesn't leave. He starts to undress and I have to try and stay stock still as a jumper and a T-shirt fall to the floor about a foot from my face. I scrunch my eyes up into a ball when the jeans join them. It's okay though, because he's getting changed, right, which means he's probably going somewhere. No, it's going to be okay. I just need to not move, not cough and not sneeze, which is totally cool because I vacuumed under this bed before Dan arrived and it is dust free under here.

'I want Mommy.'

I open my eyes again. Jack's feet are now in the frame alongside Dan's now sockless ones.

'Is she downstairs watching *Columbo*?'

How does he know I watch *Columbo*?

'No.'

'Do you know where she is?'

Please don't say under the bed, Jack. Please don't say under the bed.

'Under the bed.'

Whatever it was I did in a previous life, it must have been very shitty.

'You mean in your room?'

'Noooo, silly. In yours.'

Screw you the Big Bang and everything you have ever caused to unfold since. Jack drops to his knees and points at me. Dan follows suit. I consider closing my eyes again. If a face could launch a thousand confused memes, Dan's is it.

'I was looking for Jack,' I say.

'Well, he's right there.' Dan effortlessly lifts the bed up for me to get out more easily from under it.

'I know, he was... I was... He was...'

Now I'm upright I can see the full length of his body. I believe the term the kids would use to describe it is 'hench', although I'm always out of touch on the latest lingo. Maybe 'buff'. Every muscle is delineated, like a Michelangelo drawing, his obliques so well defined that they're like that bit on a Ken doll where his hip joints attach. He's almost as smooth as plastic too, and still tanned enough that his ridiculous choker shell necklace stands out like chopped nuts on caramel.

'I'm sorry, can you put something on?'

'I don't know, can you?'

'Wha—' a strangled cry escapes my lips. I'd forgotten I wasn't wearing any trousers. I pull my jumper down, but it barely passes my crotch. I don't recall what pants I put on this morning, but they are almost certainly not good ones. 'This isn't how it looks. I took them off under the bed.'

'Did you now?'

'I… It's… They…' Oh my god. I think my pelvic floor is going to give way.

'Here.' He tosses me the towel hung on the back of the door. I hastily wrap it around myself, but Dan doesn't make any moves to cover himself up. Mind you, if I had a body like that, I'd probably feel comfortable enough in it not to bother.

'Do you make a habit of hiding half-naked under my bed when I'm not here?'

'Of course not.' My voice is slightly hysterical. 'Jack was under your bed and I was trying to get him out, wasn't I, sweetie?' I look around for Jack. Typically, he's nowhere to be seen. My shoulders slump. Why does it all have to be so bloody difficult?

'Hey.' He's clearly sensing my life force seeping away. 'It's okay. I believe you.'

'Do you?'

'Yes. You are free to go. No further questioning.'

'Okay. Cool. Thanks.' I get to the door and even though I really want to get out of here, I'm struck by the need to ask him something. 'Dan. Those books. Are they for show?'

'What?'

'Have you read all of them?'

A puzzled look passes his face. 'Of course! They're my favourites. I keep them to refer back to now and again.'

'You like to read about science?' There's too much disbelief in my voice.

'Is that such a bewildering construct?'

'It's just that you look like…'—I gesture to him—'that.'

'A lot of that's luck.'

'That's what I've been saying!'

'You been talking about me behind my back?'

'No.'

He raises an eyebrow but then quickly returns his face to a neutral expression. 'You can borrow them if you like. I'd be interested in your thoughts.'

'Oh, really? Okay.' Yeah, I can't imagine Dan and I doing book club together. I'm about to shut the door behind me when I'm struck by another question I probably should have asked before. I pop my head back in the room. 'Dan.'

'Yep?'

'What do you do for money?'

He winks. 'Anything you like!'

My cheek furnaces fire up.

'Sorry. Stupid joke.' He leans against the bed's metal footboard, holding onto the top bar in such a way that his triceps pop. How easily he'd lifted the whole thing up. 'A long while back I created this course in blockchain that you could take online. There weren't many around at that point and it did pretty well. I invested that money in crypto, which also did pretty well. I got out during a peak, and now it's all in peer-to-peer lending. I skim some interest off the top for my monthly expenses.'

'Are you rich?'

He laughs. 'Far from it! But I'm comfortable enough.'

Thoughts ping around my head. He's taught people about blockchain? I tried watching a YouTube video on cryptocurrency once and my head damn-near exploded. And he's into science? Not any science, but quantum mechanics, the area of science where someone said if you think you understand it, you definitely don't understand it. Why the hell would he be doing a media studies course?

'Why are you studying media studies?'

'How do you know I'm doing media studies?'

It's a fair point. We've never spoken about it specifically.

'Sindy told me.'

'So you *have* been talking about me?'

Another hot flush makes its way up my face like an inkblot. At least with Dan around I get to experience what the menopause will be like.

'A bit.'

A wry smile starts to nudge at the corners of his mouth, but he tries to disguise it by stepping over to the wardrobe, opening the door, and finally taking out a top to put on.

'I don't know,' he says turning back to me. 'Broadcast media, social media, it's all having a bigger impact on society than anyone imagined. I thought it might be interesting to go behind the scenes, as it were.'

'Oh.' I thought he was going to say because it was a doss.

'Why do you want to study science?' he asks.

'How do you know I want to study science? Have you been talking about me?' Hah. My turn to do sassy.

'No. You left a pile of stuff on the table about a week ago and it still hasn't moved.'

Mental note: never do sassy. 'I'm curious about how the world works.'

'I guess that makes two of us.' He pulls the top over his head and pulls it down to his waist, covering that taut stomach.

'I don't suppose you want a sandwich or anything?' I ask. I

owe him something for invading his privacy. 'I was in the middle of lunch before, erm…'

'No. Thank you though. I really need to go to the gym.'

I close the door behind me, taking care that the latch has caught. An image of that preposterous body flashes before my eyes again. Yeah, he really, really doesn't.

Chapter Twelve

$\mathbf{M}$e and the kids have come to the local nature reserve for some fresh air, by which I mean I've come to walk off a mild hangover from movie night with Sindy. I fell asleep watching TV after she got a cab home last night and woke up on the sofa with a blanket over me. I didn't put it there.

'Can we get ice cream?' asks Eric, despite the cold weather.

'Only if you take Jack in with you to fetch them.'

They run into the park café, their mouths tiny cloud machines as their warm breath mingles with the frosty late autumn air. One of the joys of being a solo parent is that there's no one to step in when every morsel of your being is resistant to the notion of uprightness, and there's still a whole day to get through. I savour the precious five minutes until the boys re-emerge and we head into the woodland.

'This is like *Lord of the Rings*, Jack,' says Eric once we're some way in. The overhanging branches have been strangled by ivy, creating a canopy through which barely any light penetrates. The *Two Towers* was the last movie we watched with Gaz. We still haven't watched the *Return of the King*. 'I hope there are no orcs.'

'Norks?' says Jack.

'Not norks. Orcs.' *Please, don't start saying norks*, I mutter under my breath.

'Why, what are norks?' asks Eric.

'It doesn't matter.' It's Aussie slang for large breasts and I really don't want Jack using it at nursery.

Eric stops walking. 'It does matter,' he snaps. 'What are norks?'

'He said *orcs*,' I reiterate to Jack, but his focus is fixed on Eric.

'What are *norks*?' Eric asks again.

'Can you please stop saying that?' Another one of the joys of going it alone is not having anyone else to tell your kids to do as they're told. I attempt to walk on.

'Norks!' shouts Jack.

I turn back. 'Please, don't say norks Jack. It's orcs.'

'But what *are* norks?' Eric crosses his arms over his chest for added emphasis.

'I'm not telling you.'

'Norks!' shouts Jack again, warming to his theme.

'Look, can everyone stop saying norks? We were talking about *orcs*, Jack.'

'Wot are they?' Jack asks.

'A race of creatures used as henchmen in *Lord of the Rings*. They're ugly and evil and they hate everything.' Eric clutches at Jack, who recoils in fear and bursts into tears.

'Come on, Eric, don't take it out on him.'

I give Jack a cuddle and tell him Eric's only joking and

there are no orcs, but he's having none of it and unleashes huge, snotty ice-creamy sobs into my hair.

'Hey, Jack! Jack, look!'

'For God's sake, Eric, give him a second!'

'But check it out!'

I look up. There's a cavalcade of bubbles overhead, an ever-shifting spectrum of light floating majestically amongst the leaves.

'Oh blimey. Yes. Jack, look!'

He does, and the crying instantly stops.

'Where are they coming from?' asks Eric.

'Shall we find out?' I ask brightly, relieved the subject of norks has been dropped.

We make our way towards the source, the delighted shrieks of as-yet unseen children helping to guide our way through the wood.

'Hey, Jack, I was wrong before. *These* are orcs.' Eric tries to redeem himself.

Jack looks at him, uncertainly.

'There's no such thing as bad orcs,' says Eric. 'These are nice orcs. Similar to fairies, okay?'

Jack nods and licks his ice cream with renewed vigour.

'I think there are more through here,' I say.

Jack races ahead of me, ice cream thrust in front of him, the remains wobbling precariously on the stick. I tell him to slow down, but he swiftly disappears through a small clearing. He's only out of sight for seconds before a sustained scream echoes around us. Following him I come out into a tree-free area and quickly take in the scene. There's a large, heated gazebo, kids in fancy dress, a lot of bunting, a 'Happy Birthday, Maisie' banner in expensive floral fabric and a bubble machine. There's also a group of adults staring at me in horror and, directly in front of me, a bright pink castle-shaped birthday cake with a toddler's footprint right in the middle of it. And kneeling on a woollen rug, holding a box of matches, dressed as Princess Fiona from Shrek, with a chocolate ice cream melting into her cleavage, is Belinda, the perfect mom from nursery.

'Norks,' says Jack.

Yes, I think, staring at her sticky décolletage. *Yes they are.*

Even under normal circumstances, the awkwardness of ruining a three-year-old's party is fairly agonising. But when that party has been meticulously put together by someone who clearly hates you, it's monumental. And Eric laughing really isn't helping.

'I'm really sorry,' I say. 'It was an accident. We had no idea you were here.'

Belinda looks from the ice cream to the birthday cake and then up at me.

'Like I say, we didn't know you were here.'

As she stares, her daughter Maisie spots the demolished cake and starts crying.

'Want ice cream,' says Jack above the dull roar of Maisie's tears, and tries to take it back from Belinda's chest.

'No, the ice cream's gone sweetie.' I try to grab his hand and accidentally smear more ice cream across her chest.

'Ice cream is there, Mommy.' He jabs a finger into one of her boobs.

Another howl of laughter from Eric, matched only in magnitude by Maisie's cries.

'Technically, yes, but you can't have it.'

Belinda continues to stare mutely in disbelief.

'I think I've got some baby wipes in my bag,' I say.

Still nothing. But then a man wearing a deerstalker hat and clutching a cardboard tray of takeaway drinks appears. It's Belinda's husband.

'Good god, what happened here?'

'Daddy! My cake! My cake, Daddy,' cries Maisie, grabbing onto his leg. He deposits the drinks on the floor, lifts Maisie up and puts a protective hand on Belinda.

'Darling, are you okay?' His voice wavers with emotion.

Belinda nods weakly.

'What have you done?' he asks me.

'She's ruined everything, is what,' whispers Belinda, standing up.

'Look, it was an accident. I'll happily pay for a new cake. And dry cleaning.'

At this point Belinda's demeanour changes from one of stricken victim to one of self-satisfied heroine. She lays a hand on my arm. 'Oh, we couldn't expect *you* to do that.'

'Why not?' I ask.

She pats me as you might an unwanted cat you're about to have euthanised. 'I heard about you getting dismissed from Brookdene'—she surveys the circle of parents, raises an eyebrow and very deliberately says—'for drinking on the job.'

There's a collective murmur from the other parents as Belinda squeezes my arm in understanding, although her mask of concern almost cracks when she spots Jack and Eric now scooping cake into their mouths.

'*Boys*,' I hiss, praying for a sinkhole to open beneath us.

'If you're replacing it, this one belongs to us, doesn't it?' says Eric.

'It must be terribly difficult for you being on your own,' Belinda says, her words mimicking sympathy, but her face willing me to punch her high cheekbones until they face inwards. 'It's no wonder the kids are out of control!'

Okay, she's criticising my kids now. You need to say something, Cath. Something erudite. Something that proves you are an intelligent woman, perfectly in control of her children, her emotions and her life.

'First up, the booze thing is bollocks.'

I sense a collective grimace around me.

'Secondly, I'm sorry that we crashed your bullshit party.'

Someone covers a child's ears.

'But let's get some perspective here. This is not the scene of some disaster movie or deliberate sabotage by marauding kids. It's only some accidentally squished cake and a couple of sticky tits.'

'Squished cake and sticky tits,' shouts Jack, folding the words over like a Dr Seuss tongue twister.

I have a sudden longing for the good-old *nork* days. Yep, nice one, Cath. That should do it.

By the time we get home my dial of self-loathing has been turned up to eleven. Why couldn't I have handled that better? Why do I care so much what they think of me? And why the hell was Jack the only kid from nursery not invited to the party? I know he won't have cared—for now at least—and I know I'm not entitled to everything I want for him, but I can't help but wonder what might happen if he ends up at school with this lot? Do bumpy roads lie ahead? Should I somehow have played the game differently? The whole thing is not just heart-breaking, it's totally and utterly demeaning, and I'm not sure what to do with all the pent-up frustration rattling around in my head. I scoop up the Open University stuff and dump it into a bag. Who the hell am I kidding? Everything I try is destined for failure. I can't even make friends, so how could I possibly alter the course of my existence? Perhaps it's no wonder those moms don't want me around. I'm not Dan, able to glide effortlessly through life. I'm Cath. Graceless. Aimless. Useless. I shove the bag into the bottom of the kitchen dresser. We'll get through Christmas and then I'll get a job.

Chapter Thirteen

A week later I run to a precinct a couple of miles away for a change of scene. It's a bargain basement type of place, made up of independent shops selling wilting vegetables, padded greetings cards and plus-sized clothing from behind yellow filmed windows, all arranged in a horseshoe around a central flagged area peppered with empty flower boxes. It's by one of them I spot a figure I recognise. It's Reggie, and despite it being a Tuesday and term-time, Reggie is not in uniform and, more tellingly, not in school. I sneak up and tap him on the shoulder as he's undoing his bike lock.

'Shouldn't you be at Brookdene?'

He straightens up, muscles tense, but then relaxes when he sees it's me.

'I could say the same thing to you, Miss.'

'Ah, but I'm officially not allowed on the premises. What's your excuse?'

'Got better things to do, ain't I?

'Like hanging around a bargain biscuit shop. Very rock and roll!'

'I'm picking up supplies.' He lifts a plastic bag and puts it back down.

'To take where? The park? Going to drink some pop and go on the seesaw on your own?'

He looks at me darkly, suddenly not in the mood for any banter. 'I've got mates who aren't at school you know.'

'I'm sure you have.' Yep, I know the kind of mates. The dimmer, less talented ones, hell-bent on wasting their days by getting wasted and taking an aimless kid like Reggie along for the ride. 'I know I'm going to sound totally mom-ish when I say this, but you should be in school. You're smart. When you apply yourself.'

He hangs the bag off his handlebars and I spy the bright lettering of a cheap cider brand through its thin white plastic.

'There's no point, Miss. The system's not set up for people like me, is it? Struggling to read? Remedial class. Struggling to concentrate? Remedial class. Asleep at your desk because the neighbours were arguing until four in the morning? Detention. It's rigged.'

When I began teaching Reggie two years ago, I had been told he displayed classic ADHD symptoms. He was inattentive, disruptive in class, prone to fighting and would not shut up. I very quickly realised he was mildly dyslexic and very bored, so I'm not buying this woe-is-me routine. 'Cut the crap, Reggie. This is me you're talking to.'

He cocks his head. 'Yeah, well. Better to play the part you've been typecast.'

My heart aches at how readily he could write himself off. 'That's you copping-out.'

'I'm taking the path of least resistance, Miss. You taught me about that.'

'That only works in simple systems.'

'I know. Yours was the only class I paid attention in.'

'You paid attention in my class?!'

At last, there's a glimmer of a smile.

'That's more like it. Come on! What about wanting to be a nurse?'

His face darkens again. 'Not gonna happen though, is it?'

'Why not?'

'Because to be a nurse you need a degree. And to get a degree you need money. And I'm not exactly your monied type, Miss. So I take your *why not*, and I raise you a *screwed-up societal hierarchy that keeps the likes of me and mine in our place.*'

'Get your science GCSEs and take it from there.'

'I know you mean well, but you don't get it. Even if I wanted to do the right thing, I can't do it on my own. I still need help. And since you left us, there's no one to give it to me.'

He swings his leg over his bike and settles himself into the saddle.

'I didn't leave you, Reggie. I didn't have a choice. I was sacked.'

'What, all 'cos Powell's an alcoholic?'

'How do you know that?' I wonder if the truth has finally come out, and right now Mr Gerald is preparing the formal apology that will enable me to return to school and to my normal, slightly less messed-up life.

But Reggie cuts through the fantasy. 'Easy. I've got one of them at home.'

Do you know in films when the lead character has an *a-ha* moment? When all the disparate pieces that they couldn't quite put together suddenly converge into a moment of absolute clarity and the hero knows exactly what she must do to move forward? Well, this wasn't like that. After Reggie told me what he told me, I told him I was sorry, watched him ride off, went and bought some tinsel, and ran home, trying to come to terms with the fact that he was one in a long line of smart kids with a crappy background who'd already decided he would never amount to anything. Then when I saw Sindy next, I told her what had happened. She reminded me that I was also one in a long line of smart kids from a crappy background, who had decided I'd never amount to anything, so perhaps I was responsible for sustaining the cycle of shit and that I should be ashamed of myself and go and get my degree already. So I'm going to do it. I'm going to bite the bullet, accept that I'm going to have to spend some of our savings, that Jack is going to lose some of his hours at nursery, and properly try and become a teacher. And I'm also going to get Reggie through his science GCSEs if it kills me. Exactly how I intend to do this has yet to be worked out, but no more procrastination or equivocation. As of January, assuming he returns from the trip he's taken home for the holidays, Dan's not going to be the only undergraduate in the house.

PART II
WINTER

Chapter Fourteen

I'd always been a huge fan of Christmas before Gaz died. There's no spiritual connection, but any calendar entry that allowed me to consume my own body weight in cheese was alright with me. The last few years have understandably been different, each of us limping towards its inevitable sadness with the enthusiasm of a condemned man heading to the gallows, but with Jack now being of an age where he 'gets' the whole thing, Leanne being home again for a few weeks, and having made a decision about the future, it felt like there was reason to celebrate again.

'Not bad,' says Leanne, referring to the roast beef Christmas dinner we've just polished off.

'Why, thank you.'

I still couldn't bring myself to cook turkey. It doesn't seem right without Gaz here to carve it for us. He used to stand at the head of the table holding the electric knife, pretending to be some demented murderer, yielding shrieks of fear and laughter from Eric and Leanne as he made the blades buzz and whir.

'How many points do you think that was?' asks Sindy who has joined us this year since Dave is still away.

'I'd give it ten out of ten.' Geoff winks at me.

Sindy laughs. 'I think we should have a toast.'

'Yes, I want toast,' says Jack, prodding his rare beef as if it was roadkill.

Sindy raises her glass. 'To absent loved ones.'

'To absent loved ones,' we say in unison.

The low winter sun glints off the urn I've snuck into the dining room to Leanne's consternation. At least I know exactly where Gaz is, but the only thing Sindy knows is that Dave is somewhere in Baghdad, one of a small group of soldiers providing training and equipment to Iraqi and Kurdish security forces, a role not without its risks. I don't know how she copes with the uncertainty. A thoughtful silence ensues.

'I'm going upstairs for a bit,' says Eric.

'But you haven't had pudding!'

'I've got a stomach-ache.'

I open my mouth to say more, but Leanne mouths to let him go. He's been on such brilliant form all morning, I could almost convince myself he hasn't been thinking about his dad. I must remind myself that for children, even ones as precocious as Eric, grief is something they jump in and out of like puddles.

'I'll save you some for when you're ready.'

I'm almost relieved when our collective melancholy is punctuated by the smell of my youngest son's bottom.

'I done a poo,' says Jack.

'Evidently,' says Sindy, also happy for the distraction.

'I thought we agreed you were going to go on the potty,' I say to him.

I'm trying to potty train Jack. Everything I've read online suggests he should be ready, although they should ask, *are you ready?* because the process is a regular pain in the frequently unleashed and seldom-compliant arse.

'How's that working out for you?' asks Geoff.

Badly. Trouble is, he also objects to having his nappy changed now, so I'm screwed either way. I reluctantly take him into the lounge and attempt to get him flat on the changing mat. He writhes around making a high-pitched nasal whine, like someone slowly letting the air out of Kenneth Williams. Leanne appears at the door.

'Need a hand?'

'I reckon he has Ass Changing Deficit Disorder.'

'No change me, Mommy. No change me.' Jack tries to roll over.

Leanne kneels to tickle his belly to distract him. 'Perhaps it's Freudian. Boys might be more likely to get trapped in the *anal stage* than girls.'

'They're definitely slower to toilet-train. Look at your dad. He was forty-two and he still hadn't learned to put the seat down.'

'And he'd practise going to the toilet for half an hour every day!'

We both smile at the memory. Some of Gaz's sessions on the loo were legendary.

Jack tries to make another break for it. I quickly whip the nappy away and replace it with a fresh one.

'He's not getting any easier, is he?'

'Not much. Did I tell you on the last day of term he called a book a *total*—' I spell out the c-word for her.

'Ouch. What was the book?'

'Where's Spot?'

'Oh, well that is a total c-u-n-t.'

I laugh. That's exactly what I thought. I'm sure the story has made it round to the perfect moms by now, but I'm trying hard not to think about that.

'Have you considered he might be a little bit more than just *spirited*.'

'He's certainly got more energy than you and Eric ever did. Or maybe it's that I have less?'

'Are you concerned?'

'No. I'm still hopeful he'll grow out of it, but even if it is something like ADHD, we'll cross that bridge when we come to it.'

Leanne puts her arms around me and gives me a big squeeze.

'Oi, pass me those trousers will you. We're almost done.' I wrestle Jack back into them and he immediately jumps up and runs from the room shouting 'I done a poo, Granddad. Granddad, I done a poo.'

'And what about Reggie?' asks Leanne. 'What's the plan there?'

Hmm, what indeed. 'Let's get through Christmas first. Then I'll worry about that.'

Chapter Fifteen

'Hey, Miss!'

I've opened my front door to find not only Reggie waiting for his first lesson, but a few more of the rowdy rabble I used to teach.

'Hope you don't mind; this lot got wind of the private lessons you offered me and wanted in.' Reggie gives me a *what are you gonna do* shrug. Over his shoulder Bradley, Jada and Malik are scraping a smattering of snow off the top of my bins and throwing it into each other's faces.

'Er, okay. Hey guys.'

'Cheers for this, Miss.' Bradley crouches to duck under the door frame, rubbing his hands together to get them warm.

'Yeah, Powell is all the awfuls, so when Reggie mentioned you were back on his case, we thought we'd tag along,' says Jada.

I'm completely taken aback. 'Do your parents know you're here?'

'My stepdad thinks I'm at football. He'd be really mad if he knew I was doing school stuff,' says Bradley.

'Mine don't mind, so long as I stay out of trouble,' says Jada.

'Mine told me I needed to come,' says Malik.

'Well, come in, I guess.' I lead them past the front room where Jack and Eric are watching television. Well, Eric is trying to watch television and Jack is stood resolutely in front of it, naked except for a disposable nappy sagging from his bottom, ignorant of Eric's pleas to move out of the way. 'Eric, I'll be in the kitchen if you need me. Will you keep an eye on Jack?'

'He's not leaving me with much choice.'

Eric spots the visitors behind me and makes an exaggerated *peace out* sign at them, which is almost as excruciating as a politician trying to speak patois, but the big kids seem amused. In the kitchen I offer squash and biscuits, stalling for time as I'm unsure of what I'm going to do with them. It's not as if I have loads of equipment at home to perform real experiments. I had thought that Reggie and I could maybe begin with some mock exams and we could focus on any areas of real weakness, but with three extras in tow, I'm not sure that approach is going to work. I'll need something they can all see, so I fetch Jack's free-standing chalkboard which also has a roll of paper attached to it and prop it up on a kitchen chair.

I've just got them to stop punching each other in the arm and to sit still when the door opens and Dan walks in. He's been away for two weeks and the details of his face had started to recede from my memory, but there he is again, looking like he's stepped straight off the slopes as he unzips his large puffer jacket and shakes snow from his hair. He stops short when he sees the assembled rabble.

'Oh! Hey.' He seeks me out with a questioning look.

'Hi. I thought you were back tomorrow.'

'Change of plan.'

His face is more tanned save for paler rims around the eyes where his goggles must have been. It would make most people look silly, but he looks as striking as ever.

'These are some of the kids from my old school. I was planning on doing some private tuition. Only it turned out not to be so private.'

'And we ain't paying,' says Malik confidently, but then looks doubtful. 'We ain't paying, are we?'

'No. You're *not* paying.'

'Oh cool,' says Dan. 'That's really cool.' He gives me a little sideways nod like he couldn't imagine the word 'cool' and something I'd do could go together. 'Well, hey everyone. I'm Dan.'

'Hey Dan!' They chant in unison.

'I'm going to head upstairs and chill for a bit.'

'I'm sorry, I can do this at a time to suit you, next time.' It must be a lot to walk back into and it's his place too.

'Cath, it's fine. It's more than fine. Great job.' He seems thrilled that the kitchen is full of teenagers. Weirdo. 'Have a nice day everyone.'

'Have a nice day, Dan!' they chirrup together.

'Is that your husband, Miss?' Jada asks when he's left the room.

'No. I'm way too old for him.'

'Oh. So you like him, but you're too old for him?'

'No, I didn't mean that.'

'Ooooh! Miss fancies Dan!'

'Keep your voice down or he'll hear you.'

'If you don't fancy him, it doesn't matter if he hears us,' says Bradley. They all snigger.

'I don't fancy him.'

'He's pretty fit for an oldie though,' says Jada.

'There's more to finding someone attractive than their having a good face.'

'Are you looking for someone hench too?' She winks at me.

Oh, he's hench too. 'Can we get on please?'

'Are we gonna start with reproduction?' says Bradley. They snigger again. Reggie tells them to cut it out. I take a deep breath.

'Right, who knows what mitosis is?' I ask. It's as good a start as any.

'Is it the thing on the end of your footis?' says Bradley. More laughter.

'Very amusing. Come on, this always comes up in exams.'

'Cell division,' says Reggie.

'Not bad. Anyone know the stages?' There are blank faces all round. I unroll some paper and write the words 'Prophase, Premotaphase, Metaphase, Anaphase, Telophase, Cytokenesis' on it. By the time I'm done, Bradley has his phone out and is typing away.

'Phone away, Bradley.'

'Sorry, Miss.'

Hmm. How can I bring this to life? 'Did you all bring your textbooks?'

Reggie has. The others merely look apologetic.

'Okay, Reggie, here's some paper and there are felt tips over there. I want you to copy out the pictures of mitosis from your textbook as large as you can. Don't worry too much about the detail, the key elements will do.' I tear the paper from the roll and pass it over along with some scissors to Jada. 'I want you to cut these out.'

'What about me?' asks Malik.

'Think of a way to remember the order of the words, however you can. Make it a poem. Make it a story. Make it the hierarchy of people in that programme with all the dragons and boobs for all I care, but find a way to remember the words and the order.'

'What, like Princess Prometaphase is the daughter of Prophase?' he asks.

'Exactly.'

'What shall I do?' asks Bradley, hunched over his phone again.

'Try and stay off your phone.'

What follows is effectively a high-brow kids' party game. I get them to shuffle the pictures, shuffle the words, try to match the two up correctly and then use Malik's mnemonic to put all of it in the correct order. This is all done to the soundtrack of constant beeping from their mobiles. The whole thing works. Barely. But it takes an hour for us to get to the point at which anyone can do it confidently or recognise any of the elements independently of the entire sequence, which is what will be required come exam time. The doubts resurface. Was I mad to think I could do this?

'How much of this do we have to know?' Reggie flicks through the textbook.

'All of it.'

He flips to the end. 'Two hundred and thirty pages.'

'Yes.'

'And today we've done a bit over a page.'

'Yes.' I see where this is going.

'And we have, what, about twenty-one weeks to go?'

'This was a particularly hard topic,' I try to sound reassuring.

'Even so. You really think you can get us through this?'

No, I'm thinking. No, there is no way I can get you through this. Your pals didn't even think to bring a textbook today. Or a book. Or a pen. They're not stupid kids, but they're easily distracted, ill-disciplined, and would rather spend time looking at gifs on their phones than consider how the hell said phone works. In fact, I suspect that unless someone invents a social media app called GCSEme or SnapStudy they'd be happy to stare at it for eight hours a day, we are royally screwed, my friend.

And then, as I'm thinking about how I can worm my way out of this, I have the germ of an idea. Something that might just work. 'Leave it with me,' I say.

Chapter Sixteen

'So how goes it?'

I'm sat at my brand-new second-hand desk in my bedroom, all of the textbooks I'm going to need for my course piled up on top of it.

'I'm all set.' I tell Leanne. 'Official kick-off in two weeks. I even found my old scientific calculator and it still works. Amazing!' I tap out the digits 5318008 on it and flash it upside down at the phone.

'It's the little things, isn't it? And what about Reggie and co?'

'You know how during the first session they absorbed more radiation from their phones than they did the lesson?'

'Yep.'

'Well, afterwards I had this idea. Rather than trying to compete with social media, what if I embraced it? Use it to engage them.' I explain how I've bitten the bullet, got myself on various social platforms and have been doing things like setting puzzles that disappear once viewed to strengthen their memory, creating multiple choice polls they vote on to answer questions, posting some quick and easy meme-style stuff for mnemonics, that kind of thing.

'I figured that if I introduce bits of learning into a habit they already have, we might cram it all in. It also means we won't be limited to once a week.'

'I love it!'

'I don't really know how the platforms work, properly, but nothing ventured…'

'It's a great idea. I'm sure you'll nail it. Send me some links so I can check it out.'

'Will do. Also, did I tell you we're going to Granddad's caravan for half term?'

'You're going to the caravan?' There's a note of disbelief.

'I thought it was about time.'

'I think so too. Wow. It's all happening!'

'Yeah. I feel much more positive about everything.'

'Even Dan being around?'

'Shh, he might be able to hear.'

'Sorry.'

'It's my new year's resolution to not feel so awkward around him.'

'How's that going?'

I tap out 4517734 and hold it upside down for her.

'Hellish?'

That's not strictly true. It's not too bad when the kids, or Sindy or Geoff are around. I get to sit on the side-line and not draw attention to myself. But when it's the two of us, it's different. I've always been incapable of small talk. I find the pressure to perform too crushing, and I either say something accidentally offensive or else I end up fibbing in a misguided effort to get some random stranger to like me. I once told Gaz's boss that I too was a fan of Lynyrd Skynyrd and had really enjoyed *his* latest album. I only found out later that *they* were a band, not some bloke with an old-fashioned name. I was a therapist's wet dream, even then. Thankfully Dan is out a lot.

'Fair play to the guy though. He's stuck around.'

'Only to prove a point.'

'Hmm. That seems a bit of a stretch. Maybe he likes it?'

'Also a stretch.'

I have no idea why he's still here. It looks like I might get some help with my fees, which will soften the burden on my dwindling finances, but he's free to go whenever he likes.

'Perhaps he's some crazed madman on the run from the FBI? Wasn't there a film about that. Kate Winslet. Josh Brolin. She falls in love with him in the end.'

'Anyway, I'll let you go,' I say.

'You mean you want to go?'

'Yep. I need a cuppa. And for this conversation to be over. Love you, bye!'

I pop my head outside the bedroom door. No sign of Dan. I sneak along the corridor to check in on the boys. Jack is having an afternoon nap, his peaceful face half hidden beneath the comforter toy he now insists goes everywhere with us, and I can hear various chords being strummed in Eric's room. Brill, I have ten minutes to myself. Downstairs in the kitchen I make tea, grab the biscuit tin and sit at the breakfast bar to make a list of what I need to organise for our holidays. Too bloody much. I'm licking the filling out of half a custard cream and telling Gaz how all car-related prep should be his job, when Dan comes in. He is wearing a black leather jacket over a grey hooded top, Levi jeans and an oversized woolly hat. The man's ability to put an outfit together would put David Beckham to shame.

'Hey, Cath.'

'Oh, I didn't think you were in,' I say, with all the guilt of a woman who has been found talking to an urn and licking the filling out of half a custard cream.

'Yep, just back. Is it okay if I put some laundry on?'

'Yep, no problem.' I concentrate really hard on my list so I don't have to say anything more.

'Eric mentioned you guys are off on holiday soon.'

Hmm. This focusing intently thing isn't a strong enough disincentive to chit chat.

'Yep, his Granddad Geoff has a caravan in Wales we used to visit when he was younger. We've not been for a while.'

'Sounds great. I'll have to head to Wales at some point. Do they have border control?'

'Christ, no. Just a dragon made from stones on a motorway embankment. The only way you know you're in a different country is the signs are in two languages and someone has stolen all the vowels from the Welsh ones.'

He laughs.

'I don't know if I'm speaking out of turn here, but I wondered if it was okay to have some people over whilst you're away?'

'Do you mean have a party?' My shrill tone is probably evidence enough that this would, as far as I was concerned, be speaking out of turn.

'No. Nothing like that.'

'Phew.' I return my voice to its normal register. 'I've seen what those fraternities get up to. I'll come back and someone will be duct-taped to the back of my bedroom door vomiting into a nose bag.'

'I'm not a teenager, Cath!'

I note the hoody and beanie and wonder if he really believes that.

'There's some guys I've got friendly with and thought it might be fun to watch sport together.' He's been in the country for little over eight weeks and already has more mates than me.

'What's the one where they dress in a mattress, throw a dinosaur's egg around for five seconds and then stand around it for fifteen minutes as if they're waiting for it to hatch?'

His dimples make an appearance. 'You mean American Football. The season recently ended with the Superbowl. I was thinking more soccer.'

I can't think of a reason why he shouldn't have a few friends over.

'Great. Also…'

He makes this odd gesture with his hands, like he's fondling an invisible football. I think it might be the outward manifestation of discomfort, but it's not an emotion I thought he had in his repertoire.

'I know this whole arrangement wasn't really what you had in mind, so I've been looking for a room. There might be something coming up, but it wouldn't be until after Easter; think you can hang in there for that long?'

I note the *you* in that sentence, the emphasis being on *my* inability to deal with this situation. God, the man is so self-possessed, it's infuriating. Time to practise my new year's resolution. I can do unruffled and easy-going.

'Of course.' I try to pass a grimace off as a smile. 'It's all cool.' I shrug so hard that I spill some of the tea I'm holding onto the bar top.

Dan looks uncertain.

'Totally chilled,' I repeat, grabbing another biscuit and confidently breaking it in half for effect.

'Okay, well as long as you are. I'd hate for you to feel uncomfortable.'

'No way,' I screw half my face up in what is meant to be a dismissive look but may well resemble Bell's Palsy. 'I'm totally laid back about the whole thing!' I lean back and give him a lofty wave, but realise too late that I'm sat on the bar stool that doesn't have a back to it. Unable to stop myself, I do an awkward half somersault off it and land on my knees on the tiled floor. Ouch! That smarts, emotionally as well as physically.

Dan comes to my rescue.

'I'm fine.' I wave him off.

Dan points to the ceiling. 'I'll go upstairs and get my laundry then.'

'Yep. Yep, do that. I'll...' I don't finish the sentence out loud, but if I did, it would be with *never stop replaying this incident in my head for as long as I live*. Seriously. FML to the power of a hundred.

Chapter Seventeen

I normally begin the February half term with a fruitless five-hour online search, looking for some form of genuinely enjoyable weatherproof entertainment that won't cost a fortune, so at least I'm being spared that this year. Geoff has often asked us to join him at the caravan since Gaz died, but the idea of returning to a place where we once took family holidays together has been too painful. But it's time to think about the future, and that means coming to terms with the past.

'Are we nearly there yet?' asks Eric.

We're still in the driveway.

'Don't be a pain. I'm relying on you to keep Jack occupied.'

'He's occupied kicking the back of your chair.'

'Stop that please, Jack. Mommy needs to concentrate on driving.'

'Why can't I sit in the front?' asks Eric.

'Because I need you to keep Jack occupied.'

'But I get car sick in the back.'

'Since when?'

'Since you said I had to keep Jack occupied.'

He's growing up to be exactly like Leanne. I check Jack out in the mirror, maniacally sucking on his comforter toy as if his life depended on it. I have no idea what he's growing up to be like, but I'm not sure it's human.

The journey to Aberystwyth passes without incident save for a nappy change (Jack), a snack stop (Eric) and an emergency wee stop (me), and we arrive early afternoon. As I spot the faded fibreglass cowboy statue that heralds our arrival, its resin nose and fingertips worn down to the mesh beneath as if eaten away by frostbite, I get a bit choked up. So little has changed about the place, and yet so much has changed about us. Keeping my eyes on the path I stretch my arm towards the back seat, seeking out Eric's hand, but it promptly gets kicked away by Jack.

Geoff is sat outside the caravan reading the paper when we arrive 'I'll get the kettle on, shall I?'

'Don't suppose you have anything stronger?'

'Absolutely. Come on in, lass.'

The caravan is as I remember it, a riot of patterns and hardwearing fabrics with so much chintz, pelmet, and netting at the windows that opening one is like wrestling the 1980s.

Geoff hands me a beer. 'This do you?'

'Perfect, thanks.' I gratefully take a sip and gaze at all the photos. Everywhere I look there are pictures of Gaz staring back at me. Gaz with Leanne as a baby; Gaz and me standing by a BBQ on the decking of the caravan; Gaz and Eric, backs to the camera, walking through a field together; Gaz, himself a child, with his dad. We used to joke about how he could have been a girl when he was younger, his delicate features and big blue eyes peeking out from under a mop of wavy hair. I catch Eric looking at them too. I take another swig of beer. 'Are you okay, dude?'

'I'm going to the amusement arcade,' he says.

'If you hang on half an hour, we'll all come. I want to get the car unpacked first.'

'I'm going on my own.'

Geoff puts his hand on Eric's shoulder, who flinches slightly at the contact.

'There's a bag of two pennies on the side there. Why don't you take those and we'll see you back here in half an hour for your tea?'

Eric quickly wipes his nose on his sleeve, grabs the bag and leaves without another word.

The thing about grief is that it never really goes away, it simply shape-shifts. Sometimes it's as sharp and heavy as a hatchet blow, the pain exquisite and all-consuming. Other days it's a feeling of not quite there-ness, like watching a film of your own life but ever so slightly out of focus and with dodgy dubbing.

Jack is blissfully unaware of the emotional turmoil around him. He empties a box of dominoes onto the floor with a clatter, attempts to skate on them, and promptly goes arse over tit, erupting in a frenzy of outraged tears.

'I think I might join you,' Geoff says, nodding at the beer.

Later that night I'm lying on the sofa-cum-bed listening to Geoff gently snoring through the paper-thin walls. The boys are spark out in their twin room, but I cannot get to sleep. The mattress is so hard, it's cut off the blood supply to my feet and I'm reminded of the silly teenage boy masturbation technique of letting your hand go numb so you can imagine someone else is doing it. There is a lot less pleasure to be had in feeling like someone else is wearing your socks. There's a cross on the wall above my head, an intricate structure of coloured stones and wire at the centre of which sits a glass cameo of Jesus looking like he's breastfeeding a lamb. Geoff's wife, Janet, was a firm believer who found great sustenance in her faith, and there are times I wish I had the comfort of religion to fall back on, but I can't and don't believe in a higher power. There's no sense in trying to sleep, so I sit up and take in some of the room's other details that were once so familiar. It's funny, I was never that keen on caravan holidays; that whole *home away from home* thing only really works if you usually live inside a fitted kitchen on a badly upholstered corner sofa, but I would now give anything for us all to be back here together, me trying to make dinner on a two-ring burner whilst Gaz and the kids play board games on the foldaway table. I pick up one of the pictures of Gaz and stare at it until the photo blurs and my tears splash on the glass. Yep, today is a hatchet kind of a day. Let's hope things get a little easier.

The next day is dry and crisp, the low sun finding its way through the clouds, so we've come to a forest for some good old-fashioned outdoorsy fun before the spell is broken. There's something so restorative about being in amongst the trees, nature's own soothing lullaby provided by the gentle creaking of their swaying boughs. The trees are all but bare, the sharp buds at the ends of their twiggy branches the only sign of the life to come. We are in a patch of headland overlooking a five-mile-long estuary, the single wooden track of Barmouth Bridge's railway viaduct a matchstick construction in the distance. The view is so majestic that I'm feeling much better than I did last night. I'm not even bored of playing hide and seek yet which, given Jack's complete inability to understand the rules of the game, has involved pretending not to see him in plain sight for the last ten minutes, whilst he stands with his hat over his face attempting to pick his nose through the wool.

'They're growing up so quickly,' says Geoff.

'I wish Jack would hurry up a bit more.'

I pretend to stumble across Jack by accident and go through the motions of acting surprised that I've found him. He runs off shrieking with Eric to find another 'hiding' place. I watch through slightly parted fingers as Eric unsuccessfully tries to persuade him to crouch down behind a small bush. In the end Eric sets off alone in the direction of a fallen tree trunk.

'I'm glad you came,' says Geoff. 'I know it's not your ideal family holiday, but it's lovely to be able to spend some quality time with you all.'

'I'm glad we came too.'

Eric, who returned last night full of beans having made a new friend, shouts that they're ready for us to come and find them again. Jack immediately tells us his whereabouts, which is ten metres away with his back to us, but we make the appropriate searching noises in between snatches of conversation.

'*Coming, ready or not…* So what's going on with you? Any more dates?'

'*Wherever can Jack be?* Actually, I wanted to talk to you about that.'

We walk up to a large clump of bracken. '*Is he in here? No!* Ooh, sounds interesting.'

'*Could he be in here?*' Geoff gently kicks a large pile of soggy leaves. '*Nope. Not here.* Yes, I've actually started seeing someone.'

'*We'll never find him at this rate...*' I stroke my chin in mock bafflement. 'What, seeing *seeing* someone?'

'*Is this him?*' Geoff walks over to a moss-covered pile of stones. '*Oh no, that's not him.* Yes, her name's Sheila. We hit it off from the outset.'

Jack giggles loudly as we pretend to look for him.

'And how many times have you met up?' I ask Geoff, stopping to listen to him properly.

'Half a dozen or so. But time's ticking. I like her. She likes me. We're not kids any more. We've agreed that that's enough and we should see how things go.'

It's like someone has thrown a damp tea towel on my mood.

'Are you actually looking for us,' Eric shouts from somewhere beyond our eyeline.

'YES!' I shout back. 'But you've hidden too well.'

We turn back towards Jack who is now staring straight at us and waving furiously.

'I think that's great, Geoff. I really do.' I'm happy for him. But also disquieted by my emotional reaction.

'*Ooh. Is that a blue coat I see up ahead?* Thanks, Cath. It won't affect how much time I spend with you and the kids.'

'*Is it? I can't be sure. Let's go and investigate.* We'd understand if it did.' I really hope it doesn't.

'*Or is it the sky through the trees.*' He peers intently in Jack's direction. 'It really won't.' He touches me on the arm. 'I'm not going to get all obsessed with some fancy woman and disappear, okay?'

Geoff knows my dad left without saying goodbye, a cowardly act for which I will never forgive him, not that he has ever sought forgiveness as I still have no idea where he is or even if he's still alive. It's not fear gnawing at me; I know Geoff won't do that. No. It's the unmistakable pang of envy that's skittering like a cockroach across the linoleum of my psyche.

'In fact, Sheila's mad keen on meeting you. She's very sociable. You'll get on.'

If I'm envious that Geoff has someone else, by default doesn't that mean I wish I had someone else too? I bury the thought. The news is a lot to take in. Everything is changing. We're in Wales after a long time away. Little wonder I feel unsettled.

'Well, we should get something sorted for when we get back… *Oh hang on. Turns out it* is *a blue coat. Hey everyone, it's Jack.*'

Jack squeals as I pick him up and twirl him round.

'Thanks, Cath. That would be great. Right, let's find Eric and head back.'

We've been back at the caravan an hour when calamity strikes.

'Where's Stripy Big Nose?' asks Jack.

Stripy Big Nose is Jack's comforter toy. His beloved cannot-get-to-sleep-without-it comforter toy.

'Probably in the car.' But when I check, it isn't. It isn't in the bedroom either. In fact, a frantic search of the entire caravan reveals that it isn't anywhere. 'Did we take it to the forest?' I ask with a creeping sense of dread.

Eric thinks for a moment, lips pursed, then frowns. Not a good sign.

'Uh oh. He was pretending to hide it when we were playing.'

'Oh arse.' I instinctively look for a swear jar that isn't there. I cast my mind back to the route we took and the area we covered. We'd gone off-piste, traversing the overgrown forest floor rather than keeping to the gravel paths provided.

'I want Stripy really bad.' Jack's face threatens to crumple into tears. I'm about to join him when I remember I brought a back-up Stripy for such emergencies.

'It's okay,' I tell him. I rummage through the bags I still haven't unpacked, manoeuvring my hand around varying folds of fabric, but come up empty handed. Undeterred, I painstakingly unpack each bag properly, item by item, checking tiny pockets and inside trouser legs in case it has somehow worked its way inside some clothing, but still no luck. I'm racking my brain trying to think where it could be when it treats me to a brief flashback: it's one of Stripy Big Nose 2 on the kitchen table, deliberately placed there as a visual reminder to not forget it since it hadn't made the first wave of bag-packing, and ends with Jack crapping vertically beyond the boundaries of his nappy, distracting me long enough for that tactic not to have worked. Curse it.

'I want Stripy,' says Jack again. Pity his memory isn't as awful as mine.

The thing about comforter toys is you have no control over what your child will get attached to. Give them an easy-to-replace muslin and they will cast it aside with contempt. Accidentally leave a pair of post-pregnancy knickers on the floor, and chances are they will clutch them to their bosom as they might a long-lost relative who comes bearing sweets. So strong is the power of the comforter, that if your child decided tomorrow that they *absolutely must have the holy shroud of Turin* before they felt able to put their shoes on, you would find it, you would steal it, and you would cut it up into handkerchief-sized bits. In Jack's case, he settled on Stripy Big Nose as his must-have soother, a half-hanky-half-elephant with knots for hands and feet, a duplicate of which was promptly bought to allow for regular decontamination without any break in comforting continuity. But now we have neither, and judging by Jack's increasingly pained cries, this is not a good thing.

'Can we buy one locally?' Geoff asks.

'I got the spare from off the internet. We'd be very lucky to find the exact same thing, especially in the kind of shops we have nearby.'

Jack's cries take on the tone of an American cop car, a high-pitched wail growing in intensity until the need for breath forces a temporary change in pitch and volume.

'I could go and look for it in the forest?' Geoff suggests.

I'm tempted to send him out on this mercy mission, but even with Jack's pathetic attempts at hiding things, he could be there for hours. I look at the clock and calculate there'd be barely an hour left of daylight by the time he got there. Nope. That's not an option.

'Hang on.' I crouch down level with Jack. 'Jack, sweetie. Stripy has headed home because he forgot we were at the caravan.'

He eyes me curiously, stifling his tears to listen and taking in great gulps of air that catch in his lips.

'We're not going to see him for a few days, okay? We'll see him when we get back home. He can be keeping your bed warm for you, can't he?'

Jack bursts into tears again, his eyes scrunch shut whilst his wide-open mouth emits another ceaseless bawl.

'I know, I know, it's very sad.' I give him a cuddle. 'We'll see him soon.'

He fights my embrace, appalled at this turn of events. Geoff and Eric look on, helpless.

'He'll settle down in a few minutes.'

Only he doesn't settle down. He carries on crying. We count the minutes. At two, I still have faith he's going to stop. At five, Geoff picks him up and paces up and down, shushing pointlessly and barely audibly into Jack's ears. At fifteen, Eric's face has taken on the haunted expression of someone being tortured.

'Can we order one on a next day delivery?' Geoff shouts to be heard above the noise.

'How about if we sent for Stripy and he was with us tomorrow?' I say to Jack, repeating myself to ensure he's heard me.

He stops crying for a second. 'Want Stripy now,' he says hopefully.

'I'm sorry, darling, but he has to come all the way from where we live.'

His face collapses into sobs again, huge tears rolling down his bright red cheeks.

'We might have to go home.' I don't know what else to suggest.

'Not fair,' says Eric, grunting and kicking the bench. 'I'm meant to be meeting up with Grace later.'

Grace is the twelve-year-old girl from four caravans down who Eric has befriended, and tonight there's a Valentine Ball (essentially a disco with a few sugar paper hearts stapled to the walls of the clubhouse) that they've agreed to attend together.

'Don't kick that!'

He kicks the bench again.

'What do you suggest? If *he* doesn't sleep, *we* won't sleep, and that is no fun for anyone.'

'Why can't you go and get it and we'll stay here?' asks Eric. 'You're the one who forgot it.'

'Because that's a five-hour round trip!'

'Better than us spending the holidays at home.'

I consider the Dan factor, and all of us being in the house together for a prolonged period, and instantly want to emigrate. He's right, even though I don't want to admit it to him.

'It'd be a shame to have to cut things short,' says Geoff, who has taken to jiggling Jack up and down like a colicky baby.

'Okay, I'll go, but only if Jack stops crying and you don't mind looking after the kids.'

'Not at all. I could take them to the pool. Take Jack's mind off it.'

I take Jack from Geoff and smooth his wet fringe away from a face so slimy it looks like he's been attacked by a colony of slugs.

'Jack, do you want to go swimming whilst I go and fetch Stripy?'

'Shwimmin?'

'Yes, swimming. And when you get back, Stripy will be back too.'

He insta-stops crying, the heightened emotion switch flicked back into the *off* position. Kids make it look so easy.

'We'll go to the chippy for tea,' says Geoff. 'That'll drag it out a bit.'

'You're sure?'

'Go. You need to move now if you're going to be back by any reasonable bedtime.'

I don't wait to be told twice.

With the radio cranked up and no arguments coming from the back seat, the journey home flies by and I'm almost euphoric by the end. Once home I head straight upstairs for a pee, the journey having taken its toll on my bladder. I'm sat typing a text to Geoff to let him know my progress when a noise, a bit like a bin lid hitting the floor, comes from downstairs. It could well be next door, but we once had a fox come through the now-defunct cat flap, so better to investigate. I head downstairs, roll up a magazine that's on the side, creep up to the kitchen door and listen. Yep. There's something moving around in there. There's a faint intermittent scraping sound, hard to tell what, something being dragged along the floor perhaps. I ready myself, slowly turn the door handle and then throw open the door as forcefully as possible, magazine raised.

'GET OUT, YOU LITTLE SHIT BAG!'

Only there is no fox. There is no wildlife at all, unless you count Dan's one-eyed trouser snake and the beaver of the young lady he's screwing over my kitchen table.

'Oh my god!' the girl jumps about a foot into the air and almost falls over a chair. 'Is this your mom?'

Cheeky cow! How old does she think I am? I don't have time to take this up with her because Dan is now completely exposed by the absence of nubile youth covering his groin. I try not to look at his penis, but the damned thing is looking at me and so my gaze is hypnotically drawn in that direction. It hasn't yet cottoned on to the gravity of the situation and continues to stand to full attention.

'I'm really sorry, Cath, I didn't know you were coming back.'

'Clearly,' I attempt to focus on anything but his perfectly proportioned appendage and fail miserably. I'm no expert in penile matters, but if dicks were a species, Dan's would be at the pedigree end of the spectrum. 'Was the soccer a bit too unsexual intercourse-y for you?' I ask, miffed by this new evidence of his physical superiority. And how old is the girl now retrieving her pants from the kitchen floor?

Dan grabs the first thing he can to cover his modesty. Of course, this happens to be Stripy Big Nose 2, which was sitting exactly where I left it.

'Are the boys here too?' He peers shamefaced over my shoulder into the hallway.

'No. I came back to collect a spare comforter toy for Jack.'

'A what?'

I point to what he's holding and he looks down at the soft fabric of Stripy Big Nose 2 draped over his willy. I'm not even sure I want to collect it now.

'Oh my god. This is horrible.' He frantically looks around for a replacement covering. His inside-out boxers are lying discarded near my feet. I hesitate, then bend down to pick them up as Dan does too, and our foreheads crack together. He recoils more quickly than me and for a second I come eye-to-eye with his cock, which is peeking around the side of Stripy like a game of peek-a-boner.

'Should I go?' asks the girl, in a way that unbelievably isn't rhetorical. She's still only wearing a bra and pants. The confidence of youth.

Dan looks at her, further dismayed by her need to ask. 'Yes, yes, I think you should go. I need to have a word with my *landlady*.'

Finally cottoning on, she picks up her dress, pulls it on, retrieves her shoes and backs out of the door mouthing 'message me', before turning and walking up the hallway to let herself out. As the door slams behind her I turn back to Dan, who is now dressed in shorts, his hard-on finally diminishing. I can't tell if the red cheeks are the result of embarrassment or the effort he was putting in before.

I take the comforter toy from his hands. 'He'll never be able to un-see that,' I tell Dan. Nor will I.

'I don't know what to say.'

'It's fine.' I have to get back. I pop the toy into my handbag.

'No, it was disrespectful and completely out of order.'

I don't want him thinking I'm some kind of prude, and it's not the fact he brought someone back to the house that's bugging me.

'Dan. You're a man. With needs. I get that.' What's irritating is the fact that she was so young. 'But tell me. Have you ever tried sleeping with someone your own age?'

'Of course. But not for many years!'

He tries his winning smile. That's not washing in this situation. I cross my arms.

'Sorry. Stupid joke. I'm nervous.' He rocks on his feet, discomfiture resting on him as awkwardly as an ill-fitting suit.

'Did you know the singer, Tony Bennett, had a photo taken with his wife before she was born?'

'What?'

'Some woman came to his concert with a baby on board, a baby he went on to date when she turned nineteen and he was fifty-nine.' True story, I read it in one of Sindy's magazines. I got in a flap about it then and feel the same emotions arising now. 'Tony Bennett! He's just a sultana with a singing voice. Whilst perfectly decent women watch their romantic options shrink as they age, men can ... I don't know ... wander into their local maternity hospital and hand out business cards to be used in a couple of decades!'

Dan tries to look understanding. I'm reminded of those Athena posters from the 80s, where sensitive half-naked men stared meaningfully at the camera.

'I'm sure you could sleep with younger men if you wanted to.'

'I wouldn't want to! Most of the eighteen-year-olds I know couldn't find their arses with both hands, let alone a clitoris!'

He laughs. I don't.

'Okay, the Tony Bennett thing is horrible. But for the record, she's not eighteen, she's twenty-seven. And a lecturer.'

Is she? God, that makes me hate her even more.

'And we're just having some fun.'

'Does she know that?' I remember the images of Dan that Sindy and I found online. All those different faces of pretty women.

'I never make promises I can't keep.'

'Yeah, right!' I scoff.

He seems genuinely hurt by my scepticism. 'Look, Cath. I wouldn't start something I couldn't finish. But yes, I have sex with women. Glorious, satisfying, casual sex. Not all of us are lucky enough to meet *the one* at college, get married, have kids and live smugly ever after.'

I glance at the urn and Dan follows my gaze.

'Sorry, that was insensitive.'

'For the record, we weren't married. Gaz wanted to. I didn't.'

Gaz asked me to marry him three times. The first was when I was pregnant with Leanne, but it was out of some misguided sense of propriety that neither of us really bought into. The second was when Eric was born, but we needed a new kitchen and that seemed like a better investment. The third was on the twentieth anniversary of our first date, and whilst I'd been tempted, I also figured we could do without all the admin. He was fine about it. Little did I know within months I'd be drowning in admin when he died without a will, and I found out the term *common law wife* counts for nothing in common law.

'Oh. I'm sorry.'

'It's fine.' It's not, but I really need to get out of here and back to the boys. 'But perhaps next time you should go back to their place?'

He grimaces. 'Of course.'

'Okay. Well, see you, Dan.' I turn to leave.

'Wait! Can I make you a tea? Or get you some biscuits for the journey.'

Tempting as it is to have my own butler in the buff, I really do need to be heading back. 'Sorry Dan. Gotta go.'

'Okay. I'll see you when you get back, yeah?' He asks this like it might be negotiable.

'Yep. I'll see you when I get back.' With that I head back to

Wales, still mortified at what's happened, but I can't resist a little satisfied smile wondering whether it might be his turn to feel a bit uncomfortable around me for a change.

***Five days later and I'm in our hallway again, this time making sure to announce our arrival as loudly as possible. I'd also texted ahead. Dan comes downstairs, sheepish as you like. He high-fives Eric as we make our way inside.

'Good time away?'

'It was great,' says Eric. 'I've been practicing my scales. Can we move onto chords now?'

'Eric, Dan has a course he needs to study for; you shouldn't impose on him.'

'He doesn't mind, do you?' he says, running up the stairs.

'I really don't mind.'

'Pick up.' Jack tugs at Dan's jeans. Dan picks him up.

'You don't have to humour them, you know. It must be full-on having them around.' After a restorative week of sea air and Geoff helping with Jack, I'm feeling generous of spirit, even towards Dan.

'I like kids, Cath. They have a way of reminding you what's important in life.'

'Like sweets and video games?'

'I was thinking more speaking your mind and being yourself. And I enjoy being out of my comfort zone.'

'If you ever want to really immerse yourself, come to soft play. That's enough to push you out of your comfort zone and off a cliff.'

Jack squirms to be put down again.

'I'll take your bags up,' says Dan.

'No need.'

'It's the least I can do.'

I'm in the kitchen packing some bits away when Dan returns. He looks out at the still-frosted lawn, his breath forming and reforming ever decreasing circles of condensation on the patio doors. He steals a glance at me that I pretend not to notice. I think he wants to mention our run-in. Schadenfreude! His increased discomfort has correlated with a slight downward shift in my own.

'Oh Dan. I've got my school reunion next Saturday.'

Turns out Gaynor is leaving me no choice but to go. In fact, her *driver* (puke) is picking me up so we can go together. She'll be doing it for the same reasons brides choose bridesmaids uglier than themselves—so she'll look even more striking on arrival.

'It's some swanky affair,' I say, embellishing unnecessarily. 'Geoff is babysitting. I imagine it'll be a very late one.' Again, an unnecessary and untrue detail, but I'm enjoying appearing to have a life.

'Cool,' he says.

I fuss around a bit more, wondering if he'll say anything else. He doesn't.

'I'm going to order a takeaway. Do you want anything?'

'No, thanks. I'm off to the movies.' He turns towards me. He has his jumper sleeves pulled down and is fiddling with the cuffs. 'But I made you a pie.'

'What, like an apple pie?'

'A cowboy pie.'

'Does it have horns coming out of it?'

He doesn't get the Desperate Dan reference.

'It's only beans and sausages topped with potatoes. You don't have to eat it.'

'You made us dinner?' *He's made us dinner?!*

'Yeah.'

'You don't need to do penance you know.'

'I know. I thought you'd be hungry and tired when you got back.'

'Are you still trying to make a point about altruism?'

'No!' A pained look. 'What I'm trying to do is make friends.'

'Oh.' I'm momentarily lost for words. No one has asked to be my friend for a long time. 'Well, food is a really good place to start.'

He smiles. 'Cool. I should get going. Just heat it up.'

'Okay. Thanks.'

'No problem.' He walks towards the hallway and stops briefly at the kitchen door. 'I hope you get a good rest,' he says before disappearing.

When I'm sure he's gone, I open the fridge. Sure enough, there's a Pyrex dish with cowboy pie in it, and forked into the mashed potato topping is the word *sorry*. I smile and pop it in the microwave, closing the door with a flourish. It's been a very long time since anyone made me dinner.

Chapter Eighteen

If I'd felt relaxed by the end of the holiday, I've been a mass of nerves leading up to the reunion. I could barely concentrate when Reggie and the team came for their lesson today, but they're finally on board with the social media stuff. I even tried my hand at a quick video, involving Jack on a roundabout to demonstrate centrifugal forces. It was less successful than the other content, but I'll work on it. Right now, I need to work on the deep-seated feelings of failure to which my conscience is subjecting me, not helped by my looking at pictures of Gaynor on socials for the last twenty minutes instead of getting ready.

'Got any sweets, Granddad?'

Geoff has arrived and is being accosted by Jack in the hallway. There's half an hour before Gaynor is due to collect me. Where's Armageddon when you need it? Geoff pops his head round the door.

'Shouldn't you be getting ready?'

'I suppose so.'

I head upstairs to see if any clothes I might want to wear have magically appeared in my wardrobe. They haven't. But Sindy's lent me a Victorian style black lacy blouse she can't get into anymore, which I can pair with black jeans. My black heels are looking very sorry for themselves, but the only shoe polish I find has dried out to a hardened little hockey puck of uselessness, so I colour the scuffs in with one of the kids' markers. I don't normally bother with makeup, but Leanne's left me some of her old stuff to try so I attempt a vampy kohl effect eye shadow, mattifying foundation and a slick of dark red lipstick. I make my already messy hair work for me with a spot of extra mussing.

For the final five minutes, whilst Geoff gets the kids their tea, I torture myself further with more pictures of Gaynor in exotic locations. Gaynor is less child-challenged than I am, to the power of three kids, which means her body's as impeccable as her face. Every shot of her lying on a beach, or standing in the surf, or sitting at a bar (and there are hundreds) is flawless. I've even zoomed in to see if I can find a single trace of cellulite on her thighs and can't. She always was attractive, taller than average but not freakishly so, with a curved athletic body that did exactly what she told it to. Long dark hair fell in soft waves about her shoulders, framing a face freckled in all the right places, as if they'd been painted on deliberately to accentuate her delicate features. Back then she seemed to have it all, and from the vision of perfection that is currently making its way up my pathway, it appears she still does. I take a very deep breath, not to steady my nerves, but to make my waist look slimmer, and go to open the door, determined to make an amazing impression and to not feel intimidated.

'Cath! After all this time!' She air-kisses me dramatically

and then steps back to look me up and down. She's taking in the hair I had ruffled only minutes earlier, the carefully applied makeup and the slimming black clothes. If I've judged this correctly, she's thinking *not too shabby for a mom of three.*

'Have you become a Goth since I last saw you?'

Goddammit! Gaynor, by contrast, has all the sheen of an understatedly famous person, which is exactly what she is. Because of her job in the media and her excellent breeding, she regularly appears in the society pages of glossy magazines, often alongside a minor royal or a major douchebag. Her hair is shorter than it used to be, but she's still as beautiful as Anne Hathaway on a good day.

'I'll get my bag and we can go.' My voice is slightly strained as I'm even more determined not to breathe out.

'No rush.' She reaches into an oversized Burberry handbag and pulls out a bottle of champagne. 'We have ten minutes. We could have a quick drink.'

Suddenly the world stops, drains of its colour and the blood rushes out of my head to be replaced with a repeated violin screeching akin to the shower scene in *Psycho*. I had not prepared for this eventuality. My lounge flashes before my eyes. There are toys strewn across the floor, a pile of Jack's nappies I've not yet taken out to the bin, a cluster of flies belly up on the windowsill. When I snap back to my senses Gaynor is looking concerned.

'Is there a problem?'

I don't say anything immediately; I'm too busy trying to think of a good enough excuse to not let her in.

'Come on, I insist.' She links arms and leads me down the hall.

The overpowering stench of fish pie that Geoff's reheating

brings me back to my senses and by the time we reach the lounge I've rallied. I motion to the only chair that doesn't have detritus on and fetch some glasses. In the kitchen I collect my thoughts, kiss the kids, pour the bubbles, gesture to Geoff that some disaster of a non-specific nature has befallen me in the adjoining room, and return to the lounge ready to be brilliant. I find her looking at my computer, applying a squirt of antibacterial gel to her all-year-round tanned hands. There is a close-up of the lower half of a body on screen, a contextless dismembered mid-section from belly to knee.

'I have that bikini,' she says, slowly rubbing the gel into her palms.

'What a coincidence!' I muster.

'And that beach towel.'

'Well, I never.' Shame prickles my cheeks.

'And that exact same tattoo. In that exact same place.'

She turns and stares at me. I stare at her. We stare at each other. I must come clean and confess to the simple misdemeanour of trying to find evidence of a bit of orange peel flesh on her. Experience has told me that in situations such as these, no matter how cringe-worthy, you must step up and tell the truth.

'I'm so sorry,' I begin, passing her a glass of champagne. 'The kids must have been messing around. That looks a lot like Eric's idea of a joke.' I take a large glug of my own drink, try to ignore my moral compass going crazy, and hope to goodness that Eric didn't hear me throw him under the bus.

Things don't get easier en route. Gaynor asks about the kids, tells me she thinks it's interesting how I'm trying to teach with social media, but the conversation invariably comes back to how wonderful her life is, how wonderful her husband is, and isn't it remarkable how widely our lives diverged after leaving school. She seems to have forgotten how different they were for the time I was there too. It's only when we pull up to the bottom of the long sweeping driveway that leads to Redlands High School for Girls that she finally shuts up, and we both watch in silence as the imposing façade of our former seat of learning comes into view. The building is as unlike Brookdene as is possible, built in the forties to look like an oversized medieval manor house, the elegant façade beset on all sides by creeping ivy and inset with leaded windows.

'There it is,' says Gaynor. 'I can't believe it was nearly thirty years ago we first arrived.'

I will never forget the day I walked up this driveway for the first time, the final stages of a three-bus journey that had brought me from an estate on the outskirts of town to this lavish structure in the countryside. I stood beneath the huge carved stone coat of arms that hung above the great oak front doors and read the words *Dieu et Mon Droit*. I didn't have the faintest idea what they meant, but I was hungry to hoover up whatever knowledge lay beyond them. I cast a glance at Gaynor. In the seven years we were at school together, we were always competing, each of us with our own reasons for wanting to be top girl in our year. We were never firm friends —we came from too different worlds for that—but we gravitated towards one another as outliers tend to, her an abrasive prodigy prone to rubbing people up the wrong way, me the cheeky working-class buffoon who never quite fitted in.

'I wonder if you still have to wear those awful uniforms,' she says. 'I say, Jonathon.' She taps the driver's shoulder. 'Can you imagine me in anything so drab as a brown blazer and straw boater?'

Judging by his non-committal reaction, he doesn't seem that tuned in to her sartorial preferences. Jeeves he is not.

Academically Gaynor and I matched one another almost like-for-like back then, slowly gaining acceptance and eventually even sharing the title of 'most likely to succeed' in our final week in sixth form. But then over the summer holidays, as she took on a sponsored place at a university in Sydney, I'd fallen pregnant. It's little surprise we largely drifted out of each other's lives; whilst she was jetting halfway around the world and expanding her horizons, I was sat on my mother's interest-free-credit sofa with an expanding belly. And before I knew it, the whole episode became a part of my life BC —Before Children—the line drawn, the past a distant echo that had nothing to do with the here and now, all packaged up into a box marked UNWANTED. But we can't shrug off our old selves like skins we've outgrown. Instead, they lie dormant waiting for the opportunity to sneak up, tap you on the shoulder and shout, 'SO, HAVE YOU GOT ANY REGRETS?' into your ear. I'm suddenly gripped with a sensation so strong I might choke on it. I try to open the window, but I'm confused by the buttons in the door console and they swim before my eyes.

'Are you okay?' Gaynor is in a different place to me, her words ringing and remote.

'I need some air.' I claw at the door. Where's the handle? How do I get out? 'Stop the car.' I'm pressing my whole weight against the door, willing it to open, when suddenly it does, and I fall at the feet of Gaynor's driver. He tries to help me up, but I recoil from his touch. My skin is burning and I have an urgent need to run away, only I can't feel my legs.

'Don't feel well.' I stumble to my feet and rest my hands on the car roof. 'Be okay in a minute.'

I'm aware of other cars passing ours and I get the sensation that everyone and everything is looking at me, pointing at me, pulling me in a billion different directions. And then Gaynor is behind me.

'I think you're having a panic attack. Try to breathe.'

I vomit, great heaves of acrid champagne splashing noisily onto my scuffed shoes. A few minutes pass in this state, me sucking in air through my constricted throat, then the physical symptoms begin to subside and not dying seems more and more likely. My breath comes slower and my eyes clear enough to note its misty vapour disappearing into the dark night. It's a chilly evening, but the cold is soothing.

'Feeling better?' Gaynor asks.

'I'm so sorry, that's never happened to me before.'

'Well, they say you should try everything once,' she chirrups, a rare attempt at light-heartedness. Gaynor never was one for jokes; she was too tightly wound up in herself to laugh much.

'Do you want to go inside?' she asks.

The panic rises again, even at the thought of doing so. 'No, I'm sorry Gaynor. It was a mistake to come.'

'But I'm sure everyone would love to see you.'

I swallow hard, tasting bile. She's being kind, but I can't do it.

'I need to go home.' I brace myself against the cold and face down the drive.

'At least get a lift back.'

I used to get three buses to school. I don't have the energy for that. 'Are you sure?'

'Absolutely.' She pours more antibacterial gel into her hands. 'But maybe take your shoes off first.'

I ask Jonathon to drop me off a little way from mine so I can compose myself before I head in. Geoff's car isn't in the driveway, which means he may have taken the kids back to his for the night. However, when I open the door the TV's on. Strange. I pop my head round the lounge door to find Dan lying on the sofa holding a giggling Jack in the air above him. Eric, who is sat cross-legged on the floor, catches sight of me.

'You look like the Joker.'

So much for looking collected.

Dan deposits Jack on the floor. 'Jesus, are you okay?'

'Where's Geoff?'

'He felt out-of-sorts, so I offered to take over. He said he'd message.'

'I've not looked at my phone.'

'We weren't expecting you back so soon.' He looks genuinely concerned. 'Cath, has something happened?'

I get what this might look like. Distressed, dishevelled and shoeless.

'Oh no! I just had a weird episode.' I wish Geoff was here.

'Why don't I get Jack to bed and then if you want to tell me about it you can.' He scoops Jack up in his arms.

'I'll do it.'

'It's fine. I'd started some hot chocolate. Maybe you can finish that and I'll be down in ten minutes.'

Ten minutes getting Jack to bed. A bit ambitious.

'Eric, time to go to your bedroom, buddy,' he says.

Eric drags himself to his feet, the unfairness of having his evening cut short etched on his face.

'Why don't you rent a movie on your tablet?' I suggest.

'Cool.' He brightens. 'Can I take some crisps up too?'

'Okay.'

They head upstairs and I start to relax, then I remember I'm a mess so I tidy my face with a baby wipe. The drinks are ready when Dan returns only five minutes later.

'I put a story podcast on for him. We'll see if it works.'

It almost certainly won't, but it's not a bad idea. He grabs his drink and sits at the opposite end of the sofa. I grip my cup, letting the heat burn my fingers until they tingle. I'm not sure I'm up for polite chit chat—I'm still a bit shaken—but I also don't want to be alone. Silence wedges itself between us. I steel myself to say something.

'Dan...'

'Cath...'

Our words tumble out simultaneously.

'You first,' he says, smiling.

'No, you. I didn't really have anything to say.'

'Someone popped round earlier, from down the road. Said she knows you from nursery and wanted to return Jack's T-shirt. Some clothing mix-up or other. It's in the hall.'

I don't put Jack's name in any of his clothing, half in the hope that one day he'll turn up wearing something better than I sent him in, so I know it isn't his. Word must have got out about Dan and Belinda's come to look for herself.

'Did she ask who you were?' I'm sure she'd be thrilled to know I need a lodger.

'Yep. I told her I was your live-in lover.'

I nearly drop the cup. 'You did not!'

'I did. I figured if she was a friend she'd know I wasn't. She's not a friend is she?'

'No.'

'Didn't think so.'

'There's no way she'd have bought it though.'

'Why not?'

'Because…' He must know we're in different leagues.

'Well, I'm happy to pretend to be sleeping with you any time you like, even if you wouldn't return the favour.'

I blow on my drink, my breath indenting the wrinkled skin that's formed on top. I gently move it to the side of the cup and take a scalding sip, washing away traces of bile.

'Do you want to talk about why you're home early?' asks Dan.

'Hmm. Turns out I wasn't ready to revisit the past.'

He waits for more, but I don't really know where to begin.

'Did you have a rough time at school?'

'Not especially. I wasn't well off, unlike most of the other girls, but it wasn't a big deal. We were there to learn and that's something I was good at.'

He nods but says nothing.

'I guess I'm feeling a bit underachiever-y and sorry for myself. I was once voted most likely to succeed. Now look at me.' My chin wobbles. I really don't want to cry in front of Dan, but he hands me a tissue and I'm so grateful for the small gesture that the tears fall anyway.

'I'm so sorry. You really don't need to be hearing this. I'm not normally a blarter.'

'Blarter?'

'Cryer.'

'Ah. Well, maybe you should blart more. Let it out a bit.'

'I'm not into that hippy dippy stuff.' I attempt to stem the flow of tears in a way that doesn't spread even more mascara across my face.

'I'm pretty certain crying is not hippy dippy. It's a natural reaction to feeling bad.'

'But everything's fine.'

'Is it?'

I blow my nose, a long honking sound that I hope might signal an end to this line of questioning.

'Seems to me you've already been through a lot. On top of that you lost your job; you're raising two children on your own; your eldest has recently flown the nest, and your deceased partner is in a vase in the kitchen. It's understandable you lose it every now and again.'

'Life didn't turn out as planned. Whose does?'

'Nobody's. But as an outsider looking in, I don't think you're an under-achiever. You're raising great kids, and now you're giving other people's kids the chance to do something with themselves.'

'Isn't it all a bit kid-based?' I sniff, pick up a bag of popcorn from the floor and take a handful. 'It's not as though I'm out there saving the ice caps.'

'I personally couldn't give a damn about the ice caps. I do have a soft spot for children though. If there's a burning zoo and I can save a polar bear or a kid, I am voting kid every time. For a start, they are way easier to carry.'

I laugh, a bubble of snot emerging from my nostril. 'Sorry!'

'You've seen me do far worse.'

I squeak at the memory of walking in on him naked, and hide behind a cushion.

'Seriously though. You have great kids.'

I grab another tissue. 'Thank you.'

I pass Dan the bag of popcorn. 'I envy your ability to jet off at will. Decide you want to try somewhere new and go for it.'

'Do you?'

Up until this evening, I'm not sure this was something I'd been able to admit to myself. It's like having committed myself to momming, I wasn't allowed to deviate from that script. I ask Dan to tell me about some of his favourite places and he regales me with tales of kayaking in Vietnam, playing board games in cafés surrounded by the Himalayan mountains, and cooking curries on a handmade stove in a Pakistani homestay. He relates the stories with such warmth and appreciation I can't quite imagine how I've felt such resentment towards him in the last couple of months.

'The closest I've come to adventure is trying to run away when I was nine,' I tell him. 'It was disastrous.'

'How?'

'We were at a holiday park, and things weren't great between my mom and dad.'

Dan waves a bag of sweets at me. 'More chocolate?'

He tosses the bag and I snaffle a few before continuing. 'They'd been up all night arguing and I imagined the horror of finding me gone would bring them closer together.'

'A kid's twisted logic.'

'I sneak out really early whilst they're asleep and head for the park exit. But then I pass a fully inflated, unsupervised bouncy castle.'

'What are the chances?'

'Exactly. It's too good an opportunity to pass up, so naturally I climb on. After a while I try a somersault.'

'Uh-oh.' He expertly tosses a piece of popcorn into his mouth.

'Only my bum and my feet land at the same time, and I knee myself so hard in the face I'm convinced I've punctured my eyeballs.'

Dan chuckles and nearly chokes on his popcorn.

'Seriously. They're watering so much, I think the inner jelly's leaking out and I've blinded myself. Imagine being in excruciating pain, completely disorientated and trying to get out of a bouncy castle. I reckon it's easier to get out of the Church of Scientology.'

He guffaws. 'What happened?'

'Eventually I do, then I'm stumbling around, arms outstretched, like something out of the zombie apocalypse. Someone found me and took me to the medical centre. They calmed me down, assured me my eyes were fine; I just needed to try and open them through the swelling.'

'And your parents?'

'Initially confused about how I'd got two black eyes whilst I should have been asleep, but then quickly blamed each other for my disappearance.'

'Oh dear.'

'Yep. My one attempt at escape. Total failure.'

Dan smiles. 'It's a great story.'

'Why, thank you.'

'And it's nice to have a proper chat. Just the two of us.'

Under normal circumstances this would be greeted by some awkward excuse, but it has been nice.

'I'm sorry I've been standoffish. It's been a bit weird having a grown-up around.'

'It's cool. But I should remind you I am no grown-up.'

'True.'

I check the time. We've been talking for nearly two hours, and Jack hasn't reappeared. I tell Dan it's a miracle.

'Well, if there's anything I can do to help whilst I'm here, ask.'

I decide to take the plunge. 'Do you know what? There might be something.' I explain what I'm doing for Reggie and co. Some of the quick videos I rattle off are fine, but some require a bit more set up, and me and a selfie stick aren't cutting it. Given Dan's course, I ask for advice on a more professional setup. He goes one better: he tells me it sounds like the perfect topic for a research project he hadn't yet got around to deciding on, and perhaps he could develop a thesis around the use of film and media as a teaching aid. He says he'd be happy to shoot and edit some videos so long as I was happy to share with him my experiences of their effect.

'But what if I'm too nervous?' I ask him.

'There's an easy fix for that. You need to imagine me naked.'

Now that I can do.

PART III
SPRING

Chapter Nineteen

I 'm in the café section of a garden centre that sits on the edge of the countryside skirting Birmingham, to meet Geoff and his new girlfriend. It's one of those places that's diversified from selling plants and flowers and now does a roaring trade in garden tat. In my line of sight there is an entire aisle of garden gnomes, a section dedicated to tin signs filled with twee statements such as *a beautiful garden is a work of heart*, and a series of ever more expensive water features. Jack has been watching a poor replica of the Mannequin Pis for five minutes and has finally decided to try and drink the water straight from the cherub's penis.

'No, Jack.' I drag him back to his seat and try to coax him into compliance with a pack of animal shaped biscuits. He proceeds to reject each one on the basis of it missing a limb or head.

'I apologise for my child, Sheila.'

'Yes, Geoff said he was a handful.'

I cast Geoff a look. '*You traitor,*' my eyes say, although he is. Sadly Eric isn't here to parade as the clever, precocious one.

'Kids need a father figure, don't they?' says Sheila.

'Well, he'll have to make do with an action figure,' I retort, rather more defensively than I should. 'Anyway, it's nice to finally meet you,' I continue, not meaning it.

She's not at all what I expected. She's dolled up to the nines, bouffant blonde hair and bright red lips in stark contrast to the wholesomeness of our bucolic surroundings. She's wearing a low-cut black T-shirt and black denim skirt, and a gold pendant necklace that's in danger of being engulfed by a crêpey tanned bosom that rests on the table in front of her.

'You too. I've been pestering Geoff for weeks, haven't I, Love? But you know what men are like!' She throws her arms around Geoff's neck and gives him a sloppy kiss on the cheek. Far from looking embarrassed, Geoff returns the kiss, this time on the lips.

'Geoff told me about your partner. I was sorry to hear what happened. I lost my husband a few years ago.'

Have you checked your cleavage? I want to ask.

'I found Zumba really helped. Have you tried it?'

I shake my head.

'It's brilliant. There's something wonderfully healing about shaking your hips and letting the grief go.'

Is she for real? That's like expecting a dog to be able to rid itself of worms by dragging its bum along the carpet.

'I've been trying to get Geoff to come with me, haven't I?'

'She has. She's trying to get me into all sorts, this one. It's like I'm working my way through a bucket list but someone forgot to tell me I'm gonna cork it!'

Sheila places her hand on the back of mine, a gesture of

familiarity I'm hugely uncomfortable with. 'If you ever want to come with me, say the word. Give us a chance to bond a bit, maybe?'

'That's very kind. I'll bear it in mind.' I subtly try to withdraw my hand from hers, but she tightens her grip on it, turns it over and looks intently at it. Don't tell me she's a palm reader.

'Did Geoff tell you I'm a palm reader?' she asks.

'He did not.'

She traces the lines on my hand with a bright scarlet nail. 'You have a water hand,' she says. 'You're very emotional and artistic.'

'Round and round the garden,' cries Jack. 'My turn! My turn!'

I try to move my hand again to pass Jack another biscuit, but she's got a fair grip on it. 'I'm more of a scientific bent, actually.'

'But science *is* an art, isn't it?' says Sheila.

'No.'

'Perhaps what Sheila means is it's about exploring our world in a way that brings new meaning to it.' says Geoff. He knows we're on shaky ground.

'Round and round the garden,' Jack shouts again. 'My turn.'

'Of course, I prefer to explore the world spiritually,' says Sheila.

'I prefer to deal in reality.'

'Scientists. They think everything can be proven by facts!'

'Err, everything else is pure conjecture!'

Jack gets bored of waiting and tickles his own chin.

'Well, it doesn't matter if you believe in it or not, it's all

169

here. You've got a high Saturn mount, which means you're stubborn and cynical.'

Geoff chuckles. 'That's true.'

She traces the line from between my thumb and forefinger down to my wrist. 'This is your life line,' she tells me. 'People think it shows how long you'll live, but that's not true.'

Because it would be scientifically testable to see if people who keel over early in life still had a long one, perchance?

'There's a break here. You're going to experience a major change in lifestyle.'

'Perhaps Eric's going to learn to pick up his own pants.'

Geoff casts me a *be nice* look.

Sheila now has a pen out and is drawing on the side of my hand. 'This is interesting, this faint mark on your affection line. A new attachment may deepen over time.'

'Or I move my hand a lot and it's gotten wrinkled.'

'You may mock, but this has been practised for thousands of years.'

'So has female genital mutilation, but it doesn't make it right.'

She draws my hand to one of her fleshy breasts. I think it's meant to be against her heart, but we can't get that close. She closes her eyes. 'Spirit guides, may you help Cath find the lightness within and illuminate the opportunities without. May she tune in to your wisdom and protection and enjoy the influence of you, every day of her life.' She then stays still long enough for me to wonder if she's fallen asleep.

I turn to Geoff. '*Leave her a second,*' he mouths. '*I want to take my hand away,*' I mouth back, shifting uncomfortably in my seat. The movement is enough to bring Sheila out of her trance.

'Would you excuse me? I'm going to the bathroom. Using

my abilities takes it out of me. And I need to pee.' She provocatively shimmies past Geoff when she could have gone round the other side of the table. He slaps her on the bum.

I think about Gaz's mom, a slight, reserved woman who never wore a scrap of make-up and held herself with a quiet dignity that lasted right up until the day she died of breast cancer. I can't help but wonder where the attraction lies. Geoff reads my thoughts because as soon as she's out of earshot he turns to me.

'I know. She's a bit different from Janet, isn't she?'

'Worlds apart. Possibly galaxies.'

'That's sort of the point, love. There's no point trying to replace J. I couldn't if I wanted to. But Sheila's got energy. She's got get up and go. She's got this daft old sod doing things I never expected to be doing at this time in my life. It's all very —what's the word?—refreshing.'

I'm not sold, but it's his choice. I can't imagine that I'd deviate so far from Gaz if I ever dated again. I promise him I'll be on my best behaviour for the rest of lunch. I can't vouch for Jack though, who's attempting to pull his trousers and nappy over his shoes, possibly to emulate the peeing statue.

'Pass him over,' says Geoff. 'I'll take him for a wander whilst you try and be nice to Sheila.'

For once, I'd be grateful not to have my youngest son taken off my hands.

Chapter Twenty

'What's it for today?' asks Dan.

We're at the breakfast bar, about to film our fourth video. The first one was horrible: he was chief camera operator whilst I tried not to die of embarrassment as I explained homeostasis with reference to trying to maintain a stable state in our house environment despite the constant efforts of the kids to put it out of whack. The second and third were marginally less cringe-worthy efforts about the brain and electricity. Today I'm hoping to cover off testing for ions, but I'm struggling to make the information memorable.

'I was considering creating mnemonic poems or something, but it's not working.'

I hand him some notes to scan through.

'Hmm. Yep. Not much impactful about them.'

'I'm really struggling with this one.'

'Could you sing them? Find a tune to put them to?'

'Small issue. Can't sing.'

'I've heard you sing in the shower.'

I've been singing in the shower? 'I don't sing *well* in the shower.'

'You self-deprecating English. How did the British Empire ever happen?'

'We were really polite.' I adopt my most plummy accent. *'Er, do you mind awfully, we're going to invade your country now and steal your wealth.'*

Dan affects a bad cockney accent of which he's grown fond. *'Crack on, your worship.'*

'I don't think we ever colonised the East End of London.'

He tuts. 'Pedant.'

'How did you get so confident?'

'Guns.'

'Not Americans! You, personally.'

He rests his chin on fingers, flutters his eyelashes and offers me his most dazzling smile.

'Oh please. Didn't you go through a gawky phase? Some period of self-doubt?'

'There was a small window between conception and embryo. Head was too big, my body too small. But after that, nah.'

'A tiny protein tweak and you could have looked like the elephant man.'

'Some might say there are parts of me that are elephantine.' He raises an eyebrow provocatively.

'I'd say it was more invisible man.'

'Ouch! Anyway, I think you should do them as a rap.'

'Hah! And I think you're out of your mind.'

'I'm serious. You want memorable. And with these kids... Reggie would love it.'

Of course, he's also endeared himself to Reggie and the other kids.

'Give me those.' He grabs the notes and studies them for a minute, mouthing words. Then he jumps up. 'Okay, I might have something. You know the song 'Ice Ice Baby'?'

'I've not been in a cave for the last thirty years.'

'So how about this.' He adopts a classic rapper pose, fingers of his left hand curled around an invisible microphone, right hand held out horizontally as if counting beats. 'Yo, stop, collaborate, eat chowder, add NAOH and some aluminum powder. Mix it up and I'm telling you, stir in some litmus paper and it's gonna go blue.'

He was properly going for it, so I repay him with zero reaction.

'You hate it.'

'It's aluminium, not aluminum.' My face cracks. 'And it's borderline genius.'

'Yeah?' His face lights up. 'Because if it's genius, you gotta do it.'

'Not a chance. Far too humiliating.'

'Not sure you could embarrass yourself in front of me any more than you already have.'

My cheeks burn. 'Don't remind me.'

'If you want it to stick, you've gotta put some effort in. I could add some effects.'

'Why can't *you* do it? You already look the part.'

He's wearing a blue and red hockey jersey and a frayed NYC baseball cap.

'You're not getting off that lightly. Here.' He tosses the cap to me, then pulls the jersey over his head and throws that too. 'Clean on this morning.'

Riiight, because that's what went through my head with his muscly chest all up in my face. I focus on meeting his eyes and not his nipples.

'Jesus. Did you not get enough attention as a child or something?'

'Are you trying to psychoanalyse me, Cath?'

'Why, would it make you uncomfortable if I did?' I try to sound sassy.

'No! It would make *you* uncomfortable if you did.' His eyes glitter.

I switch my gaze to a cobweb on the ceiling.

'It's only a body. You've seen it all before. In fact, may as well take the jeans too.'

I cover my eyes. 'Not necessary.' I check through my fingers he's only feigning taking them off and get side-tracked by his torso. I drop my hands in surrender.

'How do you have so many muscles?'

'I go to the gym and I've started gymnastics.'

'Really? I didn't realise.'

'That's because you never ask me what I've been up to.'

'That's because I dread to think what you've been up to.'

He grips his hands together and makes his pecs dance.

'Dan, think of Doris next door. The shock of seeing you like this could kill her. Cover yourself up.'

He throws on the gingham apron from the back of the kitchen door. 'Better?'

'Sindy will be gutted she missed this.'

'You should take a photo. *For Sindy.*'

'You're such a moron.'

Since our post-reunion chat, I've come to realise Dan is anything but a moron. He's smart, kind and far funnier than he

175

has any business being given the superior fleshy outer layer he also inhabits. Some people have all the luck.

'Don't leave me hanging. Where's your phone?'

'I'll get a shot later.' I pull on the jersey. It smells of my fabric softener and his body spray, a mix of florals and spices. 'Looks like I've some rapping to do first.'

He winks mischievously. 'That's the spirit!'

'You sure about this? Normally when Dave leaves we eat a family-sized trifle for breakfast and then watch back-to-back Julia Roberts movies.'

This is the first time I've seen Sindy in ages. She and Dave spent the first week of his time off in bed together and the second at a seaside B&B. Now he's gone, she's turned up wanting to do some exercise, of all things.

'I feel bad enough as it is. I don't need food guilt piled on top as well.'

She cuts a sorry figure. Even though she's wearing a floral Lycra two-piece that would put Mr Motivator to shame, her face is one of abject sorrow. Sindy and Dave took the decision early on in their relationship that Sindy wouldn't follow him to his stations, but that he'd come to her for his holidays. The intention had been that they'd start a family and the stability for the children would be more important than stolen moments between tours. The children never came, but to upend everything now would be an admission that they never will, and neither of them are ready to concede defeat. The first week without him is always the hardest.

We move the coffee table to one side, stick the laptop on it, and pull up a low impact full body workout on YouTube. Given my new-found appreciation for what goes into these videos I feel bad fast-forwarding through the it-would-be-so-amazing-if-you-could-subscribe bit, but needs must.

'Where's Dan?' asks Sindy, circling her arms like she means business.

'Upstairs.'

'Maybe I should check on him.'

'He'll be down at some point.'

'Have you got any outtakes you can share?' Sindy says under her breath in the rest period. 'You know, where he's filming you but then accidentally gets naked?'

I should never have told her about the kitchen incident. Or the stripping off thing. Or let her force me into describing every inch of his damned-near perfect body. She joked about hiring a police photo-fit expert to create an artist's impression from my description.

'He's in a video I've got going up today. No nudity, but I'll show you after.'

Despite all the running I've been doing, it doesn't take long to get breathless, so we spend the next twenty-five minutes in silence, save for the odd puff, groan and creak of middle-aged bones.

'Phew. I'm as sweaty as a bag of salad on a hot day,' says Sindy, once we've been patronised for doing a *good job* by someone who's barely raised a bead of sweat. Sindy high-fives me, only then the instructor tells us that's the warm-up done and to grab some water before the workout begins.

'Sod that,' says Sindy. 'I need a reward.'

We sit at the island and Sindy watches a video in which Dan and Jack are playing with a bottle launcher rocket kit, used to demonstrate displacement, velocity, acceleration and motion.

'It's already got loads of likes,' says Sindy.

'It's mad, isn't it?'

'You should sell merchandise with Dan on. I'd be happy to handle the goods ... and the merchandise!' She cracks up laughing, then rewatches the video, this time in slow motion. Dan's kneeling, bicycle pump in hand, slowly and somewhat pornographically sliding the handle back and forth as he forces air into the bottle. Of course, he chooses this moment to come downstairs.

'Sindy.' He grins.

'Dan.'

'Cuppa?'

'Yes, please.' She bats her eyelashes at him. I've come to learn over the years that joking about other men is her way of coping, and if she ever got the chance of a bit on the side, she'd run screaming in the opposite direction.

As he makes tea, Sindy pauses on a still of Dan's face almost childlike in its delight. 'Did you film this?'

'Yeah. Why?'

Her face does something weird.

'What?'

'Nothing.' She un-pauses it. 'You've got loads of comments too.' She scrolls down the growing list of responses that I only ever have time to reply to a few of. 'Hang on, is this Gaynor from school?'

'What?' I grab the phone and note the profile picture. 'Yep.' I read the comment.

I see your socials are really 'taking off'. I remember my first

5,000 followers. Just! Smiley face.

'Miaow!' says Sindy.

'That's Gaynor.' I'm secretly pleased she's noticed my following has increased.

'You've got a DM as well.'

'Have I? How do I access it?'

'Here.' She shows me the icon in the corner of the app that I'd assumed was an update notification, clicks on it and reads the message.

'Dear Science Mom. I'm writing from the Luxury Lodge in Sutton Coldfield. We were wondering if you'd be interested in a free spa day and makeover for you and a friend in return for a #sponsored post? We're looking to work with local influencers to promote a range of school prom / school graduation packages we offer and, given your audience, thought this could be a good fit. Let me know if you're interested.'

She looks up at me, eyes a lot brighter than they were half an hour ago. 'They called you a local influencer. They want to give you free shit.'

'Oi. Swear jar.'

'Bollocks to that.'

Dan places two mugs in front of us. 'Read it again'.

She does.

'I know I've amassed a few followers, but not that many.'

'I've always wanted to go there,' says Sindy. 'Can we, please?'

I'm not really a spa kind of gal. I remind her how I got a

proper massage for my birthday once and I spent the whole time lying with my head through a padded toilet seat trying not to fart. It wasn't in the least bit relaxing.

Dan laughs. 'That sounds like you.'

'You could have a manicure, or a facial,' says Sindy.

'Who's looking after the kids?'

'We could go midweek whilst they're at school.'

'Or I could look after them,' says Dan.

I couldn't do that to him. And I'm not sure about posh hotels and being waited on and all that. It's weird enough when they bring the food to your table in McDonalds.

'Come ooonnnn,' Sindy whines, pulling her best sad puppy look. 'I know it's not your thing, but it's my thing and you're my best mate, and I'm depressed about Dave going away.'

I instantly feel bad. How could I be so selfish? 'Okay, I'll call them.'

'Cool!' She opens the fridge and grabs the kids' treat box. 'Can we pinch something? I reckon we've earned it.'

That's my Sindy.

'What's it going to be. Pretty Woman for the six hundredth time?' I ask.

'Yeah, I'll leave you to it,' says Dan.

'What about that documentary on the Hagrid Collider?' says Sindy.

I have visions of tiny Robbie Coltranes being smashed together to reveal secrets about the subatomic world. I'll jot it down for later use.

'I know you're super busy with your course. That way you won't feel you're completely slacking off.'

I'm touched by her thoughtfulness. She really is the best friend I could ask for.

Chapter Twenty-One

'So, that's my news, dare I ask how it's all going with you?'

Leanne has called for a long-overdue chat. There's been a lot to get through.

'Surprisingly well. Reggie and the team like the whole approach and their knowledge is coming along. The exams are barely two months away.'

'The production quality has certainly improved.'

'I have Dan to thank for that.'

'Well, he's doing something right because you look like you're having fun.'

'I am. I may as well take advantage of his expertise for as long as he's around.'

'And you've got more followers than me now.'

'I know, can't quite get my head around that.'

The whole thing has stretched beyond my initial expectations. I tell her how I'm also managing to keep up with my self-imposed uni schedule.

'Amazing. I'm proud of you, mom.'

I'm proud of myself.

'How's Eric? I've been getting gifs instead of replies to the messages I've sent.'

'He's doing okay. He likes having the older kids around.'

'What about Jack?'

Hmm. What about Jack? He's settling down a little, but I worry he may be getting a little too attached to Dan. I tell Leanne about how, when he fell and scraped his knee yesterday, it was Dan's name he shouted for comfort, even though I was there waiting to administer soothing cuddles.

'But your granddad says he'll be too excited by the mountain of chocolate in the house at Easter to miss him when he moves out.'

'Pity I won't get to meet him.'

'He'd probably try and sleep with you, what with you being young and gorgeous.'

'He'd have a job. And they're fifty percent your genes too you know.'

Dan hasn't actually mentioned his *alternative arrangements* since the day I fell off the bar stool in front of him, and I've been reluctant to raise it with him. But presumably his well-meaning altruism can only extend so far.

'And how's Sheila?'

The groan tells her everything she needs to know.

'Remember what I told you about the negativity bias.'

'Yeah, yeah. I'm making an effort. Will you be back for Easter?'

'No, but got a mate heading that way mid-April I can cadge a lift with. Okay if I pop home then?'

'That would be brilliant.'

After we sign off, I reflect on how odd it is that Leanne

hasn't yet met half of the people I talk about, and equally how she has all these new people in her life that I don't know either. The ties that bind us have been loosened; the apron strings cut. It would have been far more difficult to come to terms with if Dan hadn't been around, and not for the first time I count my lucky stars that he is, and then count the days until he may well not be.

A week later I'm dragging the kids around the Black Country Museum, a huge twenty-six-acre open air experience that shows what life was like during the Industrial Revolution. Answer: very rainy. Dan's joined us, claiming he's interested in finding out more about the rich heritage of the West Midlands, but given that so far the only cultural question he has asked is why we Brummies say 'mom', but on British TV shows everyone says 'mum'—answer: no one really knows—I reckon he's really tagged along to see women dressed as wenches. We've just emerged from the limestone mines on an open-top narrow boat tour and are presently watching raindrops the size of bullets bounce off our helmets and the Dudley Canal that surrounds us.

'A horse and cart could only transport a couple of tonnes,' the guide tells us, struggling to be heard above the downpour. 'Whereas a barge could do thirty. It was quicker, easier and safer.'

'And didn't poo everywhere,' says Eric.

A middle-aged couple in front of us turn and regard him disapprovingly.

The guide goes on to tell us that our earliest canals go back to Roman times; however, rather than carefully maintain the incredible transport infrastructure they put in place for us, we let most of the canals and roads fall into chronic disrepair.

'A bit like renting your house out to conscientious tenants,' Dan whispers loudly, 'then crapping on your own bed when you move back in.'

The couple glance back again, lips curling.

'Like father, like son,' the woman mutters. Dan winks at Eric. The boat moors and we alight onto the towpath, the rain now falling harder than ever.

'Time for lunch?' I point in the direction of the main visitor centre.

'Good idea.' Dan grabs Jack and makes a run for it.

We're in the Worker's Institute Café trying some traditional faggots (sausage meat crossed with foot odour and fashioned into a large inedible ball of horrible) when something odd happens.

'Mom, that woman's pointing at us,' says Eric.

Sure enough, there's a woman, probably mid-fortyish, whispering to a friend and gesturing in our direction.

I nod my head at Dan. 'I think you have a couple of fans.'

He looks across and smiles.

'Don't you ever get bored of being so noticeable?'

After a further exchange, one of the ladies gets up and heads for our table.

'Sorry for bothering you, but could I get a photo?'

Dan runs his hand through his hair and smirks at me. 'Well, this is novel.'

But then the woman passes *him* the phone and puts her arm around *my* shoulder.

'My son's not going to believe this. Get a few would you.'

It all happens so quickly. The fake clicks of the shutter, Dan returning the phone, the woman walking back to her friend triumphantly waving her mobile.

'Er, what was that about?' asks Eric.

'I have no idea.'

'Has that happened before?' asks Dan.

'Never.'

'She was acting like you were famous,' says Eric.

The only time I came close to notoriety was when a wasp tried to sting my face during a Christening. I was shrieking and flapping my arms so much, the vicar thought I'd had a religious conversion. It made the parish newsletter.

'I know.' I should ask her who she thought I was, but she's leaving. 'Case of mistaken identity,' I say.

'Dan thought they meant him,' Eric sniggers. 'Did you see his face when he realised it was you?!'

Eric revels in other people's discomfiture. But then Jack joins in, swept along by the wave of giggles. But when I picture Dan languidly getting to his feet, I find myself tittering too.

'Oh, you may laugh,' Dan says. 'You may all laugh now.' He play-acts tackling Eric in his chair, grabbing his waist and tickling his ribs as Eric twists and squirms to try and get away, his laughter increasing in volume all the time.

The door of the café opens and the stern couple from the boat appear, casting another disapproving glance at us. I see the scene through their eyes: to the uninitiated, they could be father and son. Oh dear. I fear it isn't only Jack who's getting too attached to Dan.

Chapter Twenty-Two

'**M**iss, you need to see this.' Reggie has popped round to borrow a book from me, but as per usual he's on his bloody phone. 'See?'

The rap video I made is on screen, the thumbnail for which is a close-up on my face mid-gurn. I resemble a witch straining to retrieve a lost tampon.

'I know. As if I wasn't ridiculous enough in that one.'

'Not that. The views.'

The figure underneath the video reads 251,321.

'That's a lot of eyeballs,' he says.

'But that's ridiculous. That's fifty times what my other videos have been getting.'

'And 830 likes. Hey Dan, you seen this?'

Dan stops at the doorway to the kitchen. He's been out for a run and his face is flushed with exertion. His T-shirt clings to his chest, and the dark patch across it expands and contracts with every laboured breath.

'Looks like we've got a hit on our hands,' he says.

I'm not thinking of it as a hit. I'm suddenly thinking of it as over a quarter of a million people laughing at me. I knew I shouldn't have let Dan talk me into it.

'Don't worry. Everyone's playing nice,' says Reggie. 'There's even some comments.' He tries to show me the phone.

'I can't look.'

'Wish my mom could help me with my homework as much as this one has… Hilair and original… Deffo subscribing. People love it as much as we do.'

'That's awesome,' says Dan.

'That's easy for you to say. You're not the one looking like Eminem in drag.'

It was fine to do this for a niche group of people, and yes, it's been nice knowing it wasn't falling on deaf ears, but the capacity of three Wembley stadia? Is that why the woman in the café recognised me? How many people I know have seen them? Old friends? Former colleagues? The kids at Eric's school? What was I thinking? Why didn't I make them private?

'Chill,' says Reggie. 'It's not mega numbers.'

'Yeah,' says Dan. 'There are a hundred million people on this app every day. Most of these viewers probably aren't even in England.'

They're right. It's hugely unlikely anyone I know other than this lot have seen them. The café incident was probably a coincidence.

'Although, it looks like we've hit on a winning formula. We should probably do more like it, give The Science Mom subscribers what they want.'

'No way.'

'He's right, Miss,' says Reggie solemnly. 'Especially if they're helping that many people. It's your duty as a teacher.'

'But I'm not a teacher.'

'You ain't no rapper either,' he quips, raising his hand for a high five from Dan. 'But you can make science easy to understand and remember.' He picks up the book he came for and pops it in his rucksack. 'I'm looking forward to seeing what you guys come up with next. See you later, Science Mom.'

Dan steps aside to let him leave then turns back to me.

'Oh, boy,' he grins, 'this is going to be fun.'

Chapter Twenty-Three

S indy and I are in our bathing suits in the reception of the Luxury Lodge Day Spa. Sindy is sporting a fabulous 1950s number that pulls her in and pops her out in all the right places. As if I wasn't self-conscious enough, I'm in a fading old navy Speedo that flattens everything except my tummy. I shrug on the robe the receptionist offers me and sit on the sofa waiting to be called in, but my bottom barely touches the leather before a tall, blonde Adonis appears and calls my name in a thick Eastern European accent. Without any warning he opens my robe and peers inside. He tuts.

'Not possible to give full body massage with this in way. This have to off.'

Sindy casts me daggers, like undressing in front of this man is a treat she's missing out on. I'd offer to swop but he firmly takes me by the hand.

'Come along. Won't bite.'

The treatment room is dimly lit with an overwhelming

aroma of essential oils. I've always wondered at the name; I've managed to live all my life without owning any.

'I put relaxing music on.' The strains of pan pipes fill the room.

I want to point out that *relaxing* for me is not having to wash up. It's a takeaway on a weekend. I'm more likely to switch off to the sweet sounds of a poppadum being withdrawn from a paper bag rather than this stuff. But I don't, because I must somehow get a two-sizes-too-small Speedo swimsuit off without looking like an octopus trying to get out of a beer bottle. The masseur hands me disposable pants.

'Put on, then wrap towel round, okay?'

'I don't even know your name.' As if this is the morning-after-the-night-before, not a professional arrangement.

'It's Serge,' he smiles. 'Don't worry, I leave room.'

When he returns, he wastes no time loosening the towel and folding it so it's barely covering my bum.

'Happy I use oil?'

I nod and he pours the warm oil onto my back and begins to spread it across my skin.

'You very tense.'

'I wasn't before this massage started.'

He laughs. 'Funny lady. Now try to relax. Stress not good for the soul.'

He rubs the oil in with long regular movements, squeezing my shoulders on the upstroke and working his thumbs into the cleft of my spine on the downstroke. I let my head sink a little deeper into the bed, slow down my breath, allow my ankles to fall open and my jaw to slacken. I'm actually relaxing. Serge continues to work his magic, skilfully kneading my back, my neck, my arms. He takes each one of my hands in his, working his fingers over mine, gently pulling each digit in turn until my entire body tingles. Then the calves, the feet, my toes, pinpointing areas of tension and deftly working on each until they melt away.

'Ready to turn over?' he asks.

I'm loath to move, but I do as instructed. Serge starts with a head massage, little pulses of energy passing over my skull and down my spine, then the collarbone and upper chest, making smooth circular presses with the heels of his hands against my yielding flesh. Then my upper legs, pushing and pressing from my knees upwards, firmly rubbing outwards as he reaches the top of my thighs, drawing his palms across the ridge between my hip and pelvis. At one point he accidentally grazes a thumb across the mesh of the disposable knickers along my groin, barely a fleeting touch, but it's enough to send the stirrings of arousal around my system, a once-familiar tingle that's been lying dormant for a very long time.

Afterwards I head through to the pool to look for Sindy. She's not easy to spot given how everyone is wearing the same robes and head towels, but then 'Where the bloody hell have you been?' echoes from across the water. Some people look up from their magazines and I apologetically pick my way amongst them to Sindy, sprawled out on a sun lounger, glass of juice in her hand. She motions to another glass next to her.

'For you, madame.'

'Sorry. I must have fallen asleep.'

'How was it?' asks Sindy.

'Unexpectedly enjoyable. Yours?'

'Gorgeous. Dave's always after me giving him a massage, but I can never be bothered.'

'After what he goes through? Give the guy a massage!'

'All that faff and oil and mess? No. What I do is *pretend* that I'm going to give him a massage, do his shoulders for a minute then give him a hand job. It's loads easier and he's always relaxed afterwards. Forgets all about the massage.'

I sense my cheeks redden a little.

'If I play it really well,' Sindy says, 'I catch him before he even asks for a massage. Just straight in there with *"you look stressed, do you want a hand job?"* Who's saying no to that?'

I loosen my robe. It's very warm.

'Are you okay?'

'Yeah, fine.'

The reason I'm getting hot and bothered is that I wasn't late because I fell asleep. After Serge finished my massage, I pretended to be asleep so he'd leave me for a few minutes and then I masturbated. I'm not normally one for acts of digital pokery, but for the first time in recent memory I felt so sexually charged I needed the flush of warm release that coming really damned hard gives you. It was great, until the remorse set in.

'Reckon that's how the whole happy endings for tourists thing started,' Sindy continues. 'Double the money, fraction of the work. Are you even listening?'

I snap to my senses. 'Sorry. Miles away.'

'Clearly.'

'Do you ever fantasise about other men when Dave is away?' I ask her.

'I fantasise about other men when Dave is there … on top of me!' She bursts out laughing.

'I'm serious.'

'Why do you ask?'

'The thing is…' I quietly tell her about what happened, and

how I'd conjured up a mental image of a hand moving across my pubic bone, only intentionally this time.

'Woah! I didn't think you had it in you.'

'Oh, by the end I had it in me!' We collapse into giggles, but then guilt kicks back in.

'Mate,' says Sindy. 'You're a widow, not a monk. And Serge *was* gorgeous.'

He was. What I can't confess is that every time I tried to get a mental fix on his blonde hair and blue eyes, his features kept on morphing into someone's who looked a lot like Dan. It doesn't mean anything; it's simply the brain conflating two things in the heat of the moment, but Sindy would read too much into it.

'Come on. Let's get in the Jacuzzi,' I say.

But once we're in, the gentle pressure of the bubbles between my legs only serve to remind me of what went before. Damn my traitorous genes. Dan would be delighted to know they're capable of betraying me, even though he's the last person I'd be attracted to in real life. Isn't he?

'By the way, don't you need to be posting something if you're going to be earning this freebie,' she says.

Good point. I get out and fetch my phone. That'll give me something else to concentrate on at least.

'Did you see the look on her face? Mind you, you do look amazing.' Sindy breaks into a rendition of 'What a Difference a Day Makes'.

'Aww, thanks Sind.'

Turns out the afternoon makeover was loads of fun once I got into it. As I sat in the hairdresser's chair, looking at my shapeless mound of long matt brown hair, I decided to give the stylist carte blanche to do whatever he liked. I am now the proud owner of a fringe and a lovely chocolatey long wavy bob. The make-up lady complimented the whole shebang with soft winged eyeliner and red lips. I barely recognise myself.

'Very Uma Thurman in *Pulp Fiction*,' says Sindy.

'After she overdoses and comes to with a syringe in her chest?'

'Stop putting yourself down. You look incredible.'

Whenever I catch sight of myself in the rearview mirror, I can't quite believe the person staring back is me. In fact, as Sindy says, when we walked past Belinda at the nursery gates after collecting Jack, her jaw did seemingly drop.

'Don't like it,' says Jack, who is struggling to reconcile the new look with the old me.

'Well, I'm grateful Auntie Sindy made me go. I'm a new woman.'

This is a trope often used in makeover shows, where someone gets a haircut and new eye shadow and says it's changed her life. Yeah, right! But it does feel as if there's been a small but significant shift within me.

Sindy pulls up outside our place.

'You coming in for tea? Eric'll be starving, so it'll be something quick.'

'Got any oven chips?'

'Almost certainly.'

'I'm in.'

We head inside and, sure enough, Eric's got his head in the fridge.

'What's for tea,' he says from behind the door.

'Talk about coming down to Earth with a bump, eh? Don't I get a kiss?'

His face appears. 'What happened to your hair?'

'I had it cut. What do you think?'

'You look like the actress who plays Cersei Lannister in *Game of Thrones*.'

'Is that a good thing?'

'You looked like the actor who played Sandor Clegane in *Game of Thrones* before.'

I don't know either reference. 'I'll take that as a compliment.'

I've just popped everything in the oven when Leanne messages me and asks for a photo. I'm posing stupidly by the French doors when Dan walks in, dressed smartly, reeking of aftershave and looking at his phone.

'Cath, have you seen the stats on the latest content? They've gone—' he looks up and stops short. 'Oh my God. Where's Cath and what have you done with her?'

My stomach feels like a plastic bag left outside on a windy day. 'I fancied a change.'

'You look really different…'

'Hmm.'

'In a good way,' he hastily adds.

Sindy is doing lewd things with her thumb and forefingers behind Dan's back, which I ignore.

'You look a bit different yourself. Off out?'

He's wearing a close-fitting navy suit, the jacket of which looks like it would barely stretch across his chest, a white shirt and a burgundy and green striped tie. The effect is one of a teenager about to grow out of his school uniform, but Dan pulls it off as a style statement.

'Yeah, some faculty dinner I promised I'd go to.' He cocks his head, studies me some more. 'You remind me of Lena Headey.'

'That's what I said,' says Eric, although I'm sure he didn't.

'Want to come with me?' asks Dan. 'My plus-one fell through.'

'Gotta look after the kids.'

Sindy is now making rude gestures with her forearm. 'I'll look after the kids,' she says. 'I was only going to watch First Dates.'

I shoot her a warning glance.

'There'll be food, some music, and a guest speaker talking about critical theory, cultural studies and transnational news.'

'Hmm. You're not selling it to me.'

'It's free drink all night.'

'You had me at *free drink all night*.'

Dan laughs.

'I can't though. I've already put tea on.'

'Don't worry, I'll sort out the fish fingers,' says Sindy, who is now dry humping the worktop to Eric's disgust.

'Are you sure?' I'm not sure I want to go to a faculty dinner with Dan.

'Yep. You pair run along now.'

I suppose a night out would be nice. Especially one I don't have to pay for.

'Alight. Give me a sec.'

'No problem. In the meantime, I'll let Sindy entertain me with her delightful sexual innuendoes.' He turns to her. 'I could see your reflection in the doors.'

'I'm thrilled you were looking,' she says.

I dash upstairs and change into a black cami and jeans, throw on some chunky jewellery to dress it up a bit, stick on a pair of red wedges and I'm back downstairs within three minutes.

'Alright then,' says Dan. 'The cab's outside.'

Chapter Twenty-Four

C ontrary to Dan's predictions, the evening is proving to be quite good fun. We're in a large mahogany-panelled dining room, the perimeter of which is full of long trestle tables at which collections of students and people from the world of local media are sat. The talk mercifully only lasted for fifteen minutes before we were served some decent food and wine. Dan and I have spent most of the starter and main course massaging the ego of a brilliantly irascible old newscaster who is regaling us with tales of disastrous interviews with members of the public. He's just finished a particularly enjoyable anecdote about how a monkey pulled his wig off on live television, when he announces, with characteristic ennui, that he needs to visit the men's room as all this plebeian polemic has given him gut ache. As he lumbers away, Dan asks if I would like to forego dessert and head to the bar, as we're all out of wine.

'For sure.' I've already had enough to take the edge off any discomfort I'd been feeling, but could definitely go another glass.

Whilst he waits to order us a drink at the busy bar, I watch a DJ add the finishing touches to his setup on the dancefloor. The overhead lights dim and the disco lights fire up, occasionally blinding me as they rotate. The first song of the evening is an 80s classic and I'm once again taken back to the disco where I met Gaz, only I don't have the same sense of melancholy this time round. Sorrow's knife edge has been blunted, its wound no longer mortal. I am, dare I say it? optimistic about what might be in store, which is almost certainly tempting fate. I reach around to knock the wood of the bar for superstition's sake, but accidentally knock Dan's hand.

'I'm going as quick as I can!'

'Perhaps I should try?'

Dan makes way for me and I step up onto the bar rail and jokingly flick my hair. A minute later I've tipsily flirted my way into a bottle of fizz, even though champagne wasn't part of the free bar.

'Unbelievable,' says Dan.

'That I can use my feminine wiles for personal gain?'

'That you can be in the presence of any adult male without falling over.'

'Very funny.'

We move to a less busy bit of the bar and Dan pours us each a glass.

'I suggest you drink that quickly,' I tell him. 'I'm going to ask you a favour and you might need to be squiffy to say yes.'

He looks mildly concerned. 'What is it?'

I take a deep breath; now seems as good a time as any. 'I've been meaning to have, er, *the chat* with Eric?'

'*The chat?*'

'About … you know…'

'I know what?'

'Come on, don't play dumb. About…' I nod my head sideways.

'Neck pain?'

'No.'

'That person over there?'

'You can be such a moron.'

He laughs. 'You can say the word, Cath. You've had three children; it must be something you did once upon a time.'

'Fine. Sex. Intercourse. Shagging.'

He puts down his drink and places his hands on my bare shoulders. I try to purge post-massage thoughts from my head.

'Well done. I know that must have been difficult for you.'

'Thank you, it was.' I'm hugely conscious of the softness of his thumbs on my collarbone. Thankfully he drops his arms again, so I can get back on topic. 'He clams up when I raise it with him.'

'Not surprised with you as a mom.'

'He knows the basics, but I'd like him to have more context and not see things only from his own perspective, as it were.'

'What are you saying?'

'What I'm saying is he probably thinks a clitoris is a creature from *Star Wars*.'

Dan laughs.

'I was hoping you could, you know … but now I've said it out loud… If Gaz were here, he'd have done it … and Dave's away so much … and there's no one else … except maybe Reggie … but he's still a kid…'

Dan rests a hand on my upper arm and my skin becomes liquid. What devilry has that massage done to my body?

'I'm goofing around. I'll happily speak to Eric.'

'Really? That'd be great.'

'I'll bestow upon him the benefit of my many years of experience.'

'Just the fundamentals would be fine.'

'I'll be like Yoda, making him strong in the ways of the sexual force.'

'You're joking, right?'

'I've no problem teaching him how to wield his lightsabre.'

'That's horrible.'

'With great power comes great responsibilities.'

'You're mixing your film franchises now.'

'By the time I've finished with him, his milkshake will bring *all* the girls to the yard.'

'You're having way too much fun with this. I'm going to the toilet. Feel free to get this out of your system while I'm gone.'

I leave him singing Marvin Gaye's 'Let's Get It On' into his champagne flute.

I'm at the basin washing my hands when I spot a face I recognise in the mirror next to me. I'm certain it's the woman from my kitchen. In fairness to Dan she is a bit older than I recall her being, but she is still far too young and pretty for my liking. I wonder if they're still seeing one another. There's nothing to say he's not going to her place. But if he was seeing her, wouldn't he have invited her to this thing? Then again, if she was going to be here already, he wouldn't need to invite her, would he? She hasn't come over to him yet though, which is what you'd expect if they were seeing one another, so if it isn't her, I wonder who his plus one who dropped out is? I could ask him, but it might suggest that I'm interested in his love life and I'm not. Am I?

She finishes washing her hands, reapplies bright pink lipstick, smacks her lips together and pouts at the mirror. Perhaps I could introduce myself and ask her. I'm tipsy enough to do it, see what her reaction is. Only, another couple of people she knows have appeared and the opportunity passes. I shake my hands off, feeling every one of my thirty-nine years, and quietly pass behind them back out into the main room.

The dancefloor is now full of people bobbing along to the music. I thread my way through to get back to the bar where, as if I'd conjured them through my thoughts, Dan's talking intently to another attractive woman. She's almost as tall as him, with an angular face that would verge on severe were it not for her white-blonde hair and upward curve of her mouth. Her simple black shift dress accentuates her long lean limbs and pitch-perfect tan. All the confidence I'd felt twenty minutes ago deserts me. Should I leave them to their little powwow and find someone else to talk to? Even if there's nothing going on there, it's only fair he should want to socialise with other people tonight. I could catch a cab on my own and relieve Sindy of her duties earlier than expected. I'm wondering what the best thing to do is when Dan spots me and waves. Oh heck, it's going to be even worse playing third wheel before I make my excuses. Only rather than beckoning me over, Dan picks up the bottle and the glasses and makes his way to where I'm standing, without the woman in tow.

'Thank heavens you're back,' he says under his breath. 'That's one of the lecturers, Dr Hansen, who was treating me to an informal lesson about Paulo Freire's dialogic theories.'

'Paulo Fre— who now?'

'A Brazilian educator and philosopher who's a leading advocate of critical pedagogy apparently.'

'She sounds more geeky than me.'

'But she's drier than Arizona. At least you're funny with it.'

He thinks I'm funny!

'Let's sit over there.' He motions to an empty table in the far corner.

'Don't you want to mingle?'

'No way. I spend enough time with them.'

Does that mean he doesn't spend enough time with me?! We sit down and because it's so loud Dan scooches close to me and my thigh rests against his. I don't move it. He reaches inside the top pocket of his shirt.

'I got us some peanuts.'

'We've just eaten!'

'Force of habit. Gotta have beer nuts, even if you're not drinking beer.' He opens the pack. 'I still can't get over how different you look.'

'I know. It was a bit odd catching sight of myself in the bathroom before. Speaking of which, guess who else was in there?'

'Umm. Don't know.'

'Your lady friend from the kitchen.'

'Oh, God. Rosie?'

'Rosie, eh? Well, it's nice to finally put a name to a bottom,' I say in my best Merchant Ivory accent.

'Glad to be of service, ma'am,' he says, trying his best to match my clipped tones, but sounding more Dick Van Dyke in *Mary Poppins*.

'The young lady is around somewhere, should the gentleman need company later.'

'Thank you, but I have been somewhat reining things in of late.'

'Oh really?' The accent slips and a sensation I can't place unfolds in my chest.

'Really.' He picks out a peanut, throws it into the air and catches it in his mouth. It reminds me of the time he did the same thing with popcorn. 'In fact,' he says between chews, 'I was wondering if I could ask you a favour, since we're trading. Is it okay if I stay on at the house? I know you thought you'd be rid of me, but my other option fell through.'

The feeling blooms a little more. 'I suppose it is useful having someone else around who knows how to use a tea towel.' I try to sound nonchalant.

'That's my strongest selling point?' He pouts, accentuating his jawline.

'That and the free emergency childcare.'

'I could always find a hotel.'

'But Sindy would miss you.'

He smirks. 'I could move in with her?'

'Hmm. Perhaps you should stay. She doesn't need the money as much as I do.'

'Are you sure?'

'Yeah, it's probably for the best.' I do a little internal dance. He's staying!

His shoulders relax a little. Did he imagine I'd say no?

'May I enquire what exactly *are* you up to most evenings, then?' I ask.

'I'm in the library studying or using the editing facilities on campus. Those videos don't make themselves you know.'

'Oh!' I'm somewhat taken aback. 'Well thank you.'

He shifts away slightly and bows in his seat. '*The pleasure is all mine.* Seriously though, I'm not known for my commitment skills, but it's great having something to focus on that I enjoy.'

'And you get the credit for making me look buffoonish in front of lots of people.'

'A small price to pay for getting the job done. In fact, I think congratulations are in order.' He raises his glass.

He's right. We really are doing something good with this.

'Your methods may be unusual, and the journey an unexpected one, but I think it's safe to say that you're now a teacher … of sorts.'

We clink glasses and I let his words sink in. I really am a sort of teacher. And eventually I'll be a real one! I don't know if it's the makeover, the teaching, or the fizz, but there's a distance between the me I was a few months back and the me I am now. I'd been tethered to an idea of how I should feel and act, but I've become unmoored from this orthodoxy without realising, and am now floating in a tranquil pond of possibility.

'I'm not sure whether you put so much effort into helping me because it's useful for your course, or whether you just like to see me squirm.'

'The latter, for sure.' He tosses another peanut into his mouth.

'Oh thanks!'

'I never had a little sister, but if I did, I'd like to think I could have wound her up as easily as I do you.'

'I'm older than you!'

'I'd have been the more confident second child.'

'I never had a little brother, but if my life has proven anything, it's that I'd probably have gotten one as annoying as you.'

He grins. 'Ah, you love me really.'

'Not at all. I am entirely resistant to your charms.'

'Then you should donate your brain to medical science; there's something unusual going on in there.'

'Perhaps that's why *you* like *me* so much?' I should probably leave the cocksure banter to him, in my mouth the words sound clumsy.

He casually finishes chewing another peanut. 'That's probably true...'

I ready myself for the rejoinder that will finish that sentence, the zingy riposte that'll see him win our little verbal battle. Only it never comes.

Chapter Twenty-Five

The doorbell rings as I'm hiding the last of the plastic eggs behind pots in the garden, under a bruised sky I'm hoping won't turn into rain. We may not celebrate Easter from a theological standpoint, but the annual egg hunt is a tradition we've been observing since Leanne was tiny, with each one containing a clue that ultimately leads to a surprise gift. Some may think this bunny-hopping onto a religious event is tantamount to sacrilege, but to them I say nowhere in the New Testament did it say, '*Suffer the little children to eateth their own body weight in chocolate for breakfast, verily spooning the fondant centre out of a crème egg, that they may truly understand sin and the forgiveness thereof.*' More likely Jesus would go into the temple of Cadbury and accuse the corporate thieves of ungodly commercialism. Sheila is at the door wearing a yellow fluffy jumper, orange leather skirt, tan cowboy boots and Easter-themed fascinator.

'Come in. Geoff's already here.'

Geoff, Dan, Eric and Jack are in the lounge, watching sport

on TV. Sheila perches on the sofa arm and Geoff squeezes her thigh.

'You join us at a crucial stage love. Final innings if all goes to plan. Dan's got me into baseball.'

'And Geoff's got me into soccer,' Dan tells her.

'Nay lad. It's called football. I keep on telling you, we bloody invented it!'

He gives a good-natured chuckle. Dan smiles and returns his gaze back to the game. He's wearing a close-fitting baseball top with contrasting-coloured sleeves. His jaw is clenched, and a vein zigzags his temple. I wonder what it'd be like to be looked at with the intensity with which he's watching the screen, that chocolatey stare fixed only on you. It's weird to think that when I first saw him at the airport, I thought his looks were too showy, too ostentatious, like he knew they were something to be lorded over others, whereas now I realise that his confidence comes from being a decent guy, capable of making other people feel good about themselves, and the attractive packaging is incidental. Suddenly he erupts from the sofa, shouts *yee-haw*, punches the air, and turns to the others to pass high-fives down their ranks. He really is very cute when he's excited.

'Lovely roast chicken,' says Geoff, as I pile up the plates from lunch. 'But not as tasty as this old bird!' He grabs Sheila and gives her a sloppy kiss. Dan smirks. I warned him they'd be a bit handsy.

'You old softie,' says Sheila. 'Did you know I'm organising a party for Geoff's seventieth, Dan?'

I'd also warned him about this, and that Sheila talks about little else. I had intended to organise an intimate little family affair for him, but she's hijacked it and turned it into something the size of the Notting Hill Carnival.

'Cath told me all about it,' he replies, casting me a gentle warning look as I subtly look skyward behind Sheila's turned head.

Slightly deflated by this lack of opportunity to go on at length about it, Sheila turns her attention to Jack, who's stuck his finger into a stuffing ball and is eating it like a lollipop.

'What did the Easter Bunny bring for you?' she trills.

'We don't perpetuate the myth of the Easter Bunny,' says Eric.

'What?' she says, taken aback.

'Shush now,' I tell Eric.

Given how Sheila apparently has a fairy house in her garden, and it's not there for ornamental purposes, we probably shouldn't get into it. Still, she looks horrified.

'Eric's rather too old to believe now anyway,' I say.

'But the kids never have?'

'It's not something we ever got into.'

'What about Santa?'

'Nope.'

Sheila shakes her head like I've told her we don't believe in breathing.

'Did you know about this, Geoff?'

'I did.' He nabs a parsnip from the bowl I'm lifting from the table.

'It's absolutely fine,' says Eric.

'I guess everyone discovers the truth eventually,' says Dan.

Sheila may as well have swallowed a feather from her fascinator, such is the look of distaste that crosses her features.

'Gaz and I decided we wouldn't lie to the kids,' I tell her.

I sense she's desperate to say something else, but the mention of Gaz has silenced her, for now. She's not a bad sort, but I feel I now have the slightly judgmental mother-in-law other people complain about.

'We made it to that new market in town yesterday,' says Geoff, changing the subject. 'Sheila got a wind chime made from old cutlery.'

She nods, still regarding us with the wariness of someone meeting aliens for the first time.

'Sindy and I went last week,' I say. 'She left with a kilo of specialist salami that not even her neighbour's dog will go near, and her neighbour's dog eats its own bottom.'

Everyone chuckles, but then Geoff suddenly puts his hand to his chest and grimaces in pain.

'Parsnip gone down the wrong way?' asks Dan.

'I'll be alright in a second,' he mutters through gritted teeth.

Sheila gets up, fussing. 'Don't worry, I'll get your pills.'

'Pills?' I look at Geoff.

'It's nothing,' he says, wincing.

'It doesn't *look* like nothing.'

'Geoff?' Dan looks almost as concerned as I feel.

Sheila comes back to the table. 'He's got that, erm, angina.'

'Mangina,' says Jack, which causes Eric to nearly die laughing.

'Eric, it's not funny,' I say. 'You're granddad's obviously sick.'

The mirth stops and genuine concern takes its place.

'I'm fine,' Geoff says as he takes a pill from Sheila's

outstretched hand and pops it under his tongue. 'It happens every now and again. Don't give it another thought. Dan, tell us what Easter is like in the States.'

He tries, but the atmosphere has changed. Eric keeps glancing at Gaz's urn, which suddenly looks ridiculous with its bunny ears and ribbons hanging from each handle. I shouldn't have snapped. I go to do the washing up. A while later Geoff joins me at the sink.

'I didn't want to worry you, love.'

'You should have told me.'

'You've been doing so well; I didn't want to put a dampener on things.'

I've known Geoff for over twenty years, longer than I knew my own dad for. In that time he's been my cheerleader and my sounding board. I knew that if I called on him for anything he'd be there. And now he's confiding in someone who's come dressed as every member of the frigging Village People.

'I'm still here for you,' he says. 'Nowt's changed.'

But something has changed; he's in a relationship now and if it's going to last, it's only right that Sheila becomes the priority in his life.

'I'm sorry. I'm feeling my nose is out of joint. And I'm worried about you.'

'Don't be. I've got some pills; I'm taking care of myself and it's all under control.'

Dan pops his head round the door. 'Cath, are you coming to play Monopoly before Jack puts the top hat somewhere he shouldn't?'

I groan. The two men smile at one another. 'Okay. I'll only be a second.'

Chapter Twenty-Six

'Hello, is that Science Mom?'

'Uh-huh.'

'This is Yam Yammy Mammy, but call me Denise. Yam alright bab?'

If the name wasn't enough of a giveaway, the accent swings it. Yam Yams is what we call people from the Black Country on account of their using the term *yam* instead of *are you* or *you are*. It's one of many verbal quirks. It can't be Yam Yammy Mammy though, because it makes no sense that she'd be calling me. Yam Yammy Mammy is a celebrity in the Midlands (and possibly beyond), having built up quite a business empire, all from sharing her thoughts on shopping, motherhood and life in general on social platforms. I'm not a direct follower myself, but I know plenty of people who are, Sindy included.

'Is this a wind-up?'

'Not at all. Hope you don't mind me calling out of the blue, I was wondering if you wanted to be featured on my channels?'

'Sindy, I don't know whose phone you're using, but you can stop now.'

'It's really me. Shall I video call you to prove it?

'Yeah, do that.'

I hang up. Hah. Bet she wasn't expecting me to call her bluff. I raise my middle finger in front of my face and wait for Sindy to call me back, only when she does, she really is Yam Yammy Mammy.

'That's no way to greet people, is it?' Denise says, good-naturedly.

'Oh.'

'Yam always so mistrustful?

'I'm so sorry. I thought you were my mate.'

'Yam Science Mom, right?'

'I guess. Not that that's how I'd introduce myself at a dinner party, not that I go to dinner parties, or any parties for that matter.' My brain tells my mouth to shut up, but my mouth has its fingers in its ears and keeps on going 'blah blah blah' except in words that are conveying I have three children, I'm a widow and I don't get out much. When I finish, Denise is looking at me with an air of detached bemusement.

'Call me Cath,' I say.

'Well, it's nice to meet you.'

She looks immaculate, exactly as she does when I've seen her on TV. Her long dark wavy hair is perfectly styled in large barrel curls and she has a full face of makeup, including magenta lipstick. Even though she's staring down into the camera, she still only has one chin. It's disconcerting, because she looks like minor royalty but sounds like nails down a blackboard.

'I've not got long; I've gotta decorate twenty bleeding

cupcakes in the next hour; some new copycat *Bake Off* they want promoting. I called to ask if you'd do a Q&A with me? Only a few questions about yourself, how and why you got started, that kind of thing. I think my followers would be dead interested in hearing more about what you've been up to.'

She's walking as she's talking and I catch glimpses of her equally groomed house.

'I'm so sorry, you've caught me a bit on the hop,' I tell her. 'Why would they be interested in me? The most fascinating thing I've ever done is find a crisp that looked like Kermit the Frog. It was in the newspaper, but that was thirty years ago.' In my imagination my brain rolls its eyes and walks out of my head in shame.

'Riiiight,' she says.

'Sorry, I'm rambling. You go.'

'Basically, a load of my Yammers—them's my followers—they've got teenage kids, so they wanna know how they can help 'em during their exams. What yam's doing is great for that.'

'Thanks'.

'Yam definitely doing summat right. It's like yam a normal mom, but yam also dead smart and don't mind making a fool of yourself. That thing you did about centrifugal forces was cowin' hilarious.'

Ah. That. I was spinning a glass of water upside down inside an old macrame plant hanger, demonstrating how the water didn't come out. I got the whole thing going okay but wasn't sure how to stop and it flew off into a coffee jar, breaking both the jar and the glass. I felt obliged to use the footage to honour their sacrifice.

'I've got quite a few followers, so I'm happy to help in any way I can.'

'Really?'

Quite a few followers is an understatement; Denise's numbers must dwarf mine by a significant margin.

'Us Midlands momfluencers need to stick together, don't we?'

'I wouldn't really describe me as a m...' I can't bring myself to say the word. 'I'm in it more for the kids. I'm honestly not fussed about all the followers' thing.'

So maybe I did get excited when one of my first videos hit fourteen thousand views. That's the capacity of the Birmingham International Arena, give or take some seats. Even if ten percent of those got something useful out of it, that's four times the number of kids at Brookdene.

'You should be fussed. How long you been going?'

'A couple of months,'

'That's quick growth. Thought about monetising?'

'No.'

'Oh bab,' she shakes her head, but in a magnified way, like someone on a shampoo advert. 'I'll advise when we speak properly. Yam interested?'

Am I interested? It's an opportunity to reach more people, which can't be a bad thing. 'Yep, I'm interested.'

'Brill. I'm gonna send you a link to an awards thing you should enter an' all. It'll be good to raise your profile, deadline's soon.'

'Okay. Thanks.'

'No worries. Right, better go. These hundreds and thousands won't sort themselves.'

Is she talking about the cupcakes or all the money she allegedly makes?

'Good luck with the decorating.'

'My assistant does that, but I ensure she makes it look like I've done them.'

'Wouldn't it be easier for you to do them?'

'Oh my goodness, yam adorable, honestly. Do them myself?' She shakes her fine head of hair once more. I get the impression she spends her life acting like she's being watched, which I suppose to a certain extent she is.

'I'll ask her to drop you a note, get something in the diary for next week, alright?'

She hangs up and I digest what just happened. Do I now have Yam Yammy Mammy's phone number in my call log? Is her assistant really going to call me to arrange something? And how much is Sindy going to lose her shit when I see her next?!

Chapter Twenty-Seven

'Hey honey, I'm hooooooome.'

Leanne has let herself in, back for her flying visit. I rush to give her a large squeeze.

'Where are the boys?' she asks.

'Upstairs. Let's leave them until they start fighting.'

'Good idea.'

I'm giving her another squeeze when Dan comes down the stairs. He's wearing khaki cargo shorts and a tatty NYPD T-shirt that looks like it's seen some frontline action. He stops at the bottom step, hand on bannister, casual as you like.

'Oh hey. You must be Leanne.'

'Guilty as charged, officer.'

He smiles. 'Your mom said you were sharp.'

'Naturally!' says Leanne.

'It's great to meet you. Should we shake hands? I'm not sure of the British etiquette.'

'Nah,' says Leanne.

'Too formal?'

'Not formal enough. I was thinking you could salute.' She catches my eye and smirks. Is she testing him?

Dan laughs fully this time. 'We like to do that where I'm from.' He gives his best *all in a day's work ma'am* tip of his imaginary hat.

'At ease,' she says.

'You guys look a lot alike,' says Dan.

'We do not!' I say.

'Yeah,' he studies our faces. 'Definitely in the shape of the eyes and the fullness of the lips.'

Only Dan can make an innocent observation sound like seduction.

'Leanne has better legs,' I say quickly.

'They are pretty awesome.'

Her prosthetics have been completely covered in intricate tattoo-style drawings.

'Did you do that?' I ask.

'No, some girl I met. She's pretty cool actually.'

'Is she now?'

'Yes, she is now!' says Leanne.

'Do I need to ask her what her intentions are?' Call me over-cautious, but I'm keen for Dan to know her tastes lie with the fairer sex.

'Mom!'

'Come on.' I say, relieving her of the need to spill more.

'Are you joining us, Dan?' says Leanne.

He casts me a glance. 'Is that okay?'

'Sure.'

I pop the kettle on whilst they get themselves settled at the kitchen table.

'It's about time I met the man who's been getting my mom to embarrass herself so effectively,' says Leanne.

'I'm not sure she needs my help for that.'

'That's true. Did she ever tell you about the canal barge story?'

'No, she did not.'

'Cup of tea, anyone?' I say loudly.

'Yes!' They chime together.

Leanne pulls her chair up closer to Dan's, conspiratorial already.

'Are you hungry?' I ask.

'Starving,' says Leanne.

'I'll make some lunch, shall I?'

'Lovely,' says Leanne. 'I'm practically a vegan now, by the way.'

'That's brilliant,' I say, 'because I got bacon in.'

Her eyes light up. 'That's brilliant, because being vegan is soo boring.'

I make lunch whilst Leanne tells Dan the story of when Gaz and I took her and Eric on a canal holiday. Within an hour of being onboard, I'd tripped over a bucket, lost my balance, and ended up in the water. I'm not the best swimmer and there were loads of reeds, so I'd been thrashing around in a panic when Gaz, between hysterics, had pointed out that the canal was armpit high, and I could in fact walk to the boat. But rather than help me back up on deck, he'd first taken several photos, the best of which he'd made into coasters for Christmas gifts for our friends. Leanne fishes out the only one we still have.

'Dad said she looked like the creature from the black lagoon!'

Dan is happy to join in on the joke. 'Brilliant. Your dad sounds great.'

Leanne glances at the urn. 'Yeah, he was the absolute best.'

'Right, grub's up!' I hand them their sarnies.

Leanne takes a massive bite and doesn't even look guilty.

'Vegan, my arse,' I say.

'That's twenty pence in the swear jar,' says Dan.

'I'll do it in a minute.'

Between mouthfuls, Leanne tells us she likes the latest content.

'Thanks.' It's continued to be popular.

'And you're making a regular appearance, Dan?'

Dan has been acting as a more regular sidekick, because why should I be the only one being publicly ridiculed? His guitar playing is proving useful for the music-style videos, plus he helps with experiments, or man-handles Jack in some amusing way to demonstrate a point.

'Yep. Cath begged me to be in them.'

'Oi!' I hurl one of Jack's plastic cups at him that he easily catches. 'You needed no persuasion.'

'Indeed,' says Leanne, head inclined quizzically.

'He was like a rat up a drainpipe, as Geoff would say.'

'Hmm. Speaking of rats, any chance of one appearing today?'

'It's funny you should ask that,' says Dan.

'Nooo,' I moan. 'We agreed we'd never mention it!'

Dan ignores me. 'You know she drove that one she found to … what's that park?'

'Cannock Hill.'

'That's it. She set it free in the undergrowth. Problem is, in an uncharacteristic act of organisation, that very afternoon she went through the mountain of mail on the kitchen table and she finds … hang on…'

He comes to the drawer on my side of the table. I try to stop him, but he easily opens it and removes a folded piece of paper.

'…this.'

I console myself by chewing my fist as he slowly and deliberately opens the paper, in the centre of which there's a picture of a rat. Leanne reads the words.

> 'Missing Rat. Have you seen Neville? All black. Likes to hide
> in shoes. Gentle and friendly. Went missing on Ambleside
> Road. Dearly missed. Please call…'

The penny drops and she sniggers. 'Oh shit!'

'Swear jar!'

'Oh … that … is … priceless!' The words escape through snorts of laughter.

Dan also creases up.

'Classic Mom,' says Leanne.

'Yep. Turns out we didn't have rats. We had *a* rat. Neville.'

Leanne re-reads the poster, enjoying it even more the second time round. Dan, still laughing, puts a consoling hand on my shoulder.

'It's okay. He probably met some rat friends.'

'I've kept the table clear since,' I tell Leanne.

'Was worth it just for that!' says Dan. 'Right, I'm heading to the library. Leanne, great to meet you. Sorry it was so short and sweet.'

'You too.'

'And thanks for the room loan. This is the most fun I've had in years.'

We watch him go. I'm keen to know what Leanne thinks of him but hesitant to ask.

'You two seem to be getting along well,' she says.

'Yeah, he's grown on me.'

'Has he now?'

'Not like that.'

She holds her hands up, all innocent. 'I didn't suggest anything.'

'Well, if you were, he's hardly my type.'

'You have a type?'

'Well … maybe … I don't know … I've not thought about it.'

Leanne looks like she's thinking about it. 'Can't lie, it's a bit weird watching the two of you. Reminded me of when Dad would tell funny stories. I'd forgotten he'd do that.'

'He was brilliant at spinning a good yarn.' Back when we had friends, before they disappeared into the mist of discomfort that surrounds unexpected death, Gaz would often be found at gatherings, beer in hand, sharing a funny anecdote to someone's amusement.

'What else have I forgotten?' Her gaze seeks out the urn.

'You've got your own life now; it's natural that some of that immense brain space of yours will get occupied with other things.'

'It's just a bit odd. And Dan's nothing like Dad, but it was a faint echo of what it was like having him around.'

'Are you okay?'

'I'm fine. Just processing it.'

She doesn't get much chance though, because at that point, Eric and Jack come barrelling downstairs and demand her instant attention.

Chapter Twenty-Eight

I t's an unseasonably warm mid-April day and I'm in the garden watching a baby squirrel take a tentative outing from its dray. Turns out being interviewed by Yam Yammy Mammy isn't the only unusual thing to happen to me this week. After I dropped Jack off at nursery yesterday, Belinda waved at me. I assumed she was waving at someone else because I've not spoken to any of them since Jack left a footprint in that birthday cake, but no, the wave was promptly followed by an approach and a question.

'Hey Cath, how are you?'

'Fine,' I replied warily.

'Loving the new look. Completely different. Must be that new man in your life, eh?'

I didn't say anything.

'Ask her...' prompted one of the others.

She glared back. 'Yes, thank you, Clare.'

'Is everything okay?' I thought perhaps Jack had been

causing problems, although none of the staff had mentioned anything. 'Is this about the party? Only I realise we never...'

Belinda cut in quickly, keen to avoid reminding everyone present of that debacle. 'All completely forgotten,' she said with the mania of someone who has relived it in their head over and over again. 'The thing is, crazy question, but this isn't *you*, is it?'

She held up her phone, and on it me, dressed in full eighties neon gear, half-singing a bastardisation of Duran Duran's *The Reflex* in a video created to help describe the actions of neurons in the nervous system. Posted three days ago, and it's already got scary viewing numbers.

'Yep, it's me.' I waited for the bitchy comments.

'And do you know Yam Yammy Mammy?' she asked.

'I'm a big fan,' said another of the moms called Clare. 'That's how I found this.'

'Yes, reasonably well. I've been to Denise's house.'

Clare looked ecstatic, whereas Belinda spent several seconds bearing the expression of a woman who's just enjoyed a top-notch tasting menu in a posh restaurant only to then be told every one of the courses was made from animal testicles.

'How charming,' she said, as you might to a child describing how to make a bogey sandwich.

But then Clare put her hand out to shake mine.

'I have a fifteen-year-old doing mocks. Soooo helpful.'

Then the others chimed in. A chorus of 'we had no idea' and 'how clever of you' and 'whose idea was it' and, from Belinda, 'would you like to come to this little thing I'm having?'

'I thought you said they were twats,' says Sindy, to whom

I've described this sudden stock improvement (she was way more excited about Yam Yammy Mammy).

'I think one of them still is, but I'm trying to be more open-minded. Leanne's been lecturing me on overcoming my negativity bias.'

'Your nega-what?'

I open my mouth to explain.

'On second thoughts, yes to whatever she said. Are you going to go?'

It's some organic beauty product party. 'Will you come with me. You love all that stuff.'

'I like Ann Summers parties. How's that the same as some vegan bollocks?'

'That vibrator you bought hadn't been tested on animals.'

Sindy pulls a face. 'That is grim.'

I laugh.

'I'm serious,' she says. 'I'm not going to be able to use it again without thinking of some animal pleasuring itself with it.'

'Any particular animal?'

'Got a mental image of a kangaroo bouncing on it. You've ruined it for me.'

'Please come,' I wheedle.

'Not with that picture in my head, I can't.'

'To the party. Go on. It might mean they'll stop treating me like a pariah.'

'Who's having the kids?'

'Dan said he'll babysit.'

She raises an eyebrow. 'You really have got him wrapped around your little finger, haven't you?'

'I have not!'

She strokes her chin. 'Haven't you?'

'What makes you say that?'

'The videos. Babysitting. The way he laughs at practically everything you say.'

'He does not!'

'I get it. You're in *Dan*-ial.'

'We're just friends.'

'Yep. Just two single, attractive, got-loads-in-common, living together friends.'

An email notification pings on my mobile.

'You can make anything sound loaded if you say it like that.' Dan wrapped around my finger. As if. 'I'm the awkward goofball in that relationship.'

Another eyebrow raise.

'Friendship,' I correct. I grab my phone. 'Meanwhile, back in reality. Are you going to come to the party? If nothing else, we get to drink her wine and eat her snacks. She's the type to have good snacks.'

'Oh fine.'

'You're a pal.'

I check the email. It's not an address I recognise, but I open it up anyway.

Dear Science Mom,

I hope you don't mind my contacting you.

I work for Birmingham Living Magazine and for our next edition we're planning a feature on influencers in the area. The magazine has a monthly readership of circa 450,000 people in print and online, with the chance of syndication to the Metro and Birmingham Mail,

*so it offers great potential exposure. Fancy being part of it? We'd
love you to be involved.*

If so, please do call.

Yours,

Steve

Trinity Mirror Midland Group

I read the email three times.

'What's up?' asks Sindy.

'Read this,' I tell her.

She reads it out loud. 'Ooh. You're going to be even more
famous!'

'It's probably one of those things you have to pay to take
part in, right?'

'It doesn't say anything like that.'

'But why would anyone want to do a magazine feature
on me?'

'Don't mince about wondering. Call them.'

'Alright, but I'm going into the house; I can't have you
goggle-eying me the whole time.' I head into Sindy's dining
room, click on the number in the email, press the green call
button and listen to the dial tone. After about eight rings
someone answers.

'Yeah, hello, Steve speaking.'

Whoever Steve is, he sounds distracted, and there's a lot of
noise in the background. 'Oh hi, this is Cath Beckinsale.'

'Can you speak up, it's a bit noisy.'

'I said it's Cath Beckinsale.'

He doesn't reply.

'You sent me an email.'

Still nothing. In fact, if it wasn't for the racket going on around him, I'd assume we'd been cut off. 'Er ... I'm Science Mom,' I hazard.

'Science Mom?' Then a much warmer 'Oh heck, you're Science Mom! Hang on!'

A door closes and the hubbub almost disappears.

'What did you say your real name was?' he asks.

'Cath Beckinsale.'

'Thanks for calling me back, Cath. I was hoping you might do me a favour.'

He explains how they're running a *ones to watch* feature on rising stars in social media. He's completely honest that I wasn't their first choice, but they're up against a deadline and the vlogger they were hoping to use is now away on an all-expenses-paid trip to Las Vegas.

'You were on the reserves list though.'

He goes on to say how, as well as being in print and online, the feature would get plenty of shout outs across their own social accounts. They'd send a team to do the interview and take photos of me in my natural habitat.

'Ah. You'd need to come to my house?' I look around at the usual chaotic scene. 'That might not be such a good idea.'

'This is the best part. It's all being sponsored by the Bullring Shopping Centre, so they'd bring a few homewares and soft furnishings to zhuzh the place up a bit beforehand. A bit of product placement if you will. We'll send an interiors specialist; you won't recognise the place when we've finished with it.'

'Where's the catch?' I ask.

'No catch. You'd obviously need to say a bit about it on your own channels,' he says. 'The usual. Can I count you in?'

I take another look around the place. At the ripped paper

lantern that Eric catapulted blue tac through a couple of years ago, that I still haven't replaced; the rug that Jack has peed on several times; the table that has a chain of coffee rings going across it like an Olympic symbol that got out of control. Er, yeah, he can count me in.

Chapter Twenty-Nine

'And you said yes?!'

'Of course. It was a really good opportunity.'

I'm talking to Leanne. We missed our last catch up, so I'm only now getting round to talking her through everything that's happened since she was here.

'But it's a lifestyle magazine.'

'I know. It's a bit left field, but I got to keep some of the homeware as payment.'

The photoshoot happened yesterday, and I'm now sat on a sofa which is home to several new scatter cushions, under the dome of an arcing floor lamp, looking at a lounge that wouldn't be an insult to a Pinterest board entitled *half-decent living spaces*.

'But you hate lifestyle magazines. You said they're picture books for image-obsessed cretins who have so little imagination that they need to have other image-obsessed cretins tell them what their homes and lives should look like.'

'I don't think I'd have used the word cretins.'

'You said they were a scourge on society for promoting unsustainable consumerism and for peddling the myth that if only you had the right kind of scented candle on your hallway console table, you could finally achieve lasting happiness.'

'You have too good a memory.'

'You said they were—'

'I get it! But you agree the place needed a spruce up, right? We haven't decorated for years. Haven't you ever been the tiniest bit embarrassed bringing your mates back?'

'No! It's our home. That's how we live. What's to be ashamed of?'

It's easy for her to say—this place isn't a reflection on her or her choices—but it's a reflection on mine and I'm glad that bits of it now look nice.

'I have other news.'

'Go on.'

'I've been invited to a conference.'

'Whoa! Science?'

'No.'

'Teaching?'

'No. Like an influencer conference. I've been shortlisted for an award because of how well the posts are doing.'

Now I come to think of it, it's probably a mistake to mention this too, but ever since the Yam Yammy Mammy feature my stats have really taken off. Still, I was utterly gobsmacked to be shortlisted in the *Edutainment* category through that competition she told me to enter.

'But you also hate influencers,' Leanne says flatly.

Did she miss the bit where I said I've been shortlisted for an award? 'I do not. I've never said I hate influencers.'

'Not in so many words, but you hate phony people who

peddle a fake version of their lives and make other people feel bad about their own, right?'

'But they're not all like that.'

Okay, so maybe Denise had been a terrifyingly astute businessperson and not quite the working-class-everywoman-come-good that her posts paint her as. And maybe she had been less than complimentary about some of the other moms with whom she pretended to be close friends online. And maybe she does occasionally force her kids to appear in posts even though they really don't want to, but who am I to judge?

'May I remind you that you're all over social media?' I say.

'I know,' says Leanne. 'And I'm fine with being peddled misinformation from unqualified fame-hungry idiots. I'm saying that, up until now, you haven't been.'

'Why are you being so negative? There's a chance I could get a little back from this. And besides, I too am an unqualified idiot.'

'Not for long though.'

My ear suddenly feels hot and I shift the phone to my other one. That feels hot too.

'You are still doing OU, aren't you?'

'I've been so busy...'

There's a sharp intake of breath and I trail off. But I really have been busy.

'Jesus, Mom, this social stuff was meant to be about Reggie and the kids. How are they getting on, or have you forgotten about them too?'

'Course I haven't, but I'm not obligated to them Leanne. At the end of the day, Powell is the one who's failing in his responsibilities, not me.'

'And what does Dan think about all this?'

That's an odd question. 'Dan thinks I should do whatever makes me happy.'

'Well, perhaps Dan doesn't understand how much you wanted to be a teacher.'

A silence stretches between us, a yawning absence of words that we've never experienced before. I'm genuinely confused by her reaction to all this, out of anyone I thought she'd be happy for me, excited even.

'I'm having some fun. After everything that's happened, isn't that allowed?'

'Of course. I just think that... You know what, it doesn't matter.'

'Shall we change the subject?'

'Good idea.'

'I haven't mentioned Dan having *the chat* with Eric yet.'

Turns out Eric beat Dan to the punch on the birds and the bees thing. I tell her how Eric asked Dan if they could go out for a walk together last weekend, *man to man*, as there were a few things troubling him about *guy stuff*. Leanne responds accordingly, and even laughs when I describe how Eric had asked Dan what fellatio was, but pronounced it *fell-ah-tee-o*, but something is still amiss. When she says she has a lecture, even though it's four in the afternoon, I let her go. I wouldn't mind, but she's the one who's been telling me to do something interesting with my life. Well, now I'm finally doing something interesting.

Chapter Thirty

The rain that started as a drizzle this morning has progressed to a heavy pelt thundering against the roof of our extension, but it's still not drowning out the shouts and shrieks of the five friends I foolishly agreed Eric could invite for a sleepover. I wouldn't normally be so accommodating, but today is his thirteenth birthday.

'Did you remember the Ben & Jerry's?'

'Would I forget the ice cream for my little teenager's sleepover?'

He tuts loudly, a response he's recently adopted for most things I say. 'It's not a sleepover; it's me and some mates hanging out.'

Eric seems to have aged six years in the last three months. He's well on his way to manhood, and I have no idea how that must feel for him.

'Noted. There's mountains of nachos, pop, pizzas and chocolate. Everything's in order.' I bow.

He regards me, appalled. 'Wanna leave Jack here and you go out for the night?'

'I'm not leaving Jack here with six teenage boys, thank you kindly.'

He sighs. 'You are so annoying.'

Eric has been acting off for a few weeks now. Someone at his school got wind of the stuff I was doing and now he's being called Science Son. Ordinarily he wouldn't have a problem with being singled out—the boy actively courts difference— but he's using it as a stick to beat me with whenever he can.

'I can always cancel if you don't like the terms.'

'Ugh!' rings his guttural cry, reverberating down the hall as he heads back up to his room, passing Dan, who is sensibly heading out for the night.

'Everything okay?' Dan asks me.

'That time of the month. Again.'

'Don't be too down on him. I remember being a teenager. All that emotional turmoil. Getting to grips with your changing body.'

'I understand. It must have been hard.'

'It was.' A lascivious smile creeps across his lips. 'ALL the time.'

I throw a tea towel at him. 'I don't want to know.'

He catches it and hangs it up for me. 'Remind me when you're off to London?'

'A week next Thursday. Why?'

'I thought I might come with you. See what all the fuss is about.'

My face does something odd.

'Is that a problem?'

'No. Why would that be a problem?' Dan and I in London.

Just the two of us. Together. In London. Sindy would be freaking out if she was here.

'Excellent. I'll book a room.'

'Mom!' Eric's back. 'Can you make the nachos? Everyone's starving.'

'I'm a bit hungry too,' says Dan. 'Got any going spare?'

'Your wish is my command, gentlemen.'

Eric looks at Dan and shakes his head. I can't see what Dan does back, but I suspect it's the same.

Much later I'm awoken when Jack, who's sharing with me as the noise from Eric's room was keeping him awake, kicks me in his sleep. There's a pungent smell in the room, and for once it's not Jack's arse. It's cannabis. I creep out of my room, past Dan's (he's still out so it's not him) and along the corridor towards Eric's, not quite believing the smell could be coming from there, although it clearly is. A bunch of thoughts go through my mind: surely Eric wouldn't be so stupid to smoke dope. Or stupid enough to do so in a house I'm inside of. And then I settle for the righteous indignation of wondering how stupid does he think I am that I wouldn't notice? I prepare myself for the confrontation that lies beyond his door and throw it open. Well, if the little so-and-sos are stoned, it's not affected their ability to move. By the time the door has banged against the wall they're all on their feet, wide-eyed and waiting for what's going to happen next, human versions of those tiny wooden toys that collapse when you press the button on their base, but then spring to attention when you release it.

'Eric, come with me please?'

His friends slump, relieved whatever scene is about to unfold, it won't be in front of them. Eric walks forward but doesn't say a word. I lead him downstairs to the kitchen, pull out a chair and motion him to sit.

'What have you got to say for yourself?'

He swallows hard.

'I asked you what you have to say for yourself.'

No response, only the exaggerated swallowing.

'Are you going to be sick?'

He shakes his head.

'Then what are you do—' The penny drops. 'Open your mouth.'

He does so, and there on his tongue are the rather soggy remains of a small joint. I roughly scrape it off and hurl it into the bin.

'What the hell were you thinking?'

'I was thinking you were asleep.'

'Not about getting away with it, about smoking weed at all.'

'It's only some herbal stuff.'

'For God's sake, you're only just thirteen! I don't care if it's grass clippings, you're way too young for this. Have you smoked before?'

'No,' he hisses, flicking his head in the direction of the floor upstairs, 'but I don't want them to know that.'

'I don't follow.'

'They've been on at me for ages about it. I did it to shut them up.'

As he squirms before me, I can almost feel the peer pressure weighing down on him and I instantly know he is telling the truth. I size up what to do next.

'You can't say anything,' he says, as if reading my thoughts.

'I'll have to inform their parents.'

'You can't. They'll crucify me!'

'It's not your decision.'

His eyes are wide in supplication. 'It's not that big a deal. They occasionally smoke fake weed to feel grown up. I don't want to. Can we leave it at that?'

The instant rush of relief knowing this isn't something he's into is followed almost as quickly by the fear that this is something he'll face more of, the seemingly benign exhortations of friends and the increasing discomfort of trying to maintain your place in a group, no matter how confident you might appear to be. I make him squirm some more and eventually tell him I won't interfere. For now. But I'll certainly be more vigilant.

'Why didn't you tell me you were feeling pressured. You can tell me anything.' I try to hug him, but he shrinks from my touch and pushes me away.

'That's interesting because I've been trying to talk to you for ages, actually.'

The emphasis on the word *actually* reminds me of arguments I used to have with my own mom and I can't stop the faint smile that plays across my lips.

'Don't do that!' he hisses. 'You always do that, making a joke out of how I feel.'

'Since when?'

'Since forever.' His eyes fill with tears.

'I don't know what you mean.'

'That's because you've stopped caring.'

'I have not.'

'What about when I asked if I could have a phone and you gave me Jack's play one.'

I remember the incident. 'I was being silly.'

'But I really wanted a phone!' His voice rises beyond its increasingly low register.

'And I've bought you one for your birthday, haven't I?'

'But you didn't take me seriously at the time.'

'Because I had bought you one for your birthday. Come on, Eric, be reasonable.'

'And when I said I wanted my ear pierced, you said I'd look like Elton John. Not Brooklyn Beckham. Not Justin Bieber. Elton John. He has a face like a melted muppet.'

I did say that, but he should remain unblemished and hole-less for a while longer.

'A lot of this sounds like me simply not giving in to you.'

'Last week I asked to go see where Dad worked and you refused to take me.'

'I had Reggie coming over.'

'You spend more time with him than me.'

'I didn't think you minded him coming.'

'I don't mind the postman coming, but I don't want you to marry him.' This is such a wonderfully childish thing to say I assume he is making a joke and smile again, but his expression darkens, overcast by a cloud of resentment. 'And I especially said I didn't want to stay at Granddad's.'

Oh, not this again. For some reason that he refuses to articulate, Eric is reluctant to go to Geoff's when I head to London, and he's been playing his face about it. I've told him it's non-negotiable, but he insists on bringing it up whenever he can.

'I'll stay with friends,' Eric says.

'Not after this evening you won't.'

'Then don't go.'

'I'm going and that's all there is to it.'

He looks over at the urn and back at me, glowering. His mouth twists.

'Sometimes I hate you,' he spits. 'I wish you were dead and that Dad was here.'

He runs back upstairs and slams his bedroom door and I sink into a chair. After a moment's silence they're all laughing as though nothing is wrong. A hundred thoughts rattle through my head. Have I been neglecting him? Surely no more than when I worked. Is it just bad timing, an upswing of emotion on the chart of adolescence, intersecting with the various plot points of recent events? Is it a good thing that he's displaying his feelings in this way? Getting something out of his system. I look over at the urn. It blurs, diffusing into a fuzzy riot of colour as my eyes fill.

'Would he have been better off without me instead?'

There are certainly times I wished it had been me who died. Gaz was always better at all of this than me. Geoff and Janet had doted on him meaning he had a pristine parenting playbook to follow, whereas I had a dog-eared list of things to avoid, passed down from generation to generation of dysfunction. For the most part I thought I'd done okay. But maybe not. Maybe all this time I've been hopelessly failing at the one thing I'm meant to have had the most practice at.

'Sometimes I still hate you for leaving us,' I whisper.

After the tears have run their course and I feel their cathartic release, I head back to bed. Things are so quiet in Eric's room now that it's easy to think the whole episode didn't happen. I tell myself I'm not going to let it get to me, and I'm not changing my plans. But the truth is I couldn't have felt more winded had he punched me in the guts.

The following night is beautiful and clear and I'm in the garden, lying on a picnic blanket, staring up at a sky so peppered with stars it looks like someone has been poking holes in the vast velvety curtain of space. I would do this often when Gaz first died. I found it mildly comforting to know that, whilst my problems were expanding more quickly than the universe, they remained barely perceptible blips on the radar of eternity. But in the here and now, with Eric not talking to me and Leanne being off, I can't shake the notion that I'm going wrong somewhere, that I'm letting them down. But perhaps that's part and parcel of the guilt every mom feels if they put themselves first or do something out of the ordinary.

'Have you fallen, or are you lying there deliberately?' It's Dan.

I prop myself up on elbows and crane my head to face him. 'Fallen. Been lying here for hours. Practically starving.'

'I'll get the biscuit tin and some tea. If you don't mind me joining you?'

'No. I don't mind at all.'

I smooth my hair down and wipe under my eyes to remove any mascara that might have slipped. Dan reappears, holding two mugs in one hand, with the biscuit barrel nestled like a baby in his other arm.

'Budge up then.'

I shuffle over for him and take my tea. He's washed up my favourite mug.

'What brings a woman like you to a place like this?'

I sigh. 'I don't think my kids like me very much right now.'

'Ah. Don't all kids go through stages like that though?'

'Maybe. But that doesn't make it any easier.'

'You're a good mom.'

'Can you tell them that?'

He passes me a custard cream.

'Thank you.'

'I'm only giving you one so I can have one myself.'

I smile. 'No, I mean thank you, for everything. All the help. I really appreciate it.'

'It's okay. I've enjoyed it.'

'You've done so much though. Not only the content, with the kids too.'

'Oh that. That's easy.'

'Taking Jack to soft play is not easy.'

'All useful life skills for future adventures.'

Future adventures. The words sting a little. I lie back to look at the sky and remind myself that sooner than I think none of this will matter. Soon we'll all be in the past, like the stars above me, whose light has been travelling for centuries. Dan stretches out beside me.

'It's bizarre to think that in the time I've been lying here, without moving a single muscle, I've moved around the Earth's axis by about a thousand miles and the Earth has moved almost four hundred thousand miles around the Sun.'

'Is this a puzzle? Am I meant to be able to work out how long you've been lying here from that information?'

'Ha! No. Merely an observation.'

'Although, you go on about your weak bladder so much, I'm assuming it can't be longer than ninety minutes.'

'Do I talk about my bladder a lot?'

'It's one of your defining features. That and knowing things like how far in space you've travelled.'

243

'Sorry. I'm a geek.'

'Don't be sorry. It's what makes you unique.'

He removes his keys from his pocket and when he rests his arm back down it's barely a millimetre from mine. My hairs prickle, making the lightest of contact. Has he noticed?

'I've never been able to get my head round it,' I say. 'A hundred thousand million stars in our galaxy alone. Millions upon millions of galaxies. Earth's so small.'

'A pale blue dot. A mote of dust caught in a sunbeam.'

'That's Carl Sagan!'

'You know it?' he asks.

'Of course. I watched every episode of *Cosmos* when I was a kid.'

'Me too!' he says turning towards me as I turn towards him.

I shiver despite the mild evening air.

'Are you cold?' He removes his hoodie, drapes it over me. The gooseflesh remains. I focus hard to conjure the image to which he referred, the one that shows the Earth, as seen from billions of miles away, suspended in a beam of scattered light, a tiny speck in the immeasurable ocean of space.

'Do you know the story of how Carl Sagan and his third wife got together?' Dan asks.

'He had *three* wives?'

'Wait for the story before you judge. You know the Voyager Space program?'

'Wasn't it Voyager that took the pictures of Earth?'

'Yep. And you know about the gold records they sent up with it?'

I shake my head and my arm brushes his with each movement.

'Oh man. This is so cool.' He turns his head, the full weight of his gaze falling on me, and his arm making complete contact with mine.

'They sent up these gold discs, containing sounds and images selected to portray the diversity of life and culture on Earth, in case anyone is out there.'

'What was on them?'

'*Is* on them. They're still travelling through space. There are photographs, diagrams, humpback whale sounds, images from books, the structure of DNA, people talking in different languages, loads of stuff. It was like a time capsule, or an interstellar message in a bottle. Sagan headed up the committee that chose the contents.'

His face gets so animated when he talks about things that interest him. I wonder how many women he's laid under the stars with, telling this story.

'What's that got to do with wife number three?' I try to keep my voice even.

'I'm getting to it. There's this woman on the committee called Ann. They've known one another professionally for a while, and she's been searching high and low for the perfect piece of Chinese music to put on the record. One day she discovers a composition called *Flowing Streams*, which is thousands of years old, and calls Sagan to tell him about it. But he's not there, so she leaves a message.'

His voice has got quieter as he's been telling me this, pulling me into the story.

'A couple hours later, she picks up the phone and it's Sagan getting back to her. And he says "*I get back to my hotel room and I find this message that says Annie called, and I say to myself, why didn't you leave this message ten years ago.*" And she says to him, *"for keeps?"* And he said, *"you mean get married?"* And she said, *"yes."'*

'What?'

'They hadn't so much as kissed before, but one call later they're engaged.'

'Wow.' Is that really possible?

'Yep.' Dan doesn't flinch from holding my gaze. 'Something switched on for him. A zero to a one in the brain's processor.'

I notice the way the light from the kitchen falls across his face, emphasising the creases at the corner of his eyes and creating a crescent moon in orbit around the inky darkness of his pupils. There's the tiniest crumb on his lower cheek, a microscopic blemish clinging to the line that runs from the corner of his nose to the corner of his lips. I want to reach out and brush it away, but suddenly there's a yowl in the street beyond the house, the primal shriek of two cats fighting. I recoil from the noise, and in doing so break the physical connection between us.

'Sorry,' he says quickly. 'Now I'm geeking out on you.'

I turn my face to the ebony expanse above me. 'It's a very romantic story,' I manage.

Dan sighs. 'As Sagan himself said *"for small creatures such as we, the vastness is only bearable through love."'*

I lie in silence a few minutes more, my mind blank, my mouth dry.

'I should be going to bed,' Dan says. It sounds like a question, not a statement. He doesn't move, except for his head inclining slightly towards me. I search for The Plough in the constellations overhead. Eventually he moves more decisively.

'Goodnight, Cath.'

There's something about the way he says my name that sets

off a murmuring in my chest. 'Night,' I say back, continuing to stare at oblivious distant suns.

It's only when the bathroom light goes on that I hazard to sit up. My tea has gone cold, but I cradle it anyway, thinking about the story he shared. How odd the nature of intimacy, to go from unknowing to knowing, misunderstanding to understanding, dislike to like. Some relationships form like the Big Bang, from nothingness comes a sudden, rapid onset of feeling, a cosmic inflation of longing and desire that gives life new weight and meaning. Some form like DNA, two separate strands woven together by a series of bonds that build over time, slowly exerting their physical effect, but ultimately changing who we are forever. There's barely a month to go until Dan finishes his academic year. What happens then? Will he be moving on to those future adventures? Will I be lying under a new moon thinking about the lodger who helped me look at life with fresh eyes? It's getting cold. I pull Dan's jumper tightly around me, breathe in its fragrance. But the chill remains. I head into the kitchen and lock the door behind me. I can't quite bring myself to look at Gaz before I turn out the light.

Chapter Thirty-One

R eggie is at my kitchen table, waiting for the others to arrive for their lesson. Despite his dark complexion, there's an unmistakable purple-red swelling across his right eye. Dan, who is sat reading a magazine, has clocked it too.

'What happened?' I ask.

'Got stung by a bee.'

'In the eye? What were you doing, trying to stare it out?'

He shrugs.

'Did you get into a fight at school?'

'I did not get into a fight at school.'

'That makes me think you got into a fight *not* at school.'

He opens his book. 'No fight. Apart from with a bee that is.'

Dan looks at me. I look at him. We both know he's lying.

'Everything okay?'

'Everything apart from an angry bee.'

I narrow my eyes, entreating, but he steadily holds my gaze until I look away.

'Have you got those mock print outs?' he asks.

Shit. I was meant to do that in town yesterday but totally forgot. I tell Reggie I'll email them to him, but he rewards me with a sullen stare.

'I hope the others hurry up. Last lesson before the big day.'

The team's two science exams have been scheduled a couple of days apart in early June, two weeks away. Judging by their progress and their performance on some of the mock papers I've been setting, there's a very real chance that if the right subjects come up on the day, they'll do okay, but they have a lot of other exams to do between now and then.

'We're coming round to cram the day before though, right?' asks Reggie.

I glance at the calendar on the fridge and the three days I've blocked out for the London trip. Double shit! I forgot I'd said they could come over.

'Reggie, I'm really sorry.' I fill him in on the whole conference thing. 'At least you get to tell people you knew me before I was famous!' It's a crap joke, said because I feel bad.

'So, you're quitting on us?'

'I'm not quitting on you, you dope, I'm just not around for those particular days.'

'But you said…'

'I know. I've got so much going on at the moment.'

His face clouds.

'I'll call you to wish you luck.'

He drums his fingers against his thigh. 'You're selling out, Miss.'

'From what?'

His eyes are laser focused on mine. 'You're like Dre rapping all that ill shit, holding onto *Detox* 'cos he claimed he wanted to

SAL THOMAS

do things right, and meantime selling garbage headphones to Apple, high priests of corporate greed.'

'I have literally no idea what you just said,' I'm still trying desperately to lift the mood, but he's in the zone.

'Or Flavour Flav,' he continues. '*Public Enemy* were at the vanguard of social activism in the eighties and nineties, and then he goes and fronts a dating show. Sell. Out.'

'Come on, Reg. It's hardly the same,' says Dan.

'I might have known you'd take her side.'

Dan's eyes widen. They're usually good buddies.

'No one's taking sides,' I say. 'I've done one rap video. I'm not swopping the streets of Compton for Sutton Coldfield!'

'And what exactly did you do that video for, Miss?'

'To create an avenue for teaching beyond the classroom.'

'Oh really? Because there I was thinking you did it for me.'

I note the hurt in his eyes as he says this; that he thinks that by seizing this opportunity I'm somehow cutting him loose. Maybe, despite his confidence and bluster, it had really meant something that this had started out for him and not for the masses in the way it's turned out to be. Dan and I exchange another look. This isn't like Reggie.

'I'll call you. I promise.' I place a hand on his shoulder.

He slips it, shoves his books back into his bag, eyes glistening. 'Course you will, Miss. Course you will.' He leaves without turning back and I'm left staring at the space where he was moments before.

'You okay?' Dan's beside me.

'No. I hate the idea of him fighting.'

'Me too.'

He gives the back of my neck a gentle squeeze. It's only a

250

friendly gesture, but I'm right back on that picnic blanket outside, my whole body a sigh.

'I'd better go after him.' I get to the end of the road, the vestige of Dan's fingers still on my skin. There's no sign of Reggie, but I see the lolloping frame of Bradley, flanked by the others, coming towards me. I can only hope they know what's going on.

Chapter Thirty-Two

It's the week before my big excursion to London, and whilst I should be at home trying to get everything prepared, I'm sat in Belinda's achingly stylish and unnaturally tidy lounge, listening to her talk about lavender oil. The evening started somewhat uneasily when Belinda showed a compilation of my content through her smart TV for the benefit of those who weren't 'familiar with my work', which culminated in everyone wanting a selfie with me. Attention has now shifted to the overpriced and under-researched beauty products we came here to be guilted into buying.

'And this is absolutely perfect for getting those little ones off to sleep,' Belinda tells us. 'A couple of drops on the pillow and they're out like lights.'

'I suppose you've gotta try any old shite now they've removed alcohol from Gripe Water.' Sindy is hating everything about this except the box of wine on Belinda's fingerprint-free glass coffee table, of which she has taken full advantage.

'Do you have children?' Belinda asks her.

'Do you? Because there is literally no evidence of them here!'

Even someone stone deaf could hear the barb in Sindy's tone.

'Actually, I do,' Belinda says, equally spicily. 'They love to help me tidy up at the end of the day. My daughter has her own mini working Dyson.' She passes the oil round.

'How lovely!' says Sindy. 'Perhaps she'll be a cleaner when she grows up?'

I poke her gently in the leg. Sindy looks at me and mouths an exaggerated 'What?' Thankfully it's time for the next product demo. Belinda holds up a silver bottle with a silver domed lid.

'Finally, the dildos!' says Sindy, raising a glass in toast.

The other guests shift uncomfortably. Wrong crowd. I prod her again; she knows full well that this isn't the time or place.

'This is Gin-Chia,' says Belinda. 'It contains two ancient herbs. Golden chia from the West and ginseng from the East.' As that gets passed along she explains how they create a powerful antioxidant that erases lip wrinkles and boosts collagen.

'No, thanks,' says Sindy when it gets to her. 'When my gob gets wrinkly, I'm having fillers.' She passes it to the woman to her right, who takes an appreciative sniff.

'Really? I don't like the idea of foreign bodies in me,' she says.

'I pity your husband then!' Sindy digs her in the ribs, causing her to spill the product between her legs and onto the very expensive, very velvety, but utterly uncomfortable sofa we're sat on. Totally oblivious, Sindy stretches towards the wine box.

'Easy, Sin!'

She turns to me, eyes glassy. 'Someone's got to liven things up a bit. There's only so much bollocking on about gluten-free organic face potions we can take, eh ladies?' She looks around the room for support, but no one offers any.

'It's not an Ann Summers party, that's all I'm saying.'

'Don't I know it.'

The polite chit-chat and product demonstrations continue, the air considerably cooler for Sindy's behaviour and everybody keeps looking at me, but not in the good way they were earlier. When she leans across for yet another glass, I stay her hand.

'Don't you think you've had enough?' I whisper.

'Don't you think you've had too little?'

'I'm just saying it's a school night.'

'Jesus, Cath, anybody would think you're embarrassed of me.'

'Don't be daft.' I look around the room. Seven pairs of eyes gawp back. This was a mistake, I can see that now. I should never have forced her to come.

Sindy's jaw slackens. 'Oh my god, you are. You're embarrassed of me.'

She tries to get up, but the sofa is too low, and her heels are too high. I try and help her, but she waves my arm away, managing to get upright, but spilling wine in the process.

'What's happened to you? Is this what you're into now?' She gestures around the room and nearly topples over again. 'Is this how you want to spend your time? With these kinds of people? Because this isn't you.'

'I'm trying to be sociable.'

'Are you? Why? These people didn't give a shit about you

when you weren't big on social media. These people have made you feel this big'—she struggles to focus on her fingers as she pinches them together—'for the last year.'

I grimace. There's no need to bring that up now.

'But what does that matter, eh? Suddenly I'm the embarrassment!'

'Sindy, you're drunk.'

'That's as may be, Cath, but in the morning, these lot will still be twats.' She picks her way carefully across the feet of those seated. 'Are you coming?' she asks when she gets to the door.

I know I should go with her, talk it through. But what if I am enjoying the attention? What if I do want these women to like me? After everything that's happened, what if I am prioritising me for a change? I shake my head. Sindy tips her head back in thought, as if she's communing with the ceiling in some way. Then she hoiks her bag up onto her shoulder, opens the door, and walks out with her head held high.

I look at the women facing me.

'Someone's not going to be needing their lavender oil this evening,' I say.

And every single one of them laughs.

PART IV
SUMMER

Chapter Thirty-Three

'Y ou didn't need to do that, love!'

It's 7.30am and I'm on the doorstep of Geoff's 1930s semi, holding Jack in one arm, and using the other to hand Geoff a bottle of the peaty Scotch that I know he likes but will never buy for himself.

'I really did. Thanks for having the kids.'

'They're no trouble.'

Hmm. This is debatable. I think of Eric who is sulking behind me and his endless bickering, constant histrionics and unreasonable demands of the last couple of weeks. Still, he finally conceded to come today, albeit after I gave up every other avenue of communication and simply bribed him with a new game for his Nintendo.

Sheila appears at the door wearing a tartan dress and ostrich feather mules. She must have stayed the night, or else been up very early this morning to look so put together. She tickles Jack under the chin and asks, too loud, enunciating each word. 'What do you enjoy playing with, young man?'

'He understands you, Sheila; he's not a simpleton.'

'I like dicks,' says Jack, who hasn't yet mastered the 'st' phoneme, despite my repeated efforts. 'And balls,' he adds for good measure.

Sheila looks pointedly back at me. I hand Jack to Geoff who gives me a wink and takes him into the house. Eric drags his bag in after them with all the enthusiasm of a man about to fill out his tax return. Sheila stays put, arms folded across her chest (only just mind), eyeing me lukewarmly.

'You're placing too much pressure on him. He's not well.'

I'm a bit taken aback. When Geoff offered to have the kids, I'd asked if he was up to it and he'd assured me that the statins were doing their job. 'He told me he's fine.'

'He could be holding his severed leg in his hand and he'd tell you he was fine. Couldn't you have asked Sindy?'

'She's busy this weekend.' I haven't told anyone about our falling out, but Sheila looks sceptical, which is weird for someone who believes so much other mumbo jumbo. I glance at the cab waiting to take Dan and me to the station; I'm sure she's exaggerating for effect as she likes to fuss. 'If there's any problem at all, I'll come straight back, okay?'

'As you were,' she says, like some stern housemaid in a historical drama.

Geoff reappears in the hallway. 'Everything okay?'

'Yes,' says Sheila. 'I was reminding Cath to be back in plenty of time for your party.'

'That bloody party,' says Geoff. 'It'll be the death of me!'

Behind me the taxi hoots and Dan shouts to hurry up or we'll miss our train.

'Right. Here are all the bags. Don't let them watch too much TV.'

'GO!' says Geoff. 'And good luck!'

I shout my goodbyes to the boys down the hall and run back to the cab where Dan is waving the tickets impatiently. To London!

'Where do you want to go first,' I ask Dan, having dropped our bags at the hotel.

'I don't know, where do you want to go first?'

'I was thinking…'

'The Science Museum!' says Dan at the same time as I do.

'Great minds think alike!' we say together.

'Jinx, you owe me a coke,' says Dan.

'What?'

'You owe me a coke.'

'That's not how jinxes work.'

'It is back at home.'

As we make our way on foot overland, I'm floored by the scale of the place; the great swathes of people making their way down busy roads in a carefully orchestrated commuter dance, the grand edifices of Victorian townhouses, with extensions and protrusions dissecting each roof in a bid to squeeze even more space into every footprint. Every street we turn down unveils yet another blue plaque, eight hundred years of the city's history spread out across its surface like fading acne scars. And then we arrive in sunny South Kensington, and the lyrics of the titular Donovan song my mom loved pop into my head. I would listen to it with her in our yellow Formica kitchen, dancing around on the cheap cork tiles, thinking one day I would go to London, to university, where I would spread my wings as the song instructed. Of course I never did, and incredibly Gaz and I never made it this far south, not even for a weekend.

'You okay?' asks Dan. 'You're miles away.'

'Sorry, daydreaming.'

We turn a corner and there it is, the Science Museum, home of human ingenuity. Not as grand or ornate as the Natural History Museum with its fancy terracotta façade, but the kind of building that lets the elegance of the discipline that spawned it do the talking. I ask to take a photo of him with the museum in the background; that should get some likes.

'Why don't you give yourself the day off?'

Being on social media is second nature now, but I put my phone away.

'How come you never take or post pictures? You've done so much travelling, do you not want to remember it all?'

'I don't need to put it on the web to know it happened,' he says. 'And the problem with photos is you come to only remember what you took a picture of. The experience gets reconstructed through a false lens. I like to be in the moment.'

Inside, the place is more awesome than I could have imagined, a glorious hodgepodge of human invention and discovery. The true jewel, we're told, is the *Wonderlab,* an entire gallery of objects and installations dedicated to bringing scientific phenomena to life, and since we only have a couple of hours before closing time, we head there first.

'Cath, come and look at this.'

Dan leads me to a space in the far wing of one of the galleries where there are three huge slides, one covered in artificial grass, one made from fibreglass and one constructed from the polished timber tiles of a bowling alley, each inviting us to explore the nature of friction by projecting ourselves down them.

'I'll race you,' he says, throwing his backpack down and sprinting towards the steps.

'Not fair!' I shout, my voice echoing. 'You got a head start!' But I chase after him nevertheless.

Although he beats me to the top, he stops to let a child go before him, which means I sneak onto the quickest slide a fraction of a second before he reaches it. Undeterred, he launches himself down the same chute as me and I barely have time to catch my breath before we both come to a giggling entangled bump at the bottom.

'Och, would you look at those two love birds.' An elderly Scottish woman gestures in our direction.

'Aye, I remember when we used to giggle like school kids together,' her companion says, squeezing her arm affectionately.

'Oh, we're not together.' I accidentally put my hand on Dan's crotch as I get up.

'That's not how it looks to me, lassie,' she says, raising an eyebrow so far up her forehead even her wrinkles get wrinkles.

'She's using me for sexual gratification,' says Dan.

'Clever girl!'

I wait until they're out of sight, which takes ages because they're rather slow, and then swing my bag at Dan.

'Your face!' he says. 'You've gone so red!'

'She was an old lady; you could have given her a stroke!'

'I'm not sure that would have been appropriate. Although you are always saying I should try a more mature woman. Should I go after her?'

He makes as if to follow them, so I grab his arm. 'Oh no, you don't. I'm not having that on my conscience.'

Afterwards, Dan insists on walking arm in arm with me, calling me 'darling', and saying things such as 'please, stop squeezing my butt' when within hearing distance of other visitors. I've told him he's an immature moron with the comedic skills of a five-year-old, which he's taken as a compliment. Still, for all the innuendos, the rest of the afternoon slips by in a gratifying haze of exploration.

Later in the evening, after a cheap meal in Chinatown, I have to return to the hotel with a splitting headache. Typical. Dan offered to come back with me, but there was no reason for us both to miss out on a night in the city, so instead he's been sending through pictures of him in front of various landmarks, pointing at them over his shoulder with that goofy smile of his plastered across his face. Another one pops up. A perspective shot of him 'impaling' his finger on the top of St Paul's Cathedral. I look around the room to see if there's anything I can use to create a fun picture of my own. It's slim pickings, but I have the idea to artfully arrange my box of painkillers on the bedside table, wrap my hair in a towel, pop a folded cloth over my face, lie with the back of my hand against my brow, and pout in a pained yet stoical way whilst trying to take several selfies without actually being able to see myself. I pick the best one, send it off, and use all my willpower not to stare at my phone waiting for a reply. I don't have long to wait.

Aww. Do you need someone to feed you grapes?

Probably a rhetorical question, but I answer anyway.

That depends. Do you mean in a someone being tended to on their sickbed way, or in a Roman orgy way?

Eek. Why did I mention orgies?

Roman orgy?! I thought you said you had a headache?!

Oh well, may as well run with it; prove I'm not the huge prude he still thinks I am.

Just a ruse. Do you reckon I can get some half-dressed slave with a cherubic face and a ripped body to do the honours at this time of the evening?

The two ticks have barely appeared when he's typing a reply.

Reckon I saw that on the room service menu. Somewhere between the nuts and the foot-long hot dog.

Hah!

Okay. Well, if you don't hear from me again, I have expired during a Bacchanalian frenzy of food, fine wine and frolicking … or more likely choked to death on a Rolo from the mini bar.

He's typing again.

Don't die. I'd miss you…

Aww. I tuck my hair behind my ears. There's another ping.

...but if you do die, may I have your last Rolo?

I send an emoji back with a smile as big as my own. I reckon I could do that for him.

Chapter Thirty-Four

I wake up the next morning buoyant and refreshed. I pop the radio on through the television and have a little dance to the summery tune they're playing. Dan has already messaged to ask what time we're heading for breakfast, and we're meeting downstairs at eight. I take extra care with my make-up and hair, one, because I can without two kids mithering me and two, because I want to feel as good as possible for the day ahead.

When I get to the lobby Dan's already there. He's wearing one of my favourite tops, a well-loved grey marl T-shirt with a picture of a polar bear on a paddleboard on the front. He's also talking animatedly with the very pretty and very youthful olive-skinned receptionist. She reminds me of a cat stretching in the sunshine, overtly elongating her neck and torso as she leans into the warmth of his charm. It's such a cliché to describe someone as magnetic, but with Dan it really does describe him. You're inescapably drawn towards him as if by an invisible force, like the unseen folds in space-time that create their gravitational pull. He laughs at something she says, and I'm instantly self-conscious, like I've intruded on something. I'm so used to being within the orbit of his attention that observing that focus being directed elsewhere feels weird. But it'd be the same if I saw Sindy being super pally with someone other than me, wouldn't it? Ugh, Sindy. This is the longest we've gone without speaking, and I feel bad about what happened, but equally I feel she was being unreasonable. Some of Belinda's friends were actually quite sweet. Bloody emotions. I should probably head to breakfast and try and eat my way through them.

I'm half-way across the foyer when Dan catches up with me.

'Morning!'

'Oh hey,' I say. 'You're already here!' As if I didn't know.

'You'll never guess what. The receptionist is Honduran, which is where I did my PADI qualification. She's really sweet.'

'That's cool.' I try to smile, but it doesn't get as far as my eyes.

We enter the restaurant, give our room numbers and get seated. The smell of burnt toast mingled with eggs permeates the air.

'You survived the night after all?' he says.

'Just about.'

'Are you okay? You look a bit off colour.'

'I'm fine.' I'm not fine. I'm in a grouch.

'Is the headache back?' his face furrows with concern.

'I didn't sleep very well. First night in a new bed and all that.' More lies.

'Well, they have some grapes over there if you need me to fetch you any?'

I manage a small smile. 'Now you come to mention it, I do have some tension at the back here.'

'Do you now?'

'Yeah. And here in the temples.'

'Perhaps you'd like me to get you some orange juice too?'

'And maybe a bacon sandwich. With brown bread, and red sauce, and a hash brown if they have one.'

He stands and bows. 'Your wish is my command. I'm going to have the full English. I'm ravenous. Must have walked ten miles last night. I'm only sorry you weren't with me.'

I smile, properly this time. Feelings are so damned fickle, aren't they?

It's already oppressively warm when I leave the hotel to head to the conference, the heat a heavy cloak I can't shrug off. Two tubes and a further ten-minute walk means I'm full-on sweating when I arrive. The conference is way bigger than I thought; it's taken over the entire Grand Hall of Olympia, a cavernous space under an incredible ironwork and glass barrelled roof. From this vantage point alone there's a dozen stands featuring brands I recognise, several playing host to businesses I don't, an airstream trailer-turned-prosecco-bar and a couple of street food stalls. And that's a tenth of it. It's odd to think that an entire industry now exists around everyday things being said about everyday stuff by everyday people, hundreds of whom are flitting around the venue like excited molecules. I catch sight of myself in a reflective surface. My fringe is stuck to my forehead but the makeup I had so carefully applied has had less luck clinging to my face. I curse the Underground and my decision to wear skinny jeans and wonder if anyone else will notice the damp patches soaking into my T-shirt. I pull out the bottle of water from the goody bag I've been given and struggle to get the top off. Even my palms are sweaty. I'm not sure what I'm meant to do now. Yam Yammy Mammy (must remember to call her Denise) said the day was a good opportunity to network, the only trouble is, I have no idea how to begin a conversation with a stranger. Even role playing asking for directions in French lessons used to bring me out in hives. I amble around for a few minutes, then spot a lone non-scary looking woman sat at communal seating area and make a beeline for her.

'Mind if I sit here?'

'No, it's fine, I was just leaving.'

Balls. I sit down, ruffle my fringe and check my face in my camera app. I wish I had some face powder with me. Or different skin. Almost everyone else looks very stylish. A party of half a dozen women that wouldn't look out of place at Ascot walk past, an excitable chattering bloom of floral dresses and fascinators. In fact, everyone seems to be talking to someone except me. And there's a lot of air kissing going on. Denise said that it was a close community, but there are over a thousand people in this hall, and I can't possibly be the only one who doesn't know anyone. And where is she? She floated the idea that we'd meet up, but I've not heard from her. I take out my phone. No messages. I should probably post something. I find a good last-minute exam prep article online and link out to it via an image post. I hope the gang are knuckling down to some revision today, science exam number one is first thing tomorrow. I wander around some more, trying to look less uncomfortable than I feel. At one end of the hall a space has been partitioned off for the awards part of the day. Large round tables have been laid out with huge architectural flower arrangements in the centre of each and there's a roped off red carpet and a large easel displaying a board indicating who's sitting where. I'm on a table fairly near the back—almost certainly an indication that I won't be walking away with an award today—but it's bonkers that I've even been nominated. I carry on to the other side of the hall and come across a complimentary drinks station with picnic benches laid out around it. I help myself to a coffee and sit down at one of the empty tables. Again, everyone seems to be talking to someone. Perhaps I should leave, catch up with Dan and spend the day sightseeing instead of sitting here like a lemon. Or I could hide in the toilets. I take a sip of my drink, but it's like there's a pebble lodged in my gullet.

Okay, this is silly. Time for an inner pep talk. It's only a conference. There's obviously loads to do, so I should just imagine I'm back at school and want to learn as much as I can. I can schedule my day, work out what's happening where, and move with purpose from one thing to the other. I glance through the programme, which offers some reassurance. There are workshops on topics like managing different channels more effectively, boosting engagement, SEO and changes to channel policies that could be useful, some panel debates that sound interesting, and then the late afternoon slot is all about the awards. At least then I can stare at the stage for an hour. I'm circling a few things when my phone pings. It's a message from Dan.

Look at this!

There's a guy holding a cardboard placard with FREE HUGS emblazoned on it. I type back.

I need one of those right now. This is terrifying.

I wait for the response.

Tell you what. I'll pick one up for you and pass it on later ;0)

I'm thinking of a clever response when I hear a shrill voice above me.

'Why yam looking like the cat who got the cream?'

I look up. It's Denise, as striking as ever in a fit and flare royal blue dress, black tuxedo blazer and very pointy black court shoes. She looks like she should be running a small country, not a lifestyle business.

'It's nothing.'

'Come on, I know that look!'

'It's my lodger. He sent me a picture.'

'Oh yeah?!'

'No, it's … it's a long story.'

'I don't have time for one of those, loads of people to see, but I wanted to check you're okay.'

'Yeah, I'm fine.' I do feel fine again. It's probably hormonal. 'How did you know to find me here?'

'Instagram location feature.'

'That's a thing?'

She treats me to another of her pitying shakes of the head. 'So much to learn.'

In the minute or so since she turned up, I've noticed a deepening buzz around us; people nudging and poking each other and pointing at Denise.

'Yam been to see Foster Management yet?' she asks me.

'Who?'

'It's an agency. They're offering representation to all award winners.'

'What does that mean?'

'Some dosh potentially.'

That would be nice. 'But I'm not going to win.'

'They want to meet everyone on the shortlist. You should go.'

I suppose it'll give me something to do for the next half an hour.

'Alright bab. Gotta dash. Good luck later.'

Standing at the front of stall fourteen is a guy in a pink shirt, too-short chinos, horn-rimmed glasses and a pork-pie hat. Despite this get-up, he exudes confidence.

'Can I help you?'

'Hey'—I read the name badge—'Alex. A friend said I should come by. I've been nominated for an award.'

'Wonderful, wonderful. Won any previously?'

'No. First time nominated.'

'How long you been going?'

'About six months.'

'Interesting, interesting. Come in, come in.'

The stand is Instagram rendered in real life, the walls adorned with large square portraits of attractive women smiling like they've won in the competition of life, but don't want to look too smug about it in case they put off any followers.

'Sit down, sit down.'

Alex has a lot of energy, which presumably is why he needs to repeat himself so often. I park my bottom on a bench in the centre of the stand.

'Er, that's the table. Those are the chairs.' He points to something that looks like a bean bag and a croissant had a furniture baby. 'Fabulous, aren't they? We were going for, like, an ultra-relaxed vibe in here; we want everyone to feel comfortable.'

'Then perhaps you shouldn't have chosen those to sit on.'

He gives a half-laugh. I was serious. I honestly don't know how I'm meant to get onto it. I sort of squat and throw myself backwards and almost knock one of his displays over in the process. Within moments the blood supply to my legs stops. Alex studies me more closely.

'Is it Science Mom by any chance?'

'Uh huh.'

'Thought so. Recognise the clumsiness.'

Yeah, that figures.

'I like your vibe. Very *now*. Very *different*.' He air-quotes like the words might have alternative, more significant meanings.

'Is it?'

'Sure, sure. We're seeing a shift away from the polished performance thing, partic within the parentscape. What you're doing is interesting. It's like your discomfort is part of the charm.'

My discomfort is currently manifesting itself as pins and needles in my feet.

'There's this juxtaposition between your expertise and your awkwardness. You're a middle-aged woman not afraid to make a tit of herself. Totally refreshing.'

His intonation makes everything sound like a question.

'Should I take that as a compliment?'

'Absolutely. Look at the crop of Travels With My Father, Road Trips With My Mother type shows people lap up. Uncool parents are cool again, aren't they?'

I can't help but think that the one person for whom this uncool parent will never be cool again is Eric. I hope he's behaving himself. 'So, what is the representation prize thing?'

'In essence we'd work on your behalf to create lucrative brand partnerships for you. We're working with some of the biggest names, brokering some of the biggest deals in the influencer space right now.'

'Like what?'

'Do you know Xena?'

'The Warrior Princess?'

'No. They're a virtual influencer.'

'Does she post about virtual reality?'

'No, *they*—Xena doesn't identify with standard notions of gender—*are* virtual reality. They're computer generated.'

'They don't exist?'

'Not in the flesh, but they're very much alive on social media.'

I'm confused. 'In what way?'

'They do collaborations, hang out with people, tell you what's going on in their life.'

'But they're created by someone else.'

'Exactly.'

'Why would people follow them?'

'We're getting off topic. The point is we recently got them a fashion deal that runs to six figures. Six figures!'

'How will they sign the contracts?'

He doesn't even manage a half-laugh at that. 'Of course six-figures is rare, but ... let's think...' he pats lips with his finger. 'We've got a high-end white goods brand bringing out a connected devices range and they're looking for someone with more of a nerdy vibe going on. That could be perfect for you.'

'I'm not going to win,' I say, keen to bring this conversation to an end. I do a sort of dismount to the side of the chair thingy and then scrabble to my feet, almost certainly flashing my pants in the process.

'I don't know,' he says. 'You are, as they say, *en mode*.'

For the rest of the morning, I hit my stride a bit more. I listen to some talks, have a lovely taco lunch and then a cheeky half a cider with a food blogger I met at a YouTube adverts workshop. Before I know it, the time swings round for the awards. Back at the special cordoned off area, I'm the last person at my table. I've barely had chance to introduce myself to the others when the lights dim and the host is introduced, a well-known comedian who does a great ten-minute routine on the joys of PTAs. It then all moves swiftly along. The winners aren't required to give a speech, they just pose with the presenter, get handed a prize bag and exit stage left. By half-way through, Denise has won three out of the four awards she's been nominated for. I spotted a grimace when she didn't win in the humorous category, so suspect someone in the Yam Yammy Mammy brand machine might be getting some grief later. When we get to the Edutainment category, a tornado starts up in my stomach and I have the instant urge to wee. I try to seem relaxed, like I'm up for awards every day, but my eyes feel like they've been clamped open, Clockwork Orange style.

'And the winner is…'—the presenter slowly opens the envelope. I really do need to pee— 'Science Mom!'

There's a big round of applause. Did I hear that right? Did she really call my name out? The woman next to me is patting me on the upper arm. I unsteadily get to my feet and walk towards the stage. My legs are super wobbly, like I've taken an adrenaline shot to each thigh, made worse by having to gingerly weave between the tightly packed chairs and tables. There are far too many people looking at me. God, I wished I'd worn something different. Someone waves at me from across the room and I wave back, until someone else points out that it's because I'm going the wrong way. At the same time, a voice over the loudspeaker describes what the judges said about me and why I won. I manage to get to up to the podium without my body doing anything stupid and shake hands with the presenter. She says 'well done', tells me I have a natural gift for slapstick, gestures towards the photographer who takes a couple of photos, then indicates that I should go along to the next person who has a gift bag for me. I pick that up, totally desperate to peek inside, only I can't because someone else passes me a glass of champagne that occupies my other hand and then I'm trying hard not to fall down the steps at the other side of the stage. At the bottom I have my photo taken by another photographer, am told that the pictures are available immediately online if I wanted to share them along with the event's hashtag and then I'm funnelled into a side room where Alex invites me to pop into their offices tomorrow afternoon to discuss next steps. When I get back to my table, I post the picture of me with the comedian, then message Dan with a pic of the award.

> *Looks like we're celebrating!!! Dinner and drinks on me later. Meet you downstairs at 7.30. Couldn't have done it without you.*

My heartbeat has barely returned to its resting phase when I get a response.

> *FUCK YEAH (that is swear-box exempt given special circumstances). And you totally could. You're the brains. I'm just the brawn ;0)*

I can't really focus on the rest of awards, I'm too excited, although I do clap extra loudly when Yam Yammy Mammy takes the Grand Prix (which I discover is the award you give to people who've won the most awards, because what they really need is another award). I sneak a look at my post. It has loads of likes already and even a comment from Gaynor.

> *V impressive! Incidentally I once hosted those awards.*

I smile. She always has to go one better, but who cares? I've only gone and bloody well won it! I am now an award-winning influencer with agency representation, and unless I trip over my own feet (always a possibility) nothing is going to bring me tumbling off this big fluffy cloud of glee.

Chapter Thirty-Five

When the lift doors open onto the hotel lobby, Dan's already there, chatting to the doorman. I glance at myself in the lift mirror one last time. I was so giddy at the prospect of a proper night out, I stopped at a vast vintage emporium I passed on the way back and picked up an outfit that will probably only ever get one more wear, and that's at Geoff's party tomorrow night. I also dropped by a department store and got my face done for free at a makeup counter. I love my new dress; it's a slim-cut wiggle number with a draped back, half-length sleeves and a not-too-deep split along the thigh. I'm less certain about the leopard-print shoes as what seemed a fun pop of colour in the shop now seems a bit 1980s barmaid, but what the hell. I smooth down the dress, adjust the hold-up stockings that I'm convinced could slip and turn into baggy gossamer socks at any time, and ruffle my hair. Dan looks round when he hears the clacking of heels across the marble floor, and it takes him a moment to register that they're attached to shoes that are attached to the rest of me.

'Holy cow. Is that you in there?'

'Ha ha.'

'You have legs? Are they yours?'

Okay, I'm probably overdressed and Dan's only in jeans. 'I'm getting changed,' I say, turning back towards the lift, but Dan grabs me by the hand and pulls me back.

'Cath, I'm teasing. You look beautiful.'

My insides pitch. He looks pretty good himself. He's paired dark jeans with a close-fitting white shirt, grey tweed waistcoat and thin blue tie.

'Come on. We're celebrating. But don't walk too quickly, I can't risk my thighs getting too sweaty.'

Dan turns to the doorman. 'Oh yep, it's definitely her in there.' He tucks my arm through his as we head out into the city.

The restaurant I booked is a cute little neighbourhood brasserie, completely unassuming from the front, identifiable only by a small sign propped up in a panel of a bay window that could as easily belong to a house, but once inside it opens out into a dimly lit oak panelled dining room crammed with glossy lacquered tables and leather chairs. It's the kind of place you see in political dramas, where you can imagine, for an evening at least, that you're someone very important on whom the future of mankind rests, although thankfully the prices are less obscene than the surroundings might suggest.

'Very nice,' says Dan.

A maître d' shows us to our table, and on his recommendation we order a boozy cocktail as an aperitif.

'Cheers,' says Dan, raising his blood red Negroni to mine.

The candle on the table flickers in his eyes. He smiles that smile of his, wide, open, always with a hint of amusement.

God, he looks insanely cute this evening. I pick the menu up, hide behind it. 'Let's decide what to eat and then you can tell me what you saw today.'

He hooks a finger over the top, pulls it down slightly. 'I want to hear about your day too.' The mild buzz I'd felt at that first sip of my drink intensifies.

After we've ordered, I give Dan a blow-by-blow account of how the day went and how unbelievable it was to win an award. Dan and I have eaten together countless times now, but for some reason this feels like the first time. No kids to interrupt. No other distractions. I'm conscious I'm speaking a bit too quickly, too eager to make sure there aren't any gaps in the conversation, and when the food arrives I'm paranoid about getting food stuck in my teeth.

'I'm disappointed you didn't have to give a speech. I'm sure you would have made some brilliant faux pas if you had,' he says.

'How well you know me.' I tell him about how Sindy and Dave asked me to say a few words at their wedding, a traditional Catholic ceremony during which, rather than 'saying peace be with you', I misheard and went around pumping everyone's hand and bellowing 'pleased to meet you'. I also didn't realise I had chocolatey fingers from feeding a much younger Eric buttons to keep him quiet, so having begrudgingly made the sign of the cross on my cream dress several times, I'd given myself two brown nipples. When I got up to speak and noticed what had happened, I stumbled onto the lectern, knocked it into the font and sent a tsunami of Holy Water into the front row. Dan's laughter makes me feel less bad that I'm not currently speaking to Sindy. He goes on to tell me about his double-decker bus tour of the city this morning and afternoon river cruise up the Thames, peppered with anecdotes of other travel adventures, and before we know it, three hours have slipped by in a blink of giggles, stories and the kind of indulgent food and wine that envelops you in an aggressive cuddle from which you don't ever want to escape.

'Should we order a digestif?' I ask after all trace of dinner has been cleared away.

'You are a terrible influence.'

'Says the man in the middle of a story about sleeping with his best friend's mom.'

'I was eighteen. I didn't know any better.'

'You regretted it after then?'

'Not for a second! Wait until I tell you about the time I faked a heart attack to get out of a date!' He attempts to attract our waiter's attention.

I try to laugh, but it emerges thin and wan. I take a gulp of water, trying to douse the flame of a memory that could easily derail the evening.

'Are you okay?'

'It's nothing. Bit too much booze maybe.' I drink some more water, trying to be okay, but once the memory has popped up it won't be suppressed so easily.

'Cath, what is it?'

I look at his concerned face, uncertain whether this is a conversation I want to be having. But if not with Dan, then who?

'You know how you remember exactly where you were when really significant events happen, like watching the Twin Towers falling?'

'Yep.'

'The moment I heard Gaz had died I was dressed as an

282

avocado, being shouted at by a homeless drunk. I used to say it's what he would have wanted. He'd had a heart attack.'

Dan looks confused and apologetic all at the same time.

'We were going to a fancy dress party and Gaz was playing football and meeting us there. Then my phone rings and it's one of the football lads and for some reason I immediately know something has happened, but he can't get the words out. And all the while there's this drunk shouting at us. And I'm saying "calm down, calm down", to both of them probably, but it's like my insides have been scooped out and they'll never go back the same way.'

'I had no idea. I should have asked sooner, but I figured you'd tell me when you were ready. I'm sorry. I didn't know that's how he died.'

'Don't feel bad, I'm aware that I talk *to* him more than I talk *about* him. The alternative has always seemed too much of an admission that he's not here to defend himself, that he's really gone, if that makes sense.'

'Kind of.'

'And it wasn't what you said, it's what it reminded me of. I feel guilty about having a nice time when he doesn't get to.'

'Does that happen often?'

'Coco Chanel put it best. She said, "Guilt is perhaps the most painful companion of death."'

'I totally get that.'

'That, and always having to be the one to clear the hairs out of the plughole.'

Dan laughs, and I feel better, grateful I've stepped back from the cliff edge of mawkish melancholy.

'So how did you cope? How do you cope?'

He's the first person to ever ask me that specific question, so I tell him how at first I didn't. The stress of sudden bereavement eats away at your self-protection. The notion of dying of a broken heart is not mere romantic cliché, losing a partner has profound physiological effects, even causing the white blood cells on which you rely to fight infection to renege on their responsibilities, making you more prone to illnesses they would otherwise have held at bay. On the outside I was functioning, going through the motions of daily life, helping Eric and Leanne navigate their feelings as best I could, but inside I was bereft. No one warns you about the cognitive impact of loss either. The days spent forgetting everything from the mundane, such as where you put the car keys, to the crucial, such as what your loved one looked like when they were happy. I couldn't focus. Television held no interest; books, once so precious, were lost to me. How could I take any interest in the workings of someone else's imagination when my own was entirely absorbed with thoughts of what ifs and maybes. When I realised my periods had stopped, I assumed it was just another physical side-effect of grief, and that the paunch I developed was a result of all the microwaveable meals we were eating because I couldn't countenance the idea of doing anything as normal as cooking. When the pregnancy test told otherwise, I was lost in a new fog of grief and uncertainty.

'Did you ever consider not going through with it?'

'Absolutely,' I say, hoping he won't judge me. 'How was I going to cope? How could I summon up the enthusiasm for life when I felt dead inside? How could I coo and play peekaboo with a brand-new baby when every inch of me wanted to curl up and pretend that it, and everything else around me, didn't exist?

'So, what changed?' asks Dan.

'A bird crapped on me.'

Dan snorts with laughter and then instantly apologises for doing so.

'No, it was funny. I was out on a walk, trying to ease the pain in my back, and then whoof, all over me. It was such a brilliant metaphor for my situation, I couldn't help but see the funny side.'

'And that's when you realised you could still laugh?'

'Kind of. But it was more than that. It was more what it represented. I found the sheer unlikelihood of it comforting somehow. That that particular bird had been in the exact right position, that I had been on the trajectory I was, that I had been ambling at the velocity I had, in the direction I'd taken. And I thought, yes, everything is awful right now, but there are an infinite number of possibilities out there, and at some point fortune will gift us with something unexpected that won't be shit, literal or otherwise, and things will be better, even if only for a bit. It wasn't much of a revelation, but I suppose I was reminded to stay open to that possibility.'

Dan raises his empty glass to mine and we chink them together. Our waiter appears and asks us if we want a top-up.

'I could do with some fresh air, actually,' I tell Dan.

'Let's take a walk. We can always find another bar.'

I try to pay, but Dan insists on going halves, and we head out, taking in the city at night in an easy companionable silence. After ten minutes or so, we pass through a small square where a couple of teenagers on skateboards are attempting some tricks.

'I can do that,' Dan says.

'Why does that not surprise me?'

At the end of the square, lit up in the warm glow of Victorian-style streetlamps, lies the slim frontage of a tiny pub bedecked in vibrant hanging baskets. It beckons us in. Dan opens the door to a softly lit, welcoming little snug where there are three tables, each made more private by being flanked by two high-backed church pews. One is unoccupied.

'What's yours?' asks Dan.

'A port.'

He returns to the table with a small glass for me and a pint of the pub's own bitter that the barman talked up about being brewed on the premises. He tells me he's never had bitter before and takes a sip.

'Oh my god, that's horrible.' His face crumples so violently it could have been struck with an invisible implement. 'Why would anyone drink that? To control their alcohol intake?'

'You should get some lemonade in it, you lightweight!'

'No, I'm going to persist.' He takes another sip and grimaces. 'Hmm. Lovely.'

I laugh. 'I'm going to the bathroom. Feel free to swap it for a weak lager whilst I'm gone.'

When I return, he's absent-mindedly fiddling with a beer mat.

'Can I ask you a question?' he says. 'And I want you to be honest with me.'

'Sure. Fire away.' I've no idea what's coming next.

'Do you think I'm immature?'

I laugh. 'You generally think shirt buttons are for ornamental purposes!'

But I can see he wants a proper answer.

Do I? When we first met, I thought he was the epitome of an overgrown teenager, now I'm not so sure. 'I don't think you take life very seriously,' I say eventually, 'but I'm coming round to the idea that's a good thing.'

'My dad thought it was a very bad thing. He was always on at me to grow up and be more mature. *Take responsibility. Stop being such a child.*' He fiddles some more with the beer mat.

'What does he do?'

'*Did*. He was a corporate lawyer. As was his father before him. I was an only child who refused to follow in the family footsteps. He hated me for it.'

'You rebelled?'

'In short.'

He tells me about how he decided to take a year out of college, got into crypto, set up his online course and then went travelling to escape his father's disapproval.

'But then one year turned into two. Two into four. And before I knew it, staying away seemed like the only option to escape becoming him.'

'But you've enjoyed yourself, right?'

'Oh, I've enjoyed myself. Sometimes a little too much maybe.' He gives a wry smile. 'The trouble is the whole thing became a self-fulfilling prophecy. Any return to *normality*, as my dad called it, would have meant admitting that he'd been right. Everyone must grow up eventually.'

'So why the degree? What changed?'

'He had an aneurism.'

He tells me how his dad had fallen gravely ill on the golf course, but Dan had been in Sedona on a retreat where everyone's phones had been confiscated.

'That's such bad luck.'

'We hadn't spoken for months,' he tears the beer mat in two. 'Mom couldn't get hold of me. He lived for six days. She reckons he held on as long as he did because he wanted to talk to me, in so much as he'd have been able. He kept on saying my name over and over.'

His eyes well up with tears. This is the first time I've seen him upset and I instinctively slide my hand over the table and take hold of his.

'Sorry,' he says.

'It's fine.'

'I went back for the funeral, and it was such a shock. So many family members, who I'd assumed were living these miserable little corporate existences but actually weren't at all.'

He tells me about a cousin who designs tiny houses, an uncle who creates superhero-inspired mechanical hands for kids who've been born disabled.

'Even my dad had been spending less time at work and more on a boat he'd bought.'

I squeeze his hand.

'I'd got it all wrong. I'd spent too long trying *not* to be someone I assumed others wanted me to be. I went away with the idea of finding myself, but what I should have been doing all along was learning to live with myself.'

His leg jiggles under the table.

'Anyway, rightly or wrongly, it was important to my dad that I get a degree and I decided I'd live a little more easily with myself if I did. And if I could squeeze in a little adventure by coming to England, then even better.'

'And then you found yourself with Birmingham's answer to *The Brady Bunch* wondering what the bloody hell had happened!'

We're definitely drunk; the conversation meanders, trains of thought going every which way.

'It's funny,' Dan says. 'I've always had this fear of missing out. On fun. On experiences. Places. People. But there are two sides to that coin. I've also missed out on the kind of thing that you and Gaz had, that my parents had, however flawed it might have been. I've never had kids. I've never had someone rely on me, never understood the pleasure there is to be had being in someone else's service.'

'But you've helped us. Me.'

He fixes me in his gaze and my insides liquify.

'I know,' he says. 'That's how I know how joyous it can be.'

We're still touching. He brushes his thumb over the back of my hand.

'I'm very glad to have met you, Catherine Beckinsale. It's been far more enjoyable than I could have imagined.'

If this was a romantic movie, this would probably be the bit where the leading man leans across the table and gives the leading lady a kiss. Where their lips lock and the outside world blurs, the camera capturing the moment from a number of different angles. But this is no movie, and I'm no leading lady, so this is the bit where the bar bell rings really bloody loudly for last orders and I end up giving him a vigorous handshake instead.

'It's been really nice to meet you too,' I tell him, grimacing internally, and probably all over my face.

He chuckles. 'Do you want another one?'

I'd love to stay here all night and talk some more, but there's a shred of a sensible person left in this almost devoid-of-sobriety body, and we have to do this all again tomorrow for Geoff's seventieth. 'We should probably head back.'

When we get outside, the balmy air hits me like a gentle punch.

'Which direction?' I ask, completely unable to get my bearings.

'This way,' says Dan, heading off across the square with absolute certainty.

I catch up, but within a few hundred metres there's a stinging in my heel. 'Hang on. I think I've got a blister.' I take my shoe off to check and sure enough, there's a small patch of raw flesh on my heel.

Dan walks back and crouches down with his back to me. 'Come on, I'll carry you.'

'You can't give me a piggyback. I'm nearly forty!'

'You're right,' he says, standing up and turning round. 'Fireman's lift it is.' He throws me over his shoulder and marches on as I shriek for him to put me down, the food and booze sloshing in my belly. He doesn't stop when we get to the hotel, striding through reception and into the lift.

'I'll be fine now.' The extra plane of movement combined with the blood rushing to my head is making me double dizzy.

'No, ma'am. I'll see you safely back to your room.' He steps out onto my floor. 'What number?'

'One hundred and twelve.'

He turns and nearly bangs my head against a wall. 'Whoops, sorry!'

We get to my door where he insists on taking my key card from my dangling bag, opening the door, turning on a side light and depositing me prostrate on the bed. I flip myself over.

'Why, thank you.' I'm almost winded with laughter.

'My pleasure.' He salutes. 'Although I think I've given myself a hernia.' He falls next to me in mock exhaustion.

We lie for a few moments, catching our breath, then he turns towards me. I twist to face him, ready to say goodnight as he gets up to leave, only he doesn't get up. Instead he looks like he's trying to make his mind up about something and before I can calculate what's happening, he leans across and kisses me. A light, delicate kiss at first, a brush of his lips against mine and I wonder what's the punchline to this going to be? But he doesn't pull away or say anything, he keeps on caressing my lips with his until I raise my head off the bed to meet the pressure of his mouth, gently pushing my tongue between his lips, a small admission of desire that, up until now, I couldn't fully admit I felt. He sighs, a warm expulsion of air against my face, and pulls me towards him, his arms around my shoulders, then my back, then the curve of my bottom, before moving down to pull at the fabric of my dress. I pluck at his shirt, my nervous fingers worrying at the buttons until he takes over, removing his tie and slowly unveiling the smoothness of his chest, the undulations of his stomach muscles, the barely-there line of hair that runs from his belly to his groin and the tell-tale swell in his jeans. For a second I think, *I can't do this.* I can't lay myself bare for his appraisal or unveil my imperfect body and not be crushed by the weight of his scrutiny upon me. But then he snakes his hand up my skirt, presses his fingers against my aching vulva, and my clitoris tells my brain to hold her beer; she's going to take it from here.

Chapter Thirty-Six

When I awake, there's a creeping sense of paranoia already worrying at the edges of my psyche. I ask my brain to kindly fill me in on the details that my consciousness is glossing over, rather than simply making me aware of how much my head hurts. And like any morning after the night before, my brain tells me to go screw myself, having disowned me for wilfully destroying so many of its cells in the name of giving the rest of me a good time.

I open my eyes as best I can, but the lashes of one resist the movement. I didn't take my make-up off last night. Using my mono vision, I see I'm in my hotel room, so that's a good start, although I can't recall anything about the journey from the restaurant to the hotel. Did we come straight back after dinner? I'm also naked, which means I was compos mentis enough to remove my clothes, but too far gone to bother putting my pyjamas on. Seems about right. And judging by the tightness behind my eyes, the throbbing in my temples, and the unwillingness of my head to move so much as a muscle, I went past my upper limit of booze last night. And I definitely didn't drink any water. As I ponder on my alcohol-related powers of deduction, I imagine how great it would be to be Sherlock Holmes and simply wander through my mind palace to locate the information I need rather than piece it together from the shreds of flashback to which I'm occasionally granted access. There's a bottle of sparkling water in the mini bar though, so I ever-so-slowly roll onto my side, hoping that by doing so I might be able to trick my inner ear into not registering the movement, thus saving me the added ignominy of nausea as well as pain.

'Where are you going?' a voice sleepily mutters as a pair of strong arms pull me back into the middle of the bed.

Oh.

My.

God.

Oh yeah, says the grey matter, tutting far too loudly, *I forgot to mention that happened.*

Dan wraps his arms around me and snuggles into my neck. 'You don't have to go yet, do you?'

What.

The.

Actual.

F*ck.

I'm in bed with Dan and I'm naked. Even my addled head can put two and two together and come up with sex. And what's he saying about go yet? Go where? The cogs slowly crank and whirr. Shitting hell, I have a meeting with those influencer people this morning. I'm trying to process the magnitude of having to get up and go and deal with that, when another part of my psyche politely coughs and informs me that Dan is stroking one of my boobs whilst pressing an erect penis into the small of my back.

'Not now,' I tell it, but I say the words out loud and Dan shrinks away from me.

'Sorry,' he says. 'I thought…'

'Oh, god, no, it's not you,' I say quickly, meaning that it's not you I'm talking to, it's my own consciousness, but the instant the words come out I'm aware it sounds like I'm about to give him the 'it's not you, it's me' speech. Ugh, I'm too hungover to be alive, let alone interacting with someone on whose genitals I sat last night.

'It's fine if you don't want to,' Dan says.

Do I want to? My mind's eye offers up more details of the evening. There was clearly a bit of me up for it last night. The front bottom bit, mainly. I turn to face him. I must look terrible.

'I must look terrible.' I worry at the knots in the back of my hair with one hand as I wipe mascara from under my eyes with the other.

'It's a good look. Very Chrissie Hynde.'

'Chrissie Hynde in the seventies? I'll take that.'

'No, Chrissie Hynde now she's in her seventies.'

I pick up a pillow and hit him square in the face. I have just playfully hit a man I'm trying to convince myself I don't fancy. Classic school crush behaviour.

'Ouch,' he says. 'That is below the belt. This, by contrast, is now officially back above the belt.' He motions to his crotch area. 'Never start a pillow fight with a naked man.'

'I'll remember that.' I'm unable to resist casting a quick glance at his nether regions which are as unapologetically attractive as the rest of him. I pick up another pillow and throw it at his groin, achingly embarrassed to be in bed with him, hugely disconcerted to see the physical manifestation of his desire whilst at the same time mentally yelling, 'Look, I did that!' like a bunch of cheerleaders should break into the room and hand me a dick-arousing award.

'Oh my, it's not that bad, is it?' He laughs as I fall back onto the bed, burrowing further into a pillow as if I might be able to hide in its downy softness. Dan strokes the back of my head. 'You seemed to be quite fond of him last night.'

I scream into the feathers. 'Stop it! I'm blushing.'

'What? Let me see.' He prises the pillow away from me. 'You look cute when you blush.' He bends towards me and kisses me on the lips, his flushed face framed by his curls as he does so.

'My mouth will taste horrible.' I'm stalling for time.

He smiles mischievously, seeing through the ruse. 'Well, allow me to find a bit that tastes nice.' He shifts his gaze down my body.

I let my head fall back onto the pillow. Do I have feelings for Dan? I mean, I know I have feelings for him, but they're friendly, 'buddy, I really enjoy your company' feelings. Not *feelings*.

'What about this bit?' He kisses my neck. 'Or this bit?' He brushes his lips over my breast. 'Or this bit?' He licks a nipple. 'Or this bit?' He kisses a stretchmark on my belly. I watch him go, wanting to shout out that there's been some mistake, because men like him don't do sex with women like me. I have a body like a golf course, full of unexpected undulations and tricky bunkers and … oh my god, he's pitched it in the rough. I look down and see Dan looking back up at me from between my legs with those cheeky eyes, studying my reaction as he gently presses his tongue into me.

Fingertips of desire tighten their grip on me. As with a magnet in a coil, the electrical charge increases with every movement of his tongue inside me. I try to abandon myself to it. *Don't think too much about it, Cath. Just go with it.* Yet hadn't there been a point last night where I'd considered what it would be like to kiss him? Where I'd felt more like myself in his company than I had out of it? But there's the quiet whisper of guilt again, the notion that even by having these thoughts I have somehow betrayed Gaz, acting as an equal and opposite force determined to cancel out my desire.

'Stop,' I say to the ceiling.

'What you don't enjoy that now either?' he asks, looking up with a smile on his face which disappears as soon as he sees mine. 'Oh, you mean stop. Is everything alright?'

'I can't do this. I'm sorry.'

'That's okay.'

I sense a rising panic, a need to explain myself, but the words don't come in an order that make any sense.

'It's just that … last night I was drunk and I didn't realise that … I mean it's been such a long time and … I wouldn't normally…'

Tell him you're confused, Cath.

'You see the thing is…'

'Hey, it's okay.' He climbs off the bed and grabs his shirt from the floor. 'I get it.' But he looks a lot like a man who isn't getting it.

'No, you don't. Look at me for a second, would you?'

But he won't, he continues to grab at his strewn clothing.

'Dan, I'm sorry, I didn't mean anything by it… I was

thinking about Gaz and the fact that ... well I've never, you know, with anyone else and ... then I got a bit antsy because, well, you're the lodger and because...'

For a second I imagine he looks wounded, that perhaps it's not his ego but his feelings I've hurt, but then he slips his shirt over his head, and by the time his face reappears it's set in a look I can't interpret.

'No need to give me the big speech,' he says. 'It was just sex.'

Of course, it was. Of course, it was just sex. What else would it be? He was drunk. I was drunk. This is probably how every dinner date with Dan ends for him. And now I'm another notch on a bedpost that has been whittled down so much it must be in danger of collapsing. As if my brain isn't buzzing enough, my mobile phone joins in on the act, only I can't see where it is. I pull a sheet around me and make a big deal of looking for it. At least that way he won't be able to tell that, for a moment there, I think I wanted this to have meant something more to him than it did. I pick up various bits of clothing, searching for the source of the vibration.

'It's there.' He points to the floor near the desk. 'Cath, what I meant to say was...'

'Oh yeah!' I'm trying to sound chipper. I pick up the phone. 'I'd lose my head if it wasn't screwed on!' On the screen there's a number I don't recognise. Great, now some cold caller wants in on the drama. I answer it regardless. I'll take being told I've been in an accident that wasn't my fault over this humiliation.

'Miss?'

I recognise that voice.

'Harpal?' Of course, today's the day of the first science

exam. I was meant to call them this morning. Unsurprisingly I forgot to set an alarm.

'Reggie's not turned up and he's not answering his phone.'

'What the … how long before you need to go in?'

'Two minutes. What should we do?'

I look out of the window, at the great sprawling city, stomach sinking. 'I'm in London. Have you got his home number?'

'No, Miss.'

'Do you know his mom's name? I might be able to find her on…'

'Hang on, they're calling us. I've gotta hand my phone in.'

Oh no, Reggie. No. 'Text me after if he shows, okay?'

'Will do.'

'And good luck,' I shout after him, but the call has already ended.

'What's wrong?' asks Dan.

'Reggie's not turned up for his science exam.'

'Why would he not show?'

'I know he was acting up the last time we saw him, but I didn't expect this.' Why didn't I try harder to get hold of him?

'Has he tried to contact you?'

I quickly check all logs on my phone and across social. Nothing. I bring up his number, try the line, but it goes to voicemail. I send him a WhatsApp message, urging him to call, but he was last on the app over two days ago. Weird. I cast around in my head, seeking out inspiration on what to do, but none is forthcoming. If I was back home, I could try and find him, but I'd probably be as helpless there as I am here. I pull the sheet tighter round me.

'What time is it?' I ask.

'Nearly ten.'

Shit. I've got to be at the agency soon. 'I need to have a shower and clear my head. I'll have to deal with this when I get back.'

'I should leave you to it.' Dan picks up his shoes and makes for the door, but then stops. 'Do you still want me to meet you at lunchtime? The train's at two isn't it?'

No, Dan. I don't want you to. In fact, the last thing I want to do is to be on a train with you for two hours this afternoon in the knowledge that last night I stupidly became another one of your bloody conquests. 'Of course. I'll see you then.'

'Good luck today. If it's what you want, you deserve it.' He leaves the room and as soon as the door swings shut behind him, I fall back onto the bed.

What does he mean *'If it's what I want'*? Hadn't we celebrated it all last night? Never mind. I'm not in the right head space to worry about it. I really want to curl into a ball and sleep for several hours, but instead I need to stay upright long enough to get ready and meet Alex. Bleurgh.

By the time I get to Foster Management's offices which is luckily not far from either the hotel or Marylebone Station, the full force of my hangover has kicked in, along with the realisation that around fourteen more hours of it stretch before me until I can crawl into bed. At one point on the way here I feared I might die, but then the pain in my head got even worse and now I fear I might *not* die. Fourteen hours. 840 minutes. 50,400 seconds tick tick ticking away like a woodpecker headbutting my brain. The equivalent of doing a full day's work, plus sitting through *Lawrence of Arabia*, plus running a marathon, plus watching a school nativity play. Twice.

I head into the building, a stark grey concrete box with jutting angles and asymmetric glass windows. Inside is far less Eastern Bloc and far more hipster cake shop, with pastel velvet couches and cutesy pictures on the walls. I'm greeted by a woman wearing a tight high-waisted pencil skirt, Breton top and bright red ankle boots, hair casually flung up in a top knot across which sits a headset. I consider my own faded black jeans, grey sweatshirt and scuffed canvas pumps, the rubber of which has begun to come away from the fabric.

'Hi, welcome to Foster Management. I'm Jocelyn. How may I help you today?'

She is far too bouncy. 'I'm here to see Alex.'

'Is it Science Mom?'

More like Screwed Mom, although probably the wrong choice of words given what happened last night. 'Yep,' I tell her.

'I'm really sorry, Alex has had some major trauma on one of the campaigns that went live this morning and he won't be in until this afternoon. He was hoping you might be able to rearrange for after lunch?'

'What time?'

'Around two?'

I do a quick mental calculation, which is hard with my head in its current state. Assuming the meeting takes an hour, I would still be on a train by four and back by six. And this way I get to eat my own bodyweight in carbs beforehand, which means I might be up for the party later. 'That should be fine.'

Back out on the street the smell of car fumes makes me feel

sick, so I find the nearest park on the map (Regent's) and head for it. I pick up two breakfast croissants, a green juice, some water and a growing sense of anxiety en route. It's already super warm again, so I find the shade of a large oak tree and check my phone, half-expecting to see a message from Reggie, half-hoping to see a message from Dan. There are neither. I eat my way through my food mountain, which takes the edge off the hangover, but not the cloud of angst gathering overhead. I decide the best way to deal with this is to ignore it completely for now and get some sleep. It'll all look better after some self-care.

I awake sometime later, the pounding in my head having receded a little, overtaken by the grumbling in my stomach and an overwhelming need to find even more food. The sun is directly overhead, which means it must be close to lunch time. Which is meeting Dan time. I check my phone again and sure enough there's a text saying he's heading to Marylebone on the tube and will message when he's back above ground. No smiley faces, no kiss, no clue whatsoever as to what he's been up to this morning and whether we're going to talk about this or not. That was over half an hour ago, which means he can't be that far away, so I text him to meet me at the Pret near the concourse and, with leaden feet, head in that direction.

As I approach the door, two things strike me: the first is a sweet blast of icy air-conditioned air escaping from within; the second is the door itself, because some guy in pinstripes holding his phone like it's a Pop Tart biscuit he's about to eat, opens it onto my face.

'Owwwww! Look where you're going, douchebag.'

He's so engrossed in his call he doesn't even register what's happened and he strides away, probably back to a role as some high paid city wanker.

I rub my stinging nose and come up with fingers full of blood. Brilliant. I head into the shop, grab a handful of napkins from the condiment counter, and try to stem the flow. Seemingly a grown woman with a nosebleed in the middle of the day is an everyday occurrence around here, because no one bats an eyelid. No one, that is, until Dan comes through the door, spots me, and rushes towards me.

'Jesus, what happened?'

Some mice wearing very heavy clogs run around in my tummy.

'It's only a nosebleed.' I keep the tissue on my face so I don't have to look at him properly, or think about what he was about to do to me this morning.

'Are you okay?'

'I'm fine.'

'Here, sit down.' He steers me over to a table. 'Tip your head forward.'

He places a hand on my nape with such exquisite gentleness my whole body tingles. For several minutes we concentrate only on stemming the flow, but then the blood stops and we have to say something to one another.

'Should we grab something for the train or eat now?' he says.

Hardly the deep and meaningful discussion starter I was hoping for. Is he literally not going to mention what happened? Okay, two can play that game.

'Actually, I'm going to have to stay here a bit longer.' I explain about Alex running late.

'What about the party?'

'It's not until six-thirty. I'll get the next train.'

'You're cutting it a bit fine.'

'It can't be helped.'

It could be helped, but, frankly, I'm grateful for the excuse not to be on a train with him. We'd probably talk about the weather FFS.

'What about the kids?' Dan asks.

'Leanne should be arriving soon. I'll text her and ask her to pick them up.'

'Couldn't you ask this Alex to meet you another time? Everyone's expecting you.'

I'm irritated by the way he says *this Alex*, like he's already formed a negative opinion about him. Fair enough, I might have formed a slightly negative opinion about him too, but I've met him so I'm entitled to do so.

'Oh yeah, I'll tell him to hold off on this great opportunity because I'm going to be a few minutes late for a party, shall I?'

'It's only promoting fridges, Cath.'

There's an unexpected flare of anger in my chest. How dare he be so condescending? 'Do you know what, Dan? I'm sick and tired of doing what's expected of me or pussyfooting around people who can't deal with me having a life of my own. Why shouldn't I put what I want first? Would that be so terrible?'

He looks bewildered by this sudden outburst. I chew the inside of my mouth, conscious we must look quite the pair, having a stupid tiff in full view of everyone. 'FUUUUCK,' I want to shout. 'HOW CAN YOU BE SO COMPLETELY INTIMATE WITH SOMEONE ONE SECOND AND THEN NOT BE ABLE TO EVEN SPEAK TO THEM PROPERLY THE NEXT?'

'Only last night you said I should go for it!' I'm trying to be more conciliatory.

'That was when I thought...' he trails off.

'Thought what?'

He looks down at the crimson-stained napkins in his hands. I want to tear them from his grip and throw them across the room screaming, 'THOUGHT WHAT? WHAT IS GOING ON IN YOUR HEAD RIGHT NOW?'

'Did you hear from Reggie?' he asks eventually.

'No. Reggie has not been in touch. Turns out he's another in a long line of stupid kids prepared to give up when the going gets tough.'

'I know you're disappointed, but don't write him off so easily.'

'Why not? His life isn't perfect, but who doesn't have a decent excuse for messing up their life if they so choose? You've got to move on.'

'Like you have?'

His face is so unreadable, I can't tell if he's being genuine or spiteful. My negativity bias opts for the latter and there's a resurgence of the rage I felt before.

'Yeah, like I have. I set out to do something worthwhile and I did it. You should try it some time. Or you could stay a teenager for the rest of your life. I'm sure your dad would be so proud.'

Even as the words tumble from my lips, I want to scoop them up and take them back. To tell him that really I'm just confused and hurt and frustrated, that we slept together, that Reggie could throw all his hard work away, that everyone close to me seems to resent me. But I don't, because I want him to be hurt too.

Dan grabs his jacket from the seat beside him and lifts his bag up onto his shoulder. 'Funny, up until now, I thought I *was* doing something worthwhile.' And then he is gone, the bluntness of his statement hanging in the air, along with the certain knowledge that things won't be the same between us after today.

Chapter Thirty-Seven

I stride back to the management agency, blood intermittently boiling at him being so patronising, and running cold at what I said in return. At least I have this meeting to take my mind off things and ensure this London trip isn't a total disaster. Only Alex still isn't back, and for a further hour the receptionist makes inane chit-chat whilst I wish I could think about what has happened. Unsurprisingly, my hangover comes back with a vengeance. It's like my brain has cottoned on to the calamity it's caused and is trying to make a quick exit through the back of my skull.

Then Leanne calls. 'Where the hell are you?'

Uh-oh. I didn't text her or Geoff that I was going to be late coming back.

'There's been a hold up. I'm meeting someone from an Influencer Agency.' I'm trying to sound chirpy, as though absolutely nothing untoward has gone on and everything is under control.

'I don't care if you're meeting the Avengers! At least Dan had the courtesy to call to let us know what was happening.'

I flinch at the mention of his name. Everything in the shame and remorse department is functioning correctly.

'Oh.' If I say anything more it would probably scream, 'WE HAD SEX', and I don't want anyone to know how stupid I've been. Instead, I tell Leanne I'll be there in time for the party, I'll just have to come straight from the station.

'You better had, mom. You know Sheila's been planning this for months.'

'Don't I just? She's spoken of nothing else. Oh, hang on, apart from when she's talking about conversing with the dead and the fairies who live in her garden.'

'I don't understand why you're being so mean.'

I don't either because right now, Sheila is the least of my niggles. 'Are the kids okay?'

'They're fine. Hurry up, okay?'

I check the clock again. Five minutes past three. I am on the wrong side of an already tight timeline now, but there's a train at four-fifteen that will get me in at six, giving me half an hour to get to the party by cab. That's plenty of time. I'll set off as soon as we're done here and change into last night's outfit enroute.

About fifteen minutes later Alex appears, wearing an identical outfit to yesterday, but in different colours, and this time sporting a straw hat. He ushers me through the building into a large boardroom that has done away with a standard table and chairs and opted instead for a huge teepee. For the love of God!

'This was my idea,' says Alex.

That figures.

SAL THOMAS

We're joined by someone called James who looks a lot like Alex, only his glasses are round and clear plastic and, despite the roaring temperature outside, is wearing a beanie. He's sat cross-legged with a laptop resting on his calves. I should probably be relieved they've not gone the whole cultural appropriation hog and sported Indian headdresses.

'So, Science Mom,' says Alex. 'How are you?'

'Never better.' By which I mean things will never be better. 'I'm hungover to hell and up until two hours ago I was asleep in a park.'

'What did I tell you James? Uber real, right?'

James offers the briefest of smiles then goes back to banging away loudly on his keyboard. Are his fingers made of lead or something?

'Sorry about this morning. Ran into difficulties with a client. Behaviour not really becoming of a brand ambassador for a clean eating brand, if you know what I mean?'

'I've no idea what you mean.'

'Hah. Funny, funny. Right, we should get down to it. But first, do you want a coffee?'

Is he going to send a smoke signal up for it?

'Yes. Two please.'

He calls someone on his mobile. 'Hey, can we get a coffee with two sugars?'

'No, can I have two coffees please?' I say.

'Love it!' He orders me a coffee with two sugars.

I want to tell him it's not an act, I'm in all manner of trouble over here.

'We haven't been doing nothing this morning, though,' Alex continues. 'James has been going over your channels and crunching some numbers.'

James nods.

'And it's all amazing, honestly, but there's just one thing. A lot of it's—how would you say— dry.'

'Dry how?'

'You know, a bit curriculum-based.'

'That's the look I was going for.'

'I see that, and I totally get why that would be a thing. But if you really want to attract brands, you could do with losing some of the straighter stuff and erring more on the edutainment side of things.'

That bloody word again.

'I'm not sure I follow.'

'You know, the little experiments with your son, that resonates really well, the goofy stuff where you sing or break things by accident, the bits where your partner makes an appearance.'

He's not my partner. He's not even my friend right now.

'Good engagement there with an older demographic. The more straightforward teachery bits, less so.'

'That's because they're there to educate, not engage.'

'No, and they do that brilliantly. Didn't I say that, James?'

James nods sagely, channelling his inner Sitting Bull.

'But you can't sell stuff to fifteen-year-old school kids,' says Alex.

'Eh? What about trainers? And makeup? And fake news?'

Alex nods. 'I know all that. I mean you. You can't sell stuff to teenagers.'

Ouch. 'But I started this because I wanted to teach kids science.'

'There's nothing stopping you sticking to the day job.'

I don't tell him that there is no day job.

'Listen, I can tell that's not what you wanted to hear. It's not that you'd have to ditch the science stuff completely. But we'd need a lot more emphasis on the lifestyle piece.'

My soul dies a little. 'Wouldn't that make me exactly like everyone else?'

'Not at all. It would still be you, but a slightly different version of you; the version of you that the older audience with a disposable income are telling us they want to hear more from. The numbers don't lie, do they, James?'

James shakes his head.

'Don't forget, GCSEs are almost over for another year, there's a whole summer where you could give it a go and see what happens, yeah? Maybe try sharing some outfits—not this one obviously—and you know, talk about your feelings a bit more.'

I attempt to think through the implications of what he's asking me to do, but someone has cracked my head open and is trying to play tom toms on my pre-frontal cortex. Then my phone rings adding to the cacophony. It's Leanne again. I drop the call; I don't need her giving me more grief.

'We can give you some guidance, can't we, James?'

James nods.

'Why don't you have a think about it? You don't have to decide anything immediately, speak to some of our other clients if you like, see what they say.'

'And if I want to keep things as they were?' Like anything involving Dan is going to go back to the way things were.

'You need to decide what you want out of this. Fame and fortune, or the feel-good factor. It's a cut-throat business. Only the hungriest survive.'

I don't point out that generally it's the hungriest who die.

'Okay.'

'Okay, we'll go ahead?'

'No. I mean, okay, I'll think about it.'

My phone rings. Leanne again. I put it on silent.

'Cool. Cool, cool, cool. Don't take too long though, yeah? Things move on quickly in this world, don't they, James?'

James nods. I so badly wish there was a campfire in here so I could kick some embers into his face, just to see him emote in some way. Probably time to leave.

Half an hour into the journey back and I've racked up two more calls from Leanne. She can relax. I'm going to be on time for the party, although I'm not sure I can face the horror of going. *Hey everyone, here's Cath. So let me get this straight, you're not a teacher, and you're not an influencer. What exactly do you do? Oh, you're a MASSIVE FAILURE at everything in life. And you recently slept with your one source of income. Nice!* My phone rings again, only this time it's Sindy calling. This is a different plan of attack. Mind you, if I'm going to see her later, I should bite the bullet and talk to her now. I take the call.

'It's Sindy.'

'I know. Sind, I'm so sor—'

'Where are you?'

'I'm on the train. I'll be there soon. Listen, I've been such a—'

'Geoff's collapsed. We think he's had a heart attack.'

I try to say something, but my mouth won't work. Where the words should be, there's a horrible metallic taste.

'We've been trying to get hold of you for ages. Why didn't you answer?'

'I'm sorry. I assumed—'

Oh God. Not this again. Not now. Not Geoff.

'We're at the Queen Elizabeth,' says Sindy. 'He came in by ambulance. We're waiting to find out more.'

I gulp in air, trying to stem the panic about to consume me. The woman sat opposite does her best to ignore me, until a huge uncontrollable sob escapes my mouth and leaves her with no choice but to look up.

'Where are the kids? Oh my god, was Eric there? Did he see it? Can I speak to him?'

'Stay calm. Everyone's here. Everyone's safe. How far away are you?'

'About ninety minutes.' Why did I go to that stupid meeting? I could have been home already.

'Okay. Get here as soon as you can, okay? We're in A&E.'

'Call me if you hear anything.'

'I will.'

She hangs up. I close my eyes and try to get my breath back under control. I need to hold it together. I need to get home. I watch my phone, waiting for an update to tell me everything's okay. It was a severe angina attack, right, coupled with the excitement of the birthday party? Or Sheila over-reacting, telling everyone it was more serious than it was and insisting he go to hospital to satisfy her own anxieties. I write a text to Leanne, the words spewing across the screen, different variations of sorrys and stupids and I've let you downs, but then I remember that this isn't about me, and I delete them all to a simple any news? I hear nothing. I tell myself the text from Geoff himself, the one in which he says it's all been a big fuss over nothing, is out there somewhere, struggling to find my phone as this Faraday Cage of a train carriage, hurtling across the South-East at one hundred and twenty-five miles per hour, blocks out the electromagnetic waves required to deliver it so I can just, stop, panicking.

But then another text comes through. The one that says he's in a coma. That it's 'touch and go', three words that sound more like a playground game than the report that someone's life is hanging in the balance. I focus on the rhythmic sounds of the train as it passes over the track, but I can't stop my mind from wandering. As countryside whips past outside the window, the dread rises again, and I have the sense that the train is a metaphor for my life, out of control, running away unchecked, and it's only a matter of time before we hit the buffers and everything comes crashing in.

Chapter Thirty-Eight

I enter the ICU's family room where Leanne, Dan and the kids have gathered to await further news. I've come from Geoff's bedside where I left Sheila fussing over him, his body completely lifeless but for the rise and fall of his ventilated lungs. His condition is more serious than I dared imagine.

'You finally made it, then?' says Leanne.

I haven't seen my daughter for over two months, and my instinct is to throw my arms around her, but she's not ready. She scoops up Jack so I beckon to Eric, but he stays put, eyeing me defiantly.

'I'm so sorry. If I'd have known...'

'You should have been here,' says Eric.

'I know, honey, I know.'

'I told you I didn't want to stay there.' He drops his head, blinking away tears that fall onto his shoes and the scuffed lino floor.

So that's why he was so resistant to staying at Geoff's; he must have been worrying about him ever since we found out he was poorly. 'Oh Eric. I had no idea this was what was running through your head. I'm here now.'

'Until the next time you have to run off.'

'I know you're angry with me, but nowhere near as angry as I am with myself.' I inadvertently look up at Dan, but look away quickly, my eyes blurring with tears. 'There's nothing more we can do tonight. We need to head home and get some rest so we can come back bright and early tomorrow.'

'I'm going to stay,' Leanne says. 'In case anything changes. We parked in the short stay.' I sense she won't be persuaded otherwise, and besides, Sheila will need the company.

We drive home in silence, the only noises to be heard are the creaks and metallic groans of the car every time we stop at a light. It's only when we're passing the turning for Sindy's road that I wonder why I didn't see her at the hospital.

'She went to the venue to let everyone know what was happening,' Dan tells me. 'And she mentioned things weren't right between the two of you.'

I desperately want to turn around and drive to her place and at least put one thing right in this hot mess of a situation, but I drive on, making deals in my head about how much I'm going to make it up to everyone, so long as Geoff is okay. After I get Jack to bed, I come downstairs to find Dan in the kitchen. He hands me a cup of tea.

'I believe this is meant to help you feel better,' he says.

'Only if it has Rohypnol in it.'

'Sorry, I'm all out.'

I smile weakly and sit down. Dan doesn't move. 'Are you not having one?'

'I'm going to stay at a friend's. Give you guys some space.'

'You don't need to do that.'

'I do. Leanne will be back for a while. She'll need her room.'

I take a sip of my tea. It scalds my tongue and lips, but I don't care. 'But you're the lodger. I'm contractually obliged to provide you with a bed.' I don't mean it to come out the way it does, but I see him wince over the rim of my cup. 'And you're a friend,' I say, too late.

'I've got someone coming to collect me in a few minutes. I think it's for the best.'

I nod, noncommittally, lift my legs onto the chair next to me and look across the kitchen. My gaze lands on the urn. I can't remember the last time I spoke to Gaz and the realization tugs like a stitch under my ribs.

'I've not heard you guys chatting for a while,' says Dan, echoing my thoughts.

'I fear I've been rather neglectful of a few things lately.'

I desperately want him to say something like 'you have nothing to be sorry for' and 'this isn't your fault', but he doesn't, and the silence is broken by his phone beeping.

'My ride is here. I have to go.' He walks out and the silence in the house closes in around me.

Sheila is holding Geoff's hand, whose face is surprisingly peaceful despite the cacophony of noise going on around him. Since he collapsed, Sheila's taken to sleeping on the plastic-coated chair next to his bed, her sparrow-like legs tucked up under her, her bouffant head nestled on a herbal-scented Native American dream pillow she brought in from home. The staff asked that she keep to normal visiting hours, but when they found her performing a directed energy healing ceremony on Geoff, they realised she probably wasn't to be reasoned with. There is a change in her this morning. Her usual cheery demeanour and absolute faith that Geoff is going to be okay has slipped like a tiara from a stumbling beauty queen, and this is the first time I have seen her without makeup on. She looks older and more vulnerable.

'I thought you said we could expect some change once you warmed him up,' Sheila says to the doctor who is completing his observations.

On the night he was admitted to hospital, Geoff underwent surgery to implant coronary stents to keep the arteries that supply blood to his heart open, and doctors placed him in a state of therapeutic hypothermia to reduce his brain's need for oxygen and minimise the risk of brain injury. Twenty-four hours ago they tried to bring him out of this medically induced coma, but so far he hasn't responded as hoped.

'I'm sorry,' says the doctor. 'As I mentioned before, it's very difficult to accurately predict when, or indeed if a patient will wake up post-resuscitation. And even then, there can be wildly different outcomes as far as the neurological impact incurred during arrest.'

'I don't understand what that means,' says Sheila.

'She's saying he could be brain damaged,' I tell her as gently as I can.

Sheila looks horrified, her pale thin lips forming a wrinkled circle. 'He'd never agree to that,' she says, shaking her head vehemently.

The doctor casts me a quizzical glance.

'He's a proud Yorkshireman. It'd be worse than death for him if he couldn't come back to us the way he was.' Hell, he'd be mortified enough to know he'd had a bed bath yesterday. 'All these tests. They must be telling you something.'

The doctor takes her glasses off and looks squarely at me. 'Honestly? If I had to call it, I'd say it's unlikely he's escaped cerebral ischemia.' She looks back at Sheila. 'That's brain damage due to lack of oxygen.'

'But not impossible?' I ask.

'Not impossible, no.'

'And is there anything else we should be doing to help to bring him round?'

'Talk to him. Hold his hand. Offer comfort. But please, Mrs Bird, no more of these…' the doctor doesn't finish her sentence, she merely waves her hand in the air, a world of quackery encapsulated in a single dismissive sweep of her arm. 'At least not whilst we're trying to undertake other more'—she chooses her words carefully—'pressing interventions.'

'Noted,' I tell her.

The doctor takes me by the arm and leads me away, past all the other beds and machines that beep and hum behind the pleated blue curtains separating each of the patients in intensive care, dropping her voice so only I can make out the words above the background noise.

'Be aware, in cases where the patient shows no signs of recovery within seventy-two hours of ceasing induced hypothermia, it's customary to consider withdrawal of treatment. You might consider that a blessing rather than a curse in this instance.'

I return to Geoff's cubicle with a heavy heart. Sheila is staring at her reflection in the one window we mercifully have to gaze out of.

'Look at the state of me. What must you think?' she says.

I draw the curtain behind me and place a hand on her shoulder, all former pettiness forgotten. 'I think you're a lovely woman who obviously cares about Geoff very much.'

'I do, love.' She slips back into the chair, clutching at Geoff's hand more tightly than before, the blue veins in the back of her own prominent against her taut mottled skin. 'We've not known one another long by most people's standards.' Her anchovy-paste eyes gloss with emotion. 'But we love one another, you know.'

'I know.'

'To be gifted a special friend at a time when you think loneliness will be your only companion is a wonderful thing, Cath. I reckon we made it look easier than it really is to find someone you can run along with when you're as old as we are.' She lowers her face to Geoff's hand and rubs her cheek along the back of it. 'I'm so tired.'

I can't bear to see her so devoid of life and hope. If she stops believing, what chance is there for the rest of us? She is our frontline domino; if she falls, we'll all tumble after her, sending what little optimism we have scattering in all directions. I can't let her give up.

'Sheila, look at me,' I tell her.

She looks up.

'You should go home.'

She begins to protest.

'Hey. You should go home, get some sleep, stick on a sparkly sweater, then put your face on and come back. Because when Geoff wakes up, he's going to be horrified to see what you look like without makeup, and the last thing we want to do is give him another heart attack.'

She smiles, her first in days.

'I'm serious,' I tell her. 'We're not giving up on him, okay?'

She unfolds before my eyes, sitting up straighter and puffing out her chest once more. 'You're right. Geoff wouldn't want us moping around, would he?'

'He would not.'

'Or to write him off just yet.'

'Absolutely not,' I say.

'I could maybe bring back some hand-painted chakra scarves?'

I'm about to say perhaps not, but think better of it. 'Definitely. We could hang them up and make the place look fancy.'

She pulls on her coat and busies herself packing a few belongings before drawing back the curtain to leave. But then she stops and looks back at me. 'You're a good girl, Cath,' she says. 'Geoff's lucky to have you as a daughter-in-law.'

I step forward and give her a hug, the first we've ever shared. 'I'm working on it,' I tell her. 'I'm working on it.'

I take up my position next to Geoff's bed, hold his hand, tell him I'm there and ramble on about what has happened since I last saw him. This doesn't amount to much. I play some music through my phone, carefully placing one of the headphone buds into Geoff's ear and the other in my own as we listen to the kind of stuff he'd had on his party playlist. And I wait, unable to absolve myself of the guilt that colours every waking thought. I can't bring myself to post anything, and without the distraction of social media I have no choice but to fester over the events of the last few months and days, slowly turning them over in my mind like a jumble of clothes going backwards and forwards in a washing machine. Every time I think they might stop and I can untangle them into orderly piles, they spin again, the volume rising until I can't hear myself think. Because Leanne and I have been taking it in turns to come and keep Sheila company, I still haven't had the chance to properly speak to her. I've not spoken to Sindy either. Every day I type and retype the message that will make everything normal between us again, and each time I delete it, the blinking cursor failing to unveil the appropriate words to explain what I need to. Reggie is silent on social media and he sure as hell isn't answering my calls. Like Geoff, I'm caught in a state of limbo, wholly incapable of connecting with the people I love. I turn the music up a little more, trying to let the strains of The Kinks' 'Waterloo Sunset' drown out everything else.

Chapter Thirty-Nine

'Cath.'

His hand is on my shoulder before I register my name being spoken.

'How are you doing?' Dan crouches down next to me. I haven't seen him since he left the house that night. His eyes seem tired, and his chin is thick with stubble, giving his face a more lived-in look than usual.

'He's no longer medicated or intubated, but he still hasn't come round.'

'I know, I spoke to the nurse. I asked how *you* were doing.'

The tenderness with which he says this is unbearable. 'Don't be kind. Please. This is all my fault.' I fold forward, heavy with regret.

'Shh. You mustn't think like that.'

'I knew he had a dodgy heart, and yet I still left the kids with him.'

'He's a grown man. You didn't force him into it.' He pushes some hair back from my face and tucks it behind my ears. 'Don't punish yourself for something that's not your fault.'

'Eric's right,' I mutter, chin trembling. 'I should have known something bad would happen.'

'Come here.'

He pulls me close to him, envelops my head in his hands and strokes my hair. I want to resist but all energy has left me, so I let myself be held by him and try to suppress the memory of the last time we were so physically close.

'It's going to be okay,' he murmurs into my hair.

I so want him to be right, but I'm scared that history is repeating itself.

'If only we hadn't gone away,' I say after the tears have run their course.

He rests his chin on my head and puts his arms tightly around my shoulders. I close my eyes and breathe him in. His scent is unfamiliar, a different fabric softener from a different place. I still don't know where he's been staying.

'Please don't regret London, Cath,' he whispers.

My heart throbs with longing, my head with questions. What shouldn't I regret? Does he mean what happened in the hotel room? The things I'd said later? The fact I'd chosen the meeting over returning home earlier?

'I'm sorry I left you to come home on your own.' It seems the safest place to start.

'It's okay. I'm sorry I was so scathing.'

I snake my arms around him, press my palms on his taut back and let myself sink into the solace of his warm body against mine. I'll worry about the other stuff another time. 'I only wanted to feel special,' I confess quietly.

'Eh?' says Dan.

'The meeting. I wanted to prove I could be successful.' I say this by way of repentance, but I know immediately it's the wrong thing because Dan's arms stiffen, which means my body tenses in response too.

'What's wrong?' I ask, pulling clear of him.

He's looking at me through narrowed eyes. 'Cath, for a smart woman, you really can be stupid sometimes.'

I stare at him, dumbstruck by this sudden change in attitude. I want to be back pressed against his chest, not under his critical inspection.

'Is that what this was all about?' he asks.

'What?'

'This whole deal with social. It was about "being somebody"?' He slices the space between us in air quotes.

And it was about teaching, obviously, but he already knows that.

'A little bit, maybe.'

He looks heavenward and gently shakes his head, like I'm a child he's caught doing something very disappointing. Despite the solemnity of our surroundings, I'm hugely irritated by this; I'm the bloody grown-up here!

'What's your definition of "being somebody"?' he asks.

I gaze over his shoulder at the version of him in the window, but his body language is no easier to take from that angle. I can't even find pleasure in seeing his bottom reflected back at me.

'Come on. Tell me. What's your idea of success?'

I roll my eyes, frustrated by the stupidity of the question and confused that I'm having to defend myself for something other than Geoff's condition right now. 'With everything that's going on, what does it matter?'

He opens his palms towards me and his mouth twists. 'It matters to me.'

'Dan, I'm tired. My head hurts. I'm not sure I can even describe it very easily.'

He runs his hand down his face, over his mouth, spreads the fingers along his jawline. 'Please try.'

I look into his eyes, searching for some clue as to what's really going on here, but he's giving nothing away. I'm so confused. Dan is the one person I've never felt like I had to stand on ceremony with, or watch what I say around, the one person with whom I've been more myself in the last few months than with anyone else at any time in the last three years. So why is he starting an argument over semantics?

'For Christ's sake, Dan, we're not playing a game of *Articulate* here. Geoff could be dying, and you want my dictionary definition of what success is?'

He crosses his arms, balled fists digging into his biceps. 'Humour me.'

I look out at a sky turning as black as the atmosphere in this room. He's not going to let it go.

'Fine. Success is being popular.'

He doesn't respond.

'Okay, not only that. Being influential too.'

Still no response.

'Oh, I don't know. Having enough money to buy a gold-plated toilet if you want to!' I obviously don't mean this but say it to annoy him as much as he's annoying me. It doesn't work. He is granite-like and I consider throwing Geoff's bedside jug of water in his face just to get a reaction. 'Okay, you tell me what it is if you're so frigging clever!'

He stares at me intently, a bull fired up by the prick of a

dart in its flesh, every sinew tensed for its next strike. 'Here's my take, for what it's worth,' he says, eyes never straying from mine. 'Success is experiencing the death of a partner and coming out the other side fighting. Success is raising three great kids despite everything you've been through. Success is earning the respect of a bunch of teenagers who now want to better themselves and have a shot at actually doing so because of the time you spent with them.'

I wonder if that will ever really be true of Reggie.

'What you're defining, Cath, is *status*. And of all the people I've ever known, you're the one I'd hoped would know it's worthless.'

I open my mouth to speak but he holds up his hand to stop me.

'Hear me out. You are an intelligent, funny and gifted woman, but in your little whirlwind to be special, I cannot believe you never stopped for a second to consider that perhaps you already were.'

I note the past tense of that final word, the deliciousness of the sentiment that preceded it tainted with a bitter aftertaste. I'm trying to process what this means, or might have meant, when something brushes against my hand and there's a noise behind me. Dan's sudden movement towards the bed makes me realise it's Geoff, groggy but conscious, trying to speak from beneath his oxygen mask.

'You're awake,' says Dan.

Geoff gets increasingly agitated, grasping at the cannulas and lines running to and from him and the machines monitoring him. I carefully lift his mask off and watch his eyes slowly focus on mine, his pupils adjusting to the first light to penetrate them for almost a week. He tries to speak again, a guttural clearing of the throat that makes no sense. Perhaps the neurological damage is worse than I'd allowed myself to imagine. I lean in close to try and discern the words.

'What is it? What are you trying to say?' I whisper.

'I was saying,' he says, in a voice admittedly gruff, but very much his, 'that if you're going to have an argument, can you take it outside? Some of us are trying to sleep.'

I throw myself upon his chest in desperate relief and then back off when I remember the operation. 'It's you. It's still you.' I plant a huge kiss on his forehead instead.

'Who else were you expecting?' He turns to Dan and feigns a look of incredulity on his now re-animated face.

'Don't get up. You're hooked up to lots of stuff.'

'I'll fetch a doctor,' says Dan and he heads out of the cubicle.

'Do you want any water?' I ask Geoff.

'Have you got anything stronger?' he croaks.

'Not a chance. Do you remember what happened?'

'I remember the old ticker going a bit doolally. The rest, not so much.'

I give him a brief history of the last few days, about the stent, the coma and how we didn't think he was going to make it, then Dan reappears with a doctor.

'I'll call Leanne and Sheila,' I say, imagining how much joy each call will elicit.

'You gave us all a fright there,' says Dan.

Geoff gives him a weak salute, half-toppling a drip in the process.

'We should argue more often,' I tell Dan. 'Offer our services out to some of the other coma patients.' I really want to get back in his good books.

He offers me a hesitant smile. 'You'd probably wave your arms around and knock a really important tube out somewhere.'

'You know me!' But his expression suggests that perhaps he doesn't know me as well as he'd thought.

The doctor coughs to get my attention. She doesn't need her PhD to have worked out there's a further drama unfolding in the room.

'You'll be pleased to know all vital signs seem fine. Everything's responding as it should be. Looks like he got away with it.'

'That's incredible news.' I turn to Dan, eager for him to be a part of this.

He shifts uncomfortably in his Converse trainers. 'I should probably leave you to it.'

'You're welcome to stay.' I let myself hope that he will, and we can talk some more.

'I'll only be in the way.'

I swallow down my dismay. 'Yeah. It'll be like Piccadilly Circus in here in half an hour!' Geoff is awake and that's enough for now. Isn't it?

'It's great to have you back, buddy,' Dan says over my shoulder. 'I'll see you soon.'

I want to ask how soon, but he turns and leaves before I pluck up the courage.

Chapter Forty

A few evenings later, with Leanne out, Jack in bed and Eric playing video games upstairs, I had an unexpected urge to dig out our old photo albums, so now I'm sat next to Gaz's urn on the kitchen floor, surrounded by dusty boxes. Rooting around in the realms of nostalgia is not something I'm comfortable with. I'm always more likely to turn up murky memories of those times when I said the wrong thing or made a right royal tit of myself, rather than radiant recollections of wonderful times in which I was beyond self-reproach. But after everything that's happened, I need to take a peek. I'm not sure what I'm looking for, a few threads of the person I was maybe, before things began to unravel.

I open the first box and feel the greasy smoothness of its grime on my fingers. I pull out a frayed cardboard folder of photos and spread the contents out on the floor. The colours have become muted with age, which is just as well because the first one I pick up shows me in a shell suit so neon it's as though I've ram-raided a high-vis uniform shop and then been sheep-dipped in highlighter pen ink.

'This was when I was going through my *Fresh Prince* phase!'

I dig deeper in the box like a kid at a tombola, seeing if there are greater riches hiding at the bottom. I pull out a burgundy faux-leather album, its plastic flip wallets clinging precariously to the spine. These are from when Sindy turned sixteen, and as I flick through the images, I sense an echo of the emotions to which we were subject at the time, caught in limbo between youth and adulthood, freedom and responsibility. Another folder of pictures, this time from sixth form, a time at which I'd declared fashion to be against my feminist principles, and I'm wearing a Fruit of the Loom white T-shirt onto which I'd scrawled CHOOSE CHOICE using an indelible marker. The thing that strikes me most about these pictures is this: I had been fearless back then, less easily injured by the slings and arrows of others' opinions. What changed? Is confidence like alpha radiation, slowly and steadily declining with the passage of time, absorbed by every barrier it comes up against? Are we destined to lose sight of who we once were? I take out another pile of folders and find a piece of paper amongst them. It's a printout of an image of Leanne, Gaz, Eric and me. We'd been to Cadbury World and gone for pizza afterwards, and the waitress had taken the shot with Gaz's phone. It was barely a month before Gaz died and Jack must have been in there, a tiny nugget hiding undetected in my belly. It must be the only picture I have of the five of us together.

'Oh Gaz. What the hell am I supposed to do next?'

'Little late-night conflab with Dad, huh?'

Leanne is in the doorway.

'You're smart. Why do I make such a mess of everything?'

She plops herself on a chair next to me. 'Is this about the kitchen table?'

It has returned to its pre-Dan state of disorder.

'Are we okay? I know we've not been getting on as well recently. Have I been doing your head in like I have Eric? I feel like I owe everyone a massive apology.'

'He'll come round. As for me, it's one thing to say you want someone to move on, but then quite another when they actually do. I think I got a bit freaked out.'

'I have been rather caught up in it.'

'What's currently going on?'

I tell her about my meeting with the agency.

'And how do you feel about that?'

'Confused. I don't know what I want any more.' I haven't been able to shift Dan's words from my head. Or his face. Or the sensation of him holding me. There's still no word of when he'll be back, but with every passing day my missing him grows exponentially.

'Then take it one baby step at a time and see what feels right. Sometimes the answers show up in unexpected places.'

'Are you not going to lecture me about getting back to my course?'

'Only you can decide what's best for you.'

'But how do you know if you're doing things for the right reason?'

'Oh, *you know*,' she says with emphasis. 'But if you want the psychological explanation, you need to read up on cognitive dissonance.'

I don't need a textbook to know what she means. I pass her

the picture I'm holding and her face brightens. She gazes wistfully at the urn. It's been ten months since our chat at university, and Gaz is still there in the kitchen. Her tacit judgment hangs in the air.

'It really is time, Mom.'

She's right, and yet... 'I'm not sure I'm ready.'

'You are. You just need to come to terms with that fact.'

We continue to stare at the urn. Jack has covered it in Paw Patrol stickers, its ornate enamel embellishments punctuated by cutesy illustrations of dogs in uniforms. To be honest, it's an improvement. Leanne removes one of her prosthetics and scratches under a bandaged knee to reach an itch.

'Do you remember when I used to feel shitty about being different from the other kids?'

It's hard to imagine that Leanne was anything other than the wise, warrior-like woman she is now, but yes, there had been a time when she'd nearly buckled under the burden of such individuality.

'Do you remember what you would say?'

I don't.

'You'd bang on about the sheer volume of atoms in the universe, how long-lived they are and how I was made up of them. "The atoms that make up your body will have once been parts of a star, or a butterfly, or a princess or a dinosaur," you'd say. And you would describe how the atoms from my missing legs and fingertips were going to be recycled into trees and flowers and the best rides at Disneyland. And that rather than having lost something, I had in fact gifted the universe with these bits of myself that might not be part of me anymore, but they were off doing awesome things for other people.'

'I said that?'

'You did.' She pulls her leg back on. 'I don't know how else to put this to you, other than, don't you think it's time you let the remains of Dad's atoms go off and do awesome things too? And you need to think about what you want yours to be doing back here. Because we don't need apologies. What we do need is for you to be happy and fulfilled.' She gets up. 'You can do whatever you decide to put your mind to, Mom. For fear of sounding like a hack psychologist, life puts enough obstacles in your way, without you having to construct your own. I'm off to bed. I love you.'

Later I lie in bed unable to sleep, like I have done for the last week. Sleep deprivation is a dangerous thing; apparently, some of the biggest disasters in living memory have been because of chronic fatigue – the power plant accident at Three Mile Island, the nuclear meltdown at Chernobyl, Donald Trump's face. Tonight is different, though. Rather than the masochistic internal chatter of self-flagellation with all the focus on what I've done wrong, tonight I am taking Leanne's advice and think about what I can now do right. I tell myself how tomorrow is the first day of the rest of my life, and then I tell myself how if I ever say that to myself again, I will have to self-immolate. And then, when I accept that sleep really is going to elude me, I decide what my first baby step is going to be.

Chapter Forty-One

S mithills is a decaying former village which sits six miles to the east of the city centre gathering grime and social problems. Brookdene is a further mile in the same direction. I've arranged to meet Bradley in the hope he'll help me track down Reggie. I find his place with some difficulty; the whole area is full of identical buildings with badly arranged windows that are too tiny to admit much light, and too high to easily observe what's going on outside. Although this may be deliberate, because the only view for miles is an ownerless dog taking a dump on a tiny strip of grass verge.

'Oh hey, Miss. Come in,' says Bradley answering the door.

I feel as though I'm in a Ken Loach film as he leads me past a sitting room in which an obese man in a vest is vaping in front of a TV, to a cramped kitchen that's seen better days.

'Cup of tea, Miss?'

'Love one, thanks.' I perch at the tiny fold-down table as he makes three cups of tea, one of which he takes through to the lounge.

'Is that your dad?' I ask when he returns.

'Stepdad. Mom's working at that discount furniture place you'd have passed on the way in.'

I take a tentative sip of the tea, the milk didn't look to be the freshest, but to my surprise it tastes pretty good. 'Not bad!' I tell him.

'Not just a pretty face, you know.'

A voice from the lounge tells him he's not even that. Bradley scowls and gives the V sign to the wall.

'Have you heard from him?' I ask.

'Yeah.'

'Finally! It's about bloody time he resurfaced. What's his excuse for disappearing? Something about education performing a labour function for the bourgeoisie?'

'No. This.'

He shows me a photo on his mobile and my stomach lurches. It's Reggie. Just. One half of his face is unrecognisable, a sickening swelling pulling his features grotesquely out of shape, the white of what little shows of his pupil completely blood red. His lip is split in two places, and stitches protrude from the vermillion gashes like whiskers. I can't believe what I'm seeing. The wounds are too graphic, too appalling to be real.

'What the hell happened?'

'His mom's boyfriend is what happened.'

Bradley tells me that Reggie had been sofa surfing for a while, trying to escape his situation at home, but he'd been forced to return so he could study for his exams.

'You know his mom's an alcoholic?'

I knew someone was, but after that initial confession all those months ago, Reggie had point-blank refused to tell me anything further.

'Her bloke's not much better. Real temper. I don't think he was treating her very nicely and, well, Reggie intervened. This is what he got for it.'

My heart splinters into a million pieces at the injustice of it all. My beautiful, principled Reggie, trying to stick up for his mom, brutally beaten for doing the right thing.

'Broke two ribs and a finger as well. Couldn't have held a pen if he'd wanted to.'

He tries to show me more pictures, but I can't bring myself to look. Not yet. I'll be sick.

'Can you send those to me instead?'

'What are you going to do? He wouldn't want you to interfere.'

'Hasn't the boyfriend been arrested?'

Bradley laughs bitterly. 'Reggie's not reported it.'

'Why the hell not?'

''Cos it's his mom that'll suffer most if he does.'

I let this settle in. I'm not sure how she could have allowed this to happen, but who knows what life needs to throw you to end up with someone capable of such brutality. I'll try and keep my judgment in check until I know more.

'Don't worry. I'm going to see if the exam board will consider his case.'

'Wish you could have a word with them about me.'

'Why? How do you think you did?'

'I reckon I'll scrape it. I need a four to go to college.'

His stepdad walks in, grunts the word 'college' dismissively, grabs a packet of biscuits from the cupboard above my head and walks out again.

'I'm really proud of you guys for knuckling down and trying.'

'That means a lot, Miss.'

'Where's Reggie now? He's not answering any of my messages.'

'He thinks he let you down.'

I could weep at the irony; I'm the one who's catastrophically let him down. Bradley explains how Reggie has been staying at his aunt's, but as lovely as she apparently is, she's got a house full already, so he'll probably be back to sofa surfing once he's recovered.

'Tell him to come and see me.'

'I can try.'

'Do your best.'

Whilst I finish my tea, Bradley fills me in on what the others have been up to, and I'm heartened to hear that everyone else is still in one piece.

'Well, you know where I live if you need anything.' I get up to go.

'I'll let you know how I get on, yeah?'

'I've got everything crossed for you guys.'

I leave the house, past the broken trampoline and rusting car parts in the garden. This is like the estate I grew up on, but how easy it is to forget the kind of conditions under which most of these kids are living. On the margins, barely enough money and barely enough motivation to be able to escape the inexorable tug of the welfare state. I wonder what would have happened to me had I not got the education I did. I'm halfway down the street when my phone beeps. It's Bradley sending me the images of Reggie. It makes me more determined than ever to help him out of his situation. That's if he'll let me.

Since Geoff has been recovering in hospital, Eric has stopped being actively hostile and has instead adopted a type of passive aggressiveness whereby he goes to school as normal, comes in bang on curfew, but ignores me the rest of the time. He has been spending most evenings in his locked room playing music too loud, to the point that Jack has taken to lying outside, shouting through the gap under the door to try and get his attention. Sometimes I join him. But yesterday there was a small breakthrough. Jack and I were watching TV, treating ourselves to a spot of popping candy ice cream straight from the tub (yes, I'm comfort eating), when he wordlessly came and joined us. Credit to him, he tried hard to keep a straight face as he ate it, but it's hard to do the full moody teenager routine with a gob full of sugar and CO_2 exploding on your tongue. I have therefore decided today's the day I chance talking to him properly. I knock on his door. There's no reply. I knock again. Still nothing. I try the handle and am relieved to see it opens, so I crack the door a little and shout into the gap.

'Eric, I'm coming in, okay?'

I open it wider. He's lying on his bed, games console in hand. He turns away from me, so I get on the bed next to him. He's got so tall; he's almost as long as his cabin bed. I'll need to get a new one soon, although I'll need to earn some money first. Best not to think about that now. I lift my legs up, lean back onto his pillows and stare at his homemade *Game of Thrones* poster on the wall.

'Hey mate. I know you're mad at me, and I want you to know that I'm really mad at myself.'

He shifts slightly but doesn't try to leave the room or anything. So far so good.

'I've never been very good at the mushy stuff,' I say, 'but I love you and I want you to know that I'm sorry. Sorry that I didn't properly listen when you were trying to tell me your concerns. Sorry that I always play down how you feel about stuff. The truth is, I don't really know what I'm doing. I'm not sure any parent does, but I definitely don't. When your dad died, I went into survival mode, trying to muddle through the days. And all the time, even though you must have been in such devastating pain, you were so amazing, so mature. Then Jack arrived and you got on with it. You were never resentful of how much of my attention he took up, and you'd always give him so much of your own in return. I haven't been there for you, not as much as I should have been. It isn't an excuse, but you always seemed so together, both you and Leanne did, and everyone would tell me how resilient children can be.' I stop and take a deep breath, determined not to cry and to finish what I have to say. 'It was easier to believe that you were okay, because I'm not sure at the time I could have dealt with the alternative. But you and Leanne … you're my world … and Jack of course, but he hasn't had to handle what you have. So I wanted to say thank you. Thank you for trying to be a grown-up and for shielding me from how scared and anxious you really were. But if I ever made you feel like a burden, I am so sorry.' I clear my throat. Maybe a few tears are allowed, but I won't sob. 'Because I'm your mom, and it's my job to look after you and from here on I'm going to make a better go of it. So what do you say, buddy? Can you forgive me? Can we try and get back to getting along? I love you so so much, and I'm so lucky to have you in my life, and even if you want to speak to me as a character from one of your books, that would be okay so long as we're talking again.' The tears are now pouring down the side of my cheeks and tickling my ears.

After a few impatient seconds he turns to me and lifts his arms and I'm convinced he's going to hug me, only his hands reach for the tiny earbud headphones that I hadn't noticed he was wearing under all that hair. I'm sat here, eyes streaming and nose bubbling snot like a neglected urchin, and he hasn't heard a bloody word. He takes them out.

'What did you say?'

You have got to be kidding me. I can't possibly conjure all of that up again. But. Must. Not. Get. Angry. Must. Put. My. Game. Face. On. I take another deep breath.

'What I said was—'

'Mom, I'm joking, I heard you.'

'Eh?'

'I heard you. These ran out of battery ages ago.'

'Oh you rascal!'

His face cracks into a big grin.

'Oh my god! You absolute horror!' Relief floods through me. We're going to be okay, for now at least. I don't know whether to coddle him or throttle him, so instead I tickle him until he's convulsing with giggles. It's been a long time since I heard him laugh like that.

'Stop, I'm going to drop this,' he says.

'I don't care. You deserve everything that's coming to you.'

I eventually let him catch his breath and we lie for a couple of minutes on the bed, his head pressing very heavily on one of my boobs, but I don't want to spoil the moment by pointing this out.

'So, we're good?' I ask.

340

'Yeah. I don't hate you anymore.'

'Phew.'

'Leanne told me about Reggie. Maybe I didn't realise how lucky I was either?'

I give him another squidge. 'Friends?'

'Yeah. Friends.'

'Is it too soon to tell Jack he's allowed back in?'

'No, that's fine too.'

I swing my legs off the bed, ready to unleash the pent-up joy of a formerly snubbed three-year-old onto him.

'I do still wish Dad was here though,' he says timidly.

'Of course you wish your dad was here. That's completely natural.'

'No, not Dad, Dan. I wish *Dan* was here. Is that bad? Would Dad mind that I like Dan too?'

I sink back down, a slow puncture in my formerly fully inflated spirits. Just when I'd not thought about Dan for a nanosecond.

'Eric, your dad was one of the most easy-going, open-minded people I've ever met. He never experienced envy or jealousy or resentment. He was too busy being supremely happy with what he already had, including you. He wasn't one of those that thought love or affection was a limited resource with only so much to go around. You have nothing to be guilty about. He wouldn't have minded one little bit.'

'Is Dan coming back?'

Is he? We've exchanged a few polite messages about Geoff's health and he's asked after the kids, but neither one of us have broached the subject of what happened in London or at Geoff's bedside, and I'm starting to wonder whether we ever will. What he didn't respond to was the text I tormented myself over, telling him he could come back any time.

'I'm not sure.'

'Was it something I did?'

'No!' I can't tell him it's something that I did. 'You mustn't think that. Dan really likes you. He's told me loads how much he likes spending time with you. But this was only ever a temporary arrangement. The academic year is up now, he probably has other places he wants to go and see. I think we need to ready ourselves for him not being around much longer.' What I mean is I think I need to ready myself for him not being around much longer, but no matter how many times I google 'how to deal with unrequited feelings', no search result has thus far managed to diminish this itch that cannot be scratched. But I can't let the pain of that wound overshadow my relief at the healing of this one. 'Your Uncle Dave will be back again at some point, hopefully for a bit longer than before. You can talk to him about stuff as well you know?'

'He'll tell me to man up.'

'Yeah, he will do that! Perhaps we should get you someone else to speak to. Someone completely independent who is properly qualified to help. I probably should have thought of it sooner.'

'Yeah, that could be good.'

'Okay, I'll look into it. There's also something else I wanted to discuss with you when you're ready.'

'What about?'

'It's about Reggie.'

'Can I come down and have some more ice cream first?'

'I reckon it would be positively indecent of us not to go and polish the whole lot off.'

The door opens. Jack wanders in with one of my bras on his head pretending to swig from a bottle of perfume.

'Mmm, so tasty!'

I retrieve both items. 'Oh no, you don't. I thought Leanne was looking after you?'

Leanne comes in, also with one of my bras on her head. 'I was. Have you two made up then?'

'Yes.'

'Great. Can I have a lie down. Jack is relentless.'

'How about we all go and eat ice cream?'

'Deal,' she says.

It's good to all be together again. And if I try really hard, I can almost imagine that the last nine months didn't happen.

Chapter Forty-Two

The Christadelphian Hall hasn't changed much in the thirty years since I was last outside it. This is where I used to attend a Christian youth group, largely because there was free squash and the tuck shop was so heavily subsidised I could get twenty chewy sweets for half their recommended retail value. The noticeboard tells me that in the next week alone I could enjoy the delights of puppy training, crochet class and laughing yoga. Presumably the latter is the standard type of yoga, but someone breaks wind at the beginning and the rest of the class can't contain themselves. This morning is slimming club, and I'm waiting for Sindy to emerge with the rest of the dieting congregation currently filtering out. Some are clutching starter packs, new recruits in search of a better body, if not a better soul, ready to turn up every week to confess their *Syns* and step on the scales as public penance for their nutritional transgressions. I spot Sindy. She doesn't see me at first as she's too busy lighting a cigarette, one of the occasional weapons in her arsenal against the weight, so I call over and watch as her face brightens, darkens, and then settles into a comically forced scowl.

'What brings you here?' she says loudly enough for other people to hear. 'The stitch and bitch session isn't until Thursday.'

'I came to see how many calories there are in humble pie.'

'Is that meant to be an apology?' she pulls long and hard on the cigarette, inhaling deeply.

'Yes.'

She exhales quickly. 'Thank god for that. I've really missed you.' She puts the cigarette out, crushing it into the ground with a spiky heel, and throws her arms around me. She's wearing *Flowers by Kenzo* and it's like cuddling a vanilla ice cream sprinkled in Parma violets.

'I was so happy to hear Geoff's on the mend.'

'Me too. Shall we go for a drink?'

She pulls away and looks at me seriously. 'And for something to eat. I'm absolutely starving.' She loops her arm in mine and we decide to head to an authentic little Spanish place a few minutes away, where they sell Sangria by the jug and artery-cloggingly good tapas to soak it all up.

'Does this constitute one of my five a day,' asks Sindy, now seated by the window and examining her large glass, which is crammed with lemon slices, orange chunks and pomegranate seeds.

'Almost certainly,' I chow down on a bacon-wrapped date as sweet grease dribbles down my chin.

Sindy smears white aioli onto a chunk of patatas bravas.

'The freebies are all very well and good, but you could also end up getting trolled.'

I've brought her up to speed on events of the last few weeks. I've still not decided what to do next, even assuming I could make it work without Dan, and talking it through doesn't seem to be getting me any closer to a decision. 'The thing about people like Kim Kardashian is breaking the internet with your massive arse is fine, but if half of the world think *you're* a massive arse in the process, it's probably not worth it.'

'I only thought you were a tiny twat,' says Sindy. 'How soon do you need to let them know?'

'Soon. I need to make money one way or another when Dan leaves.' My stomach knots. I top up my sangria glass.

'Dan's leaving?'

'His uni year is up.'

'But he's become part of the fixtures, hasn't he? Like a really comfy sofa that you want to throw yourself on top of.'

I try and keep a straight face, but my rapidly reddening cheeks snitch on me, and the filo-wrapped lamb parcel that had been on its way into Sindy's mouth hangs there like a deep-fried testicle. She puts it back down again.

'You. Have. Not.'

I was going to have to tell her eventually. 'I did.'

'O. M. Fuck. Give me all the info. Leave nothing out. I need to know everything.'

'I'm sorry, I can't. Most of it's a blur.'

'Was he going that quickly? That doesn't sound like something he'd do.'

'No. It was in London. I was roaringly drunk and wasn't expecting it to happen.'

'How many times?' she asks.

'Probably once.'

'How many ways?'

'Presumably just the one.'

'Such a waste! You should be ashamed of yourself.'

'I am, but not for the reasons you mean.' I give her what little detail I remember to satisfy her insatiable curiosity on the matter, as well as filling her in on the other things I'd discovered about Dan whilst we were away. She laps it up, but I'm left fervently wishing that I hadn't joined the ranks of Dan's conquests, or that the story had ended differently.

'What's going on now then?' she asks.

'Nothing. Why?'

'Because you like each other.'

'We get on. *Got* on. But it's not like that.'

'Are you sure?'

'Trust me. Dan made it very clear that it was just sex.' It pains me to think about that morning. Whatever bond we'd had got fractured in that hotel room and every encounter since has weakened it further.

'Just sex,' says Sindy, staring into the distance dreamily. 'That's the same as someone saying "it's just a million pound win on the lottery."'

I give her a friendly slap with a light-heartedness I don't feel. 'It's really bad. I was so angry with myself afterwards that I was mean to him, and now he's really annoyed with me.' I briefly tell her about what happened post-coitus and our altercation at Geoff's bedside. 'It's all a massive fiasco. I need your advice.'

She adopts a suitably business-like posture and taps her chin thoughtfully. 'I've listened to everything you've had to say, and I think I have the answer.'

'Do tell.'

'Okay, what you need to do is this: you need to build yourself a time machine, go back to that hotel room to the precise moment before you freaked out, and then you need to let him go down on you properly.'

I snort loudly, despite myself.

'For hours. Possibly even days,' she continues. 'And then you need to come back here and tell me all about it. You'll find that makes you feel a whole lot better.'

God, it's so good to have her back.

'Got anything more constructive? I'm so sad I let a quickie get in the way of our friendship.'

'Call him,' she says.

'And say what?'

'That you have to talk.'

'Urgh. That old chestnut.'

'What have you got to lose?'

'Er, my pride, my dignity and my self-respect.'

'Yeah, but you might get a pity shag to make up for it!'

I laugh and then want to cry instead. I have had way too much sangria for a lunchtime. 'I'll think about it.' For about ten seconds. I'm too humiliated to actually do it. 'In the meantime, I have even more pressing matters to attend to.'

'Is it ordering pudding? 'Cos the trouble with tapas is the plates are a bit small, aren't they?'

'I think that's the point.'

'I know, smarty pants.'

'Okay. Pudding first. And coffee. Lots of coffee. And I might need an afternoon nap. But then there are a few other things I need to put right.'

Chapter Forty-Three

Leanne, Eric, Jack and I are sat at a picnic bench in our local park. It's so hot that my neck is prickling in protest at the roasting it's getting. Gaz is on the table, light glinting off the edges of the urn's curves which we've wrapped in a feather boa.

'Okay, I've called this family meeting because we all agree it's time to do something with your dad's ashes. The question is what? Any ideas?'

'Can we send him into space?' asks Eric. 'It'd be pretty cool if Dad was found by aliens.' Despite the searing heat, he's wearing a leather flying helmet, a tweed waistcoat four sizes too big and corduroy shorts, all bought in a charity shop. Any fears I may have had about him succumbing to peer pressure are well and truly behind me; this boy is charting his own course.

'I'd love that, but not sure we'll get him very far.'

'How about a drone?' he asks.

'Bit expensive,' says Leanne.

'Jack, do you have any idea what we're talking about, sweetheart?'

Jack has dragged part of the boa from the urn and is trying to put a feather up his nose without giggling. He's failing miserably.

'Can I have this?' he asks through guffaws.

'Will you try and eat it?' He's still going through the *put everything in your mouth* phase.

He looks sheepish, but still says, 'No, Mommy.'

'Then yes.'

He drags the boa off the urn, climbs down onto the grass, and tries to eat it.

'I suppose the disposal of the ashes of a dead father you've never met is a hard concept for a three-year-old to get their head around.'

'Some people turn them into diamonds,' says Eric, but then immediately frowns at the thought. 'Nah, he would have hated that.'

He's right. Gaz never got the point of assigning value to bits of coal or metal. He'd have taken a Mars bar over a diamond any day.

'Did you guys never talk about what to do, should the worst happen?' asks Leanne.

'Not that I recall. He did once joke that instead of being buried he'd rather be southern-fried and fed to the lions, like an enormous chicken nugget.'

We'd been lying in bed after a very sombre funeral for a distant relative when he'd suggested it would make a more interesting finale, and properly give people something to remember him by.

'That's it!' says Leanne.

'I agree,' says Eric, looking decidedly excited. 'Why not?'

There are a hundred reasons 'why not' scrabbling around in my head, but they all fail to find a foothold when I share them with the kids. 'I suppose we *could* do something,' I eventually concede.

'I'm thinking Chicken Kiev, but with ashes instead of garlic butter,' says Leanne.

'How much ash is there?' asks Eric.

'I haven't looked.'

Leanne leans across the table, opens the lid and shines her mobile phone torch inside. 'About three bags of sugar.'

'That's a big Chicken Kiev,' I say.

'We could make a few then scatter the rest as we drive around the park,' says Leanne.

'I say we do it. Come on, Mom.' Eric pulls out the emotional big guns by resting his head in the crook of my neck. I am powerless against this show of affection.

'All those in favour say *aye*.'

There is a resounding chorus of ayes. Even Jack joins in.

'I'll call Geoff and see if he wants in. Sindy will almost certainly be up for it.'

'We could get priority tickets and go in early,' says Leanne.

'It's a plan.' I lift the lid off the urn. 'Looks like we're going on one last day trip as a family Gaz. Let's make it a good'un.'

'You wanted to see me, Miss.'

Reggie's in the doorway, shifting from one foot to the other. His face no longer bears the marks of the beating he took, but he looks more fragile and he's lost weight.

'For God's sake, we're not at school now.' I want to hug the stuffing out of him, but I have no idea how he'll react, so instead self-consciously pat his afro and make a weird growling sound that hopefully conveys extreme fondness and total relief that he's okay. 'Thanks for coming.'

He smiles, so I figure he's got the gist of it. 'You're not mad at me?'

'For what?'

'Not turning up to my exam.'

'No! I'm mad at you for not telling me what was going on, and mad at myself for not making you.'

'It's not my mom's fault, Miss. What with the booze and, well—'

'I'm not judging her Reggie. But you know you don't deserve to be treated like that, don't you?'

'I know.'

'Then let's say no more. Now come in, Eric's really looking forward to seeing you. Don't be shocked though, his voice has broken, as has his taste in clothes.'

'I heard that,' comes from the front room where we find him playing video games.

Jack is holding the other controller, frantically pressing buttons and mimicking his brother. Eric looks up from his game, nods at Reggie and simply says, 'Alright?'

Reggie nods back, unzips his sports jacket, plonks himself down on the sofa and replies with an equally brief 'aight'.

'Well, now you pair are all caught up, you've got five minutes until lunch.'

While they gawp at the television, I go and take a quiche out of the oven and pop it on the table alongside all the other buffet bits I've prepared. I snap at Leanne when she dips a carrot baton in some hummus. I know what I want to say to Reggie, but I'm worried what his reaction might be.

'Stop fussing, Mom! He'll either say yes or he'll say no. It's out of your hands.'

'I only hope he takes it in the spirit in which it's intended. I know how independent he thinks he is.'

'You can only ask,' she says.

'Okay.' I swallow down my nerves. 'GRUBS UP!' I shout through to them. Then I shout again. Then again, until I finally sense movement and they reluctantly drag themselves away from the console.

'Reggie, I don't think you've met my eldest. This is Leanne.'

Reggie looks her up and down. 'Straight fire hair,' he says. 'And your legs are savage.'

'Thanks.' Leanne turns to me. 'I like him.'

'He's surprisingly likeable, considering. Although I have no idea what he said. Everyone, tuck in.'

Reggie piles a mountain of food onto his plate and gets stuck in with gusto. As we eat, Eric tells him about our plans for Gaz, of which he strongly approves, and Jack punctuates the whole thing with the occasional fart and the proud news that he's now wearing big boy pants. If only he wasn't peeing in them every five minutes, this might be cause for celebration.

During lunch Reggie steadily relaxes and by the time the table is cleared, he's practically horizontal in his chair. 'Miss, can we now talk about why there's a tent in your kitchen?'

Here's the thing: our kitchen isn't exactly huge, but by clearing out a load of clutter and the half-dead plants gathering dust by the patio doors, we've squeezed in a little pop up tent.

'It's for you,' I tell him.

'What do I need a tent for? Not exactly heading to any festivals this summer.'

'It's your new bedroom. If you want it.'

He looks at me like I've told him Beyoncé is really a cross-dressing former bricklayer named Brian.

'Huh?'

'I know you've been sofa-surfing. I thought you could stay here instead. In the tent. If you wanted to. It's not much but after we've had tea it's as private as anywhere in this house. I'll try really hard to keep the table clear so you have somewhere to study and you can use the patio doors to come in and out if that suits you better. And we have a downstairs toilet, so you know, you can...'

Now everyone's looking at me like I've turned into Beyoncé.

'I'm rambling, aren't I?'

'Yes,' says Leanne. 'What my mother is trying to say, Reggie, is that if you want to, you can stay here for as long as you like. The tent is most likely temporary. Dan is due to move out, and I'll be going back to uni soon at which point you can have my room. Until then, this is your own private space.'

A wave of melancholy breaks over me at the mention of Dan, but the delight on Reggie's face pulls me back up from the threatening riptide.

'For real?' he says, sitting upright.

Leanne nods.

'You'd do this for me?' he asks me.

'You'd need to follow house rules, and muck in on jobs.'

'There's a rota,' says Eric. 'It's lame-o.'

'But I can't pay you.'

I've done some more number crunching. It's not pretty, but

screw it, if I need to dip deeper into savings, then so be it. 'You don't need to. You just need to study for college.'

He sags back into the chair. 'I ain't going to college.'

'Don't be so sure. I've looked into the special consideration process. I think there's a case for getting your marks adjusted.'

'So, I could pass?' he says.

'Yeah, you could pass.'

He nods slowly, biting hard on his lip. 'That's pretty dank, Miss. Thank you.'

'You're welcome. But the first house rule is you must stop calling me Miss.'

'Really? That's gonna be fucking weird.'

'House rule number two. That's twenty pence in the swear jar.'

'I don't have any cash. Did you know that soon none of us will be able to carry cash? It's another way central banks are trying to curtail our freedoms. It's really fucking serious.' He looks across at me. 'Sorry, that's forty pence I can't pay you.'

I laugh. I'm just glad to have the old Reggie back.

Chapter Forty-Four

My stomach does a backflip and I'm instantly shaky, as though I'm walking a very high tightrope with no shoes, no pole and no bloody tightrope. Dan has turned up unannounced and is standing in my kitchen chatting with Reggie. It's only been ten days, but he looks different. His hair is still a messy mop of curls, but it's shorter than it was. By contrast his previous barely-there stubble is now a fledgling beard, the darkness of which accentuates the shape of his mouth, making his lips look even more plump and kissable.

'You're back!'

'Oh Cath, you're here.'

I need to say something extremely witty and insightful and fabulous and entirely not suggestive of the fact that the sight of him has made me go to pieces.

'Afraid so. Why, were you per'aps 'oping I was out?' I was aiming for Poirot intelligently deducing something, but instead sound like I've lost control of my tongue. Probably because I have.

'I was hearing that Reggie is staying with you now?'

He looks so mature. So unlike Dan. I can't stop looking at his face.

'Erm, I'd better be going,' says Reggie.

'Where?' I manage.

'I have to go walk around the block to, er, get out of your two's way.'

'Smooth going,' says Dan smirking.

Reggie shakes his head. 'I think her awkwardness is rubbing off on me.'

He leaves and then it's just Dan and me. In the kitchen. The two of us. Alone. I can't get over how different he looks.

'That's a really good thing you're doing,' says Dan.

'I should have asked you first. It's just—'

It's just how can covering some of his face up have magnified how achingly fit he is.

'Still worried about those *contractual obligations*?' he says.

I grimace. Thinking about that day still smarts.

'Don't worry, I'm not going to sue you for breach of rental agreement.' He smiles. He's trying to put me at ease.

'I should probably apologise for everything I have ever said,' I tell him.

He chuckles. 'Perhaps not everything.'

'So, what have you been up to?' I ask as neutrally as possible. I really hope it's a what and not a who that's kept him busy since he's been gone.

'Not much. Enjoying having finished the academic year in one piece. You?'

I look down at my feet. 'Oh, you know. Eating biscuits. Badly wishing I hadn't said what I said to you.'

'I wasn't exactly on top form myself,' he says, graciously

opting not to give me a harder time than I've given myself. 'So have you been making any more content?'

'No. I'd only make a hash of everything without you.' I hope he can read the subtext in this statement. These last two weeks have made me fully realise the extent to which Dan bestowed on me a confidence I would never have naturally felt in myself. 'Did you want to do more?' I desperately want him to say yes so everything can go back to the way it was.

'I don't think I can.' He casts me a meaningful glance, but I'm not sure of the meaning.

'Oh.'

'I don't know if I'm going to be around.'

'Double oh.' Time dilates. Things slow down. Even the Brownian motion of the dust in the sunbeam coming through the kitchen window seems to falter and flag. 'How come?'

'This whole thing with Geoff, it's made me think about my own situation. I don't know. Maybe it's time I went home and spent some time with my mom.'

'Well, that is a most noble and grown-up thing to do.' I bow and make a deferential hand gesture in an effort to look completely relaxed about what he's suggesting, but my sunglasses fall off my head, and I end up juggle-catching them like a second-rate circus performer until Dan steps forward and helps me out. He puts them back on my head, a gesture so intimate it's like there's a test-your-strength hammer game under my ribs, with someone going swing-crazy in there.

'Thanks,' he says, 'but who are you and what have you done with Cath? She would never describe me as a grown-up.'

'She's been doing some thinking. And she wanted me to tell you that she really does think your dad would be proud of you.'

He nods in acknowledgement of my loosely wrapped apology. 'Thank you, Cath.'

I swallow hard, not wanting to know any more about his plans, but compelled to ask questions anyway. 'But what about your course?'

'I don't need to finish it. Or I could pick something back up over there. I don't know. What about yours?'

All those modules I could have done by now, but I can't beat myself up about that. Whatever my motivations might have been on the social media front, I had so much fun creating our content together, I wouldn't trade those times for anything.

'I guess I have a lot of things I need to work out,' I say.

'I guess we both do, huh?'

He holds my gaze long enough for me to notice that there is definite gaze-holding going on, and for an instant I think there's something there. Some undeniable connection. Something, I don't know, more than just sex.

'But I'm really proud of everything we did together,' he says.

Does he mean everything? Is he alluding to what happened between us in London? If so, this is my chance to bring it up. Nice and straightforwardly. One middle-aged adult to another.

'What, even the awkward cunnilingus-ing thing?'

He laugh-snorts like a seal and shakes his head. 'Who even says cunnilingus-ing?'

I cringe and point both thumbs at myself. Where's an aneurism when you need one?

'Come here, you jackass! I've missed you.'

He envelops me in a crushing hug and I hide my embarrassment by turning my head away and burying it in the flap of his open shirt. Does he mean he's missed me missed me, or he's missed me being a balloon around him.

'I missed you too,' I whisper.

I wish I could stay tucked in here indefinitely, compressed against him, the force of his body against mine. But as I allow myself to imagine his grip becoming more insistent, more suggestive, it loosens. I turn and look at his distracted face and follow his gaze all the way to the urn.

'I see Gaz has had a makeover since I was last here.'

'Me and the kids have been having some fun.'

Now that we know we're on borrowed time together, we've all been trying to make the most of having what's left of Gaz around. This has mostly involved putting the urn in various outfits, and today he's wearing a Fez, a fake moustache and a bow tie.

'Call it our way of spending quality time with him. It's silly.'

'Why?'

'Because he's gone. For all I know, there could have been a mix up at the crematorium and it's actually someone else in there.'

'Well, whoever it is, they're very lucky to get to stay here with you guys.'

My breath catches. We're still touching. This is my chance to say something. Something better than the something I said before. Any moment now this hug is going to be over, and we're going to go about our remaining days in the house together acting as though absolutely nothing out of the ordinary happened. But something extraordinary did happen. I'm not thinking about the sex specifically; I'm thinking about how this stranger ambled into my life after a period of intense darkness and illuminated everything.

'You could stay here with us too,' I say quietly. I look up at him again.

He continues to stare at the urn and smiles forlornly. 'I think it's a little too crowded, don't you?'

He's right. What was I thinking? Of what possible appeal can this menagerie of children be? 'It is getting that way,' I concede. I pull away from his arms, business-like. 'Anyway, your room is exactly as you left it. I've done my best to keep Jack out of there.' I don't tell him that on occasion I've been sneaking in to lie on his bed and look at photos of him on my phone.

'Actually, I don't need it.' He runs a splayed hand down his face.

'Huh?'

'I've decided to do a bit of travelling, try and get my head clear on what I want to do next.'

'Oh. That's a good idea.' My tone belies that I think this is the worst idea ever. 'Where are you going?'

'Scotland. The Small Isles. I fancied a little peace and quiet. Go off grid for a while.'

'When?' My stomach churns.

He swallows hard. 'Tomorrow.'

My head becomes a whirr of mental chatter. He's leaving us tomorrow? I feel an urgent need to make today last as long as possible. There are still so many chats to be had. So many questions I need to ask him about what he said at the hospital. 'Then let's have a cuppa and I can help you pack.' I try to sound as calm as possible.

He flinches slightly. A subtle turn of the body. I follow the movement. That's when I spot it. The corner of his backpack peeking out from behind the breakfast bar. All at once the truth of what's happening dawns on me; when I walked in before, he really wasn't expecting me to be here. I'd come back from the hospital earlier than I usually would because Geoff is being discharged today. He must not have known.

'Dan,' my voice trembles. 'Were you trying to leave without saying goodbye?'

'No.' A lie.

'Were you?' I ask again.

He digs his hands deep into the pockets of his shorts. He doesn't say anything. Oh my god. He really was going to walk out without letting me know what was going on. I can't quite compute what's happening. I take hold of a chair to steady myself. I'm not sure if souls can slump, but mine has a pretty good crack at it. Thirty years roll back in an instant and I'm nine years old again, sat on our shiny floral sofa, listening to my mom ring round the hospitals because my dad hadn't been seen for three days. After a week of uncertainty one of his mates came round to put us out of our misery. He'd shacked up with some secretary he'd met at his darts club, the culmination of an affair that had been going on for months, and we weren't to expect to hear from him again.

'Did you really think you could just slip away? What about the kids?'

'I was going to call.'

'Oh, how fucking noble of you!' My grip on the chair tightens. 'A fucking phone call? You live with us for nine months. You ingratiate yourself into our household, reading books, playing games, eating with us, watching films. And you're gonna drop us a quick line to say "alright chaps, I'm off."'

He winces. 'It's not like that. I thought it might be better this way.'

'Oh yeah. Tons better. Did you know Eric, who has the emotional range of Batman, has been telling me how much he's missed you? Sindy asks after you all the time. Geoff sees you as some surrogate son, and as for Jack ... well, Jack's Jack, but he's also really fond of you in his own way.'

'And I'm really fond of them.'

'Way to show it.'

'And what about you, Cath. What do you feel?'

I want to tell him how moments ago, tucked into his chest, I was thinking how wonderful it was to have laughed with someone as much as I have with him. How privileged I'd felt to have someone to talk to about my day, or someone to listen to tell me about theirs. How grateful that he'd filled our house with energy and positivity, giving me permission to be playful and silly and worthy and goofy and smart and stupid and sad and happy and most of all alive. But that was before I knew he was trying to leave without saying goodbye, so why give him the satisfaction now? I allowed myself to be vulnerable with him once before in that hotel room and look how that turned out. We've had sex once and we've done nothing but argue since. How could I ever have imagined we were compatible as anything other than friends? And now he's finally shown his true colours. He'll never be dependable like Gaz. He'll always be moving on to the next thing, the next person.

'I'm used to having people disappear on me,' I say. 'What's one more to add to the mix?'

He steps towards me, hands seeking mine. I pull them away.

'Don't touch me.'

He stops, raises his arms in surrender. His biceps flex. He closes his eyes and rubs the back of his neck and his T-shirt rides up to reveal his ridged stomach. Even now, my scheming hormones are hoping to find an excuse for his perfidy.

'It's best you go,' I say. I'm going to cry so I turn towards the patio doors, squeezing my way past the tent so I can stare out at the back garden.

'I guess I've still got some growing up to do, hey?' he says.

'Yeah, good luck with that.'

I watch him in the reflection of the glass. He doesn't move immediately, but slowly looks around the kitchen like he's trying to take in all the detail. Then, when it seems he is satisfied that all specifics have been committed to memory, he picks up his stuff.

'Take care of yourself,' he murmurs. 'Please do give the boys my love.'

I can't speak, so instead I concentrate hard on listening to the ticks of the kitchen clock rather than the beating of my heart. After twenty-two seconds have elapsed, the front door closes behind him. After ten more his keys hit the hallway floor. I turn and stare at the empty space left by him, and blink away the tears.

Chapter Forty-Five

I t's half-raining when we arrive at West Midland Safari Park, a pernicious drizzle that demands the sort of new-fangled intermittent windscreen wiper setting that our car doesn't possess. Instead, we've had to listen to the screeching of perished rubber across a not-wet-enough glass the whole way, hoping the sunshine the forecast promised us will materialise. I come to a stop in a near-empty car park and wait for Geoff and Sheila, who are following on with Sindy in her car. Gaz is strapped into the middle of the back seat, between Jack and Eric, a portion of him still in the urn, but decanted into zip-lock sandwich bags for the second half of our 'ceremony' later. The other portion has been rolled up, as best we could, into nearly two dozen boneless chicken thighs secured with edible strawberry laces, which are in a cool box beneath Jack's feet. No southern frying in the end, we thought raw meat might be preferable to the big cat taste buds. It's been over a week since Dan left, and I've not heard from him. I've not tried to contact him either. When I told

Eric that he wasn't going to be coming back, he was disappointed, but with Reggie serving as a novel replacement, he took it far better than I imagined. I'm the one that's been moping around, relentlessly checking my phone for what I'm not sure, and trying to remind myself that my time and energy are far better spent honouring the memory of a man who didn't have a choice about the manner in which he left us.

'Do you remember when Dad fed a camel a Starburst here?' asks Leanne.

'Oh yeah. I told him it was a bad idea.'

'That doesn't sound like you.'

She's right. I'd gleefully watched him unwrap the sweet, interested to see what might happen when you mix the natural world with the unnatural one of fruit flavoured sweets. What happened was the camel chewed it for ages and then spat it back into Gaz's face, along with half a pint worth of camel spittle.

'Since you've got previous of ignoring the DON'T FEED THE ANIMALS signs, this should be a doddle,' Leanne says.

The others have arrived so we get out of the car to join them. Sheila is wearing head to foot leopard print, topped with a real fur gilet.

'I have such a connection to nature,' she says, pulling the gilet around her. 'I think I might have been an animal in a previous life.'

'You still look like one!'

'Animals don't wear clothes though, do they?' she says. 'Except those meercats off the telly, but they're not real, are they?'

I worry this is a genuine question, not a statement. Still,

since Geoff's heart attack, I've reached an easy peace with her. We are united in our gratitude that he's still around.

'Everyone knows the plan, right?' I lay out a park map onto the wet bonnet of the car. 'We'll head to the drive-through bit first, which is here, and then afterwards we find a nice picnic spot and a fair wind for the rest. Everyone cool?'

There are murmurs suggesting everyone is cool, but given the weather, they would rather be in the cars than out of them.

'We'll stay in formation. Geoff, Leanne has a box of chicken for you. I'll distribute the bags of ashes once we're out the other side. We've also got these.' I hand a Peppa Pig walkie talkie to Sindy. 'You need to press the belly for us to hear you.'

'Roger that,' says Sindy.

'I didn't know you knew the lingo,' I say, surprised.

'I was talking about him!' She motions behind me where a park keeper in short shorts and a wide brimmed hat is being carried along on a set of brown muscular legs. 'I would do it like they do it on the Discovery Channel with him.'

I shake my head. 'Not in front of the children!'

'They don't know what I'm saying,' she says.

'I think you're intimating that, given the chance, you would have intercourse with that man,' says Eric.

Sindy puts the walkie talkie to her mouth and presses Peppa's belly. 'I've been rumbled. Over. I repeat, I have been rumbled, over.' She ruffles Eric's hair, which looks ridiculous because he's almost as tall as her now. 'Only kidding. Just missing your Uncle Dave.'

Dave is not due home for another few months and she always gets a bit antsy when he's been away too long.

'Sure you're up to this, Geoff?' I ask. 'It's a jungle in there!'

'Actually, lions don't and never have lived in jungles,' Eric tells us. 'They prefer grasslands and plains. And given that most lions are found in Africa, a continent of which only a tiny percentage is rainforests, it's actually rather surprising that this misconception prevails.'

I look at Sindy and back at Eric. 'The sooner you get a girlfriend the better.'

'The sooner your jokes get less lame, the better,' he counters good-naturedly.

'You try keeping me away,' says Geoff. 'I've prepared a few words if that's okay?'

'Of course,' I say.

At Gaz's funeral Geoff, already a man of few words, had been too traumatised to speak. It's nice he'll have the chance to make up for it today.

'Alrighty then, is everybody ready for *Operation Ash Scatter*?'

'We're ready!' says Leanne. 'Come on, before we're soaked through.'

'Ready for what?' asks Jack.

'We're going to feed the lions,' I say.

'Cool,' he says. 'I love lions.'

By the time we've collected tickets and signed waivers, the sun has come out in full force. I'm not the greatest fan of zoos. I've never understood how we consider it our right as the cleverest of the species to imprison animals as a means of preserving them, when presumably the best way of preserving animals would be not to kill them or destroy their habitats in the first place. Still, there's a certain thrill in seeing a six-metre-tall giraffe chew on your car aerial and I'm nothing if not principled in a totally hypocritical way.

'Where are the monkeys?' Eric asks, after we've passed through the Wild Asia section of the park.

'They got a disease that was potentially deadly to humans, so they destroyed them all.'

'That's sad,' he says.

I remember it being on the news. It was especially sad because a clever member of the group had once disappeared for seventeen days. No one is certain how he did it, but in a similar incident in Nebraska, an orangutan fashioned a key from a piece of wire fence he kept concealed in his gums and used it to let himself out when the keeper's back was turned. It is the best anecdotal evidence I know of the extreme smartness of our simian cousins.

We arrive at the *Realm of the Lions*, a large expanse of grassland edged by a flat grey lake which, in typical theme park style, has eschewed the use of real stones and rock in favour of the fake stuff fashioned out of fibreglass. The effect is a cross between Africa and Alton Towers. Someone has seen fit to create an edifice called *Lion Rock*, like Mount Rushmore but with a lion's face.

'Perhaps it's to remind visitors what a lion looks like in case they don't get to see one,' says Leanne, because right now, there isn't one in sight.

I bring the car to a crunching halt on the gravel and take a good look around. The walkie-talkie crackles in Leanne's hand.

'Where the bloody hell are they? Over.' It's Sindy.

'Let's wait a few minutes. It's not as though we're holding anyone up.' We've raced through the other sections so we're way ahead of other visitors.

Leanne relays this to the other car and we survey the

landscape. No sign of any movement apart from moorhens skimming along the surface of the water.

'What do you say when a round of cricket is finished?' says Sindy. 'That's that over over. Over.'

'Very droll,' says Leanne. 'Perhaps we should get the chicken out. Maybe if they get a whiff they'll come over. Over.'

'Good idea. Over.'

I reach around the back of the car and flip the lid on the cool box. 'Everyone ready?'

'Go for it,' says Eric.

Leanne winds the window down a little, pops the lid off the plastic box, pulls on a rubber glove as best she can, and drops a couple of thighs out of the window. 'Here, kitty kitty. Here, kitty kitty kitty,' she coos.

I glance in the rear-view mirror to see Sindy doing the same, the pale peachy flesh of the chicken landing with an unceremonious plop onto the ground below. Leanne hums 'The Lion Sleeps Tonight.'

'Perhaps this is a good time to say a few words. Over.' It's Geoff.

'Go for it. Over.'

He clears his throat several times, already getting emotional. 'What I wanted to say was … ahem … what I really wanted to say was … erm … what I was going to say was … JESUS H CHRIST!'

I instinctively turn round to tell Jack not to repeat that when I see the source of Geoff's outburst. A lion has appeared out of nowhere, reared up against the side of their car and is trying to shake hands with Sindy through the small gap in the side window. I fumble to start the engine. The car fills with the sound of panicked shouting. I turn around again to calm the kids and realise it's coming from the walkie-talkie. Eric is out of his seat belt like a shot, kneeling on the back seat and gawping in half terror, half awe, at the events unfolding behind us. I grab the radio. 'JUST DRIVE!' I shout, then toss it back into Leanne's lap whilst I struggle to get our car into gear. In the rear-view mirror Sindy's car jerkily moves, the lion dancing alongside it like some unnatural tango act.

'What should I do about Dad?' asks Leanne, a hand full of thighs still in her hand.

'Throw them all out. See if the meat will draw that lion away from their car.'

She duly tips the box out of the window and shouts at the creature through it. It has no effect on the lion, but I notice with horror that another two lions have appeared.

'We need to provide a distraction, Leanne. What have we got?'

She leans over into the back seat, takes the bags of ashes from the urn and begins to throw them one by one as far away from the car as she can.

The animals briefly look round, but the first lion stays resolutely where it is. Sindy is leaning away from her door, screaming.

'It's not a dog,' I shout at Leanne. 'They don't play fetch!'

'Well, I'm sorry, I didn't bring an industrial-sized ball of wool!'

'This isn't funny!'

'Oh, this is funny!' says Eric.

'What if that window breaks?'

Leanne continues to fire bags of ashes out of the window, but in her haste one catches on the ceiling handle hook and the bag rips. It only takes the merest hint of a breeze through the window to send the ashes scattering across the car and all of us in it. As I'm trying to get the gritty remains of my deceased partner out of my eyes, I hear Eric, who was facing in the opposite direction of the ash cloud, tell us that, 'It's okay, the rangers are here.' Sure enough, a bright yellow Land Rover pulls up behind Sindy's car. The lion drops back onto four paws and walks away, unphased. There's heavy breathing over the radio.

'Permission to get the hell out of here before anyone has the chance to ask any awkward questions.'

'You didn't say over. Over,' I tell Sindy.

'I'll over you in a minute,' comes the retort.

Leanne takes it from me. 'Permission granted. Over.'

Five minutes later we emerge from our cars, slightly shell-shocked and wobbly, but back in the safety of the car park.

'Geoff! Are you okay? You're meant to be avoiding stress!'

'I've never felt more alive,' he says, flushed and wide-eyed. 'You lot are looking a bit grey, mind.'

I look at my wonderful children, covered in the ashes of their dead father, and wipe my hands decisively. 'Well, I think we can all agree that that went rather well.'

Geoff chuckles. 'I don't think he'd have wanted it any other way, lass.' He wraps his arm around Sheila's shoulder and looks at each of us in turn, nodding. 'Aye. I reckon we did him proud.'

He's right. I reckon we did. 'Right, anyone fancy a burger for lunch?' I ask.

'Beef, not chicken?' says Eric.

'Whatever you like, sunshine.'

And we head off in search of a café, brushing ourselves off as we go.

Chapter Forty-Six

'**A** re you sure this is okay, Miss?' asks Reggie, who still isn't calling me Cath.

'Absolutely. Sheila was insistent you came.' What I haven't told him is that, thanks to some past life regression exercise, Sheila thinks she was an African tribesman in a previous life, which manifests itself as an interest in large costume jewellery in this one. I suspect she wants to talk to him about their shared ancestry. It's fine; I'll divert her attention by asking her to do me a Hopi ear candle or something.

This is my first time at her house, and I am genuinely overjoyed at finally getting the chance to see what her place is like. The building itself is a modest little semi-detached, but unlike the surrounding houses—identikit boxes the likes of which you find on these thirty-year-old housing estates— Sheila's is somewhat of an oddity. The exposed side is covered in gaily coloured metal butterflies and the front has been turned into a paradise for ornamental garden gnomes. Leanne lifts Jack up to press the doorbell and the tinny sounds of Greensleeves as played on a child's Bontempi organ ring out. Sheila appears wearing a novelty apron over a bright paisley dress and a pair of earrings the size of dreamcatchers.

'Come in, come in.'

Jack goes first, not bothering to take his shoes off. 'Don't break anything,' I instruct him.

'Reggie, you came!' says Sheila, throwing her arms around his neck and depositing a berry red imprint of her lips on his cheek. 'You and I have so much in common. I can't wait to have a proper chat.'

I contrast the chintz of our surroundings with Reggie's drop crotch jeans, baseball cap and oversized sleeveless hoody and mouth 'you are practically twins' to him over Sheila's head. He shrugs, completely at ease in this alien situation.

'Kids, do you want a fizzy pop or something? I've got some cream soda.'

Eric makes appreciative noises. She ushers us into the lounge, where Geoff is reclining awkwardly on a chaise longue that's covered in fake crocodile skin.

'Don't get up,' I tell him.

'I bloody well couldn't if I tried, love,' he says with a chortle.

I look around the place, drinking it in. It is even more garish than I imagined, like staring into a supernova without protective glasses on.

'This place is amazing,' says Leanne.

'It's very flamboyant,' I say.

Sheila has returned, holding a tray of glasses containing bright pink pop. She hands them out. 'I could give you a few tips if you ever want to give your place a proper facelift, Cath.'

I suspect it would be the kind of facelift Donatella Versace had, the one where she should have left well alone.

'I hope everyone's hungry. I've made loads of food.' She opens the glazed double doors that separate the lounge from the dining area.

She has indeed put out quite a spread. There are mushroom vol-au-vents, cheese and pineapple on sticks, tiny triangular sandwiches with the crusts cut off, pizza slices and a three-tier cake stand crammed with French Fancies and Cherry Bakewells. There's even a prawn ring.

'Awesome!' says Eric. 'Can I have a cake?'

'You need to eat something nutritious first,' I tell him.

He takes in the table of food and then looks back up at me, raising an eyebrow, as if to say, 'and where will I find that?'

'Okay, after you've had something savoury,' I clarify.

'Come. Sit. Get stuck in,' says Sheila. 'It's all got to be eaten!'

After everyone's had their fill and the dishes have been cleared away, Sheila emerges again carrying a bottle of Cava and four glasses. 'You kids will have to sit this one out I'm afraid,' she says.

'Are we celebrating?' I ask.

Geoff stands and pulls Sheila towards him. 'Shall you tell them, or shall I?'

'You do it,' says Sheila.

'You're not pregnant, are you?!' says Leanne, much to Eric's horror.

'No, you daft sod. We're getting married.'

It takes a few seconds for the news to sink in, but as it does a glow spreads through me. For all her foibles, Sheila makes

Geoff very happy, and she'll ensure what's left of his life will be full of colour and love.

'You don't mind, do you?' Sheila says to me.

'Are you kidding me?' I get up to pull the pair of them into a hug. 'Mind? I'm over the moon!'

Leanne gets involved, too, wrapping her arms around the three of us. Eric follows suit and within a few seconds Jack is tugging at my jeans' pocket. I look over at Reggie, who seems mildly alarmed.

'Oh no, sunshine,' I tell him. 'You are not excused from this one. Come in.'

'You want me to do a group hug?'

'And you need to do it like you mean it.'

He doesn't move immediately but then shrugs and joins in, standing a good few inches taller than the rest of us.

'Congratulations, Big G,' he says. 'Do you need me to DJ at the wedding? I can do you mate's rates.'

Afterwards, we find out that Geoff popped the question whilst he was still in hospital, and arrangements are already well underway. The registry office has been booked for two weeks from now, with the occupants of this room plus Sindy invited to the ceremony. Sheila has no living relatives to speak of, but a couple of friends will attend a small gathering back at the house afterwards. A little later, as Leanne is talking wedding dress hire with Sheila, Jack is playing with some Russian dolls he's found and the older boys are diverted by a collection of *Mysteries of the Unexplained* books, Geoff takes me to one side.

'About the wedding. You can have a plus one if you want one.'

'Who for?'

'"Who for?" she says. *Who for?!* For Dan of course.'

I have been trying hard not to think about Dan and failing miserably. I can't stop imagining what an incredible time he must be having in Scotland. And several images of him in a kilt may have popped into my head whilst lying in bed at night.

'If you want Dan to come, you should ask him yourself,' I say.

'I thought maybe there was a little more to it than that.'

'I don't know what you mean.'

'I'm not wet behind the ears, lass. I've seen how you two are together.'

I wince at the term together.

'Have I got it wrong? Are you not fond of him?'

'No. Yes. I mean … if you must know, yes, I like him. But he doesn't feel the same way. You've met him; he's not exactly that way inclined.'

'So why did he stay?' Geoff asks.

'Stay where?'

'At yours? That must have cramped his style, no?'

'He didn't have an alternative.'

'How hard would it have been to find one?'

'He had something set up, but it fell through.'

Geoff tuts and frowns. 'He turned it down. I overheard him one night I was round. Said he'd decided to stay where he was.'

'What are you saying?'

'I'm saying he likes you too.'

'No more than he likes anyone, Geoff. He came round to collect his stuff and wasn't even going to say goodbye.' The sting of the memory hasn't diminished.

'Sometimes goodbyes with people we love are the hardest ones of all.'

'Oh really? Do you think that was my dad's excuse?'

'But Dan's not your dad.'

In my heart I know this, but demonising Dan helps with the feelings of rejection.

'I invited him to stay. He said it was too crowded.'

'Have you ever considered he might have been referring to our Gaz?'

I recall that moment. I'd thought he'd meant all the kids but it could have been Gaz he'd been referring to. 'But I'm ready to move on.'

'He doesn't know that. As far as he's concerned, you're still hung up on a man who no longer has the capacity to disappoint you. Some might say that's the perfect type. It's hard to compete with a memory, Cath, even the most confident of men might choose not to bother.'

Could Geoff be right? Now I come to think of it, what had my initial reaction in the hotel room been? I'd mentioned Gaz. It was then he'd been at great pains to tell me that it was just sex. And I didn't actually tell him we were finally laying Gaz's ashes to rest. I'd just told him we were spending more quality time together. My heart is beating hard somewhere near my throat. I don't dare imagine what this might mean. Could Geoff be right? Is there the tiniest chance that Dan likes me, as in *likes me* likes me, too?

'Now she gets it!' says Geoff.

'What do you think I should do?' I ask.

'You should tell him how you feel.'

I consider this, but—

'NOW!' says Geoff, sensing my reluctance.

I go and grab my phone, banishing every impulse to chicken out. I was right; there was something else there. He wasn't rejecting me in trying to sneak away; he was protecting himself. He didn't think of me as another conquest, but had instead been trying to assuage the guilt he knew I was feeling. I take a deep breath, bring his number up on my phone and mentally rehearse what I'm going to say. There is a widely disputed theory in science that says language determines our thinking. If we don't have a word for a concept we cannot fathom it, but in ascribing labels to things they become knowable to us. Love. I say the word quietly, feeling the creaminess of it in my mouth, acknowledging it for the first time. And in naming it, it takes on shape and form, no longer an amorphous ache but something purposeful, something active and concrete that I can do something about. *I think I love you.* Is it too much? Too strong? But if he really does like me like Geoff says he does, then he won't think I'm an idiot for liking him too. And I'm too old to be mincing about with childish games. Best to be honest and see what happens. I push the call button on the screen and brace myself, nerves and excitement blossoming in my throat. Within a fraction of a second I hear a voice. Only it's not Dan's. It's a formal English accent, such that a schoolmistress might adopt. 'Sorry. The number you have dialled is not in service. Please check the number and try again. Sorry. The number you have dialled is not in service. Please check the number and try again.' I rest the phone in my palm, checking I've dialled correctly. There's his picture, the one I took at the Black Country Museum and assigned to his number. I can't try again. I'm too late. He must already be back home.

Chapter Forty-Seven

For the next few days I exist in a funk of regret, unsuccessfully doing anything to take my mind off Dan. When I told Geoff I'd been unable to get hold of him, he suggested I email instead. I really did try. Draft upon draft of trying in fact. But with every attempt to commit my garbled words to screen, the whole idea of us having any kind of future unspooled into knots of self-doubt. Even if my feelings are the tiniest bit reciprocated, this couldn't possibly work in reality. Dan might have been temporarily seduced by the novelty of our domestic set-up, but what have I got to offer him long-term? He'd soon hanker for pastures new. As much as I'm ready to move on, I'm not ready for another heartbreak, so why put him under the kind of pressure a confession of love would elicit? I believe Geoff when he says Dan likes me, but now he's back home it won't be long until he's put the whole episode into perspective—that I was nothing more than an interesting confection, past its best-before date, served up on the smorgasbord of life. Nope, the kindest thing to do for both of us is to let sleeping dogs lie. Fortunately—or unfortunately —for me, Gaynor called yesterday to tell me she was in town and offered to treat me to afternoon tea at some swanky boutique hotel she's staying at, which is where I'm headed now. The fact that I accepted offers some clue as to how desperate I am for diversion.

'Cath, you're on time!' Gaynor is at the bar when I arrive, being fawned over by the manager. Her hair is pulled back into a chic bun, and she's wearing a navy shift dress that accentuates her curves without being too showy and looks as comfortable in killer patent heels as I might in a onesie. I look down at my own faded blazer, shirt and jean combo and resolve to do some clothes shopping. As soon as I have a job.

'How have you been? Any wobbles recently?'

Oh, hundreds, I think. But not of the type she thinks. 'No. Just that one.'

'Come on, our table's waiting.' She leads me over to a huge booth with gold leather studded banquettes on either side. I'm shuffling onto one when a waiter arrives, drinks tray in hand.

'I hope you don't mind. I took the liberty of ordering already. We've got lemon lavender mocktails to start.'

Ordinarily, this tendency to take charge might have annoyed the hell out of me, but today I'm thankful for it, and the drink tastes delicious.

'This place is a bit different.' The building we're in is a former derelict rope factory in a part of Birmingham that used to be thought of as rough and is now the height of cool.

'Oui, plus ça change.' She thoughtfully sips on her drink. 'I don't have many reasons to come back to Birmingham anymore. I'm never entirely sure I like it when I do.'

In a rare act of candour, she tells me how she lost both of

her parents within a few months of each other barely eighteen months earlier, how it had been a relief to finally be free of their beady scrutiny and damning expectations. The parental home (less a house and more an estate) has lain empty ever since as she wrestles with what to do with a place she never felt any emotional connection to other than a desperate need to escape it. By the time we've eaten several rounds of miniature food, she has let more slip about her emotions than she ever did when we were at school together.

'Perhaps now's a good time to show you these.' I manoeuvre next to her so we can both view some photos of us I found when going through the boxes.

'Oh,' she says, like I've produced a rotting skunk.

I persist anyway; I have a feeling it might be cathartic for both of us. We make our way through the pile, starting with one from when we performed Handel's *Messiah* at Birmingham Symphony Hall as part of the school choir. Then onto several of us all chilling out in the sixth form common room, where we'd make Cup a Soups and think it meant we'd learned how to cook. There are various sporting events, school plays, recitals and shows, exhibiting an array of faces to which Gaynor tries to put names for me, and fill me in on what they're all now up to, information she gleaned from the reunion. The last one is my favourite, an end-of-year party in which Gaynor and I are standing together in a rare show of solidarity, her arm snaked around my neck, the huge white bow of her Shannon Doherty-inspired dress half-obscuring my face. My own dress was a simple black slip that I had proudly pimped with cheap dip-dyed feathers bought from a haberdasher not far from here. I can practically hear the strains of 'C U When You Get There' by Coolio pulsing in the background as I look at it. But as I study us more closely, I notice something I haven't before; Gaynor's sleeve has slightly ridden up her arm, revealing the very edge of something around her wrist.

'Is that a bandage?'

Gaynor winces. A dim memory comes back to me.

'Was that a skiing accident?' But as I'm asking the memory resolves itself more clearly. I know full well what that bandage is hiding; Gaynor had once tried to slit her wrists. I can't believe I'd forgotten; for weeks it had been all anyone could talk about. At first it had been a rumour, some silly whisperings from one of the juniors whose dad worked at such-and-such a hospital and had recognised her parents and enquired with the staff about the daughter's wellbeing. But then there was her prolonged absence, unheard of for Gaynor. Later came the counter-story of an accident in the Alps from which she was recovering, a tale we were hungry to accept unblinkingly because the alternative was too appalling to consider. And on her return to school, she was still Gaynor, still beautiful and capable and aloof, and so we'd let the incident slip by unquestioned, none of us daring to ask what could possibly have driven her to harm a body we all coveted, or jeopardise a life we all aspired to. How lonely she must have felt then.

'Oh, Gaynor. I'm so sorry.'

She doesn't say anything, but nods briefly and rubs at the expensive cuff bracelet on her wrist.

'Gaynor, are you happy?' I ask at last.

She turns and looks at me, surprised by the question. 'Not in the least,' she says. 'Whatever gave you that idea?'

'Because…' I shrug, thinking of everything she's ever achieved.

'I got pregnant you know, before you did. Had this torrid little affair with one of father's friends.' Her mouth puckers. 'Of course, he insisted I get rid of it. Couldn't bear the idea of a scandal. But I really wanted it, unlike my parents who never wanted me.'

'I'm sure that's not true.'

'It is. What about all those holidays I wasn't taken on, being farmed off to various camps during the summer. The dinner parties where I was instructed to stay in my room. I was an impediment. That's what the bandage was about. I wanted to take back control after the abortion. I think I might also have genuinely wanted to die.'

'You never said anything.'

'I've never been good at talking about such matters.'

'That must have been horrible.'

'I've dealt with worse.'

I can't believe what she's saying. To think our lives had mirrored each other's so closely. 'Perhaps it was the best decision. Look at everything you've been able to do since.'

She sighs. 'What have I done really? I'm part of an industry that encourages people to desire lives they don't have, spending money they often can't afford to, in the hopes of a happiness that never materialises.'

I'm reminded of Dan talking about how wherever you go, you always have to take yourself. I wish I wasn't taking him everywhere with me as well.

'So, what do you want?' I ask.

'What does anybody want? To be loved.'

'But—'

'I know what you're going to say. How could someone as beautiful and accomplished as me possibly not be loved?'

It wasn't quite what I was going to say, but I let it slide.

'I'm admired by women, desired by men, and I've been in demand workwise. But I've never been loved. Not properly. Not in the way you have been by Gaz and the kids. I might have got the status, but I'd have traded it for your status quo any day of the week.'

I stop short. Dan's words about chasing success hang before me like neon signs, each one blinking into life, their looped phosphorescence casting a stuttering light that at first had been hard to take in, but is so obvious now the illumination has reached full vibrancy. Of course he was right; I'd been using my online activity as air-cover for my need to feel validated. It explains so much. The way I treated Sindy, the conflicted feelings I'd been so eager to suppress, and the backdrop of unease that grew every day I didn't submit my essays but instead posted updates about how well everything was going. I was seduced by the false sense of significance all those likes and comments gave me. I've spent half my life thinking I was a failure, never once questioning that my judgment criteria might be all wrong.

'It's okay. I don't need your sympathy,' says Gaynor, misinterpreting my silence. 'In fact, it's rather lovely to say it out loud.'

I reach across the table for her. She flinches but doesn't pull away.

'How silly we were when we were younger,' she says. 'All that competition. We could have been great allies you and I, with our noses pressed to the window wondering how to fit in.'

I've never thought of it that way before, but Gaynor is right. I spent most of my time at school secretly thinking I didn't belong, yet never fully prepared to admit how much I wanted to.

Gaynor checks the time on her phone. 'I'm so sorry, Cath, the afternoon has all but got away with us and I still haven't asked you how things are going with you.'

'That's okay. There's not really much to tell.' I had been secretly looking forward to sharing all my exciting news with Gaynor, a chance to show that I could play her at her own game, but now it transpires I won the competition a long time ago.

'What about all this influencing?'

What about it? 'Actually, I've decided I'm going to quit whilst I'm ahead on that.'

'Really?'

I really have. But there's one last video I need to do as soon as I get home.

'Hello everyone. Science Mom here. I wanted to post this video to let you know that this will be my last one. I've decided that social media isn't really my thing, even though I've somehow become quite successful at it. Although that depends on how you define success. The dictionary will tell you—yes, I looked it up—it's either "the accomplishment of an aim or the attainment of fame, wealth, or high social status." That second definition worries me, because inherent in it is the notion that we have to pit ourselves against others, that we have to be better or have more than those around us to be considered successful. And the trouble is, social media is making it easier than

ever for us to compare where we sit on this leaderboard of life. We judge how valid our opinions are by whether they get up-voted or down-voted compared to others. We judge how popular we are by how many followers we've amassed. We even judge how liked we are by the number of likes we have. And for those teenagers amongst you, this will have a much greater impact on your lives than any of you imagine. Much greater than your choice of GCSEs, A-levels, university or even career. Why? Because unless you're careful, it's going to hugely affect how satisfied you are with the choices you make. Because the picture we're getting from social media is skewed. On it people tell the stories they want others to know, but more often than not they're not real stories. We think of them as documentaries but they're as fake as any fiction movie, all carefully edited to show the actors and actresses in the best possible light; multiple takes until they get the perfect shot, deliver the perfect line, the exact intonation, and even then they get trolled for saying the wrong thing! I'm not the first person to point this out, and I won't be the last. And you know it too. You know it's not real life.

'Real life is what happens in the gaps between the highlights. Real life is dropping your phone down the toilet when you're doing a selfie in the bathroom. Or when your kid farts loudly as you're videoing their nativity play. It is not some sanitised, retouched, retaken, re-framed, resized and re-posted anodyne shit that makes your life look flawless. It's the original emotion of the moment. The time when you're not thinking about how it will look, or how it will play, or whether it will offend anyone. It's the minute-to-minute feels you feel when you forget what other people might think and concentrate only on what you think.

'And trying to put over any other version of yourself is a lie. It's worse than a lie because it's specifically designed, whether you mean it or not, to create a point of comparison. To make yourself look or feel

superior to somebody else. And why do you do this? Because you see other people living their perfectly posed lives and you think you should be able to have a bit of that too; you deserve that special brand of happiness and contentment and smug fuckery that they're peddling. And the cycle continues. But what if we ditched the leader board? What if we concentrated on our own dashboard instead? What if we measured our success, according to our own history, our own unique set of circumstances, our own progress? What if the only standards against which we judged ourselves were our own? Coco Chanel said, "beauty starts the moment you decide to be yourself". I think the reason I got so many followers was because I was myself at first. Slightly shambolic, self-deprecating and not afraid to make a total idiot of myself. But then I got seduced by that definition of success, the prospect of social status and things I didn't need. At that juncture I stopped pursuing an aim and I started pursuing fame. But I'm not a brand. I'm not Science Mom. I'm Cath, and I'm just a person who likes science and who wants to be a teacher when she finally grows up. So it's best that I don't get distracted by this, and that I do focus more on that.

'But if I can give you a single piece of advice before I sign off, it is this: try to imagine there's a periodic table of emotions from which all human experience derives. Don't let envy and jealousy be the most abundant ones. Let those hateful feelings be like Flerovium and Livermorium discovered in the Hadron Collider: things that pop into and out of existence so quickly that it's impossible to trace their impact. Work on the elements that make up love instead: respect; empathy; understanding; forgiveness. And always measure the value of yourselves in the things that you can't post on social media, because it is these that will prove to be the most indefinable, yet most precious elements of your entire lives. So thanks to everyone for watching. And thanks to Dan who helped me begin all of this, and *who also helped me see why I had to end it. Sometimes equations don't always add up in the way you want them to, but you left me with so much more than I started with, and I'll always be grateful for that. This has been Science Mom saying goodbye for the last time. Over and out.'*

Chapter Forty-Eight

T he décor in our local café is all dark wood, doilies and tasselled lampshades, with peculiar pictures of crying children on the walls. It's meant to be knowing, retro chic, but I could be at my dead grandmother's house, had she hoarded tables and chairs. I like it because the owner has thoughtfully created a little section devoted to kids where Jack is currently sat, trying to read a board book upside down and shouting the words *dinosaur* every so often, much to the startled amusement of the few people in here. I'm sipping on my decaf cappuccino, thinking about an essay I need to write, when the door chime tinkles delicately, drawing my attention. Uh-oh. Belinda and a couple of the other moms have walked in with their kids in tow. As Sindy predicted, once I quit the influencer game, Belinda blanked me again. I get the occasional hello from the others, but I suspect Belinda has warned against any fraternization. It takes her a while to spot me, the small contortion of her mouth the only thing out of place in her otherwise impeccable get-up that includes flawless muted makeup, pale blue linen jumpsuit and tan gladiator sandals. She turns quickly to the others, perhaps to suggest they go elsewhere, but they're already making themselves comfortable. Twelve months ago, I'd have felt wretched about being alienated from the group, but not now. Now, I'm happy to sit, enjoy my coffee, and revel in my newfound self-esteem. Right up until Jack spots his nursery mates, toddles over to me and points to the group.

'Mom, it's Bellender!' he says in his outdoors voice.

This is the nickname to which Sindy and I have been referring to her, seemingly within Jack's earshot. *Ye gods.*

At first there's no reaction, perhaps she didn't hear, but then Jack shouts it again, grabbing at my face to turn it in their direction so I know who he means. There are times in a woman's life when she comes to a crossroads, when she must face up to her responsibilities and be the better person, the bigger woman. I make my way over amongst the jumble of tables.

'Belinda, I owe you an apology.'

'Seemingly so.' Her eyes are burning slits of disapproval.

'The thing is, I do actually think you're a bell-end.'

There's a collective sharp intake of breath.

'It's not because you think you're better than everyone else with your picture-perfect life, or that you only wanted to include me in your little clique when you thought I was worthy enough to join. It's because we have lived on the same street for several years. You've seen my daughter walking down our road. You were home when the hearse pulled up with Gaz in. You know what my situation is; you've seen it play out every time I drop Jack off at nursery. But you have never, not once, ever thought to ask if we were okay.'

All faces turn to Belinda, who's now looking wide-eyed and flushed.

'Which, for anyone, even someone as popular and busy as you, has to be the highest form of bell-endery going. Now I'm no expert in these matters, but maybe if you got your head out of your doubtless perfectly bleached anus now and again, you might be able to see that for yourself.'

Belinda doesn't say anything. She seems transfixed by me, as if I've hypnotised rather than insulted her.

'Erm,' one of the other moms pipes up. 'Didn't you say you owed her an apology?'

I shrug my shoulders. 'I do now.' I beckon Jack. 'Come on, son, let's leave these people to it.'

For once he does as he's told, sensing that I really do want to get out quite quickly. As I take his hand, I look back. 'For what it's worth, I think the rest of you are probably okay. See you at nursery. We'll be back in September.'

'See you, Cath,' they say in unison.

The door tinkles as I close it behind me, my final glance showing their mouths hanging open, Pavlov's dogs responding to the sound of the bell.

Yes! I nailed it!

I'll just have to collect the handbag that's still hanging on the back of my chair once they've left.

Reggie and I are having a sweating competition as we drive to collect his results. I'm winning by a nose. As reluctant as I was to face Brookdene again, I was chuffed when he asked me to go with him.

'What if I've failed?'

'Then you try again next year.'

Since he moved in, Reggie and I have settled into an easy-going relationship. He is as good a kid as I always suspected. Not crazily good, you understand—I'd be worried if a sixteen-year-old was too well behaved—but in the parlance of childhood behaviour experts, he makes mostly the right decisions. Having Leanne around, serving as a reminder of the possibilities that lie ahead if he applies himself, really helps. As we pull into the car park, the place is swarming with kids, some chewing on sleeves and laughing nervously whilst others seem way too relaxed, as though this is merely a detour on the way to more important business, like hanging around shopping precincts. We get out of the car and Reggie points out Bradley and Malik, vaping while leaning against a wall, more like expectant dads waiting for the birth of a child than kids waiting for exam results.

'Reggie, dude,' says Bradley as we approach. 'How's summer camp?'

This is what they've dubbed his living arrangements.

'Sweet, bruh,' he says, seizing Bradley's hand and pulling him into a back-slapping embrace.

'You come to give us grief, Miss?' asks Malik.

'I'm hoping there won't be any need.'

'Don't hold your breath.'

'Quick, doors are opening,' I tell them.

A few stragglers I recognise pass as I pace outside, offering me puzzled hellos and obviously wondering why I'm there. I've chewed my nails to the quick by the time people start filtering out again, some tearful, some elated, some not seeming to give a toss either way. Then I notice my old pal

Daphne emerge. I'd texted her to let her know that I'd be there and hoped to say a quick hello.

'Cath. How the devil are you?'

'Oh, still out of work and penniless, so, you know, fabulous!'

She waves her hand as though this is absolutely no big deal. 'At least you have several videos of you embarrassing yourself available for public consumption on the world wide web. Coming for a quick coffee?'

'Can't. Got to check how everyone has got on.'

'Very well. But pop in before you go. The kids'll want to hang out for a while, and we have some half-decent filter stuff knocking around for once. There might even be biscuits.'

'I won't get you into trouble?'

She waves her hand again. 'Pff. It's not as if there's a restraining order out against you. Is there?'

'No,' I say quickly. No one ever did call about that car bonnet I drew on.

'Then stop being a bore and come to the staffroom when you're ready. Oh, and I think your little set might have some news.'

I turn around. Reggie, Bradley and Malik are heading my way. I can't read Reggie's face. Is he upset? Neutral? Happy?

'I'm sorry, Miss,' says Bradley, patting Reggie's back comfortingly. 'You've got some extra coaching to do.'

Reggie raises his eyes to mine, his lips set in a thin line of resignation and he shrugs at me. But then the muscles shift, the mask cracks and he's grinning widely.

'For my A Levels! I'm going to college!'

'No. No. Nooooooo!' I jump up and down. 'Agggghhh! What did you get?'

'Fours across maths, English and history.'

These are passes. They would have been around the low C's before the *Minister for Interfering in Education* decided to change the grading system.

'What did you get in science?' I ask.

'Six-six!'

These are strong passes, formerly known as B's. I'm bursting with pride and immediately want to text Dan to let him know. I bury the impulse.

'Yeah, he's a massive speccy four eyed swot,' says Bradley.

'Aw cheers guys.'

'How did you pair do?'

'All fours but five-five in science,' says Bradley.

'Blooming heck. Not bad!'

'All fours, but a six-five in science,' says Malik.

'Ooh, amazing. Do you want to do an A Level too?'

'That's a firm no.'

'Fair enough.' I'll work on him later. 'Anyone seen or heard from Jada and Hannah?'

'We're going to go find them,' says Reggie.

'Okay, well, text me when you do. I want to know how they got on. And text or call your families. I am sure they'll all be hugely proud.'

Reggie and Bradley seem unconvinced.

Contact between Reggie and his mom has been brief and perfunctory. When I called her to tell her he was going to stay at mine for a while her relief was palpable. Apparently she's still with the boyfriend, a fact I find hard to understand, but like all of us she's largely the sum of the influences acting upon her, and from what little Reggie has shared with me, those influences have not often been kind.

'Even if they don't know how to express it,' I say.

My phone pings. A message from Daphne.

Kettle's on. Hurry up!

'Right, I'm leaving you to it, but before you go, here...' I reach into my bag and pull out a few bags of coins and hand them to Reggie. 'The profits from the swear jar. Not much by actual cash standards, but way too much by sweary standards. It might get you all a Nando's or something to celebrate.'

Reggie punches me playfully on the shoulder. 'Thanks, Cath.'

He called me Cath!

'And if anyone wants any careers advice or anything moving forward, you know where I am. Sat at home. Without a job. Or any prospects of one. On second thoughts, use Google. It is way more successful than me and it has all the answers. See you later, kids.'

As I head to the staffroom, I can't quite believe it's been nearly a year since I was last here. So much has happened, and yet, give or take an extra kid at home, everything is the same. The school hasn't changed much either, apart from a few different displays on the walls, including one about the amount of sugar in fizzy drinks from which someone has stolen the sugar from the sandwich bags attached. I open the door to the staffroom.

'Way-hey. The prodigal daughter returns,' shouts Daphne.

'Someone stole all the sugar from the wall,' I tell her.

'That was us. We ran out and needed some for coffee. Come in!'

I scan the faces in the room for Powell's, but I can't see him.

Unfortunately, Principal Gerald is there and staring straight at me with what I interpret to be malicious intent. He approaches immediately.

'Daphne said you were going to be here. I wonder if I might have a word?'

I cast Daphne a look that I hope simultaneously conveys *you traitor*, and *I still want that coffee though*. She smiles back at me, like this is totally fine. I follow Mr Gerald out into the corridor, my heart picking up speed. Just don't mention drawing on his car. If he could prove it was me, he'd have come after me by now.

'Is this about the car?' I ask. Obviously.

'What car?'

'The cock car.'

'What are you on about?'

'The bonnet with the boner on.' I unnecessarily draw the shape of a penis in the air by way of illustration. He looks like a startled baby.

'Do you drive a white car?' I ask, trying to sound sane.

He mentally calculates something. 'Not for the last eighteen months, why?'

Whoops. Looks like I drew a dick on the wrong car. 'No reason.' I need to move this conversation onto less dodgy territory. I know, talk about the weather.

'How's Mr Powell?'

Now Mr Gerald looks more bodysnatching life form, trying to smile in its human host, but not sure how it should work.

'Given the circumstances of his, er, affliction, we thought it best to lighten the load whilst he seeks the necessary help for his, er, condition.'

'Are we talking about his drinking?'

He looks up and down the corridor. 'Yes,' he answers in hushed tones.

'You know it wasn't me.'

'Yes. You see the thing is, Cath—'

'It's Ms Beckinsale to you.'

'Ms. Beckinsale. The thing is—'

'The thing is, you owe me an apology?'

'Yes,' he whispers.

A huge lightness comes over me. VINDICATED!

'I'm sorry, I know that must have been hard to take, after all your efforts with the children. One particular group was very vocal about your removal.'

Go Reggie and co!

Mr Gerald looks up and down the corridor again. 'I also owe you a job,' he says.

'Say what now?'

'With Mr Powell now taking some time out to, er, practise a little self-care, we have a teacher position available for the coming school year.'

'You're offering me a teaching job?'

'I am.'

'You know I'm not qualified?'

'I know you don't have formal qualifications; it has been the subject of great debate amongst certain colleagues, but this is an Academy, and thanks to governmental loopholes, I'm able to take on anyone whom I feel is up to the job. I've watched your unconventional videos. I've listened to the testimonials of your former pupils and today witnessed the miracle you've performed with the children with whom you've been working privately. And, if I'm completely honest, I've been trying to fill the position for a while. Now I

399

know the last time we met my treatment of you was less than—'

'It's a yes.'

He seems more stunned than he should, given he's offered me a paying job.

'It's a yes,' I repeat.

'You will need to work towards a formal qualification to satisfy—'

'Still a yes.'

'Don't you wish to discuss terms?'

'Will I get paid more than before?'

'Yes.'

'Then it's a double yes. Thank you.'

His shoulders and chest lift, as if I've literally taken a weight off them.

'Shall we shake on it?'

'Yes, let's do that. Thank you, Ms. Beckinsale.'

'Actually, it's Cath.'

'Cath. Well, thank you, Cath. We'll see you in September.'

He walks off in the direction of his office, whistling. Daphne pops her head out of the staffroom door, gives me an enormous grin and thumbs up. I nod, not quite believing what has happened.

'Do you want a Baileys in your coffee?' she asks.

'Do you have Baileys on school premises?'

'Er. No?'

I smile. 'I'd love to, but I'm driving. Just the coffee please.'

And I head back into the staffroom as an actual member of staff. YESSS!!

Chapter Forty-Nine

With the mid-morning sun glinting off its huge reflective windows, the new Registry Office is more plush hotel than civic building. Back in the day it was housed in an ugly 1950s box, a former technical college, incongruously plonked between a street of elegant art deco buildings. Approaching it was like finding a pair of brown corduroy trousers on a rail of wedding dresses. The previous site is around the corner—the building demolished over ten years ago—abandoned in favour of this sleek, new purpose-built location. It's odd to consider that all of life is here, every Midland birth and death since 1837 captured and logged on microfiches and papers covering acres of shelving. Geoff stands next to me, fidgeting in suit and bow tie, trying to get a white rose buttonhole to lie straight on his lapel. It's his big day and Sheila is due to arrive any minute. It's going to be a scorcher, so Sindy, Leanne and the boys have been sent on a water errand.

'Here, let me do it. You're all fingers and thumbs.'

'How come you and Gaz never tied the knot?'

'I thought it was an outdated notion of ownership used by people too insecure to know they were being hoodwinked by society to conform to an expectation.'

'You make it sound so romantic!'

'And I couldn't be bothered getting my bank cards changed. But I sometimes wish I was officially a widow, not simply some middle-aged woman who lost a boyfriend. Who can get worked up over that?'

'Because you're middle-aged?'

'There is that. The public don't care what happens to you once you're on the turn. Read a headline about the sad but entirely natural demise of anyone under the age of eighteen and the nation is wailing about the tragic, untimely nature of it all. But if I accidentally fell into a passing operational woodchipper, my guts and brain shredded into a thousand chunks, people would be like, "that's terrible, how old was she? Thirty-nine you say? Oh well, these things happen."'

Geoff chuckles, but barely. He seems a bit strung-out, eyes darting around as if he's expecting an ambush.

'Are you okay?'

'I'm fine,' he says unconvincingly.

'You're acting like a squirrel who's lost its stash of nuts.'

'I'm fine. It's just a big day.'

Leanne, Sindy and the kids return as a white car with blacked-out windows pulls up to the drop off area. A driver emerges, walks round to the near-side passenger door and opens it, arcing his arm to beckon the occupant out. The angle of our vantage point means the door obscures our view of the passenger, but as soon as a white sequined platform sandal touches the tarmac, I know Sheila has arrived. A plume of feathers emerges before the rest of her, attached to an extravagant headdress. She smiles and waves at us, giving me a chance to take in the full ensemble. There's a strappy bodysuit with more sequins, these ones iridescent mother of pearl that glisten like a mermaid's tail in the sunlight. A feathered cape and yoke made from white coque feathers circles her neck and a skirt of white ostrich feathers cascades to the floor. She could be a Vegas showgirl who got lost on her way to work about sixty years ago. She waves to us.

'She's a game old bird, isn't she?' says Geoff.

'*Bird* being the operative word,' I say.

'You didn't tell me it was fancy dress,' says Eric, which is a bit rich given he's wearing plus fours and a Pringle sweater, because, you know, teenagers. I dig him in the ribs as Sheila is now within earshot.

'Do you have any balloons?' Jack has mistaken her for the entertainment, not the bride.

'No,' she says taking his request in good humour, 'but I have got these.' She reaches into a beaded clutch bag and pulls out three enormous, swirled lollipops, handing one to each of the boys. Reggie casts me a withering glance, but seconds later he is tucking into it with as much relish as Jack is.

'You look incredible,' says Sindy.

'You don't think it's a bit over the top?'

'Oh, it is a lot over the top,' says Leanne. 'But fabulously so. Can I borrow it sometime?'

'Of course, love. We're almost family now.'

'We are family.' I grab her arm 'May your soon-to-be daughter-in-law escort you up the aisle?'

'That would be lovely,' she says, eyes moistening.

'Come on then.'

The ceremony passes quickly but is no less sweet for that. Both Geoff and Sheila wrote their own vows, with, amongst other things, Geoff promising to do everything he could to stay as healthy as possible for as long as possible, and Sheila promising to learn how to play bridge and backgammon. Leanne read *Love Monkey* by Edward Monkton, and I read an Einstein quote that has always resonated with me.

The important thing is not to stop questioning. Curiosity has its own reason for existing. One cannot help but be in awe when he contemplates the mysteries of eternity, of life, of the marvellous structure of reality. It is enough if one tries merely to comprehend a little of this mystery every day.

I then told them that if they comprehend one another a little more every day and stay curious about life, it doesn't matter how long they've been together or may be together, they'll get to live out their days in awe. And then, everyone's piece having been said and the legally binding bits taken care of, we emerge to the strains of The Carpenters 'We've Only Just Begun' played on Leanne's mobile phone.

'Let's head to the vestibule for photos,' I tell everyone.

We start walking, but I notice Geoff is lingering behind, his back turned, sneaking a look at his phone. I walk back up to him.

'What have you got organised, Mister?'

He jumps and turns around. 'Jesus, Cath!'

'Sorry, didn't mean to spook you, but what are you plotting?'

'Nothing,' he says, with all the conviction of a guilty man.

'Come on, tell me.'

'I was, erm, checking on a horse race.'

'On your wedding day?!'

'You said to be curious about the world.'

'I think that's stretching the metaphor a little. Come on, it's photo time.'

He bundles the phone back into his pocket. I hope he's not put a big bet on, but that's unlikely. He's so careful with money, he once tried to borrow some boxers from Gaz to see if he might prefer them to briefs before he invested in a pair. There is a large central garden room in the Registry Office with a huge stone water feature that looks like a bird bath that got out of control. I really want to get a picture of Sheila next to it, but Geoff insists we should head back outside and take more photos out there.

'Yes,' says Sheila, a little too emphatically. 'The kids can run around. They've been cooped up for ages.'

'It's been twenty minutes. They don't need to run around.'

'Come on, let's go outside anyway,' she insists.

As soon as we're out, Jack and Eric sprint away from the building as if they've been in a year-long hostage situation and climb the tangled mass of metal outside the building that's meant to pass for a sculpture. Sheila gives me her best I told you so eyebrow raise. I ignore it and ask the newlyweds to walk slowly towards me whilst Sindy throws confetti at them and I get some photos. The sun has really got its shine on now and it's hard to know where to stand for the best angle. As I'm snapping away, Geoff repeatedly looks up and down the street, seemingly agitated by the continued absence of something.

He's got a surprise up his sleeve, but whatever it is, it's running late.

'I should throw the bouquet,' says Sheila. 'Are you girls going to try and catch it?'

Leanne and I exchange a competitive glance.

'I have always wanted to do this,' she says.

'Me too.' I hadn't had the chance at Sindy's wedding because I'd had to feed Eric.

'Why do we even throw a bouquet anyway?' asks Sindy. 'I've never thought to ask.'

'It used to be thought of as good luck to touch the bride at weddings, so they'd throw the bouquet to distract the crowd so the bride and groom could sneak off and get the other wedding day deed done.'

'How do you know that?'

'I thought to ask,' I say, smirking.

'Swot!'

'You don't think they're going to sneak off for a quickie do you?' says Leanne.

'In that outfit? He'd have to pluck her first.'

We watch as Sheila tentatively climbs the steps in front of us to get a better height on the whole proceedings.

'Did you say Granddad's going to pluck Nanny Sheila?' Eric is behind me, along with Reggie and Jack.

'Where did you come from?'

'From over there,' Reggie deadpans.

'He's going to pluck her?' says Jack.

Sindy tries to hide a smile.

'No, he's not going to pluck her,' I say.

'What's plucking?' asks Jack.

Leanne snorts.

'It's nothing for you to worry about, sweetie,' I say.

'Granddad, are you going to pluck Nanny Sheila?' Jack shouts.

Both Leanne and Sindy collapse into fits of giggles.

'What lad?' asks Geoff, still distracted.

'Ignore him,' I shout. 'Hey, Jack, there isn't going to be any plucking. Nanny Sheila is going to toss the bouquet instead.'

Sounds akin to fire engine sirens emerge from my daughter's and best friend's mouths.

'Is that another euphemism?' Leanne cries, doubling over with laughter and not at all concentrating on the task at hand.

'You pair are not helping.'

'You're damned right we're not helping.' Sindy snorts, dribble now hanging off her chin.

'Are you ready?' shouts Sheila, her back turned to us. 'Here we go.'

For an old gal, she gives it one hell of a welly, misjudging the distance and sending it flying up into the sky. I don't want to let her moment end in crushed flowers on the pavement, so I resolve to catch it, even if I must channel my inner goalkeeper and throw myself at it. The sun is in my eyes, bleaching my retinas to near temporary blindness, but I just about make out the bouquet as it passes overhead a foot or so beyond us. Jack continues to shout about Geoff plucking Sheila, but there are more important things at stake now. I stumble backwards reaching up to the blur of green and white foliage to grab it, but my backside makes contact with another body whose feet I trip over, sending me sprawling to the floor, bouquet-free. Bloody typical. I'm about to apologise when a familiar American accent cuts through the haze.

'I see there's been a slight improvement on the swearing thing.'

'DAN!' shouts Eric, running towards him and throwing his arms around his waist. 'You're back!'

I, by contrast, am rooted to the spot. Everything has gone into slightly slower motion than it was before. I take in the bright halo of light around his floppy hair, notice how his skin is browner than I have ever seen it, his eyes smilier.

'Dan?' I manage.

'Cath.' He takes my hand and helps me up. The bouquet is in his other hand. I look up into his face.

'I thought you were in America.'

'Nope. Off-grid in Scotland.'

'You're a bit late for the wedding.'

'I didn't come for the wedding. I came for you. And the kids. How many of them are there now?'

My throat constricts and my hands tremble. I think I hear Geoff tell Eric to give us a second, but my ears have been filled with cotton wool and water and heartbeat and frigging choir music for Christ's sake. How am I both overcome with emotion and extreme cliché? How am I thinking about thinking clichédly, or wondering if clichédly is even a word? Shut up in there, Cath, and say something out here.

'For keeps?'

'I'd like to think so,' he says.

'Me too.'

He hands me the flowers.

'But how did you know I...' Did he see the video? I secretly hoped that he'd see the video.

But no, he cocks his head towards Geoff and Sindy, both grinning like people possessed. 'Several little birds told me.'

And then he kisses me. And it's a proper romantic movie, never-going-to-let-you-go-bend-you-over-backwards, that's-going-to-ache-a-bit-tomorrow kiss. It is such a good kiss that I feel as though I'm being gently pricked by a hundred tiny needles, my skin tingling like crazy. And then I notice that some eager bystanders have mistaken us for newlyweds and that we are actually being pelted with rice. And I couldn't be happier about it.

Epilogue

We have a few good mornings in this house nowadays. The idyllic breakfasts sold to us in commercials, in which a smiling nuclear two-point-four family sit around a table listening to cereal going snap, crackle and pop may only exist in Marketing Land, but here in the real world, things are way more interesting.

'I need a wee,' says Jack, who has finally mastered the art of taking himself to the toilet. Occasionally he'll get his urine inside it as well.

'I'll take him,' says Eric in his now preposterously and constantly deep baritone. He sounds like a cross between James Earl Jones and thunder, which is ridiculous because he is all of five feet three and built like a broom you might find propped up inside a brick shithouse.

'Thank you, Eric,' I say. 'What do you want in your sandwiches by the way?'

'Crisps.'

'But then what will you have *with* your sandwiches? A slice of cheese?'

'Yeah, that would be great. Thanks, Mom.'

'Can you make sure Reggie is up as well whilst you're up there?'

'Beat you to it,' Reggie says, walking into the room, grabbing buttered toast from my hand and heading back out of the kitchen. 'Can't be late for the first day of college,' he shouts behind him.

'Well, I never.'

'You, however, are going to be late for school,' says Dan, who has come in wearing my pink bathrobe and towelling his wet hair. 'I'll finish up here.' He nuzzles into my neck.

'Sure you don't mind dropping Jack off?'

'I'm looking forward to it.'

I think about Belinda seeing Dan rock up at the nursery gates and can't help but enjoy the uncharitable thoughts that dance loudly around my head.

'Okay, I'm off.'

'Oh, just one thing I need to know,' says Dan.

'What?'

'Exactly how old are you today?'

'Damn it! I was hoping to get away with it.'

Reggie and Eric reappear at the door.

'Hah, did you think we'd forgotten?' says Eric.

'I was hoping so.'

Dan's phone rings. 'Hang on,' he shouts into the mouthpiece. 'I'm going to put you down.' He props his phone up on the kitchen table and there's Leanne's face, hair wet, one eye kohl-rimmed.

'You're up and half-ready early.'

'I have morning lectures this year. It's mightily inconvenient,' she says.

'Okay, can we get this over and done with?'

'Almost,' says Dan.

The doorbell rings.

'I'll go,' I say, stalling.

I open the door to a mass of helium balloons and three pairs of legs, one ending in a pair of brogues, one in a pair of wedge trainers and one in a laser-cut pair of knee-high boots in red patent leather.

'*Et tu*, you guys?'

Geoff's, Sheila's, and Sindy's faces appear in the midst of inflated latex.

'It's a big day. It needed a big moment,' says Sindy.

'Come in.'

I lead them back to the kitchen.

'Okay, is everybody ready?' asks Dan.

They all sing 'happy birthday', and as much as I want to pretend I'm hating it, my eyes betray me and they produce tears quicker than I can wipe them away. I suppose now I'm forty I can expect to leak as much water as I retain—call it a kind of middle-aged equilibrium. Dan even produces a crumpet with a lit candle stuck in it, which I promptly blow out.

'How do you feel?' Leanne shouts from the table.

I take in the smiling faces of the people who mean the most in the world to me and wipe away yet more tears.

'Grateful,' I say. 'Really bloody grateful.'

So there you have it. Not exactly a fairy tale ending, more the credits rolling on a gentle farce in which nobody died—not this time round, at least. Who knows what'll happen next? I still have to get a degree and prove myself as a bona fide teacher. There are teenage years to navigate with Eric, heartbreaks in store for Leanne, and Jack will almost certainly cause me no end of grief in the future. There will be illnesses to fight, bad news to withstand, and, as far as Dan and I are concerned, overseas mothers and friends to be considered along with a wanderlust that must surely return at some point. But that's in the future, as incomprehensible to me as the notion of nothingness, or infinity, or that a strawberry isn't a berry, but a banana is. Instead, all we really have is the here and now. And right now, I'm— SHIT! Right now, I'm running late for work.

Acknowledgments

Writing acknowledgments is like trying to orchestrate pass the parcel; you really don't want to miss anyone out, but if I have, get in touch and I will give you a sweet and tell you that the gift in the middle was a panic buy from Quality Save and not worth getting upset over.

First up, many thanks to the team (and extended team) at One More Chapter including Charlotte Ledger, for taking a chance on the book, Hana Rowlands and Federica Leonardis for their editing skills, Caroline Scott-Bowden for her keen proofreading, Lucy Bennett for her striking front cover and Emma Petfield and Chloe Cummings for their marketing nous.

A big shout out to my agent Kate Barker. Mumnesia means I don't recall much nowadays, but the memory of you signing me is still fresh.

Thanks to my former boss Nicky Thompson, whose commitment to flexible working meant I had the time to try my hand at writing. I also totally used the office copier for a print-out of an early draft. I owe you a ream of paper.

Much gratitude to all the friends and family who listened to me bang on about 'the book' all the time and didn't once punch me. In particular Lorraine Lee, Becky Garrod and Deborah Taylor, who went so far as to read early drafts and offer their encouragement.

They don't know me, but I really wanted to give a shout

out to K.M. Weiland (HelpingWritersBecomeAuthors.com) and Emma Darwin (This Itch of Writing) for the completely free and utterly brilliant advice they offer on writing. How they find the time to write novels too is beyond me.

Finally, to the two most important characters in my life: Jim, who puts the Rom and the Com into every single day, and who kept the wheels turning when I would otherwise have subsisted on cup-a-soups and self-doubt; and to my son Edgar, who had to put up with the words "sorry sweetheart, I'm writing" far more than any child should. As you both are at pains to remind me, I couldn't have done this without you.

ONE MORE CHAPTER

YOUR NUMBER ONE STOP

FOR PAGETURNING BOOKS

The author and One More Chapter would like to thank everyone who contributed to the publication of this story...

Analytics
Emma Harvey
Maria Osa

Audio
Fionnuala Barrett
Ciara Briggs

Contracts
Georgina Hoffman
Florence Shepherd

Design
Lucy Bennett
Fiona Greenway
Holly Macdonald
Liane Payne
Dean Russell

Digital Sales
Laura Daley
Michael Davies
Georgina Ugen

Editorial
Arsalan Isa
Charlotte Ledger
Federica Leonardis
Jennie Rothwell
Caroline Scott-Bowden
Kimberley Young

International Sales
Bethan Moore

Marketing & Publicity
Chloe Cummings
Emma Petfield

Operations
Melissa Okusanya
Hannah Stamp

Production
Emily Chan
Denis Manson
Francesca Tuzzeo

Rights
Lana Beckwith
Rachel McCarron
Agnes Rigou
Hany Sheikh
Mohamed
Zoe Shine
Aisling Smyth

The HarperCollins Distribution Team

The HarperCollins Finance & Royalties Team

The HarperCollins Legal Team

The HarperCollins Technology Team

Trade Marketing
Ben Hurd

UK Sales
Yazmeen Akhtar
Laura Carpenter
Isabel Coburn
Jay Cochrane
Alice Gomer
Gemma Rayner
Erin White
Harriet Williams
Leah Woods

And every other essential link in the chain from delivery drivers to booksellers to librarians and beyond!

ONE MORE CHAPTER

One More Chapter is an
award-winning global
division of HarperCollins.

Sign up to our newsletter to get our
latest eBook deals and stay up to date
with our weekly Book Club!
<u>Subscribe here.</u>

Meet the team at
<u>www.onemorechapter.com</u>

Follow us!
 <u>@OneMoreChapter_</u>
 <u>@OneMoreChapter</u>
 <u>@onemorechapterhc</u>

Do you write unputdownable fiction?
We love to hear from new voices.
Find out how to submit your novel at
<u>www.onemorechapter.com/submissions</u>